C000135422

SUMMER ON Louloudhia

Love, Life & Lemons on the Island of Flowers

by Antonia K.Lewis

Chapter 1

'It is therefore with the deepest of regrets, that I must inform everyone present at this meeting today, there are going to be unavoidable redundancies within this company.'

Blah. Blah. Blah.

I knew it was coming. Scarlett knew it was coming. Even the office junior in the sales department (who'd barely done a tap of work since the day she'd bagged her job as a result of her aunty once dating the financial director) knew it was coming – and she wasn't the brightest spark in the circuit, if you know what I mean.

It didn't take a NASA rocket scientist to realise that we were both on the Goodbye and Good Riddance List. Scarlett had been with the company for eight long years but her sickness and absence records were none too clever, whilst I'd only been on the payroll for the last eighteen months, having resigned from my previous steady job to work alongside my partner in crime, who had insisted it was a shrewd move in view of the higher salary, numerous perks etc., etc. In hindsight, probably not the wisest decision I'd ever made in my life...but at least we'd had a few belly-laughs in the office, toiling alongside the other minions, eating cake every day and taking the piss out of the management before the Powers That Be had fired the bullets and our futures at Gloss Homes Ltd had been blown out of the water.

Ah well, all good things must come to an end.

We had been greeted ominously at the entrance doors to the main building by Miriam, the sly old cow with the Rita Fairclough perm, who was the p.a. to the managing director; she'd smiled sickeningly and knowingly, clearly having typed our individual redundancy letters with her own fair hands, and I swear I heard her humming the music to 'Another One Bites the Dust' as we slid past her chunky frame and into the reception area. Bitch. She snottily pointed us in the direction of the boardroom, where we sat and fidgeted through half an hour of the Big Boss waffling on about hard times, and difficult decisions, and then returned to our cluttered desks to find the anticipated rectangular, white sealed envelopes awaiting us, propped up against our computer screens; names printed on the front, Thank You and Bugger Off letters neatly folded up inside.

'On a scale of one to ten, just how happy do you think my landlord is going to be, when my redundancy dosh runs out and I can't pay the rent again?' Scarlett enquired, re-plaiting her shoulder-length black hair, whilst I was carelessly swiping the contents of my emergency

1

food drawer into a tatty carrier bag and simultaneously wondering if I could sneak any printing paper out of the building under my woolly cardigan – trust it to be today, of all days, that I was without coat.

Using one hand to hold back my wayward, chocolate brown curls, I tore open the wrapper to an out-of-date cereal bar and began to nibble on it, as I said, 'Oh, you're screwed. Definitely a zero. He warned you last time you'd be out on your ear if you fell behind again, and aren't you already two months in arrears?'

'Yeah...I broke the bank over Christmas and then had three diabolical, lean months; I'm only just getting back on my feet. Somehow, I don't think he's going to be very sympathetic to my cause, is he? Especially now the kids have moved out and I can no longer claim that I have dependents needing a roof over their heads...but do you know what? I bloody hate that house, now I'm living alone. The neighbours are miserable sods, the traffic noise from the main road is horrific and I'm sick to death of groups of scruffs chucking chip wrappers and beer cans over my front hedge every night, on their way home from the White Swan.'

Scarlett chewed on her bottom lip as she contemplated her fate, smudging ruby-red lipstick onto her whiter-than-white front teeth and slightly spoiling the look of secretary-come-vamp that she'd been aiming for. Thick, black liquid eyeliner framed her piercing blue eyes and I noticed that her matching, ruby-red false nails were perfect as usual – Scarlett could have been penniless, homeless and starving but the nails would still be done. She truly was a lost cause when it came to money and prioritising but she was my best friend and I couldn't see her out on the streets.

'You do know that you can always move in with me, lovely lady,' I reassured her, anticipating that I may come to regret my generous offer, when the front door was slamming at all hours of the day and night and dishes were piled dangerously high in the kitchen sink, as she pissed away what little remained of her money on hair dyes and mascara.

'Aw thank you honey; you're such a sweetheart and I know I can always rely on you. I suppose I *could* take up residence in that newly-decorated spare room of yours and we *could* embark on a job-hunting mission and hope we can blag our way into some decent work before we become unemployable...'

She paused for dramatic effect, curling her tongue over her top teeth to remove the offending lipstick whilst waiting for me to glance up from my task in hand, at which point she continued.

'*Or....*'

'*Or*...or what? Come on - spit it out...because I can hear the cogs whirring round inside that scatty little head of yours. What madcap plans are you going to blackmail me into going along with?' Years of experience of Scarlett's well-meaning but usually disastrous schemes and spur-of-the-moment decisions meant I knew my spontaneous, slightly scary friend all too well, and I had a feeling she had something expensive and frighteningly mad up her frilly, white sleeve.

'Well...not so long ago, did we, or did we not, discuss the possibility of hopping on a jet plane and flying off somewhere hot and sunny for a well-deserved break? Yes, yes we did, is the correct answer. So the timing couldn't be more perfect really! We are unexpectedly unemployed, with not a partner between us to give a toss whether we are home or away...and we'll soon have all of that lovely redundancy money burning great big holes in our pockets...'

'Ooh, now, that actually does sound tempting,' I agreed, for once. It really did. It had been far too long since I had lazed by the sea with an ice cold beer in a frosted glass and felt the sun's rays beating down on my pasty skin; you just don't get that kind of heat in north Manchester.

'But that money isn't going to last long by the time we've forked out for flights and accommodation, and the obligatory small fortune on holiday clothes and sun tan lotion. And that's not even including any spending money, Scarlett. It won't leave us with much, even if *you* are quids-in at the moment, unlike little old me. Don't forget that I haven't even completed two full years working for this company, so my payout is going to be utter shite.'

Tying my hair loosely back with a faded scrunchie I'd discovered at the bottom of the drawer, I pocketed the few remaining bits and pieces that were still rolling around in it. Who knew when I might just need six red pens or a selection of multi-coloured paperclips?

'Yes, I know. But at least you have your dad's legacy to fall back on; I'm sure he would rather you dip into it, than struggle on and worry where your next fish supper is coming from...' Scarlett closed her hand over mine, her collection of huge, sterling silver rings digging deep into my flesh, despite her well-meaning gesture; she knew how difficult it had been for me to move on following the loss of my lovely dad.

It had been just the two of us, Frank Albert Woodward and Jessica Rose Woodward, for so very long after mum passed away prematurely, from an undiagnosed heart condition, when she was only in her late thirties, leaving behind a lost and lonely, bewildered little girl and a devastated, shell-shocked husband. As we muddled on, trying to establish some kind of routine and a future without the woman who had been the centre of our world, we were each other's life-support - dad doted on me and I worshipped the ground he walked on.

3

With dad's blessing, I finally flew the nest and left my childhood home, but only when I'd reached the grand old age of twenty-nine, and because Christian had finally asked me to share his rented flat, which eventually led to us buying a house of our own. Even though I wasn't living with my beloved dad anymore, I still visited him three times a week, rang him each and every evening and, during his last couple of years, when his health had sadly deteriorated, I had religiously fetched his weekly shop for him, dropped his newspaper off every morning en route to work, and invited him over every Sunday to eat lunch with myself and Christian.

When I had discovered him one cold, dark morning, in the deepest of sleeps he would never wake up from, the bottom had fallen out of my world and I had found it almost impossible to deal with the devastating loss.

His handsome, lined, lived-in face was gone forever, his messy grey hair would never again need a short-back-and-sides, and I wouldn't ever see those aqua blue eyes shine wickedly at me again as he removed his glasses and said, 'Come on, Jessie – let's have that second slice of cake.' Instead of treating him to a new Marks & Spencer shirt every birthday, or a bottle of expensive aftershave for Father's Day – which would always result in a shake of the head and a protest that it was far too extravagant; that he'd have been happy with a gallon of Old Spice – flowers were all that were left to give him, as I visited his graveside and wished with all of my heart that I could see him one more time, to share one last cuddle.

When I'd finally faced up to my responsibilities, I waded through all his paperwork and belongings, not anticipating there to be anything leftover from his Estate once all bills were settled, as he hadn't been a home-owner and, despite working all of his life – latterly as a porter at the local hospital – he had always seemed to be counting the pennies. Perhaps he'd been left with no alternative, as a single father and the sole breadwinner, with no other income to rely on. However, I was shocked to receive a rather nice cheque in the post from the solicitor, as a result of dad secretly sticking the odd tenner in a post office account from time to time over the last thirty years. Good old Frank.

Despite knowing full-well that he'd have wanted me to treat myself, or perhaps splash out on a new car, or even pay a chunk off my mortgage, I hadn't yet spent any of it. Somehow it just didn't feel right to fritter it away so soon, when dad had scrimped and saved and worked so hard to accumulate the balance for half of his life. Even when Christian moved out and I'd had to pay him off and juggle my finances to meet the mortgage payments, I'd still left the money untouched in my bank account.

4

'So...I'm thinking Ibiza! Or Sharm-El-Sheik! Or maybe one of the nightlife resorts in Turkey? What do you think, Jess?' Scarlett was bouncing up and down on her rickety office chair, her collection of silver bangles jingling like sleigh bells on her arm, all thoughts of clearing her desk forgotten in the excitement of planning a holiday.

Sunshine, sand and sexy waiters would be guaranteed in all of those resorts, of that I was sure, but I knew, one hundred and ten percent, where *I* wanted to go. There was one place, and one place only where, if necessary, I could plough into dad's money without feeling remotely guilty, comforted by the knowledge he would be pleased as punch that I was finally returning to somewhere that had meant so much to us; where we'd enjoyed the holiday of a lifetime and created everlasting memories.

'Well, as lovely as those destinations sound, with all the stag and hen nights, and lads flashing their arses all up and down the main drag,' I said, 'I'm thinking of somewhere else entirely...somewhere not quite so *busy*. Now, hear me out. It may not be as lively as all of those holiday resorts you mentioned, but it's equally as beautiful - in fact it's more beautiful than anywhere I've ever seen in my whole life. Right, pin back your ears and listen up. Do you know Corfu?'

'Ooh yes! Corfu! Sounds wonderful! I've heard Kavos is banging in the summer season and Naomi from accounts said there are some buzzing bars on The Strip...'

'No, no. God, no. It's not Corfu, but it *is* Greece, and it's *near* Corfu. The journey over there would take us a little longer as we would need to hop on a boat from Corfu to the island port and then make our way...'

'Sorry? I'll stop you right there...did you just say *a boat*? Ey? *What?* So let me get this straight. You want us to fly all the way over to Corfu and *then* get a boat to some tiny island that most people have probably never even heard of...'

'Not *some* island Scarlett. The *best* island. Honestly, it's on a level with paradise - if Carlsberg made islands, this would be the one. The most magnificent, magical place you'll ever visit and, I swear to God, you'll be unable to prevent yourself falling in love with it. Don't worry though, there *are* shops and bars there...you'll still be able to purchase vast quantities of alcohol!'

Frowning as she contemplated a foreign holiday without hordes of tourists and familiar burger bars, Scarlett let her hands drop by her sides and released a huge sigh; she wasn't exactly convinced.

'So what's this mysterious place called then? And why are YOU so desperate for us to go *there* when we have the whole world to explore?'

5

How could I possibly explain how extraordinarily beautiful the island was? How could I put into words what special memories it held for me; how I had never forgotten the moment when I had first arrived there, gripping the hands of my parents whilst gazing around in awe at the boats bobbing in the harbour and the magnificent view of the mountains rising up in the distance.

'My parents took me there when I was small – I must only have been about five years old but I can still visualise the twinkling of the harbour lights and recall the scent of the overflowing baskets of flowers...and not forgetting the unspoiled beaches we visited every day...and it being the best holiday I'd ever had. We never returned, but those recollections have stayed with me all of my life, even though many of the finer details are somewhat sketchy. But I'll never forget the feeling of absolute bliss as we were warmly welcomed on to this pretty little island, the days filled with joy, and our collective reluctance to return home once the holiday came to an end.'

Discussing it with Scarlett now was like travelling back in time, and I was desperate to try and make her understand what special memories the island evoked for me, the happiness it had brought to my little family unit and how it had firmly ensconced itself in all of our hearts.

'After mum died, all holidays were cancelled for the foreseeable future – we never made it abroad again and settled for the somewhat cooler Yorkshire coast. Returning to any of our previous holiday destinations without mum was unthinkable anyway, but whenever I mentioned that special summer to dad, his eyes always misted over and I could see the emotions threatening to overwhelm him.'

'Aw, god love him, he was such a sweetie. You've still not told me where it is you're going to be dragging me off to though, have you? Does this place actually have a name?'

All at once the clearest, most vivid images came flooding back and I could almost hear the sea whooshing in my ears, and feel the sun's rays colouring up my skin, as my younger, innocent self jumped again and again over the waves, squealing in pure, unadulterated excitement every single time.

Yes, I needed to return.

'Loulouthia. The name of the island is Loulouthia.'

Chapter 2

'Mother of god! I'm sweating like a menopausal horse! Look at me Jess – I'm leaking from my forehead, it's running off my top lip and my pits are damp and stinky!'

Apart from the tell-tale stains under her arms on her mint-green t-shirt, Scarlett looked as beautiful as ever. Her glossy black hair was wound up in a messy bun, her painted nails were almost the same shade as her plum lipstick, and she was wearing black jeggings that clung to her like a second skin. The overall effect with Scarlett was always sexy and dramatic – but then that's who she was. I would have killed for a figure like hers – I was altogether too rounded to squeeze into tight jeggings without ending up looking like a big, fat sausage...and my boobs were far too big to wear such a skimpy, low-cut top; honestly, I'd have been popping out before we'd even boarded the plane. Scarlett always said she would swap my curves for her flat chest any day of the week; she'd toyed with the idea of a boob job many times but had lacked the funds to pay for it; the love of her life, Darren, had told her to 'piss right off' when she'd suggested it was his responsibility once they were married, even though she'd assured him that he would benefit from it the most.

Cursed with a head full of curls with a life of their own, I longed to have poker-straight hair like Scarlett's, and I'd spent hour upon hour attempting to iron them out but to no avail – before I knew it, they were bouncing around again and all I'd achieved was a fine selection of split ends. I'd tried various hairstyles, all of which seemed to result in me looking like someone who was severely traumatised; in the end I'd given up, allowed my hair to grow down my back and accepted that I was stuck with what God had given me - which I'd actually inherited from my mum, along with my incredibly dark brown eyes and those humungous wangers.

Sighing, as I performed a quick check in my cracked compact mirror – yep, eyebrows still slightly too bushy; yep, more wrinkles than Ronnie Wood; yep, no trace of any make-up remaining on my shiny, oval face - I turned to reply to Scarlett. 'It *is* slightly warmer here than Manchester, my sweaty friend, and the reason you are positively dripping is because you have been wearing approximately sixteen layers of clothing...'

'Well, what was I supposed to do? I couldn't fit everything into my crappy old suitcase and the airlines have clamped down so badly now with their bloody rules and regulations and luggage restrictions. How on earth could I have packed all of my little cardigans and my lightweight summer jacket otherwise?'

'Er...by leaving behind five pairs of shoes and four pairs of jeans? You've got enough gear in that case to see you through for a month, never mind a fortnight!'

I really wasn't joking – since the day we'd lost our jobs Scarlett had been ordering rafts of clothes on-line and touring the shopping centres for designer bikinis and matching sarongs that came with a hefty price tag. Even though it was likely that at least half of her purchases would be returned once she'd worn them on holiday (complete with chewing gum wrappers and men's phone numbers scribbled on scraps of paper still in the pockets), it was little wonder she couldn't stump up the money for her rent. In comparison, I had spent little and was travelling light, as I still owned a selection of perfectly acceptable summer dresses and swimsuits I'd purchased optimistically over the last few years, which had hardly seen the light of day, thanks to the good old British summertime.

My bikini-wearing days were over in any event; no way was I squeezing my fat back and saggy boobs into a skimpy little top whilst feeling the unforgiving bikini bottoms gradually wrinkling and rolling down over my belly as I wandered along the beach trying to look elegant and chic. Unfortunately, the older I got, the more self-conscious I became, and at the grand old age of thirty-eight I had entered the sensible world of modest swimsuits, rather than letting everything hang out from an itsy-bitsy-teeny-weeny shocking pink or yellow bikini. Scarlett and I were the same age but were worlds apart as far as body confidence was concerned – she'd get her kit off for anyone who asked but I preferred to undress by myself in complete darkness.

I *had* splashed out on a few new pairs of shorts, a colourful selection of vest tops and some dressy flip-flops, and by 'splashed out', I mean I wandered on down to Primark the last time I was in town, when the queues weren't horrendous. That was when I'd bumped into Christian's wife, Amy, who was armed with several shopping bags and a fake smile.

She was pretty, in a homely, mumsy sort of way, with her fair hair cut into a long bob, her hazel eyes peeping out from under her choppy fringe. She wore the boring uniform of the boring bank where she had worked since she left school – navy blue trousers, a pale blue shirt and a spotty necktie that wasn't at all flattering. She'd probably still looked better than me though; I'd had tomato soup stains splattered down my white t-shirt and my greying leggings had seen better days. Kelly Brook I was not.

It still felt strange to think that my ex-partner had moved on and married so quickly after our split, particularly when he'd shown no inclination whatsoever of wanting to tie the knot in all the time *we'd* been together. Mind you, neither had I. Introduced by mutual friends, there'd been instant physical attraction and we'd thoroughly enjoyed each other's company, stumbling headlong into a relationship. When we finally bought our two-up two-down, semi-detached house together it seemed like a natural progression, but that's where the progression had ended.

Why had he never proposed to me? I often pondered on that. Maybe I just wasn't the marrying kind – perhaps I wasn't the sort of woman a man imagined spending the rest of his life with. Or maybe he hadn't asked because there had been the distinct possibility that I might actually have turned him down, because somewhere deep inside I'd had a sneaking suspicion that he wasn't 'The One'. Christian had at least eventually arrived at that conclusion before I did – or maybe I *had* actually known but unconsciously hadn't wanted to rock the boat as I'd always struggled to cope with change. After the shock of mum passing away, I'd been practically allergic to anything that could possibly alter my life in any way, shape or form. Hence the reason I guess I'd stayed with Christian as long as I did, even though we had eventually become more friends who shared a house, rather than lovers who shared a bed.

Did I regret us splitting up? No, was the honest answer. Christian, at 6'3', with his spiky, Bovril-brown hair and his cat-like, green eyes had cut quite a striking figure as he'd marched through town in his Next suit, armed with an overloaded briefcase and a take-out coffee. However, Christian at home, lounging around in his bobbly, tartan pyjamas and matching threadbare slippers, living on Chicken Korma and litres of Pinot Grigio, was not the same man. The glint in his eyes had dimmed over the years and he'd become *dreary* – spouting off about politics and clinging on to the remote control as if his life depended on it – and if the sex hadn't exactly been adventurous in the early years, it had eventually become scarily dull. We found ourselves just going through the motions until finally neither one of us could be arsed taking clothing off anymore and we'd given it up as a bad job.

'Scarlett to Jessica! Come in Jessica!' My friend's dulcet tones could be heard booming above all those of the other passengers eagerly preparing to disembark the ferry, many of whom turned to see just exactly who was making all the racket.

'Sorry...I was miles away then. I've been dreaming of a return to Loulouthia for so long now, I can't actually believe it's becoming a reality, and there's a kaleidoscope of butterflies fluttering about in my tummy. Oh my god, look at all those boats moored in the harbour and the traditional fish tavernas lining the seafront! Wow! Just...wow! It's stunning...it's every bit as beautiful and authentic as I remembered.'

It had been a long, exhausting day; Scarlett's sister, Viola, had dropped us off at the airport early morning and we'd had a four hour wait for the flight to Corfu, due to a two hour delay at Manchester - although we had numbed the pain somewhat with pints of strong lager for breakfast and a couple of flaky croissants that cost more than we would probably spend on our evening meal most nights in Greece. After a rowdy flight to Corfu, thanks to a group of high-spirited college leavers who *were* actually going to Kavos and had the t-shirts to prove it, we endured a bumpy bus transfer down to the port, where we discovered that the next ferry wasn't due to leave until 5pm, and the eventual journey over to the island, calling at two other small islands en route, was like the slow boat to China...three more hours of sweating and yawning and Scarlett whining about how she could have travelled to Australia in less time than it had taken to transfer to Loulouthia.

But it had all been worth it. The sun was already setting over the Ionian Sea and the sky was painted in shades of orange, from the palest peach to the darkest amber. Carefully, smoothly, the ferry was eased into the quaint little harbour, which resembled a picture-perfect scene off a postcard, with its lights dotted around, strung from post to post, and the huge wooden containers of trailing flowers in hues of purples and pinks, evenly spaced around the harbour buildings, the standard ginger cat snoozing on the steps of a taverna. Overflowing hanging baskets in full bloom swung and clanked about in the evening breeze; I thought I'd died and gone to heaven.

'It's hardly a bustling port is it? But I have to concede, it's a darn sight prettier than Blackpool, so I'll let you off,' said Scarlett as we finally stepped on to dry land and she reached down to rub her aching calves. Only Scarlett could attempt a full day's travelling in a pair of three inch heels. She'd redeemed herself with her last comment, as to be honest I was becoming heartily sick of hearing her moaning, although I knew it was mainly because she was over-tired and over-hungry. In many ways Scarlett was like a small child, in that she needed constant feeding, amusing and rest. And occasionally burping when she'd devoured a burger and chips at two o'clock in the morning, after a heavy drinking session down the pub.

'I can't believe it, Scarlett...it hasn't changed a bit. Even after thirty-two, maybe thirty-three years...it's exactly how I pictured it in my mind, even down to the pots of flowers and the tiny ice cream van parked over by the walkway.'

'Bloody hell, there's flowers everywhere – you'd be knackered here if you suffered from hayfever! It beggars belief that they would grow in such a hot climate...I wouldn't want to be the one in charge of watering all the little buggers!' As Scarlett hadn't yet been able to keep one single pot plant alive, I wouldn't have fancied their chances if she *had* been responsible for their upkeep.

'*Loulouthia* means 'flowers' - this little corner of Greece is apparently also known as 'The Island of Flowers' and that's why they're everywhere you look. There are billions of those tiny little ones growing wild on the mountainsides – according to the pamphlet I read on the ferry - and at this time of year all the others are in abundance too. The locals have all kinds of pots and urns full of blooms on their verandahs, and bougainvillea vines threaded through trellises on the outside walls of their homes; even the businesses have baskets hanging from the awnings and there's an annual flower festival taking place later this month...I bet that's a sight to behold!'

'Steady on, Bamber Gasgoine, with all your useless knowledge and facts! You'll find that I'm too bloody hungry anyway to listen to anything that might actually educate me. Now, let's retrieve our luggage, which I do believe they've lobbed on that barren piece of land over there – may god help them if they've trashed my hair straighteners! Then we need to grab a taxi, pronto, before my legs give way; I can't wait to get these godforsaken toe-crushers off and slip into my sandals. And I probably stink to high heaven!'

Our luggage had indeed been chucked into what looked distinctly like some sort of animal pen to the far side of the harbour, but it appeared to be fairly unscathed, so we retrieved our cases and dragged them over to where we'd seen a taxi screech to a halt just a few minutes earlier. Unfortunately, someone had obviously beaten us to it and it shot off down the road just as we approached it, leaving us choking in the fumes left in its wake.

We waited, and waited, and waited some more...and just when I thought Scarlett might actually pass out in the stifling heat before she'd had chance to acclimatise....the same scruffy, dusty old taxi pulled up again and the driver – also scruffy and dusty – cheerily offered us his services. The cases took a further battering as they were slung into the boot, which resolutely refused to close – a fact which didn't seem to faze the beaming driver, who managed to prevent it from bursting wide open by fastening some handmade rustic rope device onto what appeared to have been a tow-bar in a former life.

Collapsing onto the smoky, slightly torn back seat, the middle-aged man closed our doors with his denim-clad backside before clambering in to the driver's seat, lighting up a cigarette and introducing himself as Yiannis. After profusely welcoming us to his island, he asked in Pidgin English, 'Where you go?'

Whilst I was emptying the contents of my cluttered handbag out onto the seat in an attempt to produce the paper containing the name and address of our accommodation, Yiannis filled the silence by adding, 'You come to beautiful island...the best of the best! Only four resorts on island, on one big road. First is here – Louthlouthia Town – many stay here. When we get

11

to road, if we go left, we go to Skafos - bigger resort with more bars...more busy...has nightclub now! If we go right, two more resorts...Chaliki and Kochyli - quieter but much more beautiful...'

'Please let us go left. Please let us go left...' I could hear Scarlett chanting beside me. I finally found what I was looking for and brandished the printed piece of paper in the air before handing it to Yiannis, who glanced at it and said, 'Ah! Very good! We go right!'

'Aw...bloody hell! Have you booked us into the deadest place on earth, you muppet?' Scarlett shook her head in disgust, clearly disappointed that she wouldn't be out clubbing every night.

'Honestly Scarlett, I had no idea where we were staying; I booked it on online and it looked stunning...but I couldn't remember any details from the last time I was here, back in the 1980s, so it was a bit pot-luck really. I recalled staying in a white-washed apartment down a long sandy track with mum and dad, but that's all – and that could be anywhere on this island! Remember, I was only five-ish when I was here last – the resort names I've long since forgotten and, as pointed out to you previously, Loulouthia isn't in any of those glossy holiday brochures you picked up from the travel agents!'

'Er, maybe there's a bloody good reason why...'

'Ah....you have been before?' Yiannis interrupted, evidently eavesdropping and understanding much of our conversation. 'Then you remember the flowers, the lights...the beauty of Loulouthia? You are very lucky ladies to visit our island...I think you will have a relaxing holiday and you will return to England more happy than you have ever been.'

'Do you know, Yiannis, I think you might just be right. I have a feeling this is going to turn out to be the holiday of a lifetime - what do you reckon, Scarlett?'

Gazing out of the open window at the traditional white-washed houses with their terracotta roofs, the imposing but beautiful church with its cream coloured walls and huge bell high up in the sky, all set against a backdrop of glorious fields of flowers and rugged mountains, it was impossible for her to sulk for long – particularly when she had two weeks of sunshine and doing sod all ahead of her, drinking, eating, sunbathing, and, who knows, maybe copping off with the odd Greek shipping magnate or two. Her features softened as she broke into a smile.

'We *will* have a ball Jess! I'm sure wherever we are going has at least one bar and restaurant and we know for a fact it's got a beach...so we're practically sorted! I can't wait to soak up the sun all day long and work my way through the cocktail menu. Do you think there will be many single Greek guys here, ready to party with an aging English divorcee? And what about you? You never know, Mr Right might just be out there for you as well. Maybe that's why you've been drawn back to this place - because the man of your dreams is already here - ready, waiting and willing!'

'Stop it! Let me tell you, I ceased dreaming a long time ago when I came to the conclusion that true love is a myth, so I can assure you that I am definitely NOT on the lookout for Mr Right – not even a Mr Right Now! Anyway, I've lived with a boy and it's not all it's cracked up to be. I'm perfectly happy on my own – not answerable to anyone, not making allowances for anybody. I value my own space...and I'm just not interested in a holiday romance or trying to land myself a Greek god to make an honest woman of me...sometimes I think I'm destined to end up a mad, old spinster who watches repeats of Heartbeat and sends letters of complaint off to the Daily Mail!'

'Bullshit! We all need someone, and your perfect fit is out there somewhere. Ooh look - finally some more houses and buildings on the horizon...do you think we're almost here? Yes, look – a sign for 'Chaliki'! This could definitely be it – house, house, house - a restaurant is that? Apartments, kiosk, more apartments, bar – yes! Finally, a bar! And on the other side...gift shop, bigger bar, looks like a couple of holiday bungalows, restaurant, dog sleeping in road, a tiny little eating place with a bar attached and...oh, we're pulling up! Is this where we are staying?'

'Yes! Katerina Apartments – that's us! Looks nice on the outside anyway...flowers everywhere, of course, and not overlooking a building site...and right near the centre.'

'The centre of what? It's not exactly Las Vegas is it, sweetheart! I'm so glad to be here though at long last...what a relief! Can you take my case Yiannis? Oh, thank you kind man!'

We had requested a sea view on an upper floor, but, alas, our apartment number 2 had a garden view, on the ground floor - and there was evidence on the internal walls of a few hastily splattered insects, which slightly concerned me, and totally freaked out Scarlett. Otherwise the place looked basic but clean and the first thing we did, after Scarlett had swapped her heels for her trainers, refusing to step on the floor barefoot in case she squished some creepy-crawly making a break for it, was to have a quick wash at the tiny bathroom sink. Hair brushed, make-up roughly re-applied, we decided to abandon the unpacking until the next morning. We each had a change of clothes in our hand luggage so at least were able to slip into something clean, before leaving the apartment again to locate somewhere to eat.

The smell from Gyros Corner, the tiny grill house with the bar area attached, immediately enticed us in and before we knew it, we were each devouring one of their specialities; spit-roasted pork accompanied by fries, slices of onions and tomatoes, and a dollop of tzatziki all wrapped up in a lightly toasted pita and washed down with an ice cold beer, followed by complimentary slices of watermelon fetched out to us by an older lady who had emerged from behind the counter, and who was as wide as she was tall – presumably the owner's wife. The owner was a chirpy little man, whose name we had been unable to catch, but who would be forever known as 'Mr Toothy', as his smile revealed that he was indeed lacking in the teeth department. He was over-the-top friendly though and his laugh was even louder than Scarlett's, as he shouted greetings to passing Greeks and handed over plastic bags containing takeaway orders to young lads who'd clearly been sent out with shipping orders.

Once our bellies were filled and our thirst was quenched, we were overcome with exhaustion, and despite Scarlett's plans to 'head for the liveliest bar and get hammered', we found that all we really wanted to do was crawl into our beds and leave the drinking and exploring until the following day.

Back at the apartment, after checking her bed approximately fifty-seven times for insects, and whining about being 'conned' out of a sea view, Scarlett almost immediately fell into a deep slumber – fully dressed and snoring like a pig with a blocked snout. Despite the exhaustion, I lay awake, overfed and overtired, excitement buzzing through my veins.

I was finally here! And it was like something had clicked when I'd set foot on this island's sacred soil and took in a lungful of salty, sea air. Not merely the usual holiday excitement and anticipation – I'd been elsewhere; I'd travelled further afield and visited other countries, but nowhere else had captivated me as Loulouthia had, not even Corfu, as beautiful as it was. No, it was definitely this island, with its mountains and its olive groves and its carpet of flowers. It was almost a feeling of 'coming home', when we arrived and inhaled the warm evening air and I had a flashback of standing on that very same walkway at the harbour, sandwiched between my lovely mum and dad, smiling from ear to ear and begging them to buy me an ice lolly.

Darkness had already descended by the time we'd headed out for food, depriving us of the opportunity to see much of our surroundings, but tomorrow would officially be the start of our holiday and there would be plenty of time to explore Chaliki; to meet the locals, and swim in the emerald waters of the Ionian Sea...and I knew when my curtain of sleep eventually came down, that I would rest well, now I was finally back on the island that had stolen a huge chunk of my heart.

Chapter 3

Knock, knock.

'Helloooo...sorry to disturb you. Hello...can you hear me? Is anyone awake?'

'Man alive! Who the hell's banging on the door so early in the morning? We've only been in this room a matter of hours...that cleaner's on the ball, isn't she?' Her eyes still firmly closed – I think the mascara had glued her eyelashes together anyway – and her vest top wrinkled up almost around her neck, Scarlett didn't particularly appreciate being roused at the crack of dawn (okay, nine-thirty) after the mammoth journey we had undertaken the previous day and the degree of knackeredness she'd apparently reached.

Tap, tap. 'Hello...good morning...helloooo...'

With a groan and a sign and a sneeze that came from nowhere, I resigned myself to being the one who would have to haul myself out of bed, slip my feet into my squeaky flip-flops (no sign of any bugs yet, but I knew they were out there) and drag my tired legs over to the door to see what all the fuss was about. When I opened it, mid-yawn, I was surprised to find a buxom young woman propping up the door frame, clearly a holidaymaker as she was wearing a custard-yellow sun-dress over a multi-coloured bikini and was carrying a huge, stripy beach bag.

'Oh god, I'm really sorry to disturb you so early, when I know you only arrived last night, especially after that arse-ache of a journey to get here.'

Definitely English – bit of a North East accent going on there.

'I wanted to catch you before you went out for the day; you see...the thing is...we arrived on Sunday – me, my husband Ricky and our little girl, Bella – and they put us in apartment 3, up the stairs. And we specifically requested downstairs accommodation when we booked...but they couldn't move us then because all the studios and apartments were full – yours was only vacated and cleaned yesterday prior to your arrival...'

Rubbing my blurry eyes, I smiled politely, wondering where this was all going and why I was attempting to converse with a stranger without first guzzling a mug of strong, sweet coffee, which would hopefully line my stomach and direct its healing powers towards my fuzzy head.

'Anyway...we were hoping...if you would be so good...that you would agree to exchange apartments with us. I know it's a pain in the bum, especially if you've already unpacked – we wanted to grab you for a quick word last night but we'd had to dine out early because Bella was playing up, and you'd already been and gone by the time we got back – but we would be ever so grateful if you could make the swap with us.'

Taken completely unawares, my mind wasn't thinking straight, but I didn't fancy heaving all of our gear upstairs and sleeping between other people's sweaty, sandy sheets. Scratching my head whilst stifling a yawn, I tried to formulate an argument of sorts.

'These ground floor rooms are only really glorified studios though - if you've paid for an apartment then you don't want to be accepting something inferior. This one does have a single bed as well as a double, but they're practically on top of each other and there's not a lot of space in here...'

'Oh, we're not worried about that, pet. You see, Bella's only four and she's a real livewire and, worst of all, a climber. Honestly, you need eyes in your arse to see what she's up to. And last year on holiday, well she managed to climb over and fall off the bloody balcony – luckily it wasn't much of a drop and she had a reasonably soft landing but she still terrified the life out of us and broke her arm...so we are absolutely desperate to move to a ground floor room.'

It was difficult not to feel sympathetic once she'd explained the circumstances; she was clearly worried and came across as a decent, genuine person, and I therefore found myself reluctantly agreeing to the move without consulting Scarlett first, who was still face down on the bed in any event, drifting in and out of consciousness. Apparently, the woman, who had finally introduced herself as Mandy from South Shields, had already spoken to the cleaner, who was happy to change the sheets and give the place a quick spruce up once they were all out of the way, after Mandy had greased the canny old lady's palm with coins and boiled sweets.

After our early morning visitor had left with a 'Cheers, honey,' and a wave, I bounced up and down on Scarlett's bed until she was forced to open her sticky, sleep-encrusted eyes.

'Alright, alright! I get the message, you dipstick! I can't believe you've agreed to move...it's a bloody good job we've not unpacked already.'

'Come on, I told her to give us ten minutes and then we'd drag our cases upstairs. Get your stuff together...the sooner it's done, the sooner we can crack on with our day.'

Thankfully, Mandy's husband was a huge, pumped-up guy who insisted on dragging our suitcases up the winding staircase, thereby saving us from hernias and heart attacks. Once the happy little family had vacated Apartment 3 and moved into Bug Central, I turned the huge, ornate key in the old-fashioned door lock, hoping that this time we would have a place to call home for the next fortnight, and that it wouldn't be an absolute shithole.

I wasn't disappointed.

'Oh, wow! Scarlett, come look, quick! It's seriously MASSIVE! Same number of beds but so much *space*...and even a fridge and kettle in the corner over there – somewhere to store our bottles of beer *and* the facility to make a morning brew...yey!'

'Never mind that, Jess – get your butt out onto this balcony and take a little look at this!'

Following Scarlett outside, I actually heard myself gulp out loud at the glorious sight that greeted me. The private balcony was huge and wrapped around most of the apartment; pots of daisy-like flowers had been spaced out a regular intervals, and there were two plastic loungers positioned to take advantage of the morning sun, as well as a patio set where we would be able to down a glass of the local wine every evening whilst enjoying the sunset and admiring the view. *The view.* It was phenomenal. Dramatic mountain ranges with villages scattered below to our right, and to our left, we could gaze out beyond the bars and other businesses lining the main road through the resort, to appreciate the wide expanse of golden sand and the bluest of seas that was just begging to be paddled in.

'We got our sea view! We got our sea view!' Scarlett was ecstatic and had already started rooting around in the depths of her handbag for her trusty old mobile to take some photographs to send home and, no doubt, post on her Facebook page – because, of course, it's nothing unless it's appeared on a social media platform.

There was a brief moment when I felt sorry for the family who had moved into our old apartment, although they had seemed happy enough and relieved that their monkey-like daughter would be safe from harm. But the sympathy only lasted a few seconds, because I couldn't believe our luck; we had really fallen on our feet with this apartment and it was simply perfect. If I spent the rest of my life sitting out on this balcony, drinking in that breathtaking view, it would be a life well spent.

After unpacking our suitcases and hanging up our clothes in the obligatory pine wardrobes, which seemed to represent some sort of mathematical problem – if you have seven coat hangers but twenty-eight outfits, where the fuck do you put all of your clothes? – we filled the bathroom with our selection of toiletries and arranged our other assorted belongings on the shelves and bedside cabinets. We were taking no chances – if asked to move for a second time we would dig our heels in and say that, unfortunately, although we would *love* to oblige, we couldn't possibly pack all that shit up again.

The morning had started reasonably cool – it was, after all, only early May, the beginning of the holiday season – but it soon began to warm up nicely and we took turns freshening up in the small, but perfectly formed, bathroom, changing into clean tops and shorts, swimwear peeping out from underneath, and made our way back down the stairs, through the meticulously maintained gardens and out on to the main street.

For a moment we stopped and stood amongst the other tourists who were milling about, as we looked this way and that, familiarising ourselves with our immediate surroundings. No one appeared to be in much of a hurry; people just strolling hand in hand, chatting, unwinding, heading off to the beach. There seemed to be several other restaurants and shops further up the street, but our rumbling tummies reminded us that we needed to eat first and explore later, so we hopped over the road instead to where English breakfasts were clearly advertised in multi-coloured chalk on a blackboard propped up outside, and from where a tantalising aroma of freshly brewed coffee drifted out. The exterior of the building gave the impression that it was only a bar, but inside we discovered it opened up into an inviting restaurant at the rear. We ambled through, taking in the disco ball and cocktail lists in the bar area (I could see Scarlett making a mental note to return later in the day to sample a few of the drinks that were on offer) and the traditional blue and white cloths covering the tables in the restaurant.

Wanting to enjoy our food al fresco, we nodded to the young Greek girl who offered us the opportunity to do so and followed her through to – oh my word, a large open terrace adjacent to the most glorious of sandy beaches, and only a short walk out to the clear waters of the Ionian Sea.

'I had no idea that this was a beach-front taverna! Oh my, it's so gorgeous out here - look at that clean, golden sand! We can literally eat, drink and then roll straight out on to the beach!' Clapping my hands together, I was unable to contain my excitement, whilst Scarlett took yet more photos and bigged me up for having found such brilliant accommodation, so close to the beach and the centre of Chaliki – even if the resort was a little on the quiet side, in her humble opinion.

This was ideal for me though. I didn't want packed streets full of hungover teens and drinking establishments with names like The Red Lion and Harry's Bar – *this* was what I wanted. Peace and quiet in magnificent surroundings – although it did seem that there were more than enough places to eat and drink around this quiet village to satisfy anyone's needs. Even Scarlett's.

'I love it here, Scarlett, I really do. I don't know what it is but I feel so *connected* to Loulouthia, and in particular to Chaliki - like I *belong* here, and I've only just arrived! This is on a par with paradise to me and I'm so happy I finally returned and that you're sharing all of this with me.'

'*Kaliméra*, beautiful ladies...good morning to you both!' I was interrupted by the arrival of our Greek waiter, who was all teeth and mad black hair, but who had the warmest smile I'd ever seen.

'Allow me to introduce myself. I am Apostolis and I welcome you to our traditional Greek restaurant, where the food is of the best quality you will find anywhere on this island! Please tell me your names and we will be less formal with each other...'

We duly obliged and explained we'd only just arrived on holiday – clearly evident by our milk bottle legs and beach towels that still smelled of fabric conditioner rather than stale sweat - and Apostolis kindly wished us a very Happy Holiday and scribbled down our orders on his faded little notepad.

After gut-busting English breakfasts and settling a bill that somehow just didn't seem enough for everything that we'd eaten, we thanked and tipped Apostolis and he recommended that we return in the evening to drink in the roadside bar – the best bar on the island, he said! We assured him we would certainly be back and then left, eager to flop down on the beach and begin the serious business of tanning ourselves to a crisp.

We both agreed that Ammos Beach was the most beautiful stretch of sand that we had ever set eyes on; it was so fine and pure, broken up by only the odd seashell or smooth white pebble that had been washed up on the shore. The waters were crystal clear and incredibly shallow for such a long way out; it was almost impossible to wade out to above chest height, which was just tickety-boo, neither of us being particularly strong swimmers. And you could never say that it was crowded – there were a few families and several older couples dotted about, but it was hardly Benidorm. We had our pick of the sunbeds and chose the nearest ones to the water's edge, so we could almost trail our fingertips into the sea when we were lying face down with our hands dangling down at our sides.

The only noise, apart from muted conversations or the odd squeal from an excitable child, was a little Greek music tinkling away in the distance and the voice of a doughnut seller, who must have made a hundred trips up and down that beach, advertising his wares – 'Cream, Vanilla, Banana, Cherry! Doughnuts! Come and get your tasty doughnuts!' Every so often we would repeat his sales patter, laughing as we tried to imitate his accent, and, despite the fact that we had declared that we would never eat again after breakfast, in the end he wore us down and we each purchased a delicious, sugar-coated vanilla doughnut, which slipped down a treat with the beers Scarlett had wandered back in and ordered from a chirpy Apostolis, who promised he would charge us 'Asda Price'.

It was a thoroughly relaxing and rejuvenating day – just what the doctor ordered after the stresses and exhaustion caused by the lengthy journey over to the island. On balance, it had definitely been worth it.

Following an afternoon siesta back at the apartment – who knew lying on a beach all day and floating about in warm, peaceful waters could make you so tired? – we each took a freezing cold shower and decided to glam up for our first full evening in the resort. Strolling up the hill, determined to tour the area before we dined out, the first restaurant we came to, Elpitha, was a traditional taverna that was both inviting and smelled amazing, so that was as far as we got. Oh well, there was always tomorrow.

After a mouth-watering meal of barbequed and skewered chicken *souvlaki,* which was accompanied by roasted Greek potatoes and a medley of vegetables, we slunk back into our chairs, sipping our incredibly potent Baileys coffees, feeling like we had all of the time in the world; no rush, taking it slowly – '*Sigá, sigá*', as the Greeks would say.

Eventually we wobbled back over to Sunrise, the bar we had ventured into earlier, which was now considerably livelier, with locals wandering in and out and young families sat around an eclectic mix of tables - it looked like someone had just visited all of their relatives, scooping up every piece of their dining room furniture as they went, and then plonked each item down in this bar, but somehow it worked. It was quirky but comfortable and it just wouldn't have been the same if it had been filled with the more regimented tables that were out on the beachfront terrace.

Noticing the young girl who had led us to our table that same morning, I gave her a cheery smile, but she looked thoroughly bored off her trolley and all I received in response was a raised eyebrow and a tilt of the head. Maybe not then. In contrast, as we made our way over to the bar area we heard a man's confident, deep voice shout out 'Hey! Beautiful ladies! We have new arrivals everyone...gather round and give them a great big cheer!'

Slightly embarrassed at the over-the-top welcome, I shyly followed behind Scarlett, who was lapping up all of the attention, pretending to take a bow. When we reached the bar area, two stools were immediately yanked out for us by a female member of staff, who was possibly in her late twenties or early thirties and who was, quite frankly, stunning. The woman introduced herself as Sofia and then disappeared behind the bar to work alongside an equally good-looking man, he of the shouty mouth, who beamed at us and said in a heavily accented Greek voice, 'Good evening ladies...I am Alex and I am the owner of this bar and this is my beautiful wife Sofia...and we are here to make sure you have the BEST time on holiday and that you never leave this establishment sober!' He handed us both a welcoming shot, which looked distinctly like Peach Schnapps, a drink that usually made me feel queasy, and instructed us to join him in a toast. As we gulped it back, feeling the burn, Alex slammed his glass on the bar top and said loudly, '*Yamas*! Bottoms up!'

'Cheers!' we sang out in unison, chuckling whilst nudging each other, suspecting that we had probably, by accident, stumbled upon the liveliest bar in the village and thoroughly anticipating we would be in for a corker of a night.

'Two Amstels please!' ordered Scarlett, as I self-consciously attempted to smooth down my natural curls whilst gazing in wonder at the beauty of Alex's wife. She was olive-skinned, tall, slim and toned and her glossy waist-length hair was highlighted with bronze-coloured streaks that *looked* expensive, as if she had stepped right out of the pages of a fashion magazine. Her nails were long, filed and painted in a sparkly bronze colour and she wore a selection of gold bangles on her wrists, a cross on a chain around her neck and small, gold hoops in her ears. Dressed in skin-tight, black jeans and a burnt orange, silky camisole top, she was the image of perfection, and I became very aware of my own wobbly bits and distinct lack of style and grace. But then again, this woman would put anyone in the shade. To give Sofia her due though, she was funny as well as friendly, and certainly had the personality to accompany the looks. No wonder she had snared a husband like Alex, who put me in mind of a lusted-after, sexy Greek popstar, in his fitted black t-shirt and bum-clenching black jeans, his dark wavy hair tumbling into his warm, melting-chocolate eyes. What a gorgeous couple they made.

'What are your names, English ladies?' asked Alex, leaning forward over the bar as if to whisper conspiratorially.

'I'm Scarlett...like the colour red!'

'Then I think I shall call you Scarlett Fever! And your beautiful, blushing friend here...what is your name?'

'I'm Jess...short for Jessica...but to my friends I'm just Jess.'

'HEY EVERYONE!' Alex raised his hands in the air and commanded the attention of everyone in the bar, as he shouted, 'Let me introduce you to SCARLETT FEVER AND JUST JESS!' His whole audience erupted into applause, and we soon discovered that every customer was allocated a name, typically that of a famous celebrity. Within minutes of our arrival, Bob Hope, Charlotte Church and Steven Seagal had joined us and before long we became accustomed to hearing, 'HEY! IT'S JACK NICHOLSON! WELCOME BACK, MY FRIEND!' or 'JAMIE OLIVER...WHERE IS MY FOOD?'

Three beers, two cocktails and several shots on the house later, it was safe to say I had lost my inhibitions along with my sobriety. We had roared with laughter and danced on the bar alongside the staff, made friends with the locals and informed at least eight total strangers that we really, really loved them. Every time Alex had shouted '*OPA!*' every member of the crowd had cheered and banged their shot glass on the nearest table and knocked back whatever concoction he had poured for them. At some point during the proceedings both sets of double doors to the building had been firmly closed to contain the noise, and when we finally decided to call it a night, after much merriment and appalling dancing, we were surprised to find the road outside deserted and in deadly silence, as we spilled out on to the cracked pavement, Scarlett stumbling down the crumbling kerb.

'God, those massive doors really do their job don't they, Jessie baby?' slurred Scarlett, holding on to me for dear life after she tripped again and almost landed in a prickly bush.

'It's something to do with Greek noise laws, my little Scarlett,' I hiccupped. 'Sofia said the local bar owners are handed out whopping great big fines if the music is *really* loud...but, apparently, there's about three policemen on the whole island and they don't give a tiny little shit!'

For some reason, we both found that particularly hilarious and shrieked with laughter as we gradually made our way over the traffic-less road, through the scented, watered gardens and up the stairs to our lovely new apartment, the latter part of the journey taking far longer than it should have done, due to us literally collapsing in giggles halfway up the steps, whilst loudly reminding each other to 'Sshhh!'

When I finally reached the sanctity of my bed, I expected to fall asleep before my head even hit the pillow but instead found that my mind was racing and determined to keep me firmly in the wide-awake-club. So I lay there, unable to resist comparing myself to the sophisticated and sultry Sofia – big mistake.

Once I'd acquired a tan, I would lose some of my obvious Britishness and could probably almost pass for a local, with my dark, curly hair and even darker eyes. I wasn't huge but could definitely benefit from losing a few kilos – I blamed Terry's Chocolate Orange and every decent red wine manufacturer for that. Everyone said I had a beautiful smile, and my skin wasn't bad for a woman who'd done some serious partying and drinking for a couple of years solid back in the day. I suppose I was about average...and that probably came from lack of confidence and effort on my part to keep appointments with hairdressers and nail salons. Scarlett still couldn't get her head around the fact that I'd never in my life had a spray tan or my eyebrows shaped professionally, or even had any part of my body waxed, when practically all of her free time was filled up with pampering and preening.

Sofia oozed confidence and obviously spent a shed-load of money making sure she was the whole package, whereas I was definitely NOT...more of a little parcel that had been battered about in transit.

I totted up in my head a rough estimate of how much I would have to spend each month to keep on top of beauty treatments and self-care and the final sum made me wince.

Bugger that...if I did meet anyone – not that I wanted to or intended to – they would have to accept me for who I was – hairy legs, cellulite, chipped nails and all!

Chapter 4

'Holy mother of God! Who the devil let all the frantic little men with whacking great big lump hammers into my head overnight?' Scarlett attempted to raise herself off her sweat-soaked pillow but then thought better of it. 'Flippin' eck, it's hot in here this morning!'

'Good grief, that's because it's eleven o'clock already! I can't believe we slept so late...we've missed almost half of the day Scarlett!'

'It's understandable really...that mammoth journey over here left us absolutely pooped; I feel almost jet-lagged – that and the fact that we were up shockingly early yesterday morning.'

'No, it's because we got off our faces on cheap alcohol last night, made the fatal mistake of mixing our drinks and were giggling like a couple of naughty school girls all the way back – which is an extremely short journey so I don't know why it took us about an hour to get here - and then I was tossing and turning until the sun came up. Christ! I know last night was brilliant and hilarious but I want to savour every precious minute of this holiday and I've just missed half a day, as well as breakfast...'

'Eugh...please don't mention breakfast, sweetie pie, unless you want to come face to face with last night's evening meal again. Bloody hell, I'm sticking to wine in future...those cocktails were lethal!'

Despite my body screaming out in protest, I prised myself out of my surprisingly comfortable bed and staggered over to slide open the patio doors. The air that came in was hot, but at least it was air. Remembering just in the nick of time that tap water was to be avoided at all costs, or else be prepared for a two day excursion to the toilet, I was seriously thankful for the small bottle of fizzy orange I'd shoved into the fridge the night before. It may have cost a small fortune at Manchester airport but it was worth its weight in gold now. Popping a couple of headache pills out of the foil packet, I swallowed them with mouthfuls of orange, before chucking both the pills and the pop at Scarlett, nearly planting them in her face in the process.

No amount of persuasion or threats could drag Scarlett out of her bed - unless she was in a fit state to apply make-up and sort out her hair, she was going nowhere - so I stood briefly under the shower, only to discover that water was trickling out as and when it felt like it, and when it did grace me with its presence, it was still freezing cold (apparently there was a two hour window somewhere around late siesta time when the solar panels had heated up the water sufficiently, but you had to dive in quick before the other guests did - according to Sofia).

Bikini on, sundress on, flip flops on - and after a failed attempt to calm down my Diana Ross-style hair, which had taken on a life of its own - I made my way gingerly down the stairs, avoiding all eye contact with the pensioners chatting on the pathway, and wandered up to the little grocery shop I'd seen next to Elpitha.

The hand-painted (presumably by a toddler) sign above it read 'Supermarket' – it was wishful thinking on the owner's part as it seemed to sell very little and could barely be considered a 'mini' market let alone a 'super' one, but that was fine. After I'd spent all of three minutes browsing around, I purchased a massive container of water, two big bottles of fizzy pop, loo rolls, bread rolls, sliced ham, the biggest watermelon I'd ever seen in my life, and a few other random bits and pieces, and then had a slight panic attack about how I was hoping to stagger the short distance to the apartment block and up those steep stairs with all of the shopping bags, let alone the fifty litre (or thereabouts) container of water. The young boy behind the counter clearly noticed me sweating and fretting because he smiled and said 'You stay at Katerina Apartments? I help,' and without waiting for a response, he picked up the container as if it was weightless, grabbing a heavy carrier bag from me to balance himself out, and set off, whistling and scuffing his feet along the dusty pavement, as I trailed behind him, staggering under the weight of the water melon, but feeling distinctly like Baby Houseman in 'Dirty Dancing' – although perhaps a tad older, fatter and poorer.

Protesting feebly when he insisted he would also haul everything up the stairs, but hoping to god he wouldn't say 'Oh, okay then, ta-ta now,' and abandon me, I was mightily relieved when he behaved like a young gentleman to the end, assured me I was very welcome when I thanked him profusely, and ran swiftly back down the stairs again to return to work. It was only as I was unlocking the door to our room that I realised he'd left his shop unmanned and his till unattended while he'd come to my aid. God love him; if he'd done that in Manchester, the place would have been ransacked in the time that he had been absent. And another thought struck me as I backed into the apartment door to shove it open with my bum – he only looked about twelve. Bloody hell, they do start them young here.

Finding Scarlett in the same position as I'd left her, I yanked her up from her pillow by the tangled, damp hair on her head to check she was still alive and breathing.

'Piss off!' was the not very polite response I got, as she rolled over to the far side of the bed, but I knew just the strategy to get her moving.

'Mmmmm...I have coca-cola, bread and chocolate...come and get your tasty chocolate...mmmm...' I sang into her ear, whilst waggling a Bounty Bar in front of her nose, which totally did the job as Scarlett shot up, pressing one hand to her aching head whilst holding the other one out like a starving Oliver Twist begging for his supper.

After a rather strange meal of bread, ham and melting chocolate bar – all on one plate - Scarlett made it out as far as the balcony but had to decline the invitation to accompany me over to the beach, not wanting to stray too far from our bathroom in her delicate state – although she was still complaining loudly about having to stick her used toilet roll in the small bin by the loo rather than flush it down the drain, as was the norm back in Blighty ('I mean, for the love of god...there's basic and there's *basic* Jessica'). Feeling pretty delicate myself, but in desperate need of a decent coffee and a flomp on the beach, I once again descended the staircase, telling myself this was the first and last time I would let the excesses of a night out dictate the pace of the following day. My beady eye had spotted a small snack bar along from the supermarket, so I made my way there, waving at my young friend in the shop as I passed by.

My god I was getting brave! Here I was in a foreign country daring to wander about and explore on my own; to sit in a cafe by myself sipping coffee and watching the world go by. Of course the snack bar owner, who must have been about one hundred and twenty years old, wanted to know my entire life story, and he in turn revealed that he was the grandfather of supermarket boy – 'He – Spiros. Me – Spiros.' I had a feeling I was going to meet a heck of a lot more locals named Spiros, along with a few more Alex's and Apostolis' on this holiday; it appeared there was a very limited name pool amongst the Greeks. It was a pleasant coffee break and I enjoyed the chit chat, the revelation that Young Spiros was actually sixteen not twelve, and Old Spiros' personal recommendations of places we should visit on Loulouthia. At this rate, we would be lucky to see the entirety of Chaliki, let alone hike up to his cousin's taverna in the mountains, where you could apparently buy the best red wine on the island.

Sauntering over to the narrow pathway which led directly down to the beach, waving at Apostolis who was hopping onto a battered old scooter further down the street and yelling *'Yasoo!'* to a baseball-capped Alex who was unloading a stack of boxes from a car boot, I smiled contentedly to myself. I'd been here less than two days and already I was on first name terms with half of the village.

Surprisingly, Scarlett eventually staggered over to collapse onto the bed next to mine and we discussed potential plans for the upcoming evening and for the duration of our holiday. It was Scarlett's birthday during our second week and - surprise, surprise - she wanted to head on down to Skafos, the livelier resort at the other end of the island, to let her hair down in the bars there and finish the evening off in the one and only nightclub. Once a clubber, always a clubber.

We were racing each other back from a quick dip in the sea, which had done us the world of good and almost made us forget our stinking hangovers of earlier, when we heard a familiar voice shout out, 'SCARLETT FEVER AND JUST JESS! THE PARTY ANIMALS ARE ON THE LOOSE! HOW ARE THE HEADS THIS AFTERNOON?' and looked up, squinting against the dazzling sunlight, to see Alex and his wife dancing around on the terrace with the mop, clearly attempting a few of the embarrassing drunken moves we had so proudly demonstrated the previous evening on the bar top. The few people still remaining on the beach turned to look and laughed – it was clearly the norm and everyone graciously accepted their allocated celebrity nicknames and would, no doubt, remember their evenings partying or getting quietly sozzled in Sunrise for the rest of their days.

Craving big, fat, calorie-laden pizzas that particular evening, I recalled that the old boy from the snack bar had recommended we take a stroll down to Mama's, the pizza and pasta restaurant at the far end of the village, and ask for the Mediterranean Feast which, he had assured me, was popular with holidaymakers of every nationality. We were approximately half way through our second slice each, cheese and oil dripping messily down our chins, dubious sex noises escaping from our overstuffed mouths as we sighed and wallowed in the spicy deliciousness of the pizza, when two chairs were suddenly pulled out and dragged up to our table and a pair of good-looking men chose that precise moment to join us.

Desperately trying to mop my chin with a paper napkin, I uttered a shy 'Hi', while Scarlett merely laughed and said 'Well hello boys! Would you like to sample a slice of my pizza?' The smutty innuendo wasn't lost on them and did a great job of breaking the ice. Their names were Lawrence and Simon, they were English, and they had intended to spend their summer working their way around Greece – except when they had landed on Loulouthia, after an initial week's holiday on Corfu, they had felt compelled to stay, finding jobs further down the coast. Simon was strawberry blond, slim, recently divorced and waiting tables at a taverna at the harbour – and he made a beeline for Scarlett. Lawrence – 'Just call me Lorry,' he said, 'everyone does' – was blond, spectacularly tanned, apparently single and usually worked morning shifts at the new car hire place just off the main harbour road. They looked young and they were – Simon was twenty-seven and Lorry was even younger – just twenty-five years old. My god! I was almost old enough to be Lorry's mum! Granted, I would have been a gym-slip mother but, still.

Scarlett was flirting as if her life depended on it and Simon responded by becoming increasingly touchy-feely, resting his hand on her exposed thigh and leaning in to brush strands of her jet-black hair from her face. I definitely wasn't looking for a man or a relationship – however brief it may be – but Lorry was thoroughly good company, easy to talk to and we laughed about everything from the nineties clubbing scene to the cheek of his potential customers, wanting to hire cars for the price of a loaf of bread, some of them even minus their driving licence.

When it came to leaving the restaurant, it was decided without too much discussion that we would make our way up to our favourite bar again. The boys had clearly visited Sunrise before as we were greeted with shouts of 'SCARLETT FEVER MEETS SIMON LE BON...OOH LA LA! BUT LAWRENCE OF ARABIA WITH JUST JESS? – JUST NOOOO!'

In an attempt to avoid Lorry getting the wrong idea – that I was on the market and up for a quick snog and a cheeky feel - I left Scarlett with our two new acquaintances and sloped off to order more liquid refreshments, perching my ample backside on a stool at the bar to chat to Sofia, and thus allowing myself a little breathing space.

'So...you have new boyfriend!' Sofia said, clapping her hands together and dazzling me with her brightest smile. 'I think he is a very good-looking boy...lucky Just Jess!'

'Oh no, no, no! We've only just met these two guys! I don't have a boyfriend, I don't *want* a boyfriend. I was in a relationship for an awfully long time, so these days I am positively lapping up my freedom! No, I am definitely and deliberately single Sofia - not searching for love at all, or even just a holiday romance. Yes, Lorry is handsome and a bit of a catch but maybe for someone a little younger rather than a cynical old bird like me...'

'Hey, Just Jess!' Alex interrupted, expertly sliding four shot glasses down the bar, as if he were working in some Wild West saloon. The glasses stopped abruptly in front of me and he leant over to pour a thick green liquid into them – I didn't like to ask what it was but, I have to say, it did look fairly similar to stuff I usually wash my dishes with. Under no circumstances would it be travelling past *my* lips – after last night I had sworn to myself that I would be taking it easy – no more wasted mornings festering in bed. A couple of beers and maybe one cocktail would be my limit tonight, although I was pretty sure Scarlett would be off her face again by midnight.

'So, you are looking very beautiful tonight in this sexy, shimmering dress of yours, with those pretty flower clips in your hair...and I think Lawrence of Arabia is a very lucky man indeed!' Alex continued, winking as he placed the shot glasses on a tray, ready to carry them over to Scarlett, Lorry and Simon, who were eagerly awaiting their freebies.

'Thank you, but no thank you!' I said, waving him away when he waved the shots under my nose as he was passing. 'I was drunk from the knees down last night and I don't particularly want a repeat performance this evening! Scarlett will have mine – I'm pretty sure of that.'

I spent my night alternating between chatting with my friendly hosts at the bar and catching up with the others at their table, Scarlett and Simon becoming noisier by the minute. Occasionally I'd notice Lorry watching me closely, looking hopeful with his spaniel eyes; I didn't mean to be rude, so towards the end of the evening, as Scarlett and Simon were tangoing around the tables, I pulled up my chair next to him and we shared a pleasant half hour, when he told me all about his life in Essex, where he had worked for an insurance company and had an on-off girlfriend called Carly, who had keyed his car when they had split up. Great, a psychotic ex-girlfriend! Who doesn't want one of those?

A glance over at Scarlett and Simon confirmed they too were getting to know each other better, seemingly by ramming their tongues down each other's throats whilst grinding to the strains of Whitney Houston, and I sincerely hoped Lorry wasn't expecting a dose of the same. He was an attractive guy, a good six feet tall with an admirable physique, but for god's sake he was barely out of short trousers, and I DEFINITELY wasn't looking for a man. Realising the situation could become awkward unless I made a break for freedom, I swiftly returned to the bar and bade Alex and Sofia goodnight, refusing Alex's offer to see me back, before exiting the building quickly and quietly.

No matter how hot he was, I had no intention of sharing a bed with someone when I didn't even know their surname! In fact I couldn't imagine sharing my hot, sweaty mattress with anyone for the duration of the holiday, thank you very much. I had dragged Scarlett off to one side to put her in the picture, whispering that I would see her later; she was slurring her words and trying to remember all of the actions for the 'YMCA' dance routine at the time, so I very much doubted she would have any recollection of our discussion. However, it was agreed that she would ring my mobile, if I didn't hear her knock at the door when she returned. Who knew what time that might be? I'd be bloody lucky if she even remembered where we were staying, let alone how to use her phone.

Once I was out of the building, I slowed down and sauntered casually over the road and down the pathway to our apartments. It occurred to me as I was walking through the barely lit gardens, surrounded by fruit trees and, of course, a multitude of multi-coloured flowers, the silence only broken by the occasional chirping of a cricket and the odd rustle in the bushes, that I would never have put myself at risk like this back home in Manchester. Here I felt so safe and relaxed and could actually appreciate peaceful, solitary moments rather than clutching on to my rape alarm and preparing myself to knee an attacker in the nads.

Glowing with a warmth that wasn't just courtesy of the sunburn, I realised that I was already basking in a sense of belonging here - which was seriously unchartered territory for me, as I'd never felt that I belonged *anywhere* throughout all of my adult life.

This was my time.

Chapter 5

'Jess, wake up! JESS!' An urgent hammering at the apartment door rudely awoke me from my much-needed beauty sleep and resulted in an unexpected tumble out of bed - smack-bang on to the hard tiled floor.

'JESS! Let me in for god's sake, woman!'

Stomping and cursing, dressed in only my ancient Winnie the Pooh pyjamas, I flung the door open only to be roughly shoved aside by Scarlett, who was clearly anxious to avoid being spotted by any of our neighbours in the other apartments, particularly as she was, of course, wearing a slightly more rumpled and stained version of the clothes she'd looked so fabulous in the previous evening. Oh, how we'd all experienced that walk of shame.

'Where the hell have you been?' I barked at her. 'I was awake until about four...and then again at five-thirty...and your bloody mobile was dead and...er, 'scuse me...is that sand in your cleavage?'

'Busted! Sorry to worry you and all that...but I've had an *amazing* night, Jess. Aw...little Lorry was gutted you disappeared into the night and he departed shortly after you left...and then Simon bought a bottle of Prosecco and we took it down on to the beach with a couple of glasses from the bar – Sofia and Alex said well done you, by the way, for being sensible and heading home alone before the bewitching hour – and we talked for hours, all about his life in England and his shit divorce and his shit job...and then we watched the sun come up and it was so god damn beautiful and romantic...'

'Well, I have to admit that sounds wonderful Scarlett...and you'll probably remember that experience for the rest of your life. At least all the talking and admiring of the view meant that you didn't do the dirty deed then...thank goodness for that!'

'Oh yeah, course I did *that!* Simon's bloody gorgeous and he's a really nice guy...let's face it, who wouldn't?'

'Oh *Scarlett!* What have I told you about allowing them to get to first base on night number one? You know how it always turns out!'

'Oh I know...but this is different Jessie, I can just feel it! However, I can also now feel a whole load of sand scratching the insides of my thighs so I think it's best I have a shower before I crawl back into bed for the morning.'

For the sake of my trusting and frustratingly naughty friend, I truly hoped that this time it *would* turn out to be different. Because mopping up the tears and listening to the roaring and raging for weeks on end was heart-wrenching and draining, and seemed to be happening more and more often of late.

Scarlett did indeed decide to retire to her bed for a couple of hours rest and recuperation, so I took the opportunity to explore the village; as compact as it was, there was still plenty we hadn't seen, and I didn't want to miss a single thing. Waving at Young Spiros in the supermarket and Old Spiros in the snack bar as I passed, I headed up the hill, enticed by the smell of fresh bread wafting down from somewhere in the distance.

The bakery was in fact only a few doors up, past a cluttered gift shop and also a cafe that appeared to sell ice cream products and soft drinks, and nothing more. Attached to what seemed to be someone's two-storey house was the source of the mouth-watering aroma and, using my limited Greek, I bought some fresh rolls and a sticky pastry to enjoy with my coffee later. Besides apartments, there didn't seem to be much after the bakery, so I crossed over the road, watching out for cars racing down the hill at the speed of light - despite the locals' 'slowly, slowly' attitude to life, they always seemed to be in one hell of a rush to arrive at their destination whenever they got behind the wheel of their car.

Another bar...and an expensive looking shop selling gold jewellery and brightly coloured sarongs; this was adjoined to quite a sizeable restaurant named Horizon, which was advertising traditional beef stew on a chalkboard outside as its Special for the day. A gap between buildings and then a bike and scooter hire shop, more holiday accommodation and a small children's park area...and then I was back at the bar where-everyone-knows-your-name (sort of) where I wandered through to the terrace like a true native, noticing for the first time the sign above the door – *Taverna Sofia* – presumably named after Alex's drop-dead gorgeous wife. A beautiful name for a beautiful restaurant in the most perfect of locations; how lucky this couple were to have their own successful businesses in this most scenic of resorts on this divine island, and right on the beach! The view sure beat the one I'd had of a scruffy multi-storey car park in my last job.

After a frappé on the terrace – basically a cold coffee, something I'd never have ordered in England, but which hit the spot when you were basking in the sweltering temperatures of Greece - which was served by the sulky Soula, who was apparently Sofia's niece, I peeled off my sun dress, kicked off my flip-flops and retired to my favourite spot on the beach to stretch out and snooze in the sun. When I awoke I found the sunbed next to my own fully occupied – by Lorry, rather than Scarlett.

'Aah, Sleeping Beauty is finally awake! Good morning Jessica! I thought I would slide over to see if you were around, as I've been delivering a hire car to a customer in Chaliki – I'm just waiting for my lift back to the office.'

Shading my eyes with my hand, I noticed that rather than sporting standard beach wear he was actually dressed rather less casually in beige trousers and a white open-necked shirt – clearly the closest you got to a uniform when you were working on Loulouthia for the summer - and it suited him down to the ground, showing off his tan and his lean physique. He was very easy on the eye and if I wasn't careful I might be led into temptation...

'And may I say how fit you look clad only in your animal-print swimsuit...even if you *were* snoring and dribbling like my nan while you were asleep!'

'I was not, you cheeky bugger!' I lobbed my floppy sunhat at him, laughing as it knocked his sunglasses off his handsome, chiselled face.

'Your friend not with you then today? She's a bit of a one isn't she?' He glanced around as if expecting Scarlett to pop up from somewhere to clatter him.

'If, by that, you mean she likes to party until dawn then you're absolutely right – and all the more on holiday. What about *your* mate though...he seemed to be getting fairly carried away himself - he almost mounted poor Scarlett in the bar!'

'Don't...I didn't know where to look! Simon's actually pretending to work at the moment...although he's probably minging after all the beers and the tequila shots last night. What have you done with Scarlett the Harlot then?'

'Oy, you're not too pretty for a slap, you know! Last time I saw her, she was comatose between the sheets again, catching up on sleep she missed last night when they were misbehaving until all hours. She'll probably come round just as it's time for us to go out again tonight!'

'Ah...I see. Unfortunately, we won't be down this neck of the woods tonight as I've agreed to do an evening shift, so my opposite number can have his night off.'

'Aw that's a shame.' It was and it wasn't – as much as I'd enjoyed their company, I didn't want an immediate repeat performance; to be tied to two guys for the entire duration of our holiday rather than Scarlett and I enjoying some quality time together, meeting a variety of interesting people and venturing a little further afield, if the mood suited us.

'Yes. It really is,' he replied, grinning and leaning over to take a cheeky drink out of my small bottle of water. 'Because I was thoroughly enjoying getting to know you, Jessica Woodward. Oh, here we are – my lift's arrived – I'd better hop on before he zooms off without me. Hopefully see you tomorrow?'

'Er...I'm not sure what we're doing tomorrow, to be honest...we're thinking we might do a bit of exploring, so we may not be around.' We had actually agreed we would jump on the bus to Loulouthia Town, to make a withdrawal from the cash machine there and hopefully see a little more of the area than we'd glimpsed when we'd docked into the harbour. But I didn't know Lorry *that* well yet; for all I knew, he could be a common thief or a scammer who intended to rob us blind, so perhaps best not to mention that we would be carrying a wad of Euros around Town with us. It still made me giggle that it was actually called 'Loulouthia Town' when, as beautiful as it was, it was hardly packed with shops and entertainment venues. It was the smallest town I'd ever seen, that's for sure.

Much later, after I'd applied several layers of sun tan lotion but sweat out practically every liquid I'd consumed over the last three days, Scarlett appeared by my side, looking incredibly perky for one who had been rolling around the beach up to no good all night long.

We decided to eat early, in Sofia's, where we had the most delicious barbequed lamb chops and Greek salad I'd ever tasted and Scarlett spent most of the mealtime texting Simon and providing me with details I was sure I hadn't asked for concerning his lower body parts. Yack.

The evening saw us heading off on a pub crawl up and down Chaliki, if you could call four bars a pub crawl, but it was good fun and we were royally entertained by the different bartenders and staff and met some real characters who were holidaying on the island.

Our local was full to the brim when we finally made our grand entrance, so we exchanged greetings with Alex and Sofia, invested in a large carafe of rosé wine and hit the beach again, removing our strappy shoes and tiptoeing barefoot across the sands. Sipping a glass of ice cold wine on a balmy night, relaxing on a sun-lounger whilst listening to the rhythmic sound of the waves, with the soft music from the restaurant tinkling on in the background – it's what memories are made of. Gulping back a glass of lukewarm, cheap supermarket plonk whilst slaving over the ironing board and watching Eastenders in my dressing gown, well it just couldn't compare.

After an indeterminable length of time, when Scarlett and I had lapsed into a comfortable silence, merely staring up at the inky night sky, each of us lost in our own thoughts, we heard footsteps padding through the sand behind us and turned to see Alex approach with another small carafe of wine and a third glass.

'Ladies,' he said, topping up our glasses before pouring just a little into his own. I'd quickly cottoned on to the fact that's what he did every time - just drank a little to everyone else's lot, to stop himself getting rat-arsed every night. 'I bring you more of the local *krassi* and we will raise our glasses and share a toast.'

We obediently lifted our glasses and chinked them with his as he said, 'To a lifetime of pleasure and peace, sprinkled with a little of the magic of Loulouthia...may all our stars forever shine as brightly as those up there in the sky tonight.'

Simple words - and if they'd been blurted out of the mouth of some Mancunian Likely Lad, I would probably have peed myself laughing - but there and then, in the moment, I was incredibly moved and felt a lump forming in my throat, and even Scarlett remained quiet, which was a miracle in itself.

For a time there was just the ocean and the music and our heartbeats.

And then normal service resumed.

'*Yamas!*' cheered Alex. 'Enjoy your evening, Scarlett Fever and Just Jess. *Yamas, yamas, yamas!*'

Chapter 6

Simply heavenly was how I would describe the days and evenings that followed. The trip into 'Town' was a revelation. There was much more to it than at first glance, with its incredible architecture and rich history, and we kept stopping to look at this building and that – the huge church with its fifty steps, the peculiar-shaped museum, the bustling Town square where the Beautiful People sat sipping their Espressos from tiny cups. We passed the morning strolling up and down by the harbour, admiring some of the enormous, luxurious yachts and laughing at a dilapidated, little fishing vessel that had been optimistically named 'The Queen of the Seas'; we became lost in the maze of roads and pathways and were almost flattened by a speeding Mercedes racing towards us up a narrow side street; we ate grilled sardines and salted calamari at a table overlooking the sea, where the whisper of a breeze cooled us down and we could hear the hum of the watersports in the distance, drifting across from Skafos beach.

And we also found ourselves sharing yet another carafe of locally produced wine, lounging outside a *cafeneion* amongst a pack of squabbling pensioners, while Scarlett draped herself over Simon and I tried to fend off a persistent youth selling cigarette lighters disguised as pistols, who later attempted to persuade me that my life would be incomplete if I didn't also purchase an egg-shaped torch for those late night returns to the apartment. At least I think it was a torch.

Funny how Simon just happened to be there when we were walking past. Mmm. We also stumbled upon Lorry, who was in the process of renting out a Suzuki Jimney to a family who really didn't look as if they would fit in it. I decided to hang around to talk to him, while Scarlett admired expensive leather handbags in the shop next door. Conceding that I *did* quite like Lorry, and not wishing to appear rude, when he asked for my mobile number I gave it to him, without hesitation. His persistence must have been unconsciously nibbling away at my defences – that and the fleck of amber in his soft brown eyes and the way the muscles in his back rippled through the thin fabric of his shirt as he leant over to deal with a sheaf of paperwork. I really must stop perving.

We lazed and tanned our way through the sweltering Greek days, and laughed and boozed our way through the humid Greek nights. Simon blew hot and cold, drifting in and out of our holiday lives, sometimes attentive and passionate towards Scarlett, sometimes worryingly vacant and seemingly unable to hear his mobile whenever she rang him, repeatedly. She responded by playing him at his own game and snogging a hairy old Greek guy who kept patting her on her behind and who wore a nifty line in seventies catalogue clothing. Somehow, I don't think Simon would have been too jealous.

Lorry was consistent. If he said he would be there, then he was. More often than not, he tried to buy my drinks, although I always insisted I would prefer to pay my own way. He never crossed the line - he didn't throw himself at me and expect sex on tap - but he did make it perfectly clear that he wanted me, very much, and was desperate for something to develop between the two of us. Back home he would have been way out of my league and the age difference meant I would never have considered him as potential boyfriend material...and I'm bloody sure he wouldn't have looked at me twice - funny how foreign climes can lower boundaries and standards...and how everyone appears so much more exotic on holiday.

Much of my time was spent in Sunrise and Sofia's and I was almost part of the furniture. Some customers obviously thought I *was* a paid member of staff because on more than one occasion I was asked for a round of drinks as I sat at the bar, propped up on my elbows, sharing life experiences with Sofia. In fact, on the Saturday night I *did* get off my backside and get stuck in, helping out when the place was heaving and Alex and Sofia couldn't keep up with the drinks orders and Soula had gone AWOL, as was par for the course. She seemed to have a knack for that. I'd never done bar work but was at least able to clear tables for them, pop a few bottle tops off and deliver bills to customers waiting to settle up and leave.

Tuesday came around quickly; the day of Scarlett's birthday. For someone who was seriously sleep deprived and permanently pissed, she was up frighteningly early, merrily singing Happy Birthday to herself and reading out funny texts from her kids. They'd purchased her presents well in advance, and wrapped them up and stuffed them in her luggage before she'd left England (customs would have a bloody field day with her); she was chuffed to bits to discover that they'd pooled their money to buy her a gorgeous owl charm for her Pandora bracelet, along with a pair of pretty, silver teardrop earrings and a flimsy, cut-off top from New Look.

We'd agreed I would buy her a gift on the island, to save carting anything over on the plane and ferry, but although I'd had plenty of time to take off on my own to choose something suitable, in truth there wasn't an awful lot in the shops here *to* buy that would be Scarlett's kind of thing, and that wouldn't set me back a few hundred Euros. I'd therefore settled for a litre of Jack Daniels and a bag similar to the one she'd admired in town, a small wad of money concealed within, supposedly as a bonus surprise. This had led to a frantic search of the bin some time later when it became apparent that Scarlett had unwittingly chucked it out along with the ball of tissue paper padding.

She'd told literally everyone everywhere that it was her birthday, which reaped its rewards as Mandy had slipped a card under the door to our apartment, there had been shouts of congratulations from the two pairs of pensioners who were our nearest neighbours, and the cleaner greeted her on the path with a kiss on both cheeks and a bag of lemons. We ate doughnuts on the beach for breakfast, drank beers with Apostolis and Alex in the bar at lunchtime and wherever we went, people wished her 'Happy Birthday' and she was positively glowing. For all her outer shell of confidence, I knew buried deep inside there was a soft centre riddled with insecurity and I realised how much all of this would mean to her.

Post-siesta, after an almost lukewarm shower experience, we titivated ourselves singing along to the latest dance tunes blasting out of Scarlett's mobile - hopefully the OAPs in the next apartment would forgive us on this very special occasion. It was bloody hard work, slapping on the make-up at the earlier time of seven, rather than eight-thirty; it was still *so* hot and we were minus air conditioning – we'd opted not to pay extra to use the unit in our room, figuring that the heat was doable so early on in the season, particularly when the showers were usually mind-numbingly cold and there was a light breeze in the evening that blew through the apartment when we propped both doors open, hoping there wasn't some opportunist rapist or burglar lurking out there, waiting to catch us off guard and run in and do their worst.

Lorry came to collect us in the finest of the fleet of hire cars (I do hope his boss never finds out) and drove us in style over to Skafos which, although very far removed from the likes of Ayia Napa and Benidorm, was far busier than Chaliki and even Loulouthia Town, and had a variety of restaurants and bars on the main strip, one with live entertainment, another with karaoke and all with louder music than was ever heard on the streets of our much more timid resort.

Scarlett was in her element, bouncing around like Tigger wherever we went, often grinding with all shapes and sizes of men, and a fair few women, while I took various pictures of her posing and sticking her tongue out. Simon and Lorry caught up with us in the karaoke bar, which we left abruptly after they murdered a Lionel Richie classic, and as they showed us the way to the sole nightclub on the island, Lorry took my little hand in his much larger one and I didn't put up any resistance. Maybe it was the alcohol, maybe it was the party atmosphere and the birthday celebrations, but I decided there and then that I actually enjoyed close contact with him and felt no desire to pull away.

Only when the balls of my feet were burning so intensely that they were in danger of actually catching fire, did I finally call it quits with the dancing, although Scarlett was still leaping around and showing no signs of slowing down. I stepped outside for a breath of fresh air and Lorry followed close behind; apparently he wanted to ensure I was safe and not about to disappear into the night. Despite my determination not to lead him on, I sank into his strong arms and tilted my chin up so he could kiss me fully on the lips. It was good – he tasted of Metaxa and freshly chewed gum – and he didn't slobber all over me as I'd known other men to do – like they were licking around an ice cream cone and scared of missing any blobs they'd stumped up good money for.

All things considered, he was pretty talented in the kissing department and I could have happily carried on chewing his face off until we were forced to come up for air, but I knew one thing would have led to another, and we'd have ended up spending the night together...and right then my need for my own bed was greater than any need to have intimate relations with a man I'd known for less than a week. Pushing him gently away as his hands began to wander and the warning bells started to ring in my danger zone, I said, 'Thank you for that...and thank you for a really lovely night...but right now, I badly need some sleep. Let's go and drag the others off the dancefloor and then we can head back. And don't forget, YOU, my boy, have work in the morning!' Christ, I sounded like his mother.

Of course Scarlett decided she would be staying overnight with Simon – I'm not sure that he had a say in the matter – and so when we finally flagged down a taxi ('Oh hello Yiannis! What a coincidence that we're jumping in *your* taxi again! What? There are only two taxi drivers on the island? Well no bloody wonder then!'), I ejected them all at the top of the road leading down to the harbour, as it was only a short walk from there to the boys' apartment (I wished Lorry the best of luck, attempting sleep in the next bed to those two going at it hammer and tong all night), and I continued on to Chaliki. At least I felt safe with Yiannis, although my stomach lurched a few times as he flew over the bumps in the road and I prayed to god we wouldn't meet any other vehicle coming in the opposite direction. After I'd paid him and said goodnight, I rolled out of the taxi outside of Sunrise, and was dragged in for a nightcap by Alex and Sofia who were just in the process of closing up.

'You are very tired I think, Just Jess,' said Alex softly, stating the bleeding obvious as my eyelids began to close in the middle of our intelligent conversation about who had the biggest feet amongst us. They insisted on escorting me back and depositing me in my room, Sofia checking that the balcony doors were safely locked and that I had water by my bed for when I began to dehydrate – because it was going to happen - and this lovely couple even waited outside until they'd heard me turn the key in the lock and shout 'Night night, Awesome Alex and Sofia Loren! See you in the morning peeps!'

Rolling contentedly into my bed and pulling the sheet fully over me to guard against mosquitos, I mumbled to myself, 'I bloody love you two, my new lovely-jubbly gorgeous and sexy friends. *Kalinichta,* beautiful Greek people. Good night.'

Even as I was muttering on, my heavy eyes were already drifting shut again and I let my head fall to the pillow, irrespective of the fact that once more I was still fully dressed, allowing the waves of sleep to wash over me, like the waves on Ammos Beach.

Chapter 7

You know what I hate? I hate that the second week of a fortnight's holiday speeds by like a superfast train running seriously behind schedule. The first week seems to tootle by so slowly and it feels like you have all the time in the world ahead of you to appreciate the beauty of your surroundings and to consume enough alcohol to give your liver a wobble. The days stretch out before you and you spend half your time giving it, 'Is it Wednesday? It is, it's only Wednesday you know – we've still got a week and a half left, can you believe it?'

The second week is a bastard - racing away from you like the clappers, and you're trying to play catch up all of the time and panicking about how much you still want to do and see...and all the while, time is running out. Tick tock.

Once the birthday celebrations were over, the days felt like hours and the hours felt like minutes. With the exception of the post-birthday hangovers, we made a concerted effort to stay longer on the beach and to drink more in Sunrise - it was our favourite place after all. We also made sure we'd visited every bar, restaurant and shop in the resort and we were desperately trying to work our way through all the food on the menus that had taken our fancy, even if it meant we would be returning home two stone heavier and with a serious addiction to olive oil and feta cheese.

Home. I didn't want to think about it – it didn't seem possible that we would soon be back in cold, old Manchester, no doubt watching the rain lash down every day whilst fat, skint and miserable, and all this would just be a distant memory, which would inevitably fade over time.

Lorry was still being incredibly sweet to me, although if he'd been hoping for a repeat performance of Kissygate, then he was sadly disappointed. He seemed confused by my keeping him at arm's length, particularly when we seemed to fit together so nicely, and especially with my impending departure drawing ever nearer, but I couldn't explain it to him as *I* didn't even know what was wrong with me. He was attractive and funny and generous and a whole other load of plus points all condensed and rolled into one, although I did feel somewhat of a cougar when we were sat together and I cringed as I wondered if people would think he was my son, but I saw plenty of stranger looking couples out and about. Whatever it was that was holding me back, I just wasn't in that place with him yet and I wasn't sure if we would get it together properly before I was on that ferry and flight back to the UK on Monday. Gulp.

Simon was being Simon – sometimes sarcastic, often elusive and I think I liked him less as every day passed by. He seemed to have got the message that his bullshit didn't wash with me and any conversation between us usually went like this:

'Hi, *Jessica*...still chubby then.'

'Hi, *Simon*...still a dickhead then.'

We were civil when Scarlett and Lorry were around though, on our best behaviour for the sake of our friends.

Three days before we were due to return home, Scarlett and I discovered the Hotel Diana. If we'd just wandered further up the hill, around the next sharp bend and slightly out of Chaliki on our previous jaunts we would have literally fell upon it – a beautifully designed, ultra-modern hotel, with not one, but TWO brand new, seriously inviting swimming pools, which were open to anyone. We adored the beach, but a late afternoon breeze blew in sometimes from nowhere and whipped up the sand, which stuck to every bit of our sun-creamed bodies, so much so that we felt like a couple of those doughnuts that were being sold up and down the resort. It was therefore a real treat to de-sand under the outdoor showers at the Diana, recline on one of their more comfortable sun loungers for an hour with a fancy cocktail, and then slide into one of the immaculate, kidney-shaped pools, where there was barely a ripple in the water.

When we first entered the main building of the hotel we were greeted by an English receptionist, whose name badge told us that she was a 'Lauren'. She was polite and efficient and pointed us in the direction of the toilets and changing areas, should we need to use them. I was intrigued to hear how she had ended up on Loulouthia and longed to hear her story, so I practically swooped on her when she rocked up at the swimming pool after her shift had clearly finished, discarding her name badge, her uniform and her shoes in favour of an all-in-one lime green swimsuit and black, shiny flip-flops, her blonde hair pulled up into a top-knot. She also seemed to have discarded her polite reception manner because she was slightly frosty with me as I leant over to say 'hi' and asked her how long she'd been working at the hotel, and if she was a relative newcomer to the island.

'This is my second year working at the Diana...it's a decent place and there are definite perks to the job, such as being able to immerse myself in the pool after work if it's quieter – that's not so easy when there's lots of guests around because – even though you would think the swimsuit and flip flops would be a huge giveaway - they don't seem to realise that I've clocked off and insist on pestering me about breakfasts and air conditioning and the price of safety deposit boxes, while I'm just trying to wind down.'

My cheeks burned, and it wasn't down to the heat of the sun; I hoped she didn't think *I* was pestering her; she was a fellow English woman and I was merely interested in discovering how she came to be a resident of this jewel of an island that shone so brightly in the middle of the Ionian Sea.

'The boundaries between work and my own free time inevitably become blurred. I do like to try and have an hour of relaxation though in the quieter months – sometimes you start to take it all for granted and forget to enjoy what is all around you.'

'I've truly fallen in love with this island,' I confided in her, although I didn't know why, as she seemed so keen to move away; to abandon her sun bed and ease herself into the pool; to be by herself and refrain from disclosing details of her private life here to complete strangers who were too nosy for their own good. Maybe that was the problem - perhaps she was sick of answering the same questions that were fired at her, day in day out, by English tourists, eager to know why she made the move and envying her lifestyle. I continued anyway, with a desire to convey what emotions Loulouthia stirred up in me and a need to explain how I had fallen under its spell.

'It seems like the most perfect place on earth. Its beauty, its simplicity, its innocence...I've never been anywhere like it. And anything goes here – yesterday I saw a father, mother and young child all on one moped – and the mother was carrying three massive bags of shopping. You just don't see that anywhere else, I can tell you. I know that's perhaps as well, as it's obviously highly dangerous, but they were only pootling along for a short distance and it was clearly just an ordinary daily occurrence for them. Everyone seems so chilled here and content with their lot. Really, you're so very lucky to live on Loulouthia.'

She didn't sneer at me, but there was a definite 'Ha!' and a shake of the blonde head before she checked herself and realised she'd probably drifted far out of the politeness zone and needed to quickly steer herself back into it, before she came across as seriously rude.

'It *is* a beautiful part of the world, although I think you appreciate it more when you are on holiday rather than when you actually live here. The flowers – of course – they're everywhere, and they are colourful and wonderful, and they make the island what it is. The beaches, the mountains, the views...the harbour in particular is my favourite location and always draws me back when I have some precious free time, to sit at my favourite taverna, sipping a frappé and watching the boats come in. I always love listening to the fishermen shouting out to their customers on the shore, selling their catch and keeping a little back for themselves, to take home to feed their families. That's my personal happy place where I really feel at ease.'

She looked a little sad then, as if she wasn't allowed to be happy, which I found rather odd – she was living the dream and most people would kill to be in her position. I knew I would.

'However, despite all of those positives, I didn't come here because of any of them. I came here because I met someone, on holiday - I fell in love, but then I went home and tried to forget him.'

'But you couldn't?'

'No, for my sins, I couldn't! So I jacked in my job and left my family behind in Hereford, and I came back. I literally gave up everything to be with Andreas.'

'Aw that's a real love story – and I adore a fairytale ending! You're so fortunate; I would swap places with you in a heartbeat.'

She smiled then, and when she did, her face lit up; maybe she was a better person under all of that aloofness and, I don't know, *suspicion.*

'Yes, I am a *very* lucky lady, and I know I should count my blessings. Well, nice to meet you...sorry – I didn't catch your name...oh, Jessica...I'll bet Alex has had a field day with that...are you Jessica Rabbit? Or Jessica Simpson? No, let me guess, Jessie J?'

She started to collect her belongings from around her and I realised our brief conversation was already being terminated.

'Actually no...my friend here is Scarlett Fever – although she is mightily disappointed that she didn't get allocated 'Scarlett O'Hara' – but I only managed 'Just Jess', nothing more - I don't seem to have achieved celebrity status!'

'Well, I was Lauren Bacall when I first arrived...but not so much these days. Anyway, I literally have to get on my bike now, as I need to snatch a couple of hours sleep with Andreas before he leaves for work and then I have to resume my cleaning duties in the house - no rest for the wicked eh? Enjoy the rest of your holiday, Just Jess.'

And then she was gone and I was left thinking, well that was a slightly weird conversation – she was a bit of a strange one. Flipping 'eck, I wasn't *that* boring, and I would have expected her to engage a little more - you know, one Brit talking to another...and we could have shared a drink and possibly a few laughs together, but she seemed determined to maintain her distance. Oh well, I wasn't going to dwell on it.

Scarlett, true to form, was trying to chat up the barman whilst giggling and pulling her already flat tummy in, god love her. She waved and grinned and, happy that she was behaving herself and wasn't about to sneak into the laundry room for a quick roll amongst the dirty towels, I lay back in the sun, fantasising about eloping to a remote Greek island, where the sun always shone, the beers were always cold, and the air was always filled with the scent of wild flowers.

Chapter 8

By the time Saturday came around, even though we still had two full days of our holiday remaining, there was a permanent lump in my throat and an unrelenting ache in my heart. No one ever wanted to go home from a brilliant holiday, I was being stupid, I repeatedly told myself...but the fear of returning to a life of...*nothing*...would not evaporate; how could I ever leave this island behind me and live on just the memories – the *feeling* of being here, which itself would eventually bleed away and, I knew, would leave me with just a sense of unparalleled loss. Even if I booked to come here again next summer, how could I survive twelve whole months away from this heaven on earth that had consumed me; that had affected me in such an epic way?

Not wanting to put a downer on the last forty-eight hours of our holiday, I chose not to share my emotions with Scarlett – she was literally skipping about the place because Simon was all over her again like a rash...maybe because he was aware that she would be gone soon and he could move on to his next unsuspecting victim. My towel rolled up under my arm, my bag full of magazines and sun tan lotions, I headed for the beach after lunch while she disappeared with him to our apartment for an early 'siesta' – I bloody hoped they stayed off my bed – the thought of Simon and his hairy chest and wandering willy tangled up in my cotton sheets turned my stomach and made me want to sleep on the balcony instead, with the assortment of flower pots and squadron of mosquitos.

All of the plastic sunbeds along my favourite stretch of beach were taken, either with bums on seats or brightly coloured towels – most of the locals flocked to the best of the beaches at weekends and I hadn't been quick enough off the mark to reserve my usual spot, which meant spreading my towel out flat on the sand and enduring the lumps and bumps underneath, but I didn't really mind. I sat and hugged my knees to my chest...thinking and wondering and imagining...

'Hey, Just Jess. You look sad.' Alex had crept up behind me, holding out a bottle of Amstel and an iced glass, straight from the freezer, and indicating I should budge up on the towel, to allow him to park his rear by my side.

'What's the matter, Just Jess? Please tell me what is troubling you and it will help to ease your burden. I will be your Agony Uncle!'

'Uncle Alex? You and Sofia have been more like my substitute parents while I've been here...always looking out for me, treating me as if I'm one of your family. I can't wait to meet your son tonight, now he's back from Athens...maybe he will be like the brother I never had!'

'Mmm...I think you will like Yiorgos, he is a good child with a heart of gold. He has many, many girlfriends though...he thinks he is a playboy, but really he is a mummy's boy!'

'I bet he's lovely, just like his parents. Oh Alex...what will I do without the pair of you and everyone else I've met here? There will be a huge hole in my heart when I'm back in England that I don't think can ever be repaired...'

'You want to stay.'

It was a statement, not a question, and Alex had hit right at the heart of the problem. Yes, I wanted to stay. Despite berating myself for my silliness, and constantly repeating that I needed to pull myself together and get a handle on reality again, I couldn't stop imagining what it would be like to live here, and not - repeat NOT - in Manchester.

I'd honestly *tried* to think about what I would do when I returned to the UK, and how I would go about finding another job not too far from home that paid a decent enough wage.

But then I'd seen the sign outside of Mama's restaurant, and it had stopped me abruptly in my tracks. The owner was advertising for a waiter or waitress; he needed another member of staff now that the season was truly underway and business was picking up nicely.

And I wanted the job.

But I hadn't said it out loud before. I hadn't mentioned it to Scarlett; I couldn't bring myself to raise the subject with anyone. Maybe people would laugh at me and my other friends back home would think I had totally lost the plot...and there *was* Scarlett to consider – she had Manchester running through her like wording in a stick of rock and I was fairly sure she wouldn't want to stay, and I couldn't let her travel all the way back to the UK by herself. Besides, there were the logistics of it all to consider. Where would I live? Was it possible to manage on the money I could earn here? What about my house back in England? Christ, I was being ridiculous; it was all just a pipedream. Lucky Lauren at the pool bar – she had done it and was living the life I yearned for. But I had to put a stop to all of this nonsense in my head and accept the fact that I would be on that ferry on Monday, on the first leg of my journey back to my homeland, where I belonged.

Except I didn't belong there. Not really. I had no real family there now. No husband or partner to consider. No ties. No job. No actual desire to be there. Jesus, my head was in a mess.

I turned to face Alex and smiled sadly, 'I do want to stay Alex; I want to be around for the Flower Festival next week; I want to explore every inch of the island including those secluded bays right up at the tip that you've told me all about; I want to be here for the whole summer and not miss one single day. But I'm afraid I have to go. I'm no Shirley Valentine; I have a life, of sorts, back in England. And it wouldn't be fair to Scarlett...she only came here because *I* wanted to! No...we arrived here together and we should leave together. She's my best friend and I can't let her down.'

Alex paused for a moment, appearing to mull it all over in his head before saying, 'I like Scarlett Fever, but she does what she wants to, without considering anyone else...she often leaves you on your own like Bobby-No-Mates while she pleases herself. Where is she now? I think she is making Jiggy Jiggy with Simon Le Bon. Scarlett - she is fun, but wild...you are a very good girl – you would be happy here. I think that you have taken Loulouthia to your heart and it would hurt you very much to leave it behind. You must do what is best for you, not Scarlett. You need a family...and you have one here on this island, where we all look out for each other. Think carefully, Just Jess. Make the right decision. That is all.'

I didn't bother to correct him by telling him the saying was '*Billy*-No-Mates'; I liked the way he often got it wrong but in a cute way. A tiny part of me wondered if he deliberately cocked it up sometimes because he knew it was funny...

When he returned to the bar, which was very much open for business throughout the days as well as the evenings at weekends, I remained in the same position for some time, slurping my Amstel and wondering where my future lay. By the time I left, the beach was beginning to clear, and I wondered where all those brown-as-a-berry locals were returning to. The old stone houses with the ridiculously thick walls that were all the way up in the mountains? Or the simple, box-like, whitewashed homes that were literally dripping with flowers in the picturesque villages? Or perhaps just to more modern, first floor apartments, which were situated above their family businesses? Wherever they had come from, wherever they were returning to – how lucky they were to have this oasis of tranquillity practically on their doorstep.

Scarlett sent me a text to inform me that she and Simon had 'finished up' in the apartment and had wandered down to see Mr Toothy for a gyros in the snack bar on the corner. The 'finished up' bit made me want to throw up...but the gyros sounded perfect – I was hungry but didn't think I could stomach a massive meal, and these local delicacies were delicious. I just needed Simon to piss off pronto - which luckily he did as he was due in work within the hour - to enable me to have a chat with Scarlett, to test the waters. Or perhaps if I hinted at what was on my mind then maybe she'd put me straight, tell me what a plonker I was being, and remind me of a few of the joys of living in Manchester. Whatever they were.

'Aw god, these kebab things are the boss! I bloody love the mixture of the meat and the chips and the salad...and I can't believe I'm eating tzatziki...I'm getting proper Greek I am!' Scarlett tucked into her food like she was eating her last meal on death row; she'd clearly worked up an appetite throughout the afternoon.

I didn't like to point out that Proper Greeks probably didn't piss away half of the night and then spend the next afternoon shagging some absolute gobshite in the stifling summer heat. But, she was on holiday after all.

'I know, I won't half miss the food...but then again I'll miss everything about this place. I'm experiencing withdrawal symptoms and I've not even left! My mum and dad had their heads screwed on coming here – I mean, what a find! When all my friends were holidaying in Cornwall or flying off to Sunny Spain, my parents were wandering off the beaten track to a remote Greek island, when tourism was in its infancy and where the locals had only just got electricity! Real intrepid explorers they were, my ma and pa.'

'And you never would have thought it, looking at your dad in his cardigan and slippers!'

Shaking my head, I laughed out loud – she was absolutely right. No one who had met my dad, who had seemed so set in his ways and such a home bird, would have guessed that he had been such a keen traveller in his younger years.

'I'm so glad they found Loulouthia, and I'm only surprised that they never returned. If it had been down to me, I would have come back every year...my god, it will be such a wrench to leave here on Monday...'

'I hear you. The thought of buggering off home and leaving all this and my sexy Simon behind does not particularly fill me with deep joy.'

'Well...it's funny you should say that because...you see, the thing is...Scarlett...I've been thinking - and I know this sounds nuts and you're probably going to tell me that I've lost it - but we don't *really* have anything to go back for that won't keep, do we? We have no jobs to lose, and you're surrendering the tenancy on your house anyway...and, in the words of Beyoncé, we're both single ladies. With the exception of my Aunty Pam – and I only usually see her at Christmas and birthdays - I have absolutely no one to go back for...so...Miss Scarlett...what do you say we stay for a while? What if we delayed our departure for the time being? The last fortnight has flown by far too quickly and it seems such a shame to leave when we don't have much to go home to. Why don't we do something spontaneous for once in our lives and look for jobs right here...in Greece...on Loulouthia?'

'Excuse me? Are you being serious? Are these words actually spilling out of your mouth, Mrs-Won't-Ever-Take-A-Chance, or are they in fact my words and I'm just a brilliant ventriloquist? Because that little speech you just gave certainly sounds like something I would say. Stay here? Don't go home? People will say we're bloody crackers! And they'd probably be right...but you know what...I don't freakin' care...because...guess what...I agree with every word you've just said - I want to stay too!'

'WHAT? I mean...*what?* Really? Are you sure? Because I truly don't want to leave Scarlett...I *never* want to leave!'

'Well, hold your horses, Dora the Explorer, because we would be leaving *eventually,* at the end of the season when the work dries up and the best of the weather has been and gone...but we could easily find jobs here now Jess...there's loads of places in Skafos advertising for staff. In fact, Simon reckons they're crying out for waiters and waitresses in Town as well. We'll walk into a job! And I've already told Adam and Adele that I think we might be extending our holiday, so they're not expecting me home just yet. I can read you like a book, Jessie Girl, and your longing to stay has been written all over your face...I was just waiting for you to admit it!'

Relief and joy flooded through me in equal measures. I couldn't believe it – all that worrying and indecisiveness and all the time Scarlett had been itching to stay and been hatching plans of her own! But there were still practicalities to consider...

'Oh and before you start harping on about practicalities, my kids are clearing my stuff out of my crappy house as we speak and storing it all in Viola's garage, and she'll be keeping an eye on my two little delinquents, when they're around that is! Adam's off to Cyprus for most of the summer with his college mates, and Adele seems to have forgotten I exist since she met the wonderful Lee – although she has said they will definitely be coming over for a holiday in July if we decide to stay. No doubt Darren will hand over a wad of cash for *that.*'

Darren, Scarlett's ex, was the father of her kids, and someone who Scarlett had treated like a cash machine for all of her married life. He was a great guy, and she *had* loved him to death, but they'd clashed as a couple, always arguing and sparring and scoring points off each other. When they'd ended up actually physically fighting one night, over him supposedly eyeing up the pretty barmaid when her back was turned, Darren had said enough was enough, kissed the kids, promised them that they'd never lose him, and walked out of the door for good. He'd remarried since, was settled and happy, and adored Adam and Adele, always treating them and digging them out of holes. What he had refused to do, besides paying the necessary maintenance until the kids were of age, was to continually clear off Scarlett's numerous debts and enormous credit card bills.

'What about my house though Scarlett? I have a mortgage to pay and I don't want to leave it standing empty. I'll have bloody squatters in it by the end of summer if I don't sort it out.'

'Now you're trying to talk yourself out of staying! Look, Heather needs a place to live, now her landlord's selling up. She's decent and she's good with money and you've known her for years...Viola's got your spare keys, she can sort the place out for you and be an emergency contact over in England if any problems occur. I bet if you ring Heather now and ask her, she'll be moving in before you can say 'That's £600 a month rent please!' Problem solved!'

God yes, Heather had been served notice and was struggling to find a new place to live – she was terrified she was going to end up back at her mum's again. And she wasn't a party animal or a scammer; she'd look after my home while I was away rather than trash it.

'Can we really do this, do you think, Mrs? Surely if it was so easy everyone would be doing it!'

'Oh, of course we can! Stop looking for obstacles, you bloody pessimist! *Everyone* isn't doing it because they *do* have ties back home and because they're not as brave and adventurous as me and you. The first thing we need to do though is find somewhere to live – our apartment is fully booked for the summer...and I doubt we'd be able to afford the rent all season anyway – we need to find somewhere *much* cheaper.'

'We'd better ask around then...Sofia and Alex may be able to help...or Apostolis...hopefully one of them will know of somewhere suitable in this area...'

'Well, I'll ask Simon too, and you can ask Loverboy Lorry...although they might only know of accommodation in Town, and I'm betting you will probably want to stay in this area...'

'If we can, yes. Sorry, because I know that makes our task a little more difficult, but I adore this sleepy little resort and all the people in it...and you know what, there's even a job advertised at Mama's that one of us could go for. It's fate, it is!'

'Oh you can bloody have that job...I'm going to try my luck at one of the livelier bars in Skafos – just think, I'll be able to enjoy a few drinkies and have fun on the job as well! Although hiring a scooter will be a must if I'm working over the other side of the island – it's not far by car but I don't fancy a three hour walk home after work in the early hours of the morning – so maybe I'll save the heavy drinking for nights when Simon can pick me up.'

I inwardly cringed at the thought of a scooter ride home in the dark; so far I'd managed to dissuade Scarlett from hiring one because I was scared to death of her coming a cropper; hitting a rock in the road and flying off the bloody thing - ending up scarred for life. The medical facilities on the island were limited, as far as I could gather, and I certainly didn't want either one of us to be testing them out any time soon. But she had a point; she *would* need some form of transport if she had that journey to make day in, day out. I hoped to god she'd find someone local to employ her.

We were giddy with excitement by the time we left, too much buzzing round in our heads to rest up, so we ended up sitting out on the balcony, making plans, desperate to start putting them into place. After eventually heading indoors to spruce ourselves up and change into our best Saturday night party dresses, we descended the stairs and ambled down the road towards Achilles Bar.

As we happened to be passing Mama's anyway, I decided there was no time like the present and called in to speak to the owner, Tassos, to have a word about the job. He was sterner than I'd remembered him but I was sure he'd be a hoot when we were on more familiar terms. Before I knew what had happened, I had agreed to start the next day, at four o'clock in the afternoon...what the hell! I didn't even know what the pay was or how many hours I was supposed to work, or any other important details. As if you would ever conduct a job interview like that in England! And I hadn't liked to mention to him that I didn't even have anywhere to live yet.

When I broke the news to Scarlett that I was starting work the very next night she responded with a 'Well done you, but we're officially still on holiday so there's no bleeding way I'm going begging for employment until Monday at the very earliest...it'll be a doddle anyway..I'll get something straight away, if your job interview is anything to go by, and then we'll both have money coming in by the end of next week...sweet!'

We clinked our glasses together and toasted our spontaneity and ballsiness in Achilles whilst I panicked about waitressing in a Greek restaurant when I could only speak about four words of the language, and the fact that we could possibly end up sleeping on the street if we didn't find somewhere to live within the next twenty-four hours.

By the time we headed over to Sunrise, I was ecstatic that we weren't leaving, nervous as hell about my new job, and worried sick that we were going to end up homeless. Sofia must have noticed my look of wide-eyed terror and shouted me over to the bar to spill the beans to her and Alex. When they found out we were staying on for the summer, there were whoops and cheers and then they both came around to pull us into a group hug, congratulating us on making such a momentous decision; *they* at least seemed delighted that we would be staying – I hoped all the other locals would feel the same!

'My cousin has a small house, not far from here, and I think it will be cheap as chops,' Alex told me. 'He does not rent it out usually but I will tell him I have found nice English girls who need a home for the summer...so behave please, Scarlett Fever!' He wagged his finger at

Scarlett and she pretended to look affronted, knowing full well what a little minx she was and that there was more chance of Katie Price behaving than her.

'Why does he not rent it out already then, if he could make a packet every week from tourists?' wondered Scarlett out loud.

'Because it is older and smaller, and a little further away from the beach. But it is a great house and I think it will be perfect for you two! I will speak to him later and we will go and look tomorrow. Now, you must think about jobs...'

'Oh, I have one of those already!' I replied happily, still chuffed with myself. 'Tassos, who owns Mama's, has taken me on and I start there tomorrow! How good's that, eh?'

The look that passed between Alex and Sofia made me slightly nervous, and Sofia's comment of 'Ah well, you will work hard, stay underneath his radar and make sure you enjoy any time off,' didn't exactly inspire me with confidence. It was to be hoped that Tassos wasn't an old letch who was going to keep 'accidentally' dropping the cutlery for me to bend down and pick up...or what if he was one of those who didn't pay you for weeks on end and I would be forced to break into my dad's money, or live on fresh air? I silently prayed that all would be fine, as long as I worked my sandals off and did it with a smile on my face.

The conversation was interrupted by the appearance of Yiorgos, Alex and Sofia's only child, who unsurprisingly was as good-looking as his father and as immaculately turned out as his mother. His short-cropped hair and his beautiful eyes were typically Greek, in that they were as dark as night, and even the silly expression he adopted when he greeted Apostolis did nothing to detract from his strong jawline and his overall handsome face. And he was as articulate, amusing and amiable as his parents, as we discussed everything from grape crushing to completing National Service in the Greek army. He told me that he was currently enjoying driving for a jeep safari company but was considering a move to the mainland where there were better long-term job opportunities. Dressed in a ribbed white vest top and cut-off denims, he attracted the stares of all the female contingent of the bar, and I could quite see why he had the ladies queuing up and had apparently been voted 'Mr Loulouthia 2018' by holiday reps and British bar workers alike at the end of the previous season.

Despite repeatedly informing every man and his dog that I was definitely having no more than five drinks, I was off my head by the time Lorry and Simon joined us and we imparted our good news, throwing our arms around them and squealing down their earholes. Lorry smothered my neck in tiny kisses as he circled his hands around my waist and he seemed genuinely over the moon; Simon – less so. He just stood there with his mouth opening and shutting, looking gormless. I was beginning to think he was more Simple Simon than Simon Le Bon.

For me, it was the last night of my holiday, but the beginning of the rest of my life – a time to start living! One of the old boys produced a bouzouki from god only knows where and he began to play and sing, accompanied by his pals...and even though I had never before heard this clearly ancient Greek tune and understood not a single word, it was wonderful all the same. Less wonderful was mine and Scarlett's drunken attempts at Greek dancing when an upbeat version of Zorba's Dance was played, but at least we made everyone laugh – who needed to pay for entertainment when they had us English making complete tits of ourselves?

It was gone midnight by the time I left, but still early compared to the other nights we'd let our hair down in Sunrise. Feeling reckless, I allowed Lorry to take my hand again, hollered goodnight to Alex and Sofia, and extracted a promise from Scarlett that she would be back soon, because we had an awful lot to sort out before checkout on Monday. In the short time it took Lorry to guide me over to the Katerina, I knew I was going to allow him to kiss me again. My mood was upbeat, my guard was down...and he was undeniably lovely and doing his utmost to woo me. The kiss was tender and enjoyable - no fireworks going off in my head or my knickers, but it was nice; his lips were soft, I liked it when he flicked his tongue inside of my mouth and I could sense there was real feeling there. I still didn't invite him in though – I definitely didn't want to be regretting any actions in the morning...and besides, we had plenty of time now to get better acquainted – I was going nowhere for the time being.

When I entered the room, it was stupidly hot and sticky and in desperate need of a good airing out; I decided to make the most of our final night in the holiday apartment, slid open the patio door and settled down on the balcony to await Scarlett's return. Unable to keep the smile off my face, I found myself replaying the events of the evening in my head. We were doing it, we were actually doing it! Tomorrow I was starting my new life on the most beautiful of Greek islands – who would have thought that possible just two short weeks ago?

Chapter 9

When I awoke several hours later, Scarlett still hadn't returned to the apartment and I had been bitten to bloody death. There was a distinct line of red, unsightly mosquito bites marking out a course down the back of my right leg and a cluster of them on my left forearm...the little bastards had savaged me while I was out for the count. Scratching my newly acquired bumps, I went inside to check my phone – sure enough, there was a message from Scarlett informing me she that she was staying out to have a little fun with Simon and a bottle of cheap plonk on Ammos beach and instructing me not to wait up. Marvellous. That was a sodding pointless promise then. It was already 5.25 a.m. according to my mobile; if she left it much longer she may as well just forget coming back for the time being and I'd meet her somewhere for breakfast.

Scarlett did eventually roll in at just after 6 a.m., staggering into the bedside cabinet and not even bothering to remove her shoes before she collapsed onto her bed. I managed, ooh, at least another fifteen minutes sleep before I grumpily gave it up as a bad job and hit the shower.

She snoozed all the way through me noisily packing up the majority of my belongings – whatever happened, we wouldn't be able to stay in this apartment beyond 10 a.m. the following day, and I had a job to go to later!

Just as I was thanking my lucky stars that at least we were only leaving the apartment rather than the island, while at the same time holding on to speak to someone at the travel company in the UK to find out if we could recoup anything from the money we'd paid out for our return journey back to Manchester (we couldn't), there was a sharp rap at the door and I heard a deep voice say, '*Kaliméra*, Just Jess and Scarlett Fever! Good Morning, wakey-wakey beautiful ladies!'

'Alex!' I opened the door to our welcome visitor, who was the epitome of cool in his fitted white t-shirt and khaki, baggy shorts, with his (knock-off) designer sunglasses fixed firmly in place and his dark, wavy hair swept to one side.

'Hello, Just Jess! I am sorry to disturb you so early but I have the key to my cousin's house and we must go now to look. If you like, you can rent cheaply. Let's go! Chip, chip!'

'Chop, chop, Alex,' I corrected him, as I tried to raise Scarlett, but she was doing a fine impression of the living dead, and even Alex's prodding and shouts of, 'Wake up Scarlett Fever...FIRE, FIRE!' in her ear three times didn't do the trick. I badly wanted her to accompany me on our inspection trip of this house belonging to Alex's cousin, but had to accept that I would have to view it alone and make the decision for both of us. I settled into the passenger seat of Alex's white Serrato while he chauffeured me, up out of Chaliki, round the sharp bend past the Hotel Diana and out into a more countrified area. Just as I was praying to god that it wasn't much further, bearing in mind that I would be making this journey several times each day on foot, Alex suddenly took a swift left turn into a road that almost wasn't a road - it was more of a dusty track that didn't appear wide enough to accommodate any car and it was rough as hell but didn't seem to bother Alex, even when stones were kicking up and pinging off the paintwork. Christ, most men I knew would have a dickie fit if they were forced to risk their pride and joy climbing up this rubble-filled incredibly steep hill.

And it *was* a bloody hill as well. Oh my, I would need an iron lung to get myself up here and I'd better get my arse back into town to purchase one of those weird torch things for my late night returns. And Scarlett! She would freak when she saw how off the beaten track this was – if I agreed that we would take this place.

Eventually we came to an abrupt stop and Alex announced, 'Ta da! We are here – you must come and look at your new home, Just Jess.'

Bloody hell, it looked like an abandoned outbuilding rather than a good-to-go house, with its exterior cracks and its peeling paintwork – no wonder it was lying empty.

'It does have running water and electricity doesn't it Alex?' I asked meekly, not wanting to offend him but slightly worried that we would be bedding down with the sheep, hoinking up water from a nearby well to have a wash in, and living by candlelight once the sun went down.

'Of course it has! We have all mod cans here!' Swinging my legs out of the car, slightly downhearted at the state of the place, I couldn't be bothered pointing out that it was 'mod *cons*' and anyway, I was becoming increasingly concerned about the size of the building now – it looked frighteningly tiny!

Alex trod down and beat back a path to the front door as I ducked and squealed, trying to avoid low-flying insects. Where the bloody hell had he brought me?

Despite the somewhat off-putting exterior of the house, I was pleasantly surprised when he unlocked the front door – the interior was spotlessly clean and well laid out and it actually looked like a house rather than a cowshed. We stepped straight into a basic living area, with clean white walls and a marble-effect tiled floor, which led to an open-plan kitchen complete with oven and refrigerator. There were two bedrooms immediately off the lounge, and a tiny corridor next to the kitchen led to the bathroom, although this seemed to be a bit of an afterthought, housing the smallest of showers together with a kiddie-size sink and toilet, but it was all serviceable, and I was pleased to see the bedrooms were furnished and there was even a patio set in the lounge; it wasn't the corner settee and reclining armchair I was used to back at my home in England, but it would have to do for now. Ah well, in this heat we would be spending a hell of a lot more time outside than in.

'You will need a wood burner if you are here after the summer because there is no central heating and it does get a little cold and damp towards the end of the year. But, I think you will be very happy because, not only is it a very good house, but...there is a washing machine here, outside at the back. Voila!'

Voila? I thought I was in Greece, not France. He was right though, I discovered, as I followed him around to the back of the house – there *was* a washing machine, so that was a bonus – I didn't fancy scrubbing beach towels in the kitchen sink. There was also a large garden area to the rear; that space could be cleared and made to look pretty, I was sure. We would definitely have to invest in some flowers for the front terrace though, or else our house would stand out from the rest of the island for all of the wrong reasons!

'My cousin, he says, the fridge is almost new (well, if you class a fridge bought sometime in the last decade as new, then I suppose it was) and everything else you need is in the cupboards. I think you will like it here...somewhere to enjoy the peace and quiet after a hectic night at work!'

'Er...well...I do like it Alex but...well...but my job is in Chaliki and it seems quite far away to walk every day....'

'Ah well, turn to the right Just Jess, look!' Gripping my sagging shoulders with his firm hands, he spun me round to face me in the opposite direction.

'You see – over there near the large, gnarled olive tree – this tree is maybe five hundred years old - there is a small pathway; this leads you down into Chaliki – you must follow the this until you find yourself at the back of the Hotel Diana – so, you see – not so far! But you must not walk home alone in the dark; after work; I will be your driver - or Sofia, or maybe Yiorgos - if he can tear himself away from all of the ladies. And Scarlett Fever says she will ride a scooter, yes? So do not worry, your problems are solved! And one more thing, my darling Jessica...my cousin, Spiros...' (Jeez, how many more?), '...he says we must arrange to cut back many of the bushes at the front of your new house as they have grown far too big – and then you will have the perfect view of Kochyli to the left, Chaliki to the right and out over the emerald waters of the Ionian Sea!'

Grown too big? They had taken over and eclipsed the whole of the front of the property and I couldn't even begin to imagine what would remain once they were cut back or removed. I wasn't sure if I was doing the right thing, agreeing to take this house in Scarlett's absence, but when Alex confirmed the much reduced price that his cousin was agreeing to charge us for rent, my mind was made up. It would have been incredibly silly to turn down such a reasonable offer, and in any event it would have left us with the small issue of having nowhere to live from the very next day – we were running out of options.

So I said yes, please, we would like to take the house, whilst crossing my fingers and hoping that I wasn't making a huge mistake, whereupon Alex kindly offered to be our removal man the following morning, to transfer all of our belongings into our new home.

Scarlett was rather lacking in enthusiasm on my return when I informed her that we at least now had a place to call home, but she *was* still slightly green around the gills from the excessive alcohol consumption the previous evening. My stomach was rumbling like an earthquake (and I'd been informed by Apostolis that I could expect a few *actual* earthquake tremors while I was on the island – for pity's sake, please don't let me be home alone if and when the earth started moving), and so I nipped out again to the best little supermarket around and exchanged pleasantries with Young Spiros before picking up some fresh bread rolls and a packet of cheese slices for lunch – better start as we mean to go on and stick to a budget rather than frittering away all of our precious Euros!

Whilst grabbing a bottle of orange cordial from the back of the shelf, I noticed a familiar figure leaning over me to reach into the cooler – Lauren from the hotel, who looked a world away as she was picking up various cartons of juice and pieces of fresh fruit. She hadn't been overly friendly last time I'd spoken to her but I decided to give her another go – after all, I would be seeing her around much more now I was going to be an actual resident of Loulouthia.

'Hi again,' I said, offering her a friendly smile, despite the previous somewhat hostile reception. 'How are you?' I did wonder if she even recognised me initially because she had a pretty blank expression on her face but she eventually replied with a 'Oh...hi...erm...just getting a few bits before I have to go back to work. The fruit and juice is needed behind the bar.'

'So they've got you running around doing all of their errands then, have they?' I meant it as a joke but received a frown in return.

'I don't mind doing them; it gets me out of the hotel for twenty minutes.'

'You're a star if you can walk all the way down here and back to the hotel in twenty minutes, Mo Farrah!'

She almost smiled then; bloody hell, it wouldn't have killed her to be nice to me.

'I have a moped. Almost everyone has a scooter or moped.'

Maybe words were being rationed around the village and nobody had bothered to tell me, as she was now down to delivering eleven word responses whilst appearing desperate to escape as fast as her little sandals would take her away from me.

I pointed vaguely in the direction of our newly acquired 'bungalow' and said, 'Well, I'd better think about hiring one if I'm going to be travelling to work and back every day from our house up there on the hill.' Ha! Hell would freeze over before I hired a death-mobile, but I thought I'd just throw that one in to keep her on her toes; to let her know we would be living on Loulouthia, so she had better get used to bumping into me and accepting me as her equal.

'Aah...I see...more Brits believing that the grass is greener on the other side...making a new life for themselves in the sun, complaining when they're wilting in the August temperatures, and ordering pork pies and crumpets to be shipped in. Well, best of luck.'

Oh my god...how rude! Gobsmacked at her bloody snotty attitude and total double standards – she was a prime example of someone who had done just that, after all – I decided she needed a taste of her own medicine before she had the opportunity to dismiss me again.

'Right, well, I'd better dash - things to do, crumpets to eat, you know how it is. Oh, and I'm starting my brand new job in a few hours' time, after I've done some wilting and complaining. So...bye for now Lauren, see you around!' And then I swiftly turned on my heel and left her standing there, probably wondering what the hell had just happened. Two could play at that game, cheeky cow. Of all the people to be weird with me, I wouldn't have expected that attitude from a fellow Brit.

Lunches bought and scoffed, more packing done, further liaising with Viola and Heather, and I had a short, sweaty cat-nap before showering and dressing, and making my way down to Mama's for my first evening at work. Warning Scarlett that I would NOT be in a position to treat her to a meal on the house during my very first shift, I slung my canvas bag over my shoulder and trotted off down to the restaurant, perspiring a little as I walked, well aware that I was about to start grafting when it was boiling hot and the beautiful sunset was still hours away, when the evening breeze would blow in and hopefully cool the air a little.

'*KALI TIKI*, JUST JESS!' shouted Alex from outside of the bar, which I was later to discover meant 'Good luck!', and I received friendly waves from various locals and tourists I had become acquainted with over the past fortnight.

Pepped up by the encouragement of my new friends, I was a happy little bunny when I sprinted up the steps to the restaurant and went to take instruction from Tassos via the young Albanian boy, Lukas, who also worked there and spoke better English than I did. My little bubble of happiness soon evaporated when I was informed I would have to mop the floors before the punters came in for their evening meals, followed by a whole host of other crappy jobs the boss had lined up for me, including cleaning out the coffee machine and polishing the mirrors in the toilets. Right.

Sweat leaking out of my every pore, I wondered where they had found the industrial sized mop that weighed about five stone when wet through, making it heavy, messy work, and I cursed that no one had bothered to inform me that this was part of my job description so I could have brought along a spare set of clothes to change into. I felt filthy and stinking by the time the customers started to wander in, and no matter how many times I washed my hands, I still didn't feel clean enough to be serving food.

The meals were as fantastic as I'd remembered and my stomach rumbled along when I had to serve the huge, mouth-watering pizzas, as I'd not even managed to snatch a five minute break to devour a bag of crisps, but, oh my god, why had I never noticed before that Tassos was a mad, grumpy old bugger who thought nothing of yelling at me in the kitchen for stacking dishes in the wrong area or getting the odd order mixed up. I tried to point out that it *was* my first shift but an urgent shake of the head from my Albanian colleague warned me that perhaps it was ill-advised to have an opinion in this particular restaurant, so I shut my mouth again and just glared at him as he let rip.

The customers were a jolly bunch though and the atmosphere out front was pleasant and relaxed. When I wasn't zooming around like a blue-arsed fly, Tassos had encouraged me to make conversation with tourists passing by, in an attempt to entice them in off the street...but if I was speaking to anyone for longer than two minutes I would hear, 'Jessica! You must work now!' I resisted the temptation to punch him in the face and knock his few remaining teeth out – he was old and I needed the job. Hopefully it would get easier and he would take pity on me when he realised what a great work ethic I had; that I wasn't taking the piss.

What griped me the most was that I physically couldn't have done any more during those eight hours; I must have covered the equivalent of five miles back and forth through that restaurant, from the sweltering kitchens situated at the rear of the building to the furthest tables, right at the front of the outside eating area...and back again. Repeat x 500.

There were a number of truly embarrassing incidents as well. For instance, a lovely middle-aged lady with a fantastic perm, who was holidaying with her young daughter, requested a simple lemon wedge to squeeze over her sea bass and I replied 'of course', and off I raced, back to the kitchen to fetch one, but was intercepted by Tassos who insisted on swapping it for lemon *juice*. Feeling like a bit of a dickhead, off I trotted back to the lady again, only to have her repeat that she wanted an actual *wedge* of lemon. Gritting my teeth, I returned to the kitchen where Tassos lay in wait, refusing outright to let me have anything other than lemon *juice*, even though there are about fifty billion frigging lemons growing from practically every other tree on the island, and lovely lady must have come to the conclusion that I was actually quite bonkers, when I apologised profusely, practically threw the lemon juice at her, and made a run for it.

By the time I staggered over to Sunrise, when I finally managed to escape Tassos the Tyrant and that freaking hellhole at quarter past midnight, I was dead on my feet and my clothes were so drenched with sweat they actually needed ringing out – and that unfortunately included my underwear.

I was greeted by a 'Fucking hell, what happened to you?' from Scarlett and a 'Poor Just Jess, She needs a beer!' from Sofia. I almost collapsed into one of the vacant chairs, prising my shoes off my swollen feet and wondering how the hell I was going to keep *that* up, night after night. It had crossed my mind before I'd left the restaurant that Tassos might not want me to bother returning for a second shift, as he seemed so unhappy with my performance throughout the evening, but instead I'd got a 'Same time tomorrow Jessica,' as I'd staggered down the steps, wondering what had happened to the friendly guy who'd served us up our pizza only a few nights earlier. Bastard.

Giving up on my new job after only a single shift really wasn't an option and so, after downing my beer almost in one, I tried to ignoring the throbbing of my feet and attempted to laugh it off in the company of my friends.

Tomorrow could only get better.

Chapter 10

I'll say one thing about modern slavery – it knocks you out like a cricket bat to the head. After three beers in Sunrise, there was a pleasant role reversal when I was escorted back to the apartment by a mildly-sober Scarlett, who took pity on me hobbling out of the door, having squeezed my poor little trotters back into my sweaty, damp work shoes. I immediately fell sound asleep on top of my sandy bed sheets, still clothed in my minging work gear, only to wake six hours later, perspiring like a cling-film wrapped chunk of cheese that had never seen a fridge – my joints aching from severe dehydration.

After a Mars Bar breakfast (oh how my diet had gone rapidly downhill in the last couple of days), I had a last shivery shower, before throwing on a semi-clean t-shirt and shorts and stuffing the rest of my belongings into my case and bags. Scarlett was still packing at ten o'clock when the maid came to strip our beds and evict us and we were forced to drag all our Greekly goods down the stairs to await the arrival of Alex, fanning ourselves with trashy magazines whilst slumped in the plastic chairs, which we were lucky weren't occupied by the new family who had temporarily moved into Apartment 2, along with the insects - Mandy and family having warmly hugged us goodbye the previous morning, everyone promising to keep in touch (unlikely – sad, but true).

By the time Alex showed up gone eleven, looking chirpy and relaxed, Scarlett was hot and bothered and I was already counting down the minutes I had remaining until I had to force myself to return to work, but was grateful that he had turned up at all to assist us on moving day.

'Where the hell have you been, Alex?' Scarlett scowled at him, hardly appreciative of the fact that he'd been working until all hours and was going out of his way to help us.

'Hey, someone fell out of the wrong side of the bed, Scarlett Fever! *Ciga, ciga*...I am here now...I am your friend and will never let you down.'

'Thanks Alex...it's really kind of you to do this,' I added, to appease him, although he didn't seem to have taken offence, thank goodness.

'No problem, Just Jess...*parme* - let's go!'

Following closely behind him, I tried to hide my smile as Alex grabbed my heaviest bag and wheeled my bulging case over to his car - which was pulled up with all its hazards flashing by the side of the road, a typically Greek thing to do - leaving Scarlett to huff and puff and heave all her own stuff down the path. She probably regretted being offhand with him.

Overjoyed to be finally on our way, I breathed a huge sigh of relief as we set off for our new home, although a little sad to be leaving our spacious, modern apartment behind with its gigantic balcony and jaw-dropping views.

Scarlett was speechless for once as we turned off the main road and crawled up the track leading to our new house. I don't know quite what she was expecting for the exceedingly low rent that we were to be charged, but as she caught her first glimpse of the little old building with the dilapidated exterior, behind the masses of tangled weeds and overgrown bushes, I'm guessing it wasn't that.

'Tell me this isn't it. Tell me we're not moving into this shagged-out little cowshed and that there's a bigger, better place awaiting us, albeit slightly further up the mountain. Tell me. Jess. Tell me, *please*.' I could sense the panic rising in Scarlett by the pitch of her voice, which was becoming whinier by the second, as she nervously clutched my arm, digging her talons in and making me wince.

'Sorry babe, but yes, this is it. If you have any better ideas then please, do tell. Because if we don't take up residence here, then we are officially homeless.'

Luckily, Alex was already out of the car and unlocking the door – probably hoping to silence Scarlett by revealing the far superior interior of the property. I think she was so pleased there weren't actually cows installed in there that she was overcome with relief and even managed to treat us to a faint smile.

'Well it's not exactly the Ritz but it'll do for now! Thanks Alex, sorry I was a bit off before but it's that time of the month coming up and...'

'Whoa, Scarlett Fever! Too much information for an innocent young Greek boy like me! So...I have checked that you are connected to the water and electricity...and now I must leave, to eat with my family and sleep for a short time before I must return to work for many hours. And you must unpack and settle in before Just Jess has to go to her job. Goodbye ladies...I will see you later.'

Thanking him profusely, I felt my spirits take a nosedive as he drove away and left us to our unpacking. I was hot and I was gritty and I was overtired; wearily dragging my case into the front bedroom, Scarlett having already bagged the slightly larger one next to the bathroom, I sank down on to the bed, wondering why the hell one of us hadn't had the sense to nip to the shop to pick up more food and water while we were waiting for our lift from Alex.

Moments later, a wide-eyed Scarlett appeared in the doorway, holding the actual washing machine door up in front of her shocked face. Fantastic.

'What the hell have you done? We've only been here five minutes!'

'I haven't *done* anything, apart from take a look at the washer, attempt to open it and then have the bloody door come clean off in my hands! I think the hinges to it have rusted away!'

'Christ...I suppose that's because it's been outside and uncovered. Maybe we will be able to just slot the door back on and it will work anyway?'

'I wouldn't bank on it – the rubber seal has disintegrated and the whole thing looks like it's going to fall apart any minute. If Charlie Cairoli had a washing machine, this would be it. For fuck's sake Jessie, where have you brought us? I've never seen a bathroom as tiny as the one we've got – I mean, is it even legal?'

'Yes, I know it's a bit small and...'

'*A bit small?* I've just had to sit practically sideways on the toilet, which only just accommodates both cheeks of my arse I might add, and my bloody feet were dangling into the shower tray! I can't believe you've agreed to actually pay good money for this!'

'Oh, fuck off will you!'

'No, you fuck off!'

We both started to laugh then, the hilarity of the situation, with Scarlett stood there clutching the washer door, dawning on us and breaking the tension. Finally deciding to exhibit a bit of oomph, Scarlett unpacked her suitcase – by which, I mean she grabbed handfuls of clothes and clumsily shoved them on the shelves and stuffed them into drawers rather than actually hanging anything up - while I moved around throwing open shutters and windows, plugging the fridge in (thank the lord *that* worked), sweeping the tiled floors (no obvious sign of any infestation at this stage) and making a mental note of what we would need to buy from the supermarket. I think you could safely say, my first week's wages would be spoken for.

Singing her way through most of the *Mama Mia* soundtrack, Scarlett then moved on to wiping down the kitchen units, of a fashion, with a packet of dried up baby wipes she'd had rammed in her handbag, before lifting out crockery, pans and cutlery that had all been stored away in the kitchen. Not particularly wishing to have to iron every item of clothing I possessed whenever I needed it, I took my time unpacking and storing away the contents of my case and bags, and was just out on the covered terrace, hanging up a set of wind chimes that were supposed to have been a gift for my aunty, when I heard a vehicle heading up the track towards our house and the honking of a horn disturbing the peace.

Hoping and praying that it was an Asda delivery van, whose driver had somehow found us on this remote Greek island and who was about to unload ten gallons of water and hundred weight of bacon and bread on our doorstep, despite the fact that we'd never even placed order with them, I was disappointed to note that it was actually just an individual rid' moped, and as they came closer I was surprised to see that it was Lauren - old nowty-knickers herself. She looked equally surprised to see me and screeched to a halt, creating a cloud of fine dust that would make an unholy mess of my freshly swept tiles.

'Hi,' she said, brushing a few stray hairs out of her eyes, and clearly now reduced to one word greetings.

'Hi,' I replied, brushing aside a few imaginary stray hairs of my own, and stubbornly refusing to add anything else; waiting for her to fill the awkward silence.

'So, you're moving in here then. You're lucky...it's actually much better than the part of Andreas' family home that he and I have had to shack up in...'

Much better? Where did she live? Stig of the Dump's weekend place?

'Yes, we *are* lucky. We're only just unpacking now but we'll soon make it feel like home. Where's your house then?'

She pointed vaguely up into the clouds somewhere behind me and I glanced around at the track that snaked up the hill and then disappeared out of view. Bloody hell, she must have a hell of a commute to work then...no wonder she travelled by moped!

She hopped off in front of me, and I thought she was about to invite herself in for a brew (coffee and tea bags – more essential purchases!) but instead she grabbed a bag full of empty plastic water bottles from the handlebar and began to walk away, as if I didn't exist, and hadn't been wading my way through a stilted conversation with her.

What the heck was she doing now?

Out of interest, I followed her, and was amazed to see her disappear down a couple of steep steps I hadn't even noticed were there, and then I heard the sound of water gushing out. Of course! A fresh water spring! That was why she had all of the bottles. Relief flooded through me as I realised we had drinkable water practically right on our doorstep – wait till I told Scarlett!

Lauren glanced over her shoulder, observing me watching her every move. 'Weren't you aware that you had a spring nearby? It'll save you a lot of time and hassle, and it's handy when the water goes off in the house.'

Water goes off in the house? Were we actually still living in the twenty-first century or had ¬alled back in time and no one had deigned to tell me? I didn't think I'd mention that ˈɔ Scarlett – it might send her over the edge, and she was already teetering.

had offered up some useful information...I just wished she wasn't such specially now it was apparent we were practically going to be

Screwing the lids tightly back on all of the bottles, their peeling labels suggesting that they had already been refilled on numerous occasions, she shoved them into the plastic bag again, informed me she was just nipping home from work to feed 'the animals', and kick-started the moped again - whizzing off, leaving me standing there like a goon. Shaking my head in frustration at the peculiarities of this woman, I nevertheless rushed back into the house to impart the good news to Scarlett - that we had water we could drink, that wouldn't send us dashing for the nearest bathroom - and we both grabbed a cup and almost ran to where the spring was mostly hidden from view...knocking back the ice cold water as if we hadn't had any liquids for a week; as if it was the sweetest nectar of the gods.

The hours were ticking on, and the constant yawn-stifling warned me that I badly needed my siesta, before I had to return to work. When Scarlett and I disappeared to our separate bedrooms and I went to lie down, I could have wept. No frigging sheets! Or pillowcases! Just bare beds with bare pillows on top. The air turned blue again as Scarlett realised that this small matter was going to necessitate another purchase and that we'd have to manage without them until we could find an appropriate shop, but I kept repeating to myself that it would probably only be for one night...and I dragged out a cotton nightshirt and t-shirt to lie on, while Scarlett eventually spread out her beach towel on her bed. I didn't have the energy to point out to her that it was already a bit whiffy and was sprinkling grains of sand all over her mattress and the floor. I suppose towels were something else we needed to think about buying. Bloody hell, at this rate I would be bankrupt by June.

After a surprisingly decent sleep, I groggily awoke to the buzzing of my phone alarm, informing me it was time to scrub up, cheer up and get my arse down to Mama's to get shouted at for eight hours solid. Scarlett had made arrangements with Simon for him to pick her up at Sunrise, to take her to Skafos to enquire about a possible job there, which meant at least we could leave the house together.

We locked up and made our way down the path which Alex had said led into the resort. It was a little bumpy under foot and I was glad I'd chosen to wear my trainers, having chucked my sandals into my canvas bag, along with a change of clothes. Like it or lump it, I would be cleaning up the restaurant in my shorts and vest top combo, thank you very much Tassos, and then changing into my smarter 'work' dress later on.

The quiet, winding path was a truly pleasant route to take to work, and I loved the fact that the further we descended the hill, the closer we came to the sea. The only noise was courtesy of the chorus of cicadas in the trees and the sound of our own footsteps, and even Scarlett was silenced by the wild beauty of our surroundings.

It didn't last long, however, when we came to the end of the path and she went arse over tit on a slippery rock protruding from the ground. Grunting and cursing, she picked herself up and I dusted her down and sent her on her way to meet Simple Simon while I took a deep breath and plodded into Mama's, determined that this shift would be better than the last one. Tassos looked me up and down as I passed him, but I glared at him defiantly, daring him to take me to task about my much more relaxed approach to work clothes. My Albanian friend, Lukas, did at least greet me with a smile and asked why I hadn't eaten the food that had been boxed up for me the previous evening! Er, that's because no one had thought to tell me that I was entitled to a free meal each night!

Tassos insisted on following me round like a bad smell while I was cleaning, and I was tempted to thrash him to death with the mop, but somehow I managed to restrain myself. When he instructed me to wipe every vacant chair in the restaurant for a second time before we started to fill up, I pretended I hadn't heard him and disappeared into the toilets to wash my face and pits and change into my slightly crumpled, but most comfortable, navy blue and daffodil yellow, flowery skater dress. Still sweltering, I at least looked a tad more presentable after I'd re-tied my hair back and patted some face powder over my shiny nose and forehead.

Squirting myself liberally with what remained of Scarlett's body spray, I stuffed my cleaning clothes back into my bag, steeled myself for a grilling from Tassos and returned to the restaurant. Thankfully the old git was engaged, chatting to a potential customer out front so I hung back in the inside seating area, wrapping napkins around cutlery and piling them onto a tray. When Tassos appeared by my side, I smiled sweetly and innocently at him, as if I had been there all the time, and he eyed me suspiciously, as if he suspected me of stealing the family silver. He probably hadn't even noticed the change of clothes, so intent was he on conjuring up ways of making my life a misery.

It was a stupidly busy night which meant we were run off our feet – I was only glad I'd worn my flat sandals as I don't think I'd have survived in my shoes; I still had the weeping blisters from the previous evening. By ten-thirty most of the English customers had disappeared, and only a couple of Greek families rocked up later on, the loud and lively adults sharing huge, deep-pan pizzas and a bottle of ouzo, while the children ran circles around the tables, knocked over numerous glasses of Fanta and screamed like teenage girls at a Justin Bieber concert. While I was mopping up the latest spillage and pretending not to mind in the slightest, whilst gritting my teeth and silently telling myself I was NEVER having kids, I heard footsteps on the stairs to the restaurant, and I hoped this wasn't an order for a dozen pizzas, or some pain in the arse who would stay for hours, yacking on to Tassos, and thereby keeping me from my lovely sheet-less bed.

'*Kalispéra* – Good evening to you. Well, well...who do we have here? I think Tassos is a very clever businessman, employing a lady of such beauty to work for him in his restaurant...'

Smooth. I looked up into an impossibly handsome face; a smiling, olive-skinned Greek man dressed in a creaseless black shirt, more buttons open than were fastened, and charcoal jeans that clung to his long legs, with black shoes polished to perfection. His dark hair was cut short and his mirrored sunglasses were balanced on top of his head, despite it being late into the evening. It was allowed. It was Greece.

'I'm sorry – forgive me - we haven't been introduced.' As his rich, coffee-coloured eyes looked me up and down, he held out his hand for me to shake and I complied. Ooh, firm grip. I liked that.

'My name is Nikos – actually Nikolaos, after the patron saint of sailors, which is very apt, as I spend much of my life on the water - and I am an old friend of Tassos; we were at school together so I have known him for many, many years.'

Good god, I would never have guessed they were the same age, or thereabouts. Tassos had thinning, grey hair and an unruly, handlebar moustache – add to this his weather-beaten, leather-look skin and his tragic dress sense, and it all made him look about seventy. This attractive, self-assured man I saw before me looked much younger, and I would have put him in his mid-forties. He had definitely been at the head of the queue when looks were being handed out, whilst Tassos had clearly been lurking at the back somewhere, possibly even missing the queue altogether, and had presumably endured an unimaginably hard life.

Momentarily distracted by his innate sexiness, I finally remembered my manners, smiled and replied, 'Hi, I'm Jessica – pleased to meet you. It's only my second night here; let's hope I can make it to the third.'

My tone must have belied my smile because Nikos laughed and then moved closer to whisper, 'Tassos may be a strict boss but he is a good man.'

No he's not, he's a grumpy old goat who treats me like shit, I wanted to reply, but didn't dare, for fear of losing my newly acquired job.

'Come sit with me for a while and we shall share a carafe of wine,' ordered Nikos, pulling out a chair for me and shouting something incomprehensible to Tassos, who angrily shuffled off and brought back a *half* carafe of red wine and two *small* glasses, banging them down on the table in front of us. It gave me immense pleasure to see the twisted look on his face, knowing it must have killed him to allow me to take a break.

Expertly pouring out the wine, Nikos looked directly at me as he raised his own glass and said '*Yamas!* To Jessica, and hopefully a memorable summer on the Island of Flowers.'

'*Yamas!*' I toasted myself and eyeballed him right back, noticing again how good-looking he was, the air of sophistication, and how a girl could lose herself right there in those deep, dark pools that looked like that they were mentally undressing me. God above, it must be the climate that was affecting me...I was a hot mess!

He leant over to take my left hand, clearly checking to see if there was a telltale band of gold wrapped around my wedding finger.

'You are single, Jessica from England? Amazing. I cannot believe that someone has not yet snapped up such an enchanting, beautiful lady! You must let me take you out for dinner one evening to allow us to become better acquainted...I suspect that we could have a lot of fun together...'

Bloody hell, he was a quick worker. Slightly over the top, but somehow not sleazy. I couldn't help but mentally compare him with Lorry and his youthful demeanour and flowery swim shorts, but I felt guilty for doing so. Lorry was a kind, funny guy, who was also blessed with good looks, and he was such a genuine and honest person. Here I was being charmed by someone I'd met literally minutes ago, who might be talking a load of old bull and just trying to worm his way into my pants, for all I knew.

I could feel Tassos' beady eyes boring into the back of my head and thought I'd better remove myself from the conversation with Nikos; it seemed an appropriate point to break it off.

'Somehow I don't think I'll be allowed any evenings off any time soon, but thanks for your kind offer Tassos. And for the wine. Now, would you like to see a menu, or can I fetch you anything else to drink?'

It transpired that he'd only called in to speak to Tassos about a broken chainsaw; to share a heated conversation with him and a large measure of Raki, but he stayed awhile, and I could feel his eyes following me around as I attended to the needs of the Greek families and then divvied up the cleaning duties with Lukas once the restaurant had emptied out. At least he was keeping Tassos out of my hair and he wasn't a high-maintenance customer. In the end, I left before he did, but I made sure to drop by to say goodnight to him, and he responded with a '*Kalinichte*, Jessica. Goodnight my English Rose, sleep tight, and we will meet again soon.'

Confidence boosted, but bone-achingly tired, I slid over to Sunrise, knocked back almost half of a beer in one go, and watched Yiorgos chat up some pretty, young blonde with an annoying laugh, as I tried to keep awake at the bar. When Scarlett texted to say she'd bagged herself a job, but was staying out celebrating with Simon in Skafos, I drained the rest of my drink, grabbed my bag and quietly left the bar. I couldn't expect Sofia or Alex to offer me a lift back as they had their hands full with a crowd of over-exuberant customers, and Yiorgos was otherwise engaged. My heart sank as I contemplated the lengthier, uphill route ahead of me; I would have to walk via the main road as there was no way on earth I was risking the steep, semi-overgrown pathway on my own, in complete darkness. However, I'd only just passed the supermarket when I heard the tooting of a horn and turned around to see Sofia pull up in her car beside me.

'For goodness sake, jump in, Just Jess! Where did you think you were going on your own at this time of night? It is too far for you to walk home, especially by yourself, you naughty girl!'

Lacking the strength to argue with her, I hopped in, but did confess that I thought it was unfair for any of them to have to run me around, particularly when they were rushed off their feet in the bar.

'Nonsense! You are our very good friend now - and we must keep you safe. Now tell me about your job tonight. Did grumpy old Tassos drive you crazy again?'

I filled her in on Tassos' stalking tendancies and also the visit from his much sexier friend Nikos, probably dwelling a little too much on his handsome face and come-to-bed eyes than was absolutely necessary.

'Oh Just Jess, you must be careful! I think I know the Nikos you speak of - he is Nikolaos Georgiou who lives on the outskirts of Skafos, and he often calls in to see your arch-nemesis, Tassos. He is a striking man; very good-looking...but do be on your guard! He is older than you and sometimes a woman's head is turned by a man who is generous with money and flattering words. Stay sensible Jess, and in the meantime, don't break young Lorry's heart!'

I was touched by her concern, but I would never intentionally hurt Lorry – even though he had no claim on me. Anyway, I was nobody's fool; I wouldn't be taken in by a conman or leap into bed with someone I knew virtually nothing about.

'Okay...Just Jess, I also must give you the bag that is there, behind me, on the back seat. Take it with you when you get out – I think it will help you settle into your new house.'

Cheered at the thought of surprises from Sofia, and always a grateful recipient of any gifts, I was looking forward to delving in and discovering what delights Alex and Sofia had packed for us; I only hoped it didn't contain mice traps and fly spray – that wouldn't bode well. Unfortunately, I couldn't smell any home cooking in there and...Christ I had forgotten to pick up my free food on the way out again! By the time the week was out I would have faded away to nothing at this rate! I blamed Nikos for my forgetfulness – he had distracted me from my complimentary supper. Never before in the history of man had I ever forgotten to eat!

Kissing Sofia on her smooth, flawless cheek, I exited the car and then reached in and grabbed the overstuffed bin bag from the back seat, before closing both doors and waving her goodnight. It didn't escape my notice that she waited until I was safely indoors before driving away; this woman was a genuinely lovely person, through and through.

It felt strange to be alone in our new house, half way up a mountain, surrounded by almost complete darkness and with only the rustlings in the trees to keep me company. If I hadn't been so knackered, I probably would have been completely spooked. As it was, I barely had the strength to slip into my pyjamas and sip a few mouthfuls of a bottle of water I'd been generously allowed to take from the fridge at work when I'd been in imminent danger of collapsing from the heat.

Sinking down on to my bed, I upended the bin bag Sofia had given me and looked in amazement as the contents came tumbling out. Sheets! Glorious sheets! And an assortment of pillowcases, and big white fluffy towels that were completely devoid of foundation and sun lotion stains...and cleaning cloths and, presumably, cleaning products...and a couple of toilet rolls...and a whopping great big bag of Lays ready salted crisps! Oh my lord, this woman was my heroine!

From somewhere within, I mustered the strength to stretch a freshly laundered sheet over my bed and slipped the pillowcases on. Clutching a lovely, soft towel to my chest, I visited the tiny bathroom and washed my face and then luxuriated in the small pleasure of being able to dry it with something that didn't smell of sweat, sun cream and feet. Happily munching my way through my crisps, I perched on one of the plastic chairs in the middle of the living room waiting for Scarlett to return. At some point I must have dozed off as I awoke to her familiar drunken giggles, as she turned her big clunky key in the lock (thank goodness we'd been given one each, otherwise trying to locate somewhere on the island that could cut a second one of THOSE would have been, no doubt, an almighty challenge, not to mention yet another job to add to our ever-growing list)...and I found I still had my hand buried deep in my bag of salty Lays.

'Greetings!' she yelled as the door crashed back into the wall – shit, I hope that hadn't left a mark. And thank goodness we didn't have any immediate neighbours to offend on night number one. She clearly found that tripping up over the tiny step on the way in was absolutely hilarious as she collapsed in a heap on the floor, howling with laughter, while the contents of her handbag broke free and clattered across the room. Not wanting to invite in every sick and twisted bastard mosquito in the neighbourhood, I rushed to close the door behind her – no mark on the wall, thank god for that.

'Had a good night, did we?' I queried, my voice laced with sarcasm. My body was crying out for sleep more than ever but my mind needed to hear the details of Scarlett's new job, to satisfy myself we would definitely be able to pay the rent and other bills.

'Aw, it was ace, Jessie-Wessie! Simon Le Bon gave me a lift as promised...he's lovely isn't he, my Simon? Isn't he lovely? Don't you think he looks like the real Simon Le Bon? *'Her name is Rio and she dances on the sands...*' I was then treated to a chorus and a full verse of Scarlett singing, badly, along to Duran Duran, while I waited impatiently for her to get to the point.

'...anyways...he took me to this cracking little place called Bay Bar and I saw the manager there about the job and, guess what, he's fit as hell too! The whole time he was firing questions at me, I was imagining him naked except for a pair of the tiniest little budgie smugglers! Anyway, Spiros – that's his name...' (seriously, another bloody one) '...well he was *so* nice and straight away we struck up a really good rapport and....da, da, daaa...he gave me the job there and then – I start tomorrow night at seven - woo hoo!'

'Aw that's brilliant mate...I'm so chuffed for you. I bet you'll love working there.'

'Oh definitely...chatting to customers, dancing, larking about while I do a bit of serving and waiting on...it's right up my street! I will have to lay off the sauce though because I'm definitely going to have to hire a scooter tomorrow as apparently Simon's going to be too busy to pick me up most nights...'

Good old Simon...you could always rely on him to be unreliable.

'Fantastic Scarlett, it all sounds great...and there's some other good news. Sofia dropped us off clean bedding and towels and a few other bits...how lovely is that!'

'Aw, what an absolute shining star that woman is! I did drop some huge hints earlier that we had absolutely bugger all and I was considering sleeping stood up tonight to avoid laying out on a sweaty towel again; she must have nipped home to grab all that gear for us. Oh...sweaty towels...that reminds me...Alex said earlier that he will call by in the morning and collect all of our washing and they'll sort it out for us this time, seeing as our washer is somewhat defunct. And one of them will take us shopping later in the week to the supermarket just the other side of Skafos, which apparently is much cheaper and has a much better selection of stuff...well, let's face it, it couldn't have a worse selection of stuff than our local Spar down the street there, with its half-empty shelves and enforced child labour!'

After filling her in on my second shitty night at work, but omitting the details about the delicious but forward and fast-working Nikos – that was a story for another day – I collapsed onto my bed, uncovered, as it was already about a thousand degrees Fahrenheit in my bedroom. Scarlett couldn't have made any more noise if she'd tried, banging about in her room until it suddenly went ominously quiet – which meant she'd either fallen asleep or died, and to be perfectly frank, I was too tired to go and find out.

Chapter 11

Lord only knows what time the bloody cockerel started cock-a-doodle-doing but more than once I heard Scarlett screeching in her hoarse, still-drunk voice that she was going to ring his sodding neck if he didn't put a sock in it. That didn't seem to have much effect as he continued on and on...until at some stage I must have fallen asleep again because the next thing I knew, I was awakening from some weird erotic dream about me and Simon Cowell getting it on in a dirty cowshed, watched by several bleating goats and an excitable ram, to what sounded like a pneumatic drill at full pelt, right outside of my bedroom window.

'WHAT THE ACTUAL FUCK!'

Scarlett was awake then. At least *she* was further away from the epicentre of the disturbance. Wondering if the house was actually being demolished with us inside it, I gingerly released the mosquito blind so it shot up, almost taking my fingers off in the process, and prised open the rickety old shutters, to be rewarded with the sight of two skinny young men dressed in scruffy overalls that had clearly once been a shade of blue, completely decimating the trees and bushes currently obscuring the view from our terrace, with an industrial strimmer thing that looked decidedly lethal - and yet they were completely devoid of any protective equipment or even plastic safety glasses.

Thankfully, the noise of the strimmer had drowned out Scarlett's shouting and the creaking of the shutters, meaning the two men hadn't even realised there was anybody inside looking out on them, so I quietly closed everything back up again and wandered in to tell Scarlett what all the commotion was about, before joining her on the bed in her considerably quieter room, where we eventually both dozed off again, sleeping top-to-tail, with pillows over our heads in an attempt to keep out any noise and light.

When we surfaced again, a considerable time later, with sweaty heads and a diabolical thirst, all was quiet outside, so I ventured out to take a look.

My god. What a difference. Everything had been sliced right back...and we were left with an unbelievably spectacular view out to sea, which was as calm as a millpond on this fine, cloudless morning. It took my breath away and I knew from then on I would be out on that terrace at every possible opportunity - eating my food out there, drinking my coffee out there, cutting my toenails out there - not wanting to miss any glimpse of that view by being stuck indoors. Scarlett was equally impressed and the first thing she did was drag the old plastic chairs out and we drank pint glasses of ice cold water filled directly from the spring as if we were sampling the finest of wines from the cellar (not that we had a cellar or were ever likely to have one).

Alex arrived shortly afterwards, smelling of a heady combination of minty shower gel and Gucci aftershave, accompanied by a whistling Yiorgos, who was bearing gifts in the form of still warm, crusty bread rolls purchased from the village bakery. Devouring mine straight from the paper bag, I thanked them both profusely, whilst we stood back to admire the newly acquired view.

'It is magnificent now, Just Jess! You can see all the way down to Ammos Beach and also, if you look to the right, you can even just about catch a glimpse of the boats in the harbour. The grass must be cut down regularly anyway, to avoid fires in the hottest months of the year...and we must of course be careful of the snakes in long grasses too...'

Coughing and spluttering, I almost choked on what remained of my bread roll. I managed a 'Come again?' to which Alex replied, 'Do not worry, Just Jess...there are only a few poisonous snakes on this island...but we must keep them from moving into your new home!'

'If just one of those slippery, slimy, vicious little buggers moves into my home Alex, then *I* will be moving into *your* home,' I warned him, not kidding at all.

'We would enjoy your company,' he assured me, his grin suggesting that he wasn't taking me entirely seriously.

Swallowing the last of his hunk of bread, he then went on to stress the importance of purchasing a cheap Greek mobile from his friend's shop in town, to avoid incurring ridiculous charges and bills on our English ones. Those two lovely men, despite being freshly showered, then somehow unearthed a bent spade and a wonky wheelbarrow and moved much of the rubble from the side of the building round to the back, which immediately improved the appearance of the property, and then they both stood back to admire their handiwork whilst we threw our dirty laundry in the bin bag I'd emptied the night before. We kept back the underwear to wash ourselves in the bathroom sink, not wishing to burden anyone else with handling our smalls. Although mine weren't as small these days as they once had been, but, hey, such is life.

Once hand-washing and cleaning duties were completed, Scarlett meandered down to the village on a mission to hire a scooter and, just over an hour later, the 'put-put' noises coming up the hill signalled that she had been successful and now had her own means of transport. To be honest, I was pretty sure it should have been condemned because it looked a rusty heap of old shite and seemed to have various bits missing, but Scarlett was made up with it, so I kept quiet.

She'd also brought back fresh, juicy tomatoes and huge melons apparently donated to the Cause of Lost Brits Living on a Shoestring by good old Apostolis who, like most other people on the island, grew most of his own fruit and vegetables, and bought as little as possible from the shops and supermarkets.

I was in the best of moods, comfortably relaxing in my plastic chair on the front terrace, gazing out to the Ionian Sea, chin covered in melon juice, daydreaming of Lorry and Nikos and wondering just exactly who would have the best body when stripped naked, when Lauren arrived to fill up her multitude of bottles from the spring and put a stop to all that.

Knowing full well I should just lower my shades over my eyes and only speak when spoken to, I of course leapt up to go and say hello. I just couldn't be that person who would sit there and ignore someone who was a matter of metres away.

'Hi,' I began, wandering over. 'How's things? Been busy at work?' Christ, I sounded like a drunken customer in the back of a speeding taxi, returning home after a heavy night out on the lash. This is what she had reduced me to.

'Hi. I'm okay thanks. And work's busy as always. No rest for the wicked, as they say.'

I noticed she didn't ask how I was, and then proceeded to turn her back on me as she filled the remainder of the bottles as quickly as she could.

Bollocks to this, I thought. I live here now and she's not making me feel like a lesser citizen, especially when we're the same nationality!

I waited until she'd finished, impatiently tapping my foot on the ground, and then stood right in front of her when she reached the top step, completely blocking her path, so she couldn't possibly ignore me.

'Listen, have I done something to offend you? Or do you just not like me for some unexplained reason and that's why you're behaving like an arse? Because right from the outset you were offhand with me at the hotel...and since then, despite the fact that I've been consistently friendly and polite towards you, you've been nothing short of rude. So, if we have a problem here, I would appreciate it if you would kindly let me know what it is, and then we can move on, like adults do. Because, like it or not, I'm here for the duration, and you're going to have to endure seeing me probably every single day. So you can either be nice to me, or you can continue to behave like a gobshite and let this awkwardness drag on.'

Nothing. She stared at me and said nothing. Brilliant.

'Right, so you don't have anything at all to say to that, do you? Well, in that case I've just got one thing left to say to you then. Fuck off. Just fuck off.'

Seething, I marched back into the house and slammed the front door behind me, storming into the living room and hearing Scarlett yell out some abuse in response to the sudden bang that had disturbed her sleep, AGAIN!

Bloody Lauren! That sodding woman! Manners cost nothing and I just didn't see why she couldn't be polite. Maybe she thought I was homing in on her territory – but I had as much right to be here as she did – if not more, depending on which way you looked at it - after all, I'd visited this island long before she swooped in on it; I'd stepped foot on Loulouthian soil and appreciated all its charms when she didn't even know it existed, and I therefore had more of a link to Loulouthia, however tenuous, than she did. So there. Ah...sod her.

Once I'd made sure that Scarlett was in the land of the living and had staggered into the shower, I braved the pathway down to work all by myself, squealing and dodging as some massive mutant hornet thing kept trying to intimidate and dive-bomb me, whilst I flapped about and attempted to swat the bloody thing away with my hand. Consequently I was already sweaty and stressed to the max by the time I arrived at work and was in no mood for Tassos' shit and shenanigans. Weaving through the tables, I was pleasantly surprised though to find a gift awaiting me – an overflowing basket of flowers, made up of all shades of purples and pinks and which I knew would look perfect at the front of our once-whitewashed, but now rather dirty-looking, home up the hill. Lukas immediately informed me who the flowers were from, but I had already guessed – 'The man Nikos – friend of Tassos – he came earlier and left these for you. He said he enjoyed meeting you last night and will look forward to wining and dining you when you are available...'

Oh, the man was keen. Obviously, blooms were to be found in abundance on this island and you couldn't put a foot outside without falling over pots of geraniums and containers of assorted wildflowers, plucked from the earth in the mountains and transplanted in the resorts to give colour and scent to the streets, but still.

As far as Nikos was concerned, well I didn't even know what the man did for a living, what his actual age really was...or, most importantly, if he had a wife and children stashed away somewhere. He was too handsome to be single, I figured; too charming to have been on his own all his life. He probably shagged his way up and down the touristy side of the island every summer season and then returned to the bosom of his wife in one of the villages for the quiet winter months. And why was I even bothered? I hadn't come here looking for a man; I didn't *need* a man. Men only complicated matters and I had enough to think about at the moment, what with relocating to a foreign country, starting a new job (with an employer who was starting to remind me more and more of Mr Burns from The Simpsons as every day passed by) and not forgetting sorting out my affairs back in the UK.

And *if* I was to get with anyone, then Lorry was equally as attractive and a much safer bet, despite him still being a relative youngster and not even knowing who Wham! were; I'd be better advised to give in to his relatively shy advances, rather than getting myself tangled up with a self-assured smooth talker – albeit a shockingly attractive one. Not that I would be getting with anyone. I'd leave all that nonsense to Scarlett who was definitely looking for love, although perhaps emitting some of the wrong signals by misbehaving on the beaches and returning home in the early hours with her knickers in her handbag.

Clap, clap! Oh Jesus, here he was, my least favourite boss ever, summoning me to attention. What did he want me to do tonight, in between cleaning the place, taking the orders, serving the food, totting up the bills and generally bouncing around like a tit? Paint the outside of the restaurant? Run up a new set of curtains? Re-fit the kitchen?

'Jessica...you are a little late tonight...I think you are not coming.'

Cheeky bastard, I'd arrived early!

'Many people will arrive here soon to eat in our restaurant, and you must work very hard tonight!' Yeah, because like I didn't already do that. Dickhead.

My eyes were already glazing over as I allowed myself to drift off to a better place; imagining myself lazing on that glorious sandy beach again, soaking up the ever-present sun and delicately sipping a long, strong, fruity cocktail, while a sexy man sensuously rubbed sun oil into my bare back...

'...so from tomorrow you must come to work at six o'clock, not four...'

Oh...brilliant news! That would be so much civilised and would mean that at least I would be able to have a lie-in and then venture out when I was all refreshed, to enjoy a lazy lunch and top up my tan...

'...and then each day you will work eight o'clock until one o'clock to help with breakfasts and lunch...and you will return at six o'clock and stay until we have finished serving the food and cleared up – so, I think, maybe midnight. Do you understand?'

Excuse me? What the fudge! Did he just say what I think he said?

'So, let me get this straight...you want me to be here for eight o'clock *in the morning* and I won't just be around for the breakfast rush but will have to stay for most of the lunchtime service as well...and then I will then have to return here at six o'clock in the afternoon and work on until the early hours?' I was gobsmacked – here I was thinking I'd be getting extra time to chill and put my feet up and instead he wanted me to work split shifts...*every day...IN THE HEAT!* He was trying to bloody kill me, I was convinced.

He must have seen the look of disbelief and horror on my face because the crafty old sod quickly added, '...and I will pay you five Euros more, of course, for each day.'

Five Euros! He wanted me to work split shifts, to graft for three more hours each day and he would pay me less than one Euro seventy cents for each of those extra hours, out of the kindness of his heart!

Before I even had chance to recover from the shock and attempt to formulate some sort of sarcastic reply to this canny old git's outrageous proposal – not even a proposal really, it was more of an order – the restaurant was suddenly mobbed by various families with more kids than I could shake a stick at, and I didn't have time to turn round, let alone think, for the next few hours. Lukas and chef had obviously been informed of the changes to my working pattern as they glanced over at me a few times sympathetically...and then members of Tassos' extended family arrived unannounced and took over one whole section of the restaurant, as they all sat down together to share a huge mezé and a mountain of chips and I was unable to interrupt to ask him why he was so determined to finish me off.

Disgusted, annoyed and completely shattered, after another frantic eight hours on my aching feet, only bearable because of the genuinely sweet customers who came in and tipped well, it occurred to me that there had been no mention whatsoever of when I would actually be paid any wages, so I quizzed Lukas on the subject while I was grabbing the box containing my free pizza slices and picking up my basket of flowers. Apparently pay day was every Saturday at the end of the shift, of course, but I was to make sure Tassos handed over the correct amount I was due, as he often made 'mistakes'. When I asked Lukas why Tassos hadn't told *him* he had to work mornings *and* evenings, he informed me that he already had a second job, at a busy cafe in town...and then I felt guilty because it turned out he worked more hours than me, day in day out, and never complained or made a song and dance about it. Maybe they were made of steelier stuff in Albania than the suburbs of Manchester.

'Nice flowers, Jessica!' cried Sofia as I stormed through the door to Sunrise, swearing like one of 'The Inbetweeners' and not caring in the slightest who the devil heard me.

'But they could never smell as sweet as you always do, Just Jess,' added Alex, popping the bottle top off my statutory Amstel, and eliciting a smile I didn't think I had in me.

Hopping on to my usual bar stool, my basket of flowers at my feet, I slugged back a mouthful of beer, as Sofia demanded to know where my unexpected gift had come from and raised a carefully shaped eyebrow when I replied that the man in question was none other than the Naughty but Nice Nikos, with the attitude and the awesome looks.

'Don't tell Lorry,' she whispered suddenly, the quick dart of her eyes indicating that the man himself had arrived in the bar and was creeping up behind me. His arms slipped around my waist and he rested his chin on my right shoulder as he said, 'The elusive Jessica! I miss you, now you are working...we need to arrange a beach date one afternoon or else I'll never see you at all!'

He was the cutest, loveliest guy, he really was, and I found myself gently easing the basket of flowers to one side with my foot – pretending they belonged to Barbara Streisand on the neighbouring stool – and agreeing to meet up with him the very next day on Ammos beach, after I'd finished my first shift of the day. I just hoped he wouldn't read too much into it – and besides, I wouldn't have time to squeeze in either a love-life or sex-life, with the hours I would be putting in during the forthcoming weeks and months. Maybe the locals sensibly saved getting down and dirty for the colder winter months rather than sweating their bits off in the heat of the summer anyway.

Welcoming the relaxing effect of the strong alcohol, I stayed longer than I intended to, but I was enjoying Lorry's company and everyone was laughing as I described the washer door incident and also Scarlett's displeasure at being woken by up the loudest cockerel in the whole of Greece.

When I mentioned Lauren's name to Alex, to enquire if he knew much about her, he was non-committal and appeared keen to change the subject and shut me down. Interesting.

Eventually, Lorry offered to see me home but his face fell when Sofia insisted that I needed to take the weight off my feet and jump in her car instead; I attempted to placate him with a peck on the lips, as she grabbed the basket of flowers, as if they actually belonged to her, and placed them in the boot.

'Why don't you have a scooter or a moped like everyone else, Sofia?' I asked her as we fastened our seatbelts. 'Every Tom, Dick and Spiros on this island seems to zip about everywhere on one and I'm definitely in the minority when I say I'd much rather walk. I'm guessing you're not a big fan either?'

'No, Just Jess. No, I certainly am not! They are exceedingly dangerous and I much prefer the safety of travelling by car. Let me tell you something – a girl I once knew was involved in a horrific accident after being thrown from her scooter - not too long ago actually - and since then I have vowed never to use one again. Besides, my heels are too high to be riding on two wheels up and down the island...and the wind would mess up my hair!'

'I couldn't imagine anything messing with *your* hair, Sofia! You always look so beautiful and expertly styled...unlike me with my uncontrollable curls and occasional greys. I have to say, you always look divine, and could so easily have been a high-paid model. Next to you I feel like...I don't know...the ugly sister!'

'Oh no! You are very beautiful Just Jess...my very attractive younger sister! And I like to style hair and use many beauty products. It is something that has always interested me and I wish I could maybe have learned how to do it properly; taken some exams and then opened up my very own boutique salon...'

'So why didn't you, Sofia?'

'Ah Jess...it was my dream once, when I was a very young girl. But then along came Alex and Yiorgos... and now I must help in the businesses and also look after our home. Family ALWAYS comes first in Greece. Sometimes we have to leave our dreams in the past and accept that they will never come true. Except for you, of course! You are braver than I have ever been and you are chasing after your dreams now Jess...better late than never! You are here, where you belong, and I think life is just beginning for you...'

Whilst I appreciated the kind words and encouragement she was doling out to me, it seemed such a shame that she had surrendered her own dreams so readily. She couldn't quite hide her inner sadness; she was almost wistful, as she remembered the girl she had been before she became Mrs Alex Makris – the girl who'd still had all of her life ahead of her and who'd had a clear vision of a future doing something she loved. But, okay, she may not have carved out the career she'd planned, but she had been blessed with Alex and their son, their thriving businesses, a lovely, comfortable home no doubt, and an envious life on Loulouthia. She had so much to be thankful for!

'Do you know, I think you could be right, Sofia. It certainly feels like a fresh start and a chance to make something of my life,' I said, snapping her back into the present. 'But I fear Tassos is doing his best to end it by working me to death!'

She laughed as she pulled up outside the house and leant over to warmly hug me goodnight.

'Kalinichta, darling Just Jess! Now go and grab some beauty sleep before Scarlett O'Hara bursts in and wakes you up to tell you all about her first night at work! And don't let Tassos work YOU too hard in the morning. *Kalinichta* my friend. Good night.'

Chapter 12

Scarlett did indeed wake me up to give me the full run-down on her night's work, and she seemed determined to omit no detail. It sounded as if she'd spent much of the night openly flirting with Bay Bar Spiros, but at least she'd returned with a smile on her face and was apparently being paid nightly rather than weekly, so had money in her back pocket when she arrived sometime in the early hours, thankfully having given the alcohol a wide berth before she'd steered her scooter home and up the rough track to our house in the almost pitch black. She was practically dribbling as she was talking animatedly about her new manager and I had a feeling Simon was going to have to up his game considerably now he was in competition with this Greek Adonis. God love her, but I think I nodded off as she was still prattling on, as I awoke to the buzzing of my alarm at seven, having slept through the bloody cockerel, to find she'd considerately covered me with a sheet to try and prevent the insects from eating me alive, before she'd bedded down for the remainder of the night.

My whole body screamed out with fatigue, but I had no choice other than to drag my bum out of bed and my weary legs down to work for eight o'clock smart. After splashing cold water onto my face, and squirting deodorant under my armpits, I changed into a clean top and skirt – freshly washed and ironed, courtesy of Sofia. When I opened the front door to stagger down the path, already shading my eyes against the brightness of the morning sun, I was surprised to find a bulging carrier bag placed on the small white, plastic table on the terrace...and when I hastily inspected its contents, I found a whole host of goodies inside including oranges, melon, courgettes and half a dozen eggs, along with a note that simply read, 'Sorry'.

The one person (besides Tassos) who had anything to apologise for was Lauren, so I assumed it could only have been from her. Not one to bear a grudge for long, it cheered me up no end; if she was offering an olive branch, I would gladly accept it. Hopefully we could be friends, if she chose to let down those defences. The bag and its contents safely propped on the kitchen units, I locked up again, and was just admiring the view on this glorious Wednesday morning before heading down to Chaliki, when I heard a car making its way up towards the house from the main road. To my surprise it was Alex, clean as a whistle and all bright and smiley – how did the man do it?

'*Kaliméra*, Just Jess...I would say good morning to you both, but I am guessing that Scarlet Fever is still snoring like a little piggy in the luxury of her bed. Your taxi awaits you!' He opened the passenger door and indicated I should slide in, once he'd shifted a bag of fresh bread from the seat and brushed off the crumbs.

'Oh Alex, that's so kind and thoughtful of you. But you and Sofia can't keep coming to my rescue all of the time like this, particularly when your own lives are so busy.'

'Oh, poppycack!'

'Poppycock?'

'Yes, that's what I said. Anyway, my wife tells me that you also now have to work the breakfast shift at Mama's...so I thought that I would catch you after I collected our bread from the bakery...and now you can rest your legs for a little while longer in my car. It's no problem! Stop protesting and climb in, Just Jess!'

I briefly tried to maintain the pretence that I didn't really want a lift, but instead I was chanting a thousand silent thank yous, that I didn't have to tread the long path down the hill, no matter how stunning the view was.

'Oh that bread smells soooo good Alex...I'm so ravenous, I'll probably end up scoffing the customers' breakfasts if they don't eat them quickly enough!'

We were just slowing down to ease out onto the main road when Alex leant over with what looked like a half French stick he'd removed from the bag, and said in a mock-sexy voice, 'Just Jess, would you like to nibble on my baguette?'

It was impossible to be down when I was around Alex - God, how I loved him and Sofia! They were so adorable and kind and relentlessly cheerful and funny, without being annoying at all. Snapping the end of the baguette off, I stuffed it into my mouth before he could change his mind, choking on the crust and then accepting the offer of a sip of Alex's coffee – which nearly brew my brains out, it was *that* strong.

If I'd expected the morning shift to be any quieter, I was sadly disappointed. It was a whole lot worse, as I didn't even have Lukas to assist, just Tassos noisily making the coffees and ensuring he took all payments for bills – and therefore pocketing any tips that had been donated as well. Old swine. How I was ever going to complete another shift that day, I had no idea.

Slaving away in the heat of the day was seriously not my idea of fun either and I refused to hang about even one minute longer at the end of my shift. Grabbing a small bottle of water out of the fridge, I descended the steps, and plodded along the dusty pavement and into Sunrise; through to Sofia's and straight out on to the beach. Apostolis tried to converse with me on my way past but I merely mumbled something like 'Need to swim...must cool down...before death,' and stripped off my outer layer of clothing and dumped it in a heap on the beach, so I could wade out into the cool waters of the Ionian Sea and try to remember all of the good things about this island, and forget about how my job in England seemed like a piece of piss compared to this form of torture. Plonking myself down in the shallow waters, I closed my eyes and allowed my fingers to sink into the sand, attempting to clear my mind of all the nasty, violent thoughts (towards Tassos) that were building up in there.

My clothes were left unattended on the beach, but I didn't give a toss – if anyone wanted to steal those sweaty, grubby items then best of luck to them; they seriously needed help. Feeling sorry for myself, I remained in the sea, water lapping over my legs as the sun beat down on me for probably a good twenty minutes or so. However, when I eventually forced myself out of the water and returned to the same spot, I noticed a bottle of beer had been planted in the sand next to my clothes; when I glanced up in surprise, I saw Apostolis waving at me from the restaurant. 'From the boss!' he shouted, giving me the thumbs up before dashing off to serve another customer. Gratefully glugging it down, straight from the bottle, I released my curls from the damp scrunchie with my free hand, allowing them to fall around my shoulders, before collapsing onto an unoccupied sunbed, not caring that I was without towel and that various bits of me hadn't seen a razor in days.

My mobile was still back at the house, so I didn't know or care what time it was, but the arrival of Lorry, panting and sweating as he ran over and apologised for his tardiness, coupled with the intensifying heat, signified that I didn't have long before I needed to go and have, ooh, half an hour's shut-eye, before I had to return to work again. Bloody hell, I didn't think I could keep this up.

We passed a pleasant hour on the beach together, munching on doughnuts whilst completing some silly quiz in a magazine left behind by another sun-worshipper, Lorry insisting that he needed to slowly rub more sun lotion into my back despite my feeble protests, but all too soon we had to pack up our stuff. Fortunately, he had one of the hire cars parked out on the road so was able to take me home and save me some precious time.

My heart sank when I realised we had company at the house and found Simple Simon wandering round in his tatty Tasmanian Devil boxer shorts, burping, and scratching his bum, and I nearly lynched him when I realised he'd just necked the last of the Tango out of the fridge. Scarlett was sat up in bed with a smug smile plastered on her face; I didn't need to ask what they'd been up to in my absence. Thankfully, he was also keen to cadge a lift off Lorry, so he threw on his t-shirt and shorts and slid his ugly trotters into his manky flip-flops and was gone before I could give him a piece of my mind.

Glancing at the time on my phone, I realised it was far too late to snatch even the tiniest of siestas, and it was to be hoped that I didn't end up collapsing in a heap at the restaurant before the end of my shift. Remembering the early morning gift from Lauren, I washed and changed quickly, as I wanted to try and catch her as I left.

Leaping out just as she was passing by, I unintentionally managed to frighten the life out of her and she ended up having a serious wobble on her scooter.

'Oh god, I'm sorry, I didn't mean to startle you, especially when you're riding one of those bloody things.'

'No, it's me who should be saying sorry. Because I really am.'

'You left the goody-bag this morning?'

'Yes. And I know you've probably got lemons coming out of your ears, but it was just a small peace offering because you were quite right – I was rude - appallingly rude - and I didn't mean to be. For what it's worth, I was just trying to maintain my distance, not cause any offence.'

'But why? Am I really that hideous that you can't abide to be anywhere near me? Or are you merely sick to the back teeth of inquisitive English people asking too many questions? You're not hiding from the law are you?'

I saw her laugh properly then, for the very first time and it absolutely illuminated her pretty, heart-shaped face and she transformed into someone else right in front of my very eyes. Her blonde hair, streaked with the sun, hung like a cape around her shoulders, still wet from her post-work dip in the pool, and for the first time I noticed how bright and blue her eyes were. She looked, well, *honest* and *normal* and this Lauren I could get on board with. Not for the first time I wondered what her partner, Andreas, was like and where she hid him away as I'd never even clapped eyes on him.

'No, I'm definitely not on the run! I can assure you, I really did meet Andreas on holiday, we fell in love, and I returned to live with him here, up the mountain...amongst the lemon trees and the olive groves and the in-laws...'

'Do you know, I think that's the longest sentence you've ever said to me? So much progress made in such a short time! And just when I have to head off to work as well, although I feel like I've only been away from there for ten minutes, now he's got me rostered for doing split shifts...'

'Yes...I don't envy you, working for Tassos; I've heard he can be a bit of a tyrant. I'd better let you go then. But...maybe you, and your friend, could come up to the house one day for a bite to eat, when I can introduce you to Andreas...although, I must warn you, he's pretty quiet and I'm lucky to pin him down for five minutes because in the daytime he's usually tied up with the farm and the animals, and then he works at his uncle's bar in Town most nights – and on the busier evenings I'm down there with him – not just to help out, but to make sure I actually get to see him in the flesh! But it would be nice for you to meet him...and I can show you where we live.'

'Aw, I'd love that thank you, and I'm sure Scarlett would too. It would be nice to meet Andreas and get to know you both a little better, particularly after our slightly bumpy start.' I broke into a grin to let her know she was forgiven, and she gave me a wry smile in return. Who knew why she had been so reluctant initially to give me the time of day – maybe she had met some dodgy Brits while she'd been out here, or perhaps even had some unpleasant experiences back in England that had led to her distrusting everybody on first sight, until they proved themselves worthy of her trust. Hopefully the two of us could get along now.

Despite the exhaustion, lack of sleep and the unrelenting heat, I practically skipped down the pathway to the village, delighted at last to have made headway with Lauren, and very much looking forward to meeting Andreas. Unbelievably, I was actually twenty minutes early so made a snap decision to visit Sunrise to cool down in front of one of the huge fans in there and hopefully have a chat with one of my friends.

Soula was behind the bar when I went in, looking as cheery as ever, but thankfully Sofia was tucked away in a corner, quietly tapping on her mobile whilst sipping iced water.

'Hi Sofia, can I interrupt your quiet time for a few minutes before I start my six hours of hell?' I asked, sighing heavily and sinking into the settee next to her.

'You? Always. You look tired, Just Jess...' She placed her mobile face down on to the table, ready to give me her full attention.

'I feel it. Can I ask you something Sofia? Are all jobs here like this? Does every employer in Greece do their best to work you into an early grave? Or is it just Tassos? Don't tell me, he has a second job as a funeral director and he's trying to drum up some business!'

'Ha, ha you are so funny Jess...I think you should be on a stage telling jokes, not waitressing in a Greek island restaurant! Now, listen, my darling Jess, while I give you some useful advice. Firstly, if you live here all year round, you have the pick of the jobs that are not taken by family members or close friends. Secondly, what remains are very few jobs in a small resort like Chaliki, and by the time you began to look for work, even so early on in the season, the best of the jobs were already spoken for. Besides Lauren, I think there are only two English girls working in this resort – one who cleans apartments and one who, I believe, will be working *many* hours in Horizon restaurant from next week! Oh and there is an Irish girl, Rhiannon, who worked in Achilles last year and who is due to return before the end of the month – rumour has it that she had a dangerous liaison with Stathis, who owns the bar, and he wants to...ahem...use her services again this year. Otherwise all jobs here, and the better jobs in the other resorts, they are all gone – to Greeks, some Albanians, a few Americans and one or two other nationalities.'

'So, basically what you're saying is that we totally missed the bus on this one, and have now been left with the shitty jobs that no one else wanted? Ace!'

'Ha, ha! See, Jess – funny! I'm sorry, but unless anything changes you're stuck with Tassos - if you want to work in this resort. I'm not aware of any other jobs at the moment. I wish *I* could give you a job but I have everyone I need in the restaurant and they are good, loyal workers...and I think you would be great here in the bar but Soula...' She leant over to whisper so her niece didn't hear her name mentioned in vain. '...Soula is family and so I must give her a job. She is a very lovely girl but truly does not want to be here...and we cannot afford to pay anyone else at the moment...I do wish I was in a position to offer you a job, to allow you to leave Mama's...'

'Oh no, Sofia, I wasn't hinting...honestly, I wasn't. You and Alex have done more than enough for me...you've been so generous and I don't know how we'd have coped if we hadn't had you to lean on. I could hop on the bus down to Town or Skafos and try for a bar job there – Scarlett seems to think there's loads of them on offer – but as you know, the buses are a bit hit and miss, and I would struggle to get one back late at night. And don't you dare try to offer me a lift down there as well! Never mind, I will just have to persevere with Tassos and hope he starts to give me a break sooner rather than later...'

Sofia's concerned expression warned me that I shouldn't hold out much hope, but I really had no alternative at this stage. It was this job or relocate to another resort to follow the work...and that would kill me - I loved this quaint little village with all its quirky people. The only other option was to admit defeat – to return to England to look for a steady job there...but that was simply not on my agenda and, besides, Heather was scheduled to move into my house at the weekend!

Spontaneously hugging Sofia, I said goodbye and see you later, and dragged my already sore feet over to Mama's, wondering what fresh hell awaited me within. I *had* to make this work – I couldn't give up already when my new life here had only just started to take shape...please god let Tassos go easy on me tonight!

Chapter 13

It was fair to say that Tassos did not go easy on me on that evening or at any point during the next four shifts. Desperately wanting to prove myself, I initially tried to be overly polite towards him, keeping my head down and working like a dog; I seemed to be a hit with the customers and I gave him no reason to be constantly on my back, and yet he was. The more meek and submissive I was, the more he seemed to take advantage of my good nature, so then I chose to fight back a little instead, by mirroring his abruptness with my own, developing selective hearing when he was picking fault with everything I did, and insisting on a short break and cold drink mid way through each shift. This rebellion didn't come easy to me; I'd been brought up to believe that you always followed your boss' instructions, without question, and treated them with the utmost respect at all times.

You've got to earn respect though.

Consequently, I was one big ball of simmering tension by the time I'd hiked home after finishing lunch service on Saturday, when I'd delivered more breakfasts than I ever thought possible and, following which, I swear to god, I never wanted to see another fried egg again. Ever.

To make matters worse, it was the weekend of the Flower Festival and the long hours and split shifts meant that I was missing out on all of the fun. I'd seen old women carrying bundles of freshly picked flowers that would be cleverly transformed into wreaths for hanging on front doors, and I'd witnessed a colourful procession passing by the restaurant as I'd juggled four plates of scrambled eggs on toast, but I wouldn't have the opportunity to join the crowds in Town for the traditional Greek dancing display or be part of the late night festivities in the old Chaliki village square, where wine was free-flowing until the early hours, and petals were scattered all around, as it was believed they brought the islanders happiness and health – both of which I needed a bloody good dose of at the moment.

When I stormed into the house, dripping with sweat and ready to keel over, I found Scarlett still languishing in bed, which wasn't unusual as she worked until the early hours and then slept until lunchtime. However, I was clocking up roughly the same hours but during split shifts and surviving on just a few hours sleep, usually restless and broken. And if *I* didn't clean the house, then it didn't really get done; despite my determination that I would ensure all domestic duties were shared equally, I always gave in as I couldn't live like a tramp. Add to that having to wash clothes in the kitchen sink before hanging them out to drip dry on the makeshift line strung between two olive trees at the side of the house, and I had a pretty full day, let me tell you.

Unsurprisingly, I was mightily pissed off when I gave Scarlett a sharp nudge as I was preparing to go to work AGAIN, after an exciting afternoon of completing chores, but she simply crawled back under her sheet, whinging that she was too *tired* to get up, and muttering that she would just ring in and inform her boss she was being violently sick so couldn't possibly make it in that evening.

'Scarlett, you've only worked four nights! He's going to sack you! It's not like having a permanent job in England you know, where you at least have some rights; when you've been given a contract and they can't just fire you willy-nilly. If you don't turn in, he'll tell you not to bother coming back and sure as hell offer your job to someone else...'

'Oh stop being such a miserable old nag...I'll promise to put in a few extra hours next weekend or something and he'll be sweet. Don't sweat it - honestly, it'll be fine. I'll tell him I've got one of those twenty-four hour tummy bugs and he'll just have to suck it up...he wouldn't want me spreading *that* amongst all his workers, now would he?'

Fighting back the urge to cry, I told her to piss off and went to grab a drink from the kitchen. What I wouldn't have given for a night off. With the exception of a trip to the supermarket to do a 'big shop' with Sofia, I hadn't been anywhere – not to the beach, the pool or any place other than work and home in the last couple of days – I'd even walked back alone up to the house after work on Thursday night, rather than slip into Sunrise for a quick drink, to wait until Sofia or Alex were free to give me a lift home. Realising it would be slightly idiotic to brave the path up to the house in the dark, I had taken the longer route, up and out of the village on the main road until I could eventually turn left onto the track – I'd never appreciated what a steep journey it was on foot and I'd consequently been breathless and had reached a new level of fatigue that I'd never experienced before. Alex had given me a right bollocking about that when he caught up with me the next morning and made me promise never to do it again. I didn't think I *could* do it again.

I hadn't seen Lorry at all, or even had the pleasure of Nikos dropping by to brighten up my evenings, as he had apparently sailed over to Corfu to sort out some paperwork and catch up with family, and I felt like I'd been working for six months rather than almost a week. My skin was terrible, my eyes had huge bags underneath and I dreaded to think what state I would be in by the end of the season – if I survived that long.

But I knew if I didn't go to work then I didn't get paid, and if I didn't get paid then we would be struggling to meet our rent. It all boiled down to the fact that I couldn't afford to lose my job, however shit it was. A little voice at the back of my head reminded me that I still had dad's money tucked away in my English bank account...but I was determined not to touch it, except in an absolute, dire emergency.

Despite my frustrations, I couldn't bear it if there was even a whiff of bad feeling in the air between myself and Scarlett, and so I approached her again, to try to persuade her to get her lazy arse out of bed, but no amount of threats or coercion would do the job, and I had no choice but to stomp out and leave her there. After another failed attempt to cool down by fanning myself with an out of date Hello magazine I'd picked up in Sunrise - it seemed hotter than ever on that terrace – it was time to leave. The familiar put-put sound coming up the hill told me Lauren was on her way home and she stopped as usual to have a brief chat – it was rapidly becoming the highlight of my day, our quick natter about everything from chickens to childhood illnesses as we crossed paths at roughly the same time each afternoon.

She was funny and kind, I'd realised, and a wealth of information. She had told us all about a tiny little shop in Town that sold English bacon and bread, explained about the slightly chaotic postal system, directed us to where we needed to pay our utility bills when they arrived (hopefully not for some time yet) and warned us where NOT to eat or drink on the island. She also brought us two plastic water bottles that had been filled with Andreas' homemade red wine, which she wisely warned us tasted and smelled like rocket fuel, and she wasn't wrong. One small glass left us coughing our guts up and feeling the burn, all the way down, until I was sure it was melting our insides. Still, it was the thought that counted.

'Hi Jess, what gives? You look stressed...anything I can help with?'

'Not really, but thanks all the same. Unless you know of some well-paid jobs coming up soon, suitable for myself and Scarlett – jobs that will allow us at least a smidgeon of time off to have some sort of life while we're here...no? Thought not. It's Saturday night too, so I know the restaurant's going to be heaving, and I can already play dot-to-dot on my feet with the assortment of blisters I've acquired over the last week. If you hear the headline on the Greek news tomorrow, 'English woman slays Greek Dickhead', you'll know Tassos has sent me over the edge!'

A nasty thought occurred to me then. 'Oh shit, tell me Andreas isn't related to him! I forget that everyone on the island is connected to everyone else in some way. He's not Andreas' dad or second-cousin-twice-removed is he?'

'God, no! Don't worry, they're definitely not relatives. But do be careful, because you will find that most folk on this island *are* related, if not by blood then by a friendship that goes back decades. I know you're not a blabbermouth, or else it would have been all over the village by now...but, I can tell you, I dropped a bollock many a time when I first arrived...slagging off an old boy who I thought had ripped me off at the hardware store on the Town road, and it turned out he was Andreas' father's best friend from school...and not forgetting the argument I had with a real bitch at the pharmacy over migraine medication. She's moved over to Corfu now but not before I discovered she was Andreas' distant cousin. His mother gave me the cold shoulder for *months* over that incident, I can tell you.'

Before I had chance to reply, another vehicle came speeding up the hill creating a cloud of dust, and as I shielded my eyes from the sun I heard a cheery shout of '*Yassoo!*' and saw the wave of an ebony, wrinkly hand which had been dangling out of the window of a filthy clapped-out car of indistinguishable make and colour.

Lauren shouted back something in Greek that I couldn't quite catch, before turning to me and saying 'Andreas' father. He's a pussycat really; hot tempered but kind and thoughtful. His wife's a bit of a dragon though and I was terrified of her when I first arrived. Oh, stand back - here comes someone else...it must be rush hour up here in the mountains!'

Blinking away the grit from my eyes, I squinted in an attempt to see who it was, unused to witnessing such a high volume of traffic on our fairly remote, usually peaceful road; the vehicles that did come up and down tended to do so very early in the morning or when I was out at work, as most errands were run at the cooler times of day. From information gleaned from Lauren, I was aware that there was a handful of houses further up the road; Andreas' parents' place, where Andreas and Lauren also shared a room; the neighbouring property which was occupied by an older couple, Sakis and his wife Maria, who hardly ever came down to connect with civilisation unless it was for official business in Town, or occasionally for a wedding or funeral; the house next door to Sakis and Maria, which had been built for their daughter and family; a crumbling one storey stone building where an old lady called Angelique, who permanently dressed in black widow clothes, lived all alone, and a currently empty brick house that an assortment of animals wandered in and out of, but was likely to be renovated by the deceased owner's son at some point in the future.

But it wasn't any of those people approaching us; it was Alex, again – apparently sent up by Sofia, to collect me as she was worried about my poor little legs and didn't want me to burn myself out so early on in the season. There was a stilted 'Hi' that passed between Alex and Lauren but nothing more, and the atmosphere was supremely awkward until Lauren uttered a quick 'See you later', promised to fetch me back something flower-related from the stalls that were set up in Town for the festival, and rapidly took off up the hill, leaving me wondering why on earth these two seemed so keen to keep their distance from each other.

I didn't have much time for further contemplation as Alex raced off as soon as I'd climbed in the car, and within seconds had me warbling along with him to a popular Greek song on the radio, attempting to teach me some repetitive lyrics, in an effort to improve my knowledge of the language. I feared it would be some time before I would be chatting away like a local.

In a flash, I was at work, and after a sweaty sweep and mop around and a quick change into a clean dress, I was literally run off my feet, orders spinning around in my head like plates in the air, my nerves fraught with Tassos constantly barking instructions at me. More than once, he nearly had me in tears and it was only the ever-cheerful Lukas who got me through the evening, making me laugh at regular intervals, and saving my bacon by chasing after me and swapping plates of food over when I'd accidentally picked up the wrong ones from the pass. By the end of the evening I was completely drained, mentally and physically, but looking forward to receiving my pay and at least having something to show for my week in the workhouse.

The last thing I wanted to do was hang about after my shift but I needed my money and Tassos hadn't mentioned it once. So I waited, and hovered, and hoped he would hand over the readies before my legs gave way beneath me. Instead he just sat at an empty table, playing with his *komboloi* (worry beads! – I'd give him something to worry about one of these days) and people-watching as tourists wandered up and down the road wearing flowers in their hair, and locals stopped to chat outside of the bars. He wanted me to *ask* for the money then, I realised...it would obviously give him great satisfaction to see me practically *begging* for what I was due – and unless I did so, my wages would not be forthcoming. Scummy bastard.

Trying to adopt an air of confidence and no-nonsense, I approached him and said, in a don't-mess-with-me-you-tight-arse-git voice, 'I need my wages, Tassos.' Instead of leaping up and showering me with apologies, he sighed dramatically and thrust his hand deep into his trouser pocket, pulling out a huge wad of notes, before he then had the audacity to stand up and turn his back on me, while he counted out my wages. Begrudgingly handing them over, without so much as a thank you or a kiss-my-arse, he shuffled off into the kitchen area, leaving me scowling after him. I was about to get the hell out of there when I remembered Lukas' wise words from earlier in the week and decided to quickly check the money I had been given before I left the premises.

Forty-four Euros short, the cheeky fecker! Not wanting to cause a scene in front of the few remaining customers, I stomped into the kitchen to hunt him down and inform him of his 'mistake'. 'No, no Jessica, I have given you the correct amount of money...you are becoming confused by the Euros,' he said patronisingly, again turning his back on me, this time in dismissal. My voice went up an octave or two as *I* assured *him* that it most definitely was NOT correct, whilst scribbling down my hours worked, and money due, on a scrap of paper and shoving it in front of his beaky nose. Presumably before I knocked Tassos to the floor and beat him to death with a heavy pan, Lukas intervened and eventually Tassos handed over another couple of twenty euro notes, adopting a look on his smackable face that said I was clearly robbing him blind. *He* then pretended not to understand *me* when I told him I was STILL four Euros short, so I stalked off to the till, relieved it of four Euros, showed him what I'd done and said goodnight to Lukas before storming off the premises and fleeing to the sanctity of Sunrise.

Shaking with fury at being made to feel so small and insignificant, I gladly accepted the beer Sofia handed over to me and elected to drink it out on the beach, where I could try to calm myself down and clear my head. I couldn't believe the cheek of the man and I wanted to tell him where to stick his job but I needed an income – what the hell was I going to do? When Sofia came to join me and we sat side by side on the sand, she stroked my damp hair away from my face and said, 'Just Jess, I do not think Tassos is worth getting yourself all hot and bothered about. He is a difficult man and you need to have...how do you say...a thicker skin?'

To my horror, tears started to plop down my face and I felt incredibly stupid. 'Lots of people work horrendous hours throughout the whole of the season, so why am I so exhausted and stressed already? I feel like such an idiot!'

'Aah...the work is harder than people think, especially when you are not used to the heat. But the problem is not necessarily the hours – soon you will become accustomed to the exhaustion and the lack of time to yourself! No, the problem is Tassos and his many demands. Listen...Alex will speak to Tassos on your behalf before he leaves tonight and he will inform Tassos that you will no longer be working the morning shifts – only the evening hours, as previously agreed. And you will be firmer with him in future. Okay, Just Jess?'

'Okay,' I sniffed, 'Thank you. And I'm sorry Sofia - I feel like such a moaner. That would certainly be an improvement – if I don't have to work mornings then I can catch up on some sleep and when I'm feeling more alive I'll be able to spend a little time at the beach again, and maybe even be around for some of the other celebrations later on in the season. Please don't think I'm usually so soft and pathetic – I've always been a hard worker and I don't want anyone to think bad of me or view me as some kind of slacker.'

'Oh Jess...no one thinks bad of you! We have looked over to the restaurant many times when you are there and seen how hard you work and how conscientious you are...and that is why Tassos is taking advantage of you. It is wonderful to be such a great member of staff and to want to do your job so well, but I'm afraid the more you are doing, the more he is expecting of you. You must growl at him like a dog...look....gggrrrrr!'

My god, I'd never had to growl at an employer before...what had my life come to? Sofia's comments cheered me though and I was touched that Alex was prepared to speak to Tassos on my behalf and relieved that I wouldn't have such a gruelling work schedule in the days to come.

Once I knew that I wouldn't be grafting the next morning, the relief was immense and I was happy to return to the crowd in the bar for a couple more beers. By the time Lorry arrived, I had metaphorically and literally let my hair down and was half way to being as relaxed as a newt. I was surprised to see him accompanied by Simon and Scarlett – she'd made a remarkable recovery for someone who had been unable to leave her bed just a few hours earlier, although I had a nasty feeling Simon had jumped into that very bed within minutes of me exiting the house. Keeping my fingers crossed that there was no distant relative of her sexy boss out and about in Chaliki, I joined her on the tiny dancefloor and we leapt about and laughed like we were still on holiday.

The exhaustion, the stress, the alcohol and the dancing meant I slept like a log the next morning, only peeling my eyes open just before lunchtime. Ah, the bliss of not having to work a double shift each day! Scarlett awoke around the same time and it was a simple pleasure to be able to accompany her onto the terrace for a mug of coffee and a proper catch up. She was concerned about Simon, as even though he had been around the previous day, dipping his wick, and being his usual smarmy arsehole self, he was apparently acting all weird with her and she felt that they were on very shaky ground.

Squinting as the glare of the sun offended my eyeballs, I winced as I recalled a few hazy details from the previous evening, such as Lorry declaring his undying love for me during the journey home and my embarrassing response of, 'Don't be so silly, Lovely Lorry...you can't love me because I haven't shaved my bikini line all week and it's *totally* overgrown down there!' Undeterred, he'd taken my hand and firmly held on to it in the back of Alex's car, as he'd driven us up the bumpy road to our house, where Scarlett had then clumsily fell out of the passenger side when we'd jerked to a halt, almost colliding with the bushes as she slipped, while Simon looked on and pissed himself laughing, rather than rushing to her aid, as did Alex.

The look in Lorry's eyes was that of undisguised longing and lust; I knew he was angling for an invitation to stay the night with me. Alex had chipped in though and kindly offered to drop them back off in Town, so I'd bundled Lorry back in the vehicle, kissed him sloppily on the cheek and slurred 'Goodnight, sexy boy', before tottering round to do the same to Alex, much to his surprise and mirth.

'So why did you really send Lorry packing last night then, Jessie?' Scarlett broke into my thoughts, clearly reading my mind, as she examined the graze on her left knee, no doubt wondering how and where she'd acquired her injury.

'I don't know, to be honest, I just don't know. I mean, he's absolutely gorgeous and he's witty and funny...and just a really nice guy through and through...and most women wouldn't be able to resist that impish smile and floppy fringe...but so far I haven't felt that magical spark between us, which is a bloody crying shame, because *he* seems convinced it's there...and I don't want to hurt him or lead him on if ultimately it's going nowhere.'

'Maybe you're reading too much into it, Jess. Maybe you should take that padlock off your knickers and show him a bloody good time and just enjoy it for what it is. Just try and avoid falling for him if at all possible...because - take my word for it - it's really not advisable...and we must remember, after all, that we are only here for the summer and will be returning to the real world when October comes around.'

'Is that your way of telling me you've actually fallen for Simon and his rather fetching selection of cartoon character undies? Daffy Duck being my absolute favourite, naturally. Because you've always seemed a bit blasé about him to me...and then there's been all this flirting with your new boss...and the tonsil tickling with that old Greek guy. I didn't realise you were wading in deep with Simon Le Bon...could this actually be true love again for Scarlett Olivia Askwith?'

'That celebrity name thing has actually started to do Simon's head in! The thing is, Jess, I've been trying so very hard to keep it light and playful and to not take any of it too seriously...but somewhere along the way I seem to have developed all these feelings for him...and you know what Simon's like - educated at the School of Treat Them Mean and Keep Them Keen. He's got me wrapped around his little finger and, the trouble is, he knows it.'

'Some men are just like that though, aren't they? They think if they reveal any feelings whatsoever that it will somehow announce to the whole wide world that they have a slither of vulnerability in there! Has he given you any clues at all? Do you think he might have any similar feelings for you or are you worried it could be a one-way, dead-end street?'

'I just don't know, if I'm honest. He gives nothing away; keeps his cards very close to his chest. Hopefully he's not leading me up the garden path – I'd hate to think he's just in it for the sex. Although the sex is top drawer, it really is...the man is insatiable! Anyway, we still have the rest of the summer ahead of us...plenty of time to get to know each other better...and it could be amazing if he chooses to behave himself! I just hope my feelings *are* reciprocated and I'm not making a complete dick of myself. Anyway, stop changing the subject! What are *you* going to do about Lorry, who is obviously madly in love with you and desperately searching for any sign from you that the feeling is mutual? And - not forgetting that other egg in your basket - when are you likely to see this fast-talking, flaming hot Greek guy again – the one who treated you to the flowers and the good old ego boost?'

Winding two of my curls tightly around the handle of a spoon I'd picked up from the table, I sighed as I thought about the two very different men in my life.

'Lorry – I have absolutely no idea. Nikos – he's back on the island on Monday, and Lukas said he'd heard him instructing Tassos to give me a night off, so he could take me out. Imagine – no morning shifts and a night off as well! A girl could get used to this.'

Sliding the spoon handle out, I watched with satisfaction as the curls firstly uncoiled and then sprang up again. I knew I had quickly changed the subject, but how could I give any answers to Scarlett when I didn't know them myself?

Before long, we were joined by Lauren, who was looking very businesslike in her smart skirt, white blouse and patent shoes, but who was also bearing gifts again in the form of bread and meats from the hotel and we enjoyed a veritable feast of pilfered lunch items sat out in half-sun, half-shade, washed down with tumblers of coca-cola filled with ice cubes and slices of lemons picked from Andreas' trees. Lauren entertained us by regaling tales of bed-hopping and stolen sheets at the hotel, and Scarlett treated us to her best Dot Cotton impression, and I'm sure our squeals of laughter could be heard as far away as the tavernas on Ammos Beach.

Once Lauren had departed and Scarlett had whizzed off on her scooter, to firstly drop off our bag of rubbish at the nearest bin, and then to pick up some shopping (vodka), I took the opportunity to enjoy the peace and solitude. It had been my intention to crack on with the next chapter of a racy novel I'd borrowed, but instead I found myself lazily daydreaming and imagining a long-term future that didn't involve commuting to Manchester every day, but consisted rather of olives, ouzo and all that this idyllic island had to offer.

Chapter 14

Rather than criticising my every move in the restaurant, Tassos entered a new mentalist phase by beginning to sulk like a big, ugly baby and doing his utmost to ignore me throughout my shifts, which often caused difficulties when I needed to ask him something important or a problem arose whilst in service. Lukas thought it was hilarious; he'd never seen his usually vocal employer this timid and quiet, and my cheery work friend took to whistling and singing loudly as he flew around the restaurant pouring out wine, rattling off dishes from the specials board and delivering food to sun-kissed diners. The incessant whistling and tuneless singing drove Tassos absolutely nuts and I loved Lukas even more for it.

When Nikos returned he actually DEMANDED, in English, at the top of his voice that Tassos reward me with a well-deserved night off, and also stipulated that this must be a weekly event to allow him to show me some beautiful, unspoiled parts of the island. Unsurprisingly, my arch nemesis wasn't particularly happy about it but, not wanting to lock horns with his old friend, he eventually, reluctantly, agreed that yes, I should take Mondays off, as it was generally the quietest night in the restaurant and around the resort, and I practically punched the air and shouted 'In your face!' as he said the words out loud.

Nikos was just as handsome as I remembered and, like the time I overdosed on caffeine by consuming several litres of Pepsi and a family size bar of seriously dark chocolate, I had serious palpitations when I saw him again and wondered why on earth someone like *him* could be interested in someone like *me*. But he apparently was, and he was sexy to the core, and I imagined he would be a real goer in the bedroom department – not that I was intending to find out for real of course - so although I pretended to hesitate before agreeing to a date with him, of course my final answer was yes, and a week later I found myself being chauffeured up into the mountains, keeping my fingers crossed that he wasn't a demented serial killer with a shovel and a length of rope in the car boot, to visit an expensive restaurant with panoramic views that apparently knocked spots off all the other eating establishments down in the resorts.

The food was indeed delicious; my meal consisted of the most perfectly cooked medium-rare steak with a portion of melt in the mouth, lemon roasted potatoes and a tomato flower garnish that simply looked too damn good to eat, while Nikos tucked into pork chops the size of dinner plates. The red wine was dark but fruity (a bit like Nikos himself) and slipped down far too easily; I only saw him drink a tiny measure which clearly meant that I'd knocked back most of the bottle – that might have explained why I was mentally undressing him and wondering if his deep colour covered all of his body, or if he would have a t-shirt tan and a white bum to match - while he was telling me all about his thriving business; he apparently owned TWO boats – so he wasn't short of a bob or two as they say – which offered day excursions departing from both Corfu and Loulouthia throughout the summer seasons. He explained that he was finding it difficult splitting his time between the two islands as his home was on Loulouthia but business on Corfu was much more lucrative; however, if he was to find a special lady on Loulouthia, he might be persuaded to step back a little more from the business...

As far as his personal life was concerned, he informed me that he had been married young, but that marriage had ended many years earlier.

'I was a very bad boy Jessica,' he confided, lowering his voice and moving forward to stroke my face and twist one of my curls around his little finger, yanking on it slightly and making me go weak at the knees at the same time. Yes. God. I could imagine him being a bad boy and surprisingly it didn't put me off him one iota. Bad boys knew a lot of stuff, or so I've been told...and I had a feeling he could teach this old dog some new tricks. Hubba hubba.

'I had too many ladies, too much sex.'

Christ, I was going to be vaulting over the table and jumping his bones at this rate.

'And my wife, she told me she despised me for being unfaithful to her, but I do not blame her – I could not justify my actions. When her mother became ill she moved over to Athens to take care of her, and she did not return. We divorced some years later and I am told she is married again now, to someone who works in computer programming. I wish her well, but I think her life will be much duller now, without me in it...devoid of excitement, not so thrilling...no adventures on boats...and wherever she lives now, she could never find a more beautiful home than on this island.'

I bobbed my head up and down, like a nodding dog, whilst slicing off a portion of the honeyed sponge in front of me. It really was amazing – I'd let Nikos choose the desserts and, it had to be said, he had exquisite taste.

'But I can assure you that I am a changed man, Jessica. I am forty-seven now and a one-woman man, which means that I choose carefully. My greatest thrill these days is pleasuring the lady in my life, in fact taking her to new heights of pleasure...and loving her in ways she has never known before. Tell me Jessica, do you like to give or receive pleasure?'

Jesus wept, I nearly choked on my mouthful of cake.

'Both, Nikos,' I coughed and squeaked. 'I think you should always treat someone the way you would like to be treated yourself.' Taking the coward's way out, I'd tried to gloss over the question, pretending not to notice the sexual undertone; the conversation seemed to be heating up rapidly and was in danger of getting out of hand.

I think he was merely toying with me though, as he smiled, raised his glass and said, 'A fine wine for a fine woman. Jessica. I am so very happy that we have met and I look forward to getting to know you.'

Once the food was devoured and the wine bottle was empty, Nikos insisted on paying the (presumably) enormous bill, we slipped back into his silver soft-top Mercedes (couldn't wait to tell Scarlett about *that*) and made our way back down the mountain – slowly and carefully, as the road was rough in parts and there were a few precarious turns which took my breath away, even in my slightly sozzled state. Turning right, rather than left, when we reached the main road at the bottom, I glanced at Nikos in surprise – *this* wasn't the way to Chaliki; I hoped and prayed that he really *didn't* have that deluxe serial killer kit hidden in his boot.

He laughed when he saw the apprehension on my face and said, 'Do not worry, Jessica, I will take you home soon. We are not far from *my* home and so we will call there first, and then you will know where I am to be found, should you ever need me. I would not be so presumptuous as to think that you might stay with me tonight; that should only be when you feel you are ready, Jessica – you must decide when the time is right for you.'

To be fair, it wouldn't have taken a lot of persuasion and coercion in my current state, but I appreciated his thoughtfulness. However, *I* was nearly begging *him* when I caught sight of his house, which was behind closed gates and was practically a mansion, all majestic and massive, with stone pillars at the end of the long, sweeping driveway and a sprinkler system ensuring the mass of flower beds and plants were kept suitably lubricated.

I must remind myself to stop thinking of words like 'lubricated' when in the company of a Greek god with a line for everything and a body just crying out to be worshipped.

Gasping audibly at the sheer size of the place first of all, I then wondered if it actually *was* his house and he wasn't perhaps just the caretaker or gardener and he'd been bullshitting me all along – although that wouldn't explain away his ability to pay for five star meals at the most expensive eatery on the island. I swear to god, my thoughts must have been plastered all over my stupid, transparent face because he responded by throwing his head back and laughing, before telling me, 'This wonderful house belonged to my parents before they passed away, and now it belongs to me...and also my brother Apostolis (presumably not Apostolis from Sunrise or else he wouldn't be waiting tables for a living). He lives in one half of the house and I live in the other; we share the entrance hallway, the grounds and the swimming pool.' *Swimming pool*. How the other half live.

'I will open the gates now and introduce you to Apostolis and his wife, who I see are relaxing on the verandah...and then you will know for sure that I am telling the truth. No, no...I can quite understand why you would think I am just pretending to own this house! It is a truly magnificent building and I am aware that I am very fortunate to live here.'

Right then. That was me told.

Blasting down the driveway, having opened the electronic gates with a fob on his Mercedes keyring (how did such modern luxury make its way over to Loulouthia, which on the whole could only be described as basic and understated?), we stopped briefly to speak to his brother and wife, who were polite but spoke very little English, and whilst my Greek was coming on a bundle, and I had advanced from Holiday Greek to Supermarket Greek, it would be a bloody long time before it could ever be described as fluent.

After our fleeting visit to his house, and once I'd scooped my jaw up off the floor, he did indeed take me home as promised, and I almost wanted to royally wave like the queen to our spectators as we passed through Chaliki, with the roof down and the welcome evening breeze rushing through my hair.

I wasn't sure, but I thought I'd seen Lorry casually leaning on the wall outside of Sunrise, with Simon and a bunch of over-excited, young tourists – it still seemed strange that I spoke of other people as tourists but no longer considered myself to be one. Briefly closing my eyes, I swallowed the lump of guilt that threatened to rise to the surface and choke me; Lorry was aware that I hadn't promised him anything; I wasn't his girlfriend – and anyway, it was only one date, and it was all above board. It wasn't like I'd been getting down and dirty with Nikos behind his back...although there had been times when I'd come scarily close.

One date. But with a man scoring ten out of ten on the scale of handsomeness, one being Mr Toothy and ten being Jamie Dornan; a man who had a filthy look in his eye that seemingly drove me wild and made me forget myself.

Not wishing to remain in the car and possibly read the situation all wrong, but feeling no inclination to leave and put an end to this memorable evening, I very slowly removed my seatbelt and took an age smoothing down my skirt and scooping up my handbag out of the footwell. Nikos, the professional mind reader, simply reached over and pulled me towards him, brushing my curls away from eyes whilst looking deep into my soul, before he bore his lips down on mine and I eagerly responded.

Good god, if his sexual prowess was anything like his first kiss then the future was looking promising. His lips were soft and smelled faintly of the red wine we had shared, and his tongue was firm as it probed ever further into my mouth and made me gasp for breath. If he hadn't pulled back first then it's unlikely I would have done; I was mesmerized and it wasn't just the taste of the alcohol that was intoxicating.

'I think you had better go inside now, Jess, before we do something that you may regret in the morning.' Nikos smiled as he leant over to open the passenger door for me, allowing one hand to linger on my knee; the heat from his touch penetrating through the soft fabric of my skirt. Shakily, I exited the Mercedes and closed the door, somehow finding the words to tell Nikos to drive safely, and to bid him goodnight.

'*Kalinichta*,' he replied in his deep, sensual voice, as he manoeuvred the Mercedes to begin his descent down the track. 'Please, ring me soon, and we will share another wonderful evening. Sleep well, my beautiful Jess. Goodnight.'

I watched until the car was completely out of sight and then lightly held my fingers to my lips; I could still feel his kiss on them. Sleep well! I thought it rather unlikely in view of the fact that my heart was racing and my body temperature was through the roof, and I couldn't just blame it on the fact that I was resident in Greece during the hottest of summer seasons.

Finding a potential love interest had been surprisingly low on my To Do list when I'd first arrived on Loulouthia...and I still wasn't sure whether I wanted to be someone's steady girlfriend or throw myself into anything more serious than mild flirtation. In my experience, relationships were draining and time-consuming; I was far more interested in forming lasting friendships and exploring every nook and cranny of this picture-perfect island, rather than constantly having to take someone else's feelings into account or being distracted by the messy business of sex, however pleasurable it may turn out to be.

Although my head needed to have strong words with my heart and my body, to beat my womanly needs into submission, or else I was going to end up hurting someone unnecessarily or, as was usually the case, risk being irreversibly damaged myself.

Chapter 15

Despite strenuously reiterating to both Lorry and Nikos that I couldn't promise anything more than friendship, I found myself dividing the majority of my free time between the two of them.

Every Monday evening Nikos would drive me to another superb location that wasn't necessarily on the tourist trail – a restaurant in the middle of nowhere that I hadn't dined in before, or a rooftop bar down a tiny alleyway at the far end of Skafos that apparently served the best cocktails on the island (not true – Alex's cocktails, whilst lethal, were far superior and I was becoming ever so slightly addicted to his Sex on the Beach) and we'd also taken to meeting up for the occasional day excursion too.. He couldn't believe I hadn't yet visited the small neighbouring resort of Kochyli, just a mile and a half up the coast, and so he packed us a picnic (which looked suspiciously shop bought, but probably from the most expensive deli in all of Greece) and we drove there in style in his open-top Mercedes, and it was just a perfect, perfect time.

The beach there consisted of considerably more pebbles than grains of sand, but when we strolled to the end of the jetty which protruded out into the sea, there was an uninterrupted view of Chaliki and the harbour beyond, and the sheer magnificence of it all snatched my breath away, and I took endless pictures on my phone. There were only a couple of bars and old-fashioned family-run tavernas in Kochyli which meant fewer holidaymakers and barely anyone on the section of beach where we had opted to spread out our picnic blanket, to sample some of the lavish spread he had brought with him, washed down with more fine wine - this time a crisp, dry white, kept as cool as possible in a silver ice bucket, although the ice had melted long before we arrived at our destination.

The selection of nibbles was, of course, in true Nikos style, vast, and had no doubt cost the earth and then some. Amongst the bottle-green, parcelled-up stuffed vine leaves and the heap of crispy *spanakopita* (spinach pies to you and me), there were thick slices of feta cheese, stacks of tomato bruschetta and a variety of exotic dips, which were accompanied by a selection of marinated olives of varying size and colour, which appeared to be his pride and joy, as they had originated from the sprawling olive grove that formed part of his garden.

I hadn't the heart to tell him that, despite currently living in the land of olives, those pesky little buggers made me retch, so I had to pretend to eat them, whilst every time his back was turned I surreptitiously buried another in the sand and hoped that some rabid dog wouldn't suddenly pop up and start manically digging next to our picnic blanket and expose all of my little secrets.

While massaging my shoulders, his strong hands kneading my flesh and eliciting groans of pure pleasure, he divulged a little more about his businesses and I found myself confiding in him that I'd been practically raised single-handedly by my father after the sudden death of my mum, and how my last relationship had broken down and I'd been living alone ever since. He flattered me by saying he could not comprehend how anyone in their right mind could ever let me go, before buying ice creams from the tiny shack on the beach, slowly, meaningfully licking the drips from the cone as he handed one to me, his eyes explicitly stating what he would prefer to be licking instead, and it was a bloody good job I was already red from the sun because I could feel the blush rising up from my toes to my cheeks.

So far I had resisted his offer to sail around the island on his boat (Shirley Valentine sprung to mind, and I really wasn't sure that I should be Making Fuck with him just yet), but I really didn't know why I was fighting against it. Most women would sell their granny to be cruising round a Greek island with a handsome and charming man who wanted to spoil them rotten and treat their body as a temple; I was beginning to think I seriously had a screw loose in my head – Scarlett had often said that was the case.

It amused me to notice that every time I saw him, his hair had grown a little more and that he was revealing himself to be a natural curly-top like me. There was also the odd glimpse of silver amongst those dark hairs – he was racing towards fifty after all - but it didn't detract from his good looks; if anything it just gave him the air of someone more worldly-wise and experienced. Maybe I would take a trip on that boat after all.

Lorry was very much still on the scene; sometimes we met up for lunch at the beach and he always tried to come down to Chaliki whenever possible, popping along to Sunrise after I'd finished work to throw down a couple of beers, and they were great, good for the soul, catch-ups; he always made me laugh out loud and was as kind and considerate as ever.

One particularly stifling evening, when everyone was doing their utmost to try and keep cool, I found myself paddling in the sea with him while we were still fully dressed; we rolled up our jeans as best we could and laughed until our sides ached, kicking up the water and each soaking the other. He stole a few tender kisses in the endless darkness, as we were splashing around, enjoying the silliness of it all, and forgetting anything and everything else that threatened to dent our happiness; storing up memories for the future.

His kisses were different from those I shared with Nikos; he was ever so gentle and I loved the tiny flicks of his tongue as it darted inside my mouth, his hands cupping my face and his body pressed up against mine.

With Lorry, it was still difficult to imagine a transition from friend to lover; I'd tried to carefully explain this to him but it was tricky to convey without hurting his feelings. I'd never been one to mess people around and I needed him to understand that the situation I found myself in really was virgin territory for me. However I tried to dress it up, the bottom line was that I'd forged friendships with two wonderful men, who both wanted to move the relationship on, each undeterred by the presence of the other. What I didn't want was for it to become competitive - to be comparing one against the other when they were both so fabulous in their own unique way. But, as I stressed to Lorry, rather than hurt either one of them, and lose their friendship, I would rather keep the relationships purely platonic.

Besides, I still wasn't sure if I even *wanted* to be involved in any relationship at all...and I hadn't slept with either of them, yet, or even done anything more than kissed and, for that, I think I deserved a medal!

Scarlett had lost her job. After three sick days and one no-show, when she had quite frankly just decided they were working her too darn hard in the oppressive heat, Bay Bar Spiros had let her go. She enjoyed two nights out on the piss and then thankfully managed to pick up a job in Town, allegedly as a waitress, but she seemed to spend more time trapped in the kitchen, washing mountains of dishes, and had consequently been eaten alive by the dreaded mosquitos, who seemed to thrive in the damp, dark conditions in the back corner where the sinks were located. She was NOT happy, and it was only a matter of time before that particular job went tits up as well.

She had also nearly poisoned us both one quiet afternoon when she was actually getting stuck in for a change, making us both a sandwich and a cup of tea. After much deliberation about whether she would add onion to her ham butty or maybe a thin layer of mustard instead, she finally appeared on the balcony with our lunch. We both agreed that the sandwiches were delicious, particularly as the bread was so fresh that it was still warm and we'd also been absolutely starving.

'My, that was good...you can't say I don't make a decent butty, Jess.'

'Oh your sandwiches are great; it's the rest of your cooking that's the problem. Eugh! This tea has a funny taste though...try yours...honest to god, that doesn't taste right.'

'Bleugh! You're right!' Scarlett agreed, spitting tea out all over the table and watching it drip down on to the tiles. As she raised the cup to her nose to sniff the offending liquid, a section of her hair dipped in to the brew but she didn't seem to notice. 'What bloody milk did you pick up yesterday?'

'The same bloody milk as always!'

'Did you check the date on it? That's rank, that is!'

'Of course I checked the date...but I'm beginning to wonder if the seal wasn't air-tight or something...Christ that's disgusting...let me go look...'

Two minutes later, I emerged from the kitchen having solved the mystery of the minging tea.

'You absolute dickhead!' I told her, hands on hips, shaking my head in disbelief. 'There's nothing wrong with the milk. It's what's gone in the kettle that's the problem.'

'What are you talking about you numpty...I think all this luuuurve and attention is going to your head.'

'Scarlett, I despair of you sometimes. The tea would be fine if it had been made with water. But you...YOU...have only gone and filled the kettle with neat frigging ouzo!'

'Get out of it! I used the stuff in that big glass bottle which is on the worktop...'

'Yes, the big glass bottle that is full of the strongest ouzo known to man, that Alex kindly brought us as a gift after he had been to the warehouse last week...the fucking water bottles are on the floor near the pop!'

Oh. My. God.

The girl really wasn't safe to be let loose on her own. At least we could laugh about it afterwards, and all the customers in Sunrise thought it was side-splittingly hilarious. Definitely one to tell the grandchildren...not that I was ever likely to be a grandmother – or even a mother - but there you go.

And I think it had put me off ouzo for the foreseeable future.

Lauren also regularly dropped in at our house and I thoroughly enjoyed her company; she was rapidly becoming a firm friend who I was able to confide in, and I wondered how I'd ever managed without her. It was a real treat popping by the hotel as well, lazily floating around in the pool and enjoying the other facilities - and it provided me with an opportunity to chat to Lauren and in turn was a welcome interlude in her day. Before we headed into high season, when workers barely had time to breathe let alone socialise, we managed to squeeze in a trip to Lauren's house and met the mysterious Andreas for the first time. Except he wasn't mysterious at all – in fact the exact antithesis of what I'd expected, which was a dark, swarthy outdoorsy type – all muscles and mouth. Instead, and quite unusually for Greeks, his short, tousled hair was fair and his skin was the colour of golden syrup rather than

Mediterranean Mahogany, and he had a gentle, appealing way about him. He was of average height and build but very good-looking, in a boy-next-door way rather than man-about-town. He was clearly oblivious to his looks and charms though and he didn't say much or hang around very long, but I really liked him; he had a calming quality; a way of making you feel comfortable in his presence even when he wasn't speaking. And you could see the depth of feeling between them; the way his hand briefly touched her shoulder as he was passing; the way her eyes shone when he said her name or smiled at her. How lovely.

We managed to avoid the out-laws as well; apparently his mother had gone out to see a friend on the day we visited so I didn't get to hear her tear strips off Andreas' poor father, as Lauren assured me she often did. His wrinkly old dad, dressed in only a white string vest and a pair of dusty, baggy shorts was taking the opportunity to enjoy a snooze in his favourite chair, which meant that the only noise in the vicinity came from the bleating of the goats and the jingling of the sheep bells, and of course the ever present chirping of the cicadas from high up in the olive trees.

I repeatedly begged Lauren to join me at Sunrise, just to share the odd pitcher with me rather than sit around twiddling her thumbs, waiting for Andreas to return from his evening job, but she seemed reluctant to do so. And when I did finally drag her down there, when I happened to have a free Monday because Nikos was over on Corfu, she wasn't the same Lauren I knew and loved – she was the curt, unsmiling girl I'd first met at the hotel, avoiding all eye contact with Alex and making me seriously wonder if something had occurred between the two of them in the past that they'd prefer to forget. Surely not though – with partners like Sofia and Andreas, I couldn't imagine either of them being untrustworthy and unfaithful and going behind the backs of the people they adored the most. But it was all a bit weird.

I was a little concerned about Sofia as well; she had been absent from the bar on three occasions, and when I enquired about her whereabouts, Alex merely informed me she had important appointments over on Corfu but didn't disclose any further information. Hoping they weren't medical appointments and she wasn't seriously ill, suffering from something nasty and incurable, I tried to push my concerns to the back of my mind. I couldn't bear it if anything was to happen to this lovely woman; she was only two years older than me, and so motherly and kind and they didn't come much more glamorous than her.

The only real fly in my ointment though was the job at Mama's and Tassos' unjustifiably appalling treatment of me. Nikos had disclosed that Tassos' mother had been a real old witch who had bullied him terribly and often taken a leather belt to his behind...so perhaps he just hated all women in general as a result – although he was always the jovial host with customers, no matter their sex. Whatever his beef was, it was no excuse for treating me like shit and things had gone rapidly downhill since he'd begrudgingly given me a weekly night off, and the sulking and ignorance had now been replaced by sarcasm and viciousness. Nikos tried to stage an intervention by apparently warning Tassos that he would have HIM to answer to if I came away from the restaurant distressed even one more time – but he never really witnessed Tassos' cruelty, as he treated me normally when Nikos was around, which suggested that he knew *exactly* what he was doing and he just got a kick from behaving like an arse.

It all came to a head at the beginning of July, when it seemed like the heat had seriously been ramped up, and, apart from the true locals, who still dressed as if they were in the depths of mid-winter, if you didn't permanently feel the trickle of sweat down your back all throughout the day, and dream of standing in the rain in your underwear, then there was something seriously wrong with you.

For a Thursday night, it was reasonably quiet at the restaurant, which always put Tassos on edge and meant I was clock-watching and doing my level best to avoid him all evening.

The heat was really getting to me and making me tetchy on that particular night – my tormentor had made me wash down cupboards in the boiling hot kitchen early on in my shift, and I'd never really recovered from that. He'd complained about the number of soft drinks I'd helped myself to from the fridge (two), in an attempt to cool down and quench my thirst, and every time I'd paused to have a brief moment in front of the huge fan positioned near the till area, he'd shouted me over to give me a bollocking for some pathetic reason, like overfilling the napkin dispenser or adding too much ice to the drinks.

When he made a spectacularly holy show of me in front of a table of four elderly customers, who were even more embarrassed than I was, I reached the end of my tether. Already seriously pissed off, I'd arrived front of house just in time to hear him inform two old couples that I was a lazy woman, incapable of delivering food to tables until it was merely lukewarm, and who couldn't be trusted to handle any money - and not forgetting that I was constantly breaking his expensive dishes in the kitchen - one cheap, small plate I'd dropped. One.

He'd been unaware that I was in such close proximity; that I was right behind him, just a few feet away. Suppressing the urge to scream and shout, and slap him across the back of his head, I merely said quietly, 'I beg your pardon, Tassos', and as he swung round to face me, I saw for the first time a little fear in his expression. Maybe he was wondering if I was wearing a heavy belt under my baggy t-shirt that I was about to whip off and leather him with, like his mother used to.

But I felt an inner calmness running through me, as I handed him my order pad and pen and leant over to speak to the customers, to put them soundly in the picture.

'Please accept my apologies but this man is a compulsive liar and also quite, quite mad. The food is delicious though so do enjoy, and if you feel inclined to leave a tip afterwards, make sure you tell HIM it's for Lukas and Chef, who actually do all the hard work around this godforsaken place.'

Pushing right past him, I stalked back into the kitchen to say goodbye to my friends, grabbed my belongings, and then walked out through the restaurant with my head held high, my trusty, canvas bag over my shoulder and my dignity almost intact, finally descending the stairs to the worst place I had ever had the misfortune to work, for the very last time.

Alex and Sofia were surprised to see me appear so early on in the evening, but when I calmly told them just what had taken place, there was an initial silence and then they both roared with laughter, Alex repeatedly banging the palm of his hand on the bar top, as the assortment of customers drinking in his establishment joined in and the whole place erupted and cheered and toasted the fact that I'd finally had the nuts to stick it to Tassos and his ballache of a job.

'Oh poor Just Jess,' Sofia cried, wiping tears of laughter from her eyes. That stupid man has put you through hell but now you have the ultimate revenge – his very best member of staff gone, and just when the season is about to go crazy – he won't know what's hit him! I do wish I could have been there to witness you walking out on him like that - it's hilarious!'

Laughing along on the outside, inside I felt terrible, and not just because I'd left my friend Lukas in the lurch, with no option but to cover every single table in the place until Tassos managed to take on some other poor unsuspecting soul, desperate for a job. I was now seriously unemployed, and all the other jobs in Chaliki were taken. Crappity crap.

'Oh don't, Sofia. Even knowing it was the right thing to do, I still feel like such a failure...to give up and walk out on a job like that...it's honestly just not me! I have never, ever done that before in my life...but I just couldn't hack it anymore; it was horrendous.'

'Oh my darling girl! What are you talking about, Just Jess? You are the longest serving waitress that Tassos has ever employed! The other young girls – they lasted a week, maybe two, and then they all left, and occasionally with the contents of the till. A few only survived one day before telling him, no thank you, this job is NOT for me! He has never managed to keep a female member of staff working for him for so long...Just Jess, you are the champion – you have won first prize! Congratulations!'

The laughs kept coming as Alex continued to top up my vodka and coke and, despite the worry about finding another job, I did feel an incredible sense of relief begin to wash over me. I was free. Free from the hell that was working for that old bully. Free, but skint though. Alex assured me he would call into Mama's before Tassos closed up to collect the wages I was due, but it was hardly enough to keep me in Amstels for the week, let alone pay the bills, so I needed to find something else to bring some money in, and fast.

When the door flew open just after eleven, and Scarlett entered the room like a ferocious tornado, riled up and ready to destroy anything in its wake, I guessed she'd had a bit of a shite night at work as well. She was taken aback to see me already installed at the bar, my glass having been refilled so many times by Alex that I couldn't even begin to tell her how many measures I'd sank. She was even more surprised to hear I'd walked out from Mama's – packing jobs in was usually her forte!

By the time she was tanked up, I'd pretty much drunk myself sober and was quietly chatting to Sofia about what the hell I was going to do to earn money, besides perhaps sell a kidney or another valuable organ.

'Listen to me, Just Jess,' she began. 'I have a proposition for you. It is not ideal but it may help your situation.'

I was all ears, hoping she could wave a magic wand and miraculously pluck the perfect job out of thin air. To be fair, she kind of did.

'Alex and I have been discussing your predicament for a few days now and we have agreed that we *are* able to offer you a few hours here in Sunrise after all. At the moment Yiorgos is occupied, driving on the jeep safaris alongside his uncle, and he does not wish to work much in the bar this summer, if at all. Soula, as much as I love her, is a terrible, terrible waitress. Her heart is just not in it; she wishes to pursue a career in health and nutrition and I found out yesterday that she will be moving to the mainland at the end of summer to complete her studies. In the meantime, she is volunteering at the health centre in Town and will therefore only be working limited hours in the bar and restaurant. So, my darling Jessica, if you would like to work for us, we can offer you four nights every week, here in Sunrise, but on all of the busiest nights I'm afraid – Thursday through to Sunday – and the money is no better than working for Tassos, except you will probably earn the same overall when your tips are added to your wages. We will of course pay you at the end of each shift and we will never try to rob you as he did! So what do you say, Just Jess...do you think you can handle working alongside myself and Alexandros night after night?' '

Resisting the urge to dive over the bar to smother her in kisses to express my gratitude, I leant in to hug her instead and said, 'That would be wonderful Sofia...if you're absolutely sure. You have my word that I will never, ever, let you down.'

'I know that, and Alex knows that – otherwise we wouldn't have offered you the job. You might hate us once you have worked with us though...and it *is* only four nights a week rather than fulltime...but we may need you to do extra hours from time to time. We would love to have you join our little team Jessica...and actually you would be doing us a small favour because I do sometimes have to travel over to Corfu and I can't always rely on Soula to step in and fill the gap.'

'Sofia, you are amazing! Don't worry about the hours...I'm sure I'll be able to manage once I have tips as well, and if I fall short then I do have a little money put aside to tide me over. Whether I am working with both of you, or just Alex, I just know I will love this job...let's face it, I spend more time here than anywhere else so I'm practically one of the staff already! And I love Apostolis to bits, and all the other restaurant staff...god, I can't believe I've been so lucky, not only walking straight into another job, but to also be working somewhere so great. Thank you, both of you, from the bottom of my heart - for being so kind and handing me this opportunity...wait till I tell Lorry and Nikos – let me text them now and give them the good news!'

'Yes...of course...your two handsome men. I think they will be drinking in here more often when you are working behind the bar - along with all of your other admirers - so I am sure we will see a big rise in our profits!'

Blushing like a silly schoolgirl, I said, 'Don't be silly, I don't have any other admirers. And Lorry and Nikos...well, they are just friends...good friends who I enjoy spending time with.'

'Friends? Mmmm. Soon you will need to make a decision, I think. Follow your heart, Just Jess. Don't break anyone else's heart, but also take care of your own. I know you think you are invincible and more than happy being Beyonce's 'Single Lady', but, trust me, you too will fall in love and wish to give your everything to that one special person, because you will know, for sure, that he is the one. Just make the right choice...and if you have any doubts at all, then he is not the man for you.'

Sofia meant well but it was easy for *her* to say – she *had* found her 'one' – she'd met Alex when she was relatively young and fallen in love and her life was mapped out for her. Me? I hadn't a bloody clue. In my late thirties, husbandless, childless and clueless, I seemed to have achieved precisely nothing in my life.

And, whilst I had returned to the island of my dreams, I seemed no nearer to settling down – here on Loulouthia, in England, or anywhere else for that matter.

Chapter 16

From then on, my work life was completely transformed – I went from slogging my guts out every night at a job I despised, to becoming *that* person who couldn't wait to go to work, even on the busier nights when a fine pair of rollerskates wouldn't have gone amiss for zooming up and down behind that bar. With the exception of the night when I'd popped a few bottle-tops off for Alex and Sofia as a small favour during my holiday, I had no experience of bar work whatsoever. But I didn't let that hold me back, even promising to work for nothing on my first night, when I was learning the ropes.

Not only would Alex not hear a word of it (Sofia was away on Corfu at the time), he also dissolved into laughter when I dropped three glasses at the same time, took the mick out of me when I mixed up simple orders that even a chimp could have managed, and made sure he informed everyone who would listen that I had been completely blameless in the whole walking-out-of-Mama's incident – assuring everyone that I'd been an outstanding waitress and that Tassos' loss was their gain. He also retrieved my wages from the man himself, who unbelievably asked why I had left, and wondered if and when I would be coming back! Dear god!

Despite my appalling treatment at the hands of the sadistic little weasel, I was relieved when Alex repeated the conversation, ridiculous as it was, because it meant his behaviour had been nothing personal against me, and despite everything he'd put me through in the short time I'd worked for him, I didn't want to feel a sense of acute awkwardness every time I bumped into him or had to pass by his restaurant. It was a small island and an even smaller resort and I couldn't afford to be at loggerheads with anyone because, at the end of the day, I was the outsider; *I* knew I belonged here – I just had to prove it to everyone else.

And besides, the chef in Mama's made the best pizzas for miles around.

Following my hasty departure, I'd texted Nikos to inform him of my resignation and he'd replied that he too was surprised I'd lasted that long; Tassos was his friend and he'd known him for many years, but there was no way *he* would have worked for him! Whilst wondering why the hell he hadn't said that earlier, I was also kind of glad that it hadn't caused a rift between the two of them – friends were a bit short on the ground for the cantankerous old bugger (I still couldn't believe they were the same age!) and to know and be associated with someone like Nikos, with all his charm and obvious success, could only be good for him.

After very little persuasion, I returned to Nikos' villa with him after one of our dates, although I didn't stay over. The house was as beautiful inside as it was out and I was bowled over by the kitchen especially, which resembled something out of an interior design magazine. Fighting the urge to christen those immaculate kitchen surfaces, one way or another, I kept thinking of my old dad and how chuffed he'd been with his new marble worktops when he'd finally had the old formica ones ripped out; there was enough marble in Nikos' house to fit out fifty kitchens, and don't get me started on the banisters and the light fittings and the collectable pieces of artwork.

He'd invited me back for drinks and a tour of his half of the house, and I'd nervously accepted. Sipping champagne from a crystal flute whilst gazing around at the tasteful decor of the lounge and dining room, I recalled the previous blissful day that I'd spent with Scarlett, Lorry and Simon – who, thankfully, had been on his best behaviour – when we'd taken off to Skafos and sampled the delights of the watersports (and that *wasn't* a euphenysm)...when I'd screamed with terror as I was repeatedly dunked under the water after I'd been cajoled into paragliding and swallowed half of the ocean, but minutes later had been howling with laughter on the beach as I'd watched Scarlett suffer the same fate. We'd shared delicious, foil-wrapped gyros and plates of crispy golden fries, played a dubious game of Never Have I Ever, drank pints of draught beer from frozen glasses and returned home sun-scorched and exhausted, but bubbly and content.

This was so much more *adult* though. As I followed Nikos up the grand, sweeping staircase, eyeing up, not for the first time, his perfectly rounded arse, I fully expected the music to 'Dynasty' to start piping out, because I sure as hell felt like I was in an episode of it. Thank the lord I'd worn my sophisticated, full-length, crimson dress, although I felt slightly more elephant than elegant, as a result of packing away the chips, cheese pies and meatballs in Sofia's for the past fortnight.

When he showed me into his room (four poster bed – of course), and kissed me firmly on the lips, while gliding his hands down over my backside (not so rounded, even though I was furiously clenching my cheeks), I was thankful for the air conditioning in the room as I was heating up rapidly. It was clear that he was hoping there would finally be a little bedroom action and my willingness to follow him there had only pointed towards one inevitable outcome.

I won't lie, I let him advance to first base – I did want it, and it was bloody wonderful. He was passionate and clearly an expert on how to undress and caress but, as I felt him pulsating against me and anticipated exactly where his hands were en route to next, I started to feel panicky and pressurised and knew I had to intervene. Taking a deep breath, I held up my hands in protest and asked him if we could please stop there.

'What is the problem, my sweet Jessica? Did I do something wrong?' He looked wounded, frustrated and bewildered – poor man; I had been giving him mixed signals all evening.

'Oh no, no Nikos...you did nothing wrong. In fact you did everything right.'

His response was to sigh, over-dramatically - like a Z-list actor in a naff soap opera - before sinking down onto his sumptuous king-size bed, his strong, solid hands wearily rubbing his eyes, his face a picture of disappointment and confusion.

'It is the Lorry boy, yes? He is the issue here.'

I matched his sigh with a cracker of my own, and slowly moved to sit beside him on the bed, which felt as squidgy and comfortable as it looked, squeezing his firm thigh with my hand in a manner that I hoped said to him 'you're lovely, you are, but I just can't do this' rather than 'I'm raring to go now, do you have any condoms?'

'It's not Lorry, honestly. It's not anyone. Yes, I do love being in Lorry's company and we have so much fun together and I get to pretend I'm twenty-five again. And yes, any fool can see that he has feelings for me, and I do have feelings for him. I'm not sure what those feelings *are* exactly, but I do care about him - an awful lot. But I also love being with *you*, and we have such a wonderful time together and you're so considerate and kind, and you spoil me rotten. And you're both so god damn handsome! I've tried to be completely transparent with you both, to avoid leading anyone on or giving either one of you false hope...but it all makes me feel so icky and uncomfortable, like I'm enjoying the best of both worlds without actually giving anything in return. So I feel permanently *guilty* and completely out of my depth. But I do know one thing - I can't go on like this. For goodness sake I don't want all the locals to think I'm some little tart either, who flits from one man to another!'

'Oh Jessica, of course no one thinks that – you are an extraordinarily special woman with a good, kind heart and everyone who has met you believes this to be the case – even Tassos! You have not yet wanted me to make love to you - although I would very much like to, particularly now, when you are already on my bed and your breasts are still exposed – and I do believe you when you tell me you haven't done anything with this other *boy* – because he is just a boy, and I think you need a real man. Do not worry, I will not pressurise you, but you must make a choice soon Jess. I want you so badly and it has been very difficult for me to sit back and wait for you so long, knowing that there are times when you are sailing into another man's arms. If you do choose me though, I promise that you will have no regrets – and when we finally have the sex, you will wonder why you waited so long...'

Hastily tucking my boobs back into my bra, I whipped the shoestring straps of my dress back on to my shoulders – he was right, it was kind of difficult to show any restraint or even have a serious conversation when your tits were merrily swinging about. My bloody willpower stood me in good stead at that moment in time; I very nearly threw caution to the wind and jumped his bones there and then, what with his dark, brooding eyes and his low, gravelly voice and, not forgetting, his strong, experienced hands and the talk of all the stupendous sex...but I knew in my heart that it would be the wrong thing to do.

Despite my reluctance to sleep with him, I wanted him to know just how special he was to me. Resting my head on his shoulder I said, 'I'm sorry Nikos; I shouldn't be leaving you both in limbo like this. Maybe I'm destined to remain single; perhaps I was never meant to settle down with *anyone*. I'm deliriously happy here on Loulouthia and I've just been concentrating all my energies on building my new life – putting down roots in the very place that meant so much to my family – rather than embarking on any serious relationship. I've often wondered if it's down to my past – losing my mum so young, and my dad determinedly wearing his mourning widower's cardigan long after she'd gone – that it's left me with the need to be by myself; this ability to stand alone and fend for myself when everyone else is so happy to be part of a couple. Then again...maybe one of you *is* destined to be the person I fall in love with – the missing piece of my puzzle. I just wish I didn't like you *both* so much! It sounds pathetic, but I feel so *torn*.'

He swooped in and kissed me again then and all the worry I was harbouring, and all the decisions I knew I would inevitably have to make, were cast aside as he forced his tongue into my mouth and I retaliated by pushing mine into his, feeling a stirring inside me that left me aching for more. Maybe he was just trying to shut me up, but perhaps he was offering me a taste of what was to come, if and when he became my lover. I had no doubt that he would be passionate and fiery in bed, as he was in life, and it would be hard, fast and amazing. But there was more to finding 'the one' than just sex, I had to remind myself. That's if he wasn't just in it for a one night stand - maybe I'd never hear from him again once he'd buttered me up and got his end away. For Christ's sake, my head was in bits!

We eventually left behind the luxury of the master bedroom and returned to the relative safety of the downstairs lounge, where he sat in an old leather armchair and I clambered onto his knee and he entertained me with stories of disastrous sailing trips, and I told him about Christian and what a nice, steady man he was - just not the nice, steady man for me.

When he delivered me back to the house that night, there was an unspoken agreement that I would mull everything over and be in touch again once I had clarity as to just exactly who or what it was I wanted.

I was seriously tempted to toss a bloody coin.

Chapter 17

The next day seven days equated to a particularly bad week for Scarlett.

I'd been drafted in again to cover Soula's shift on the Tuesday, as she'd once more gone AWOL, and I'd been there less than two hours when I turned to find Scarlett stood the other side of the bar with her hands on her hips, and smoke almost billowing out of her ears. She was tomato-like in the face and did NOT look happy, as she slammed her mobile down on to the bar-top and *demanded* a shot of tequila.

You always knew that something had gone drastically wrong when she ordered tequila before midnight.

'Do you know what my no-good, cheeky bastard of a boss did tonight, do you?'

'Well, it's fairly tricky to tell at this stage...but to hazard a guess, I would say he stuck you in the kitchen all night scrubbing pots and pans, with only the mosquitos for company?'

'Oh, *no*. As if having to clean the place, wash all the dishes, tot up the bills, drag people in off the street, and just being treated like a general skivvy isn't bad enough, especially when I'm supposed to be a fucking WAITRESS...not to mention being ordered around and criticised and made to work all the hours god sends. Oh *no*...tonight he excelled himself. Tonight, the fucking TWAT decided he was going to deduct ten Euros from my wages because I'd made so much in tips! So I work my ass off and go the extra mile to deliver outstanding service to all of his customers, to make them want to come back and eat in his poxy restaurant, and persuade them to recommend us to all of their friends...and I get penalised for it! And when I had the audacity to complain, the miserable old BASTARD looked me up and down as if I was a piece of crap, muttered something in Greek under his breath and then turned his back on me! I stood there like a plank and he just IGNORED me!'

Oh dear, NOBODY ignored Scarlett and lived to tell the tale.

'So what did you do, Mrs? You're not going to ask me to help bury a body are you?'

'Ha! I *almost* launched myself at him and battered him to death but then I remembered, my daughter's arriving next week and I don't want to be languishing in a cell when she's here. Besides, prison uniform just wouldn't suit me.'

'No, I thought that. It would clash with your shoes. So go on then, what happened?'

'Yes ladies, I'm all eyes.' Alex had appeared by my side behind the bar, polishing wine glasses with his chequered tea towel; hoping to catch up on all of the gossip, seemingly oblivious as to his malapropism.

'Well I went and collected my bag and my tips and got the hell out of there...and on the way past that KNOBHEAD, I told him he could stick his crappy little job up his mean, hairy arse!'

Squeezing my eyes shut, I groaned out loud. That's one restaurant we wouldn't be eating in then. Please don't let him be related to the only doctor/dentist/mobile phone repair guy on the island.

I didn't blame her though – the sly old trick with the money would have sent anyone over the edge. Yet again, I counted myself lucky that I was working at Sunrise, and had been paid fairly and squarely for every single hour of every single shift, and my tips were all mine. In fact I'd been paid extra each Saturday night when the bar was absolutely packed out and business had been brisk, but it was a two way street – my official finishing time was supposed to be around one in the morning but I always stayed as long as they needed me, even if it meant rolling home at dawn. And after I finished each shift, I still hopped on a bar stool and joined in with all of the fun anyway; I'd be missing out on a bucketful of laughs if I ever considered leaving on time.

'I'm so sorry Jessie...that's my second job gone down the pan. You have my word though that I will be out and about looking for alternative employment tomorrow so, don't you worry your pretty little head; I'll find something to ensure sure I can hand over my share of the rent on time.'

Perhaps not tomorrow, I thought, as Alex removed the empty shot glass and began to concoct her favourite 'Espresso Martini' cocktail. Best give her a day off to recover from her stinking hangover.

She was (almost) true to her word though, as she did go job-hunting two days later and almost immediately found another position.

She caught up with me passing the time of day with Lauren at the Diana pool bar when she staggered in, all hot and sweaty and gasping for a drink. As the barman poured her a large glass of rosé, she filled us in on her trip to Town, where she'd had no luck, but been pointed in the direction of a hotel in Skafos that was looking to hire another cleaner. It wasn't ideal, but they'd taken her on without asking any pertinent questions and didn't seem to be too interested in knowing what she'd done before or whether she was likely to be an honest and trustworthy candidate – 'Honest to god Jess, I could have been a real crank and they wouldn't have given a shit.'

I worried about her nails – she'd screamed blue murder when she'd broken two of the pointy little buggers while pot-washing – but thought it was handy she'd found a job which involved working only day shifts, leaving her free to spend time with her daughter, Adele, when she arrived on the island. The two exceedingly early starts each week would be a bit iffy, particularly if she'd been out on the lash the previous evening, but hopefully things would work out.

'I'm just going to have to sweat out my beer while I'm cleaning,' she told us. 'I mean, how hard can it be?'

Lauren and I exchanged sceptical looks, each of us thinking, actually it's likely to be *really* hard. Lauren had previously done a month cleaning rooms when she'd first returned to the island and it was NOT a walk in the park – the state some dirty scrubbers left their beds and bathrooms in and the *stuff* she'd had to clean off walls...and she'd had to bottom about twenty rooms in two hours at a rate of knots, all the while thinking she was about to collapse and die from the oven-like temperatures.

Best not mention it to Scarlett.

Making a wise decision to change the subject, Lauren soon had us howling with laughter, relaying tales of spats she'd had with Andreas' mother when she was new to the island, including one particularly cringeworthy incident when she had decided to generously cook a meal for the old woman and her husband.

'So, I spent *hours* preparing and cooking these beautiful, big stuffed peppers and, I'm not kidding, they looked the business and tasted *amazing*...and you know what the awkward old biddy did? She refused to eat any of it because the peppers weren't IN SEASON! I mean, for feck's sake, wouldn't you have just kept your mouth shut, ate the god damn peppers, said they were wonderful and then had a quiet word with your son later – so he could explain that they honestly weren't trying to be offensive, but the 'in season' thing really matters to them. The least they could have done was thank me for going to all of that trouble.'

'Aw god, so what did you say to her then?' I know I probably would have just zipped my mouth shut to keep the peace but Scarlett would have absolutely blown her top.

'I said she was rude and ungrateful and that would be the last time I went to all that effort again! And I was determined to give her the cold shoulder from then on, but it's kind of difficult to ignore someone when you live in their house and eat most of your meals with them...so in the end I simmered down and just accepted that's the way it is here. You find that – you have to choose your battles. You don't always understand their way of thinking - and I often want to shout and scream at them and tell them that something's ridiculous - but in the end it's their island and who am I to come here and start preaching to them that their way of life is wrong? You really don't mess with the mother-in-law – she rules the roost, and with an iron rod. And the likes of Andreas, well they have so much respect for their elders, particularly their parents - they just don't argue with them about *anything*.'

'It's strange that you refer to her as your mother-in-law, because you're not actually married are you? Sorry – I know I'm being nosy – but have you and Andreas ever thought about tying the knot and having children and all that malarkey?' They seemed so well-suited and in tune with one another, and I knew most men of Andreas' age on the island were already married with 2.4 kids, a moustache and a chainsaw, and I wondered why they hadn't yet took the plunge.

'No, it's okay – it's what everyone expects of us...and I want kids Jess, I really do. But Andreas and I just aren't in that place yet. You see, when you're Greek, you can't just elope or else you will cause a major scandal and offend about five hundred people...and you also can't have a quiet, relaxed wedding over here either – they go all out and it costs a small fortune and it's a HUGE event. So consequently, it's advisable to know exactly how you want everything to pan out before you find it all running away with you, and you're no longer able to have a say in anything. And our situation is a little bit more complicated...'

'Lauren! You're needed at reception – the occupant of room 11 has lost her key *again*.' The barman interrupted our conversation before I could delve any further – I could understand her hesitation if her in-laws were likely to take over everything...but I loved a good wedding so I would have to get on her case!

After she'd wandered off to sort out the key issue, Scarlett and I enjoyed a leisurely swim in the pool before heading back to the house to grab a quick siesta prior to Scarlett's date in Skafos with Simon and my shift at Sunrise. Lorry was due in later and I was looking forward to seeing him as he'd been busy the last couple of nights, covering shifts for his fellow worker and even escorting a relative of his boss over to Corfu Town.

When I wasn't with him, I missed his smile and his teasing and his easy way of looking at life. Not to mention his handsome face and supple, tanned body. I was still no nearer to knowing if either Lorry or Nikos could be the one for me; still not sure that I actually *wanted* a man in my life, fullstop, when all I'd desired when I'd travelled to Loulouthia was to revisit the loveliest place on earth and connect with my past...and later, to live full-time on this island that I'd fallen head over heels in love with.

Work was pretty quiet early on, with just a few stragglers left from late afternoon, and the other potential customers still tucking into their evening meals in Sofia's or elsewhere in the resort. I was just re-stocking the fridges when there was a commotion near the door and I looked round to see Scarlett, tears pouring down her cheeks, panda eyes and make-up smudged all over her face, closely followed by Lorry, who was as white as a sheet (well, as white as you can look when you have a serious tan that you've built up over three months).

'HE'S FUCKING GONE!' she screamed as she stormed through the bar area, almost knocking Bryan Adams' (not his real name) pint clean off the table.

For one awful moment I seriously thought she meant there'd been a death in the village when she said 'gone', and I realised I hadn't seen Mr Toothy for a couple of days. Surely not though – as sweet as he was, I couldn't see Scarlett becoming hysterical about an old man she barely knew.

Alex swooped in and took the bottles from my hands as I ran around the other side of the bar and quickly scooped Scarlett into my arms, attempting to comfort her as I asked 'Who? Who's gone, Scarlett?'

She looked at me incredulously as she screeched, 'SIMON! Simon, of course! That's who's fucking gone!'

'What? Oh my god, what the hell's happened?' Simon was never my favourite person, but we'd had some laughs all together as a group and I genuinely hoped he was okay.

'Oh Jessie, I can't believe it,' she sobbed, clinging on to my sparkly top, which was shedding silver sequins everywhere, and it was to be hoped there wasn't a noticeable bald patch when she finally released her grip.

'I was supposed to be meeting him in Skafos at seven-thirty and he never showed! I waited and waited and kept trying to ring him but every time it went straight to voicemail and although I left a ton of messages, he never returned my calls. Everyone was looking at me, stood there on the corner outside of the bar like some bloody prostitute, and I started getting scared that he'd had an accident or that there was something seriously wrong. So I rang Lorry, who picked up straight away, but he didn't know where he was, and he messaged and rang Simon but couldn't get in touch with him either. So Lorry came straight over to Skafos and we searched everywhere for Simon but it was like he had just vanished into thin air.'

'Oh Scarlett...what on earth's happened to him then? Surely there must be a reasonable explanation for his disappearance?'

She started to cry again and her voice went up several decibels as she continued.

'Reasonable explanation? Pah! If only. Lorry and I were just thinking about involving the police when we both finally got a message through from Simon.'

'Oh, so he was alive and well then, thank god.'

'I fucking wish he'd been dead, the bastard. Because all that my message said was that he was sorry he was standing me up, but he was on his way home to England because he was getting back together with his wife! No '*Sorry for using you, Scarlett*'! No '*Sorry for treating you like shit, Scarlett*'! No frigging '*Sorry for breaking your heart Scarlett*'! Nothing more! And when I messaged him back, he didn't reply, and now I think he's actually gone and blocked me!'

'No! What did his message to YOU say then?' I turned to ask Lorry, who so far had remained silent but his grim face said it all.

'Just that he'd had a great time on Loulouthia but Kerry wanted to try again and he'd be stupid to miss this opportunity to get his feet back under the table. And that he would transfer some money into my account to cover his half of the rent for this month...and to enjoy the rest of my summer. And he just added a 'Sorry, mate', on the end. That was it.'

'And he's definitely gone, has he? He's definitely left the island and is making his way back to the UK?'

'Yes, definitely. When we raced back to check the room, on the surface it looked the same, but when we opened the wardrobe, all his clothes and shoes had disappeared, and he'd emptied the drawers of all his socks and boxers, and taken his bit of cash and jewellery from the safe.' He shook his tousled blond hair, clearly in disbelief that his so-called friend could have done the dirty on him too and left without even so much as a goodbye.

'I think he must have planned it,' he whispered. 'He obviously took all his stuff while I was out at work and then arranged for Scarlett to be out of the way when he would be boarding the evening ferry, so there was no chance of her catching sight of him on his way to the port, with his massive rucksack and all his belongings.'

'How could he have been so cruel, Jess?' Scarlett looked at me pleadingly, as if I would have all the answers. 'How can one human being do that to another? And for it all to be pre-meditated...I just can't get my head around it...'

Me neither. I definitely didn't want him to be 'okay' now. To leave my lovely friend in this hellish state out of pure selfishness and through lack of any conscience or morals...I wanted him to fall off the fucking ferry and swim with the fishes under the Ionian Sea...the dirty, little shit.

Sofia came to my rescue, steering Scarlett to a corner table out of the way, where she sat her down to talk to her softly and soothingly whilst she stroked her hair, directing me to pour my friend a very large brandy and ordering Alex to hold the fort. As I was filling the huge brandy glass with Five Star Metaxa, I spoke in angry whispers to Lorry, who also looked in need of a stiff drink.

'How could he do this to Scarlett? If I ever catch up with the fucking scumbag I'll nail him to a bastard door!' I warned him, through gritted teeth.

'I feel so guilty Jess...I should have known something was up. He said his ex had been messaging him and that she'd split up with her latest fella; he kept claiming she still had the hots for him but I thought he was just rattling off his usual bullshit – you know what Simon's like. He did seem really chuffed that Kerry was in touch again and I suppose he didn't really talk about Scarlett that much anymore, apart from saying when they were arranging to meet up and stuff. Honestly, I had no idea, but I feel so bad that I didn't realise what was going on...'

'Yes, you bloody idiot, how could you not have known? You *lived* with him for Christ's sake, and he was your mate from England – it's not as if you'd only just recently befriended him! How could you not have seen any of the signs?'

'Jess, he was one of my mates in England but there were about ten of us who knocked about together, and he was probably the one I knew the least. When I said I wanted to travel, he was just the one who piped up and said he wanted to come along for the ride...we were never that close back home, to be honest.'

'Fabulous! So you barely knew him at all and yet you led us to believe that you were best buds with your matching swim shorts and your stupid 'in' jokes. Well, you know what? You want to pick your friends a bit more carefully in future!' Purposely slamming his beer bottle down on the bar counter, so that the alcohol fizzed up and overflowed all over his hand, I turned away before I really let rip and let him have it. I knew I wasn't being fair to him; it was hardly his fault that Simon had behaved like a total twat and Lorry couldn't be held responsible for another grown man's actions...but I felt the need to strike out on Scarlett's behalf.

When I eventually turned around, he was practically down on his bended knees, begging for forgiveness. 'I really am sorry, Jess...please don't be angry with me,' he pleaded with his head cocked to one side and his accompanying spaniel eyes, but I was too furious with Simon to feel any sympathy towards Lorry.

'LISTEN UP, MY FRIENDS...' Alex suddenly shouted across the room. 'We will no longer refer to the love-rat who broke our Scarlett's heart and spirit as the handsome and talented Simon Le Bon! Tonight, we are banning that scambag from our bar FOREVER, and in future, when we speak of him he will only ever be referred to as...Simple Simon!'

There were cheers all round and through her tears, Scarlett attempted a weak smile but I could see her battered and bruised heart just wasn't in it. We soldiered on for another couple of hours; I was still trying to serve customers and keep the bar tidy whilst keeping my eye on Scarlett and popping over from time to offer a shoulder to cry on, all the while giving Lorry the cold shoulder. He eventually left with his puppy dog tail between his legs, feeling sorry for himself, and Sofia grabbed her car keys and told me she was treating me to a half-night off, on full pay, instructing a downhearted Scarlett to jump in the back seat with me, so she could take us home.

'Please, my friend, do not think that all men are like that charmless loser, with his loud mouth and his terrible taste in shirts,' Sofia said, as Scarlett sobbed quietly in the back.

I glanced over to Sofia, my eyes warning her that it was never a good sign when Scarlett was quiet; this must have hit her like a ten ton truck and it would be a struggle to get through to her while she was still feeling so wretched.

'You must rest, darling, and the lovely Jessica will look after you, and when you go to work tomorrow it will help to take your mind off this unfaithful bastard. And soon your daughter will be here and you will begin to recover and find the strength to move on.'

Poor Scarlett was truly devastated; even I hadn't appreciated the depth of her feelings for Simple Simon – in my humble opinion she was worth ten of him and he had always been totally out of her league. He'd apparently recently declared his undying love for her; I kept quiet about the fact that he had rarely shown her any real affection when they were out in public, focusing on mainly getting his end away whenever they were alone. I'd often wondered if he'd been secretly seeing other girls so I wasn't surprised when Scarlett told me she'd previously had her doubts, but whenever she'd broached the subject he'd always denied it and cleverly turned it around to imply she was being paranoid.

Lauren arrived, after I'd texted her for back-up assistance, with armfuls of goodies, including a huge bag of nuts and a bottle of vodka, and we sat for hours on the terrace, discussing what a first-class knob Simon was, and generally slagging off the male species in general, whilst beating ourselves up about how fast and ready we were to fall for their bullshit.

Instead of watching some banal programme on TV (not even an option for us as we didn't actually own a television set), we had to settle for staring at the family of geckos that now treated the exterior walls of our house as their home, flitting about and clinging on for dear life. It was amusing really to recall how those odd-looking creatures had made me jump out of my skin when I'd first arrived; I'd become so accustomed to seeing them everywhere now once the sun went down, that I didn't bat an eyelid even when they were in such close proximity.

No such luck with Scarlett, who said they still gave her the heebie-jeebies, which meant she had an all-screaming, all-dancing dickie fit when a tiny baby one dared to whizz past her dainty little feet and into the living room on this particular, trouble-filled evening, and we spent the best part of an hour chasing it around with a brush, trying to coax it back outside - which at least took Scarlett's mind off her man problems. We retired to her bedroom after the Gordon Gecko Incident, where she promptly fell asleep while we were still in conversation, deafening us with her snores, her mouth gaping wide open. Dropping a gentle goodnight kiss on to Scarlett's forehead, Lauren summoned Andreas by text, to stop by on his way home to collect her, and a short time later she crept out and on to the back of his scooter, blowing me kisses before they disappeared into the night.

To my astonishment, Scarlett made it up and out for work the next morning, Apostolis turning up out of the blue to give her a lift, on Sofia's instructions, as she didn't want to risk the poor, distraught girl flying around the island on a scooter while her mind was clearly elsewhere.

The next few days were a struggle for her but, like a trooper, she kept going; it unnerved me though when she was so quiet – that wasn't the Scarlett I knew and loved - and she stayed in the house for two consecutive nights on her own, hair unwashed, while I was working, rather than joining me down at the bar, or going on the piss round the resort, and *that* I never would have believed possible. Lauren was an absolute godsend and regularly called in to check that Scarlett was okay, whilst Sofia, Alex and even Yiorgos made the journey up the steep incline to our house to keep up the welfare checks.

It was a huge relief when Adele, her effervescent, ever-cheerful daughter, arrived safe and sound on the Thursday afternoon ferry with her boyfriend Lee in tow; they were a massive distraction for Scarlett. She clung, in true limpet fashion, to Adele at the harbour side, and for her part, her daughter seemed over the moon to be reunited with mum again after such a long absence. Lee was a big burly lad, short on words but large on laughs and I could tell Scarlett liked him a lot and approved of her daughter's choice in men which, she said, was a hell of a lot better than her own. Well, I wasn't going to argue with that.

Thankfully, although she was clearly still miserable about being duped and dumped by Simon - having to let go of a relationship that she had truly believed was actually heading somewhere – she slowly emerged out of her shell again when she was around Adele and Lee, and proudly took them to all of our favourite haunts and introduced them to everyone she knew, including Tassos the Twat, who gave them free garlic breads, so he really didn't hold any grudges - unless he'd spat on the bread first of course.

Adele, who was a pretty, slim girl with her mum's poker straight, jet black hair and her dad's cute little dimples, adored Sunrise and its jovial hosts almost as much as we did, and cheekily declared that if she hadn't found Lee then she would definitely have been up for a fling with Yiorgos.

Unfortunately, due to the sheer volume of ouzo she'd knocked back with Adele and Lee one particularly rowdy evening on Ammos Beach, Scarlett missed a whole day of work and was fired, yet again. And I couldn't even bollock her for it as she'd had such a tough time of it lately and I could never begrudge her the precious hours she was spending with her daughter and Lee. Even so, I worried about how she would find another job once they'd departed, especially as we were now in August - peak season - when all the jobs seemed to be spoken for, and soon bars and restaurants would need less staff, not more.

I didn't have to time to ponder for long though, as the arrival of August meant the arrival of the Greeks from the mainland for their annual holidays. The population of the island exploded for two weeks and the heat was relentless and exhausting, as were a few of the customers to be fair, who seemed to think they were entitled to one-to-one service and clearly did not believe in queuing or waiting their turn. For a short time the restaurant and bar kind of blended into one, which meant working in whichever side was busiest, mucking in and running around and barely having the chance to speak to Scarlett, let alone Adele and Lee.

To be honest, I was glad that it gave me the excuse to put some space between myself and the two men in my life. They were equally run ragged anyway; Lorry was also helping out in a bar in Town whenever he wasn't renting out vehicles and Nikos made so many trips around the island and over to Corfu, I didn't think he'd ever find his land legs again.

Besides, there were emerging issues with both of them that had really started to bug me.

Not only had Lorry royally pissed me off in the whole Simon-desertion episode, the company he was keeping of late was starting to grate on my nerves. Prior to holding down two jobs, he'd been knocking about with a couple of Australian lads who, contrary to popular belief, didn't drink very much but I'm sure were smoking a bit of the funny stuff as they seemed to giggle a lot and were great fans of practical jokes, which I was not. Their giggling and sniggering made me want to slap their faces, hard, and when Lorry was with them it seemed to highlight the age difference between us and make me question if we could ever really be more than friends.

There were completely different issues with Nikos that had resulted in Lauren literally peeing herself with laughter when I'd spoken to her about my concerns.

When we met up one night in Horizon, it was a fairly windy evening and the temperature seemed to dip a little. It was still about a trillion degrees and I never strayed far from an air conditioning unit, but Nikos - who always felt the cold, like a true local - was all wrapped up in his best winter gear and was sporting underneath...wait for it...a clingy, black polo neck top.

I hated polo neck tops on men.

To make matters worse, he seemed to have forgotten to pay a visit to the barber and his hair was longer, greyer and curlier...almost in the style of an 80s mullet at the back, with a bit of a bouffant going on at the front. The rather disturbing hairdo, coupled with the vomit-inducing polo neck, meant every time I looked at him I couldn't help but think, 'Tom Jones'.

Even worse - when he attempted to kiss me later that evening, instead of passionately responding to his advances, all I could hear in my head was 'Da, da-da...da, da-da,' and I kept picturing him shimmying around, thrusting his hips to 'It's Not Unusual' and calling me 'Boyo'. It was all a bit Alan Partridge – you know, the bit where he imagines himself dancing along in his leather underpants – but I just couldn't clear this image from my mind and it was seriously doing my head in.

And I could not, repeat NOT, partake in any tonsil tickling with someone who reminded me of Tom Jones, so I'd made excuses that I felt a tad under the weather (I wasn't lying, the whole notion of being touched up by Tom left me on the verge of being violently sick)...and even though the next time I saw him he was wearing a perfectly respectable plain, navy blue t-shirt and stonewashed jeans, I still kept experiencing disturbing flashbacks and, in the circumstances, desperately needed some time apart from him while I recovered from the ordeal.

To make matters worse, Scarlett had let Sofia in on my innermost thoughts, and every time I tried to quietly slope into work and keep my head down, I was greeted with a chorus of 'Da, da-da...da, da-da,' from staff and customers alike, and I'm sure Yiorgos kept popping in and playing 'Sex Bomb' on purpose every evening just to take the piss. I had to concede, it *was* funny, and it cheered everyone up when we were rushed off our feet, although all the thrusting was getting out of hand, particularly when old Mr Toothy started joining in.

Scarlett seemed particularly happy and carefree one evening when she came into the bar; she'd had her locks washed and blown at the hairdressers Sofia recommended, accompanied Adele on a lengthy shopping expedition to Town (Adele presumably in possession of her dad's credit card as Scarlett was now the proud owner of a sexy, turquoise strapless dress that fitted her like a glove)...and my beautiful friend almost seemed like her old self again. I was so pleased to witness the welcome return of her mojo, as she danced around with Adele and teased Alex about the knock he'd received to his head when he'd shot up from behind the bar and Soula had nearly taken his eye out with a litre of gin. As the numbers started to dwindle in the early hours, she raced around with Adele, collecting glasses and wiping down tables before grabbing two bottles of beer and leading me out to the loungers on the beach, where we could wind down and catch up.

These were the best of times - the calm after the storm, peacefully reclining on the beach with a bottle of Amstel's finest, listening to the back and forth of the sea almost lapping at our aching feet, the air still warm with the promise of another belter of a day to come – these were the moments which made me appreciate exactly where I was.

'It's beautiful Scarlett, isn't it? Just look at it...the ripples in the water, the clarity of the sky with the stars looking down on us...unwinding here surrounded by miles of sand rather than overheating in traffic jams and choking on fumes...god we're so lucky to be here, living this life. I love this beach, don't you? I never want to be anywhere else. I can't imagine Adele wanting to leave on Thursday, can you? She'll miss all this when she's back in England and we're...'

'I'm going with her Jess. It's time. I'm ready. Will you come home with us?'

She stopped speaking. She waited. She'd pulled the rug from under me.

I was speechless. I was dumbstruck. THAT I was not expecting.

Finally, I found some words.

'What? Are you kidding me? Scarlett, we live *here*...we have our house and I have this job and I'm sure you'll stumble upon another...'

'And do what exactly? Because the three jobs I've had have been utter shite and the pay is absolute pants...it's barely enough to live on for god's sake. And, let's face it, I'm really not cut out for working in this heat...and I am definitely NOT cut out for cleaning other people's toilets!'

'But...but we love it here...you said yourself, it's amazing. I know the Simon thing has probably taken the gloss off it for you recently but this summer's been fantastic...'

'It has. I've loved it. In some ways it's been like one long holiday and I'll be taking back memories that will last a lifetime...but the holiday's over now for me. The whole Simon crap brought me to my senses really; I know I'm daft as a brush and I'll always be a clubber at heart...but I need to face the fact that I'm no longer a teenager and it's time I sorted myself out. Do you know what I want now? I want to go back to Manchester to build a new life for myself there, somewhere I'm not sweating to death whilst trying to do my job; somewhere

I'm not woken up every morning either by a frigging cockerel or some guy firing his gun up into the air on his balcony; somewhere I can watch all of my favourite television programmes instead of staring at those gross-looking creatures scooting about all over the walls; somewhere I can relax on a big comfortable, squidgy settee and not perch on a PLASTIC FUCKING GARDEN CHAIR in the middle of the bloody living room! And don't get me started with the whole toilet roll in a bin palaver! I miss my home comforts babe...but, more than anything, I miss my kids.'

I couldn't really argue with that; obviously she missed her children, and being reunited with Adele had of course made her realise that she couldn't possibly wave her off from the harbour on Thursday, not knowing when she'd be seeing her again. And her son would be back from his travels soon, and she needed to be close to them both. I got that.

Feeling like I'd had my Loulouthian future blasted apart in one clean shot, I began to cry. 'I thought you were happy here Scarlett; I thought we'd made a life for ourselves here and, job situation aside, we were settled; we were putting down roots.'

She took my hand and squeezed it gently. 'No, you're settled, not me; they're only your roots. This was your dream Jess, not mine. As beautiful as this island is, I would have been just as happy to go to Ibiza, or anywhere else that was hot. For you, this was different...a pilgrimage that had a lot to do with your past and everything to do with your future. You seem to have this deep-seated connection to this place and these people and you were *born* to be here. I see you behind that bar, giggling with Alex and Sofia...and practising your Greek numbers with the old lady in the bakery...and offering the tourists pointers on the best places to eat and visit...and I can't imagine you anywhere else in the world now. I think you will stay for the whole summer and maybe return every summer to work the whole season, again and again...but I really can't do that. I just can't.'

I had a confession to make. Time to lay my own cards on the table.

'Well...I know it sounds a bit silly now...after all that you've just said...but I was actually thinking at the end of the season that we might stay on, Scarlett. It would be hard graft, I know, but there is olive picking work available and there might still be the odd bar job going in Town...'

'What? Are you out of your tiny freaking mind? Bashing bloody branches all day, every day with a big stick...it would kill me off! Lauren said it's back-breaking and even she couldn't hack it. There would be no hope for me! So, how on earth would I be able to pay my half of the rent?'

'We'd get by somehow...and I still have all of my inheritance in the account, so if our cash runs out...'

'NO WAY! I'm not taking your dad's money just because I'm a lazy swine. Yes, I'm your best mate but I would be a bloody liability! And I know I'm crap with money etc, etc, but I'm not a total scrounger and I could never let you continue to bail me out indefinitely – because that's what you've been doing these last few weeks when, let's face it, I've probably earned less than I used to get paid at my Saturday job in the market when I was fourteen!'

'But how on earth can I afford to stay on in our little house by myself?'

'Oh Jess, come on - don't kid yourself! You've been keeping us in that house ever since we moved into it – my scrappy contributions have barely been enough to cover the electricity bill. And for that, I'm really, really sorry, and I promise once I'm back on my feet in Manchester, I will reimburse you as soon as I can...'

'I don't *care* about the money...I can't imagine you leaving here and me not going with you. But, on the other hand, I'm truly not ready to say goodbye to this island just yet...'

'It was only ever supposed to be a temporary arrangement, Jess. At the end of the holiday, we agreed to stay and work the summer, but that was it – we never mentioned any plans to stay here long-term. I'm just heading home a few weeks earlier than planned...but you – you little Greek goddess, you - I knew you wouldn't want to leave when your time was up. Promise me though, you'll come back to Manchester, at the end of the season babe – I've heard the winters here are harsh and I'm worried that once all the businesses in the resorts are closed up and the locals return to their village lives you'll end up isolated and alone up that sodding hill. Give me your word that you'll be on that ferry before the end of October...'

I couldn't. In my heart of hearts I knew I'd do everything within my power to stay on Loulouthia. I was so sad that she was leaving, and I would miss her more than she would ever know, but I wasn't about to start making promises that I couldn't keep.

Shaking her head from side to side, she sighed and said, 'I bloody knew I'd never drag you back to the UK...you're more Greek than most of the locals here now – it's like you're part of the fabric of Loulouthia, and you're woven into it all in a way that I never could be. This amazing island has laid claim to you, and Manchester will always be a shit-show in comparison. I've lost my little Jessie to Greece and all its wondrous charms.'

'Don't,' I sobbed. 'You'll never lose me...but I have to give it a go. If I'm honest, I have to admit I'm a little bit terrified...but if I don't try, I'll never know. *If* I do decide to stay forever, please don't forget to come back and visit me from time to time...I realise there's a vast array of other wonderful places scattered across this world, but promise me you'll return to Loulouthia at some point in the future!'

'Oh, you try and stop me! If you're still here next summer, and I strongly predict that you will be, I'll be back to see you, for sure...and I'll bring proper English sliced bread and copious amounts of crumpets with me, along with my usual wit and good humour!'

We laughed and hugged each other tightly, neither one of us wanting to let go. When we eventually pulled apart and I wiped away the tears from my eyes, I said, 'I'll be lost without you though, Scarlett Olivia Askwith.'

'Well it's just as well you have the level-headed Lauren to look after you then,' she replied. 'I'm going to warn her that she had better take bloody good care of you and find you a decent, stable man to keep you warm throughout the winter! Because I'm not sure either Young Lorry or Old Tom Jones is the right man for the job...'

'Oh god, please stop calling him Tom! And I really don't need the presence of a man in my life, complicating everything and leaving the toilet seat up! But what I do need is to give one of them the big heave-o as all of this really doesn't sit right with me – keeping them both dangling, each hoping for something more.'

'Ooh, it's exciting, isn't it? Like the X-Factor final but with relationships at stake rather than recording contracts! Well, be sure to let me know who you plump for and I'll give you my verdict. And in the meantime, I'm going to arrange a bit of a leaving do for Wednesday night – we'll hold it right here in Sunrise and it will give me the opportunity to say goodbye to everybody whose life I've touched while I've been here!'

Gulping at the prospect of her saying those goodbyes, especially to me, I nodded and pulled her back in for another massive hug, and we stayed glued to each other like that for what seemed like forever – a simple gesture that said we loved each other and that, no matter what distance was between us, we would always remain the very best of friends.

Chapter 18

When it was time for Scarlett to leave, she refused to allow me accompany her to the port to wave her off as she knew I'd be an emotional wreck, and she might be tempted to stay, even though it was obvious her heart belonged back in the UK. At least she was going with Adele and Lee, so I wouldn't be worried about her travelling alone. Knowing Scarlett, if she'd been by herself she would probably have got pissed on the ferry and missed her flight to Manchester, leaving her stranded on Corfu.

Lauren had come down to the house and we'd packed Scarlett and all her bags and her overstuffed suitcase into Yiannis' clapped-out taxi, and I'd sobbed and clung to her before she'd eventually ejected me from the rear of the car and slammed the door shut. Yiannis had shot off down the track with his precious cargo on board, leaving a veritable dust-storm in his wake, and I'd cried in Lauren's arms and then got smashed with her on the terrace, having been treated to a night off by Alex who'd assured me they could manage at the bar for one shift, no matter how busy it was.

Thank god for Lauren. She stayed over so I wouldn't feel so lonely on my first night without Scarlett, and I'm fairly sure she was still a little bit inebriated when she went off to work the next morning, having spent the night listening to me reminiscing about a whole load of stuff me and Scarlett had got up to in the past, and all the new experiences we'd shared on Loulouthia. The steady flow of tears had turned to hoots of laughter as I'd recalled Scarlett returning from the supermarket in Chaliki looking like 'Miss Wet T-Shirt' and discovered she'd been blessed by a member of the local clergy while she was picking up emergency supplies - 'Honestly, Jess, I was just leaning over to grab some beans and next thing I knew I was piss-wet through. I turned round to clobber the bloody joker who'd done it and it turned out it was only the flipping priest!'

It felt strange to be sitting on the terrace alone, sipping my black coffee (Scarlett had of course used the last of the milk up before she'd left), and not listening out for my scatty friend or expecting her to roll home from Simple Simon's at any moment. She had texted me already to confirm she'd arrived home safely, but not before getting smashed on the plane with a nutter called Kirsty from Wigan, who'd apparently left her poor partner in charge of their little girl, because she said she'd had a 'bloody bellyful of her antics' all throughout their holiday. Trust Scarlett to make friends and have an eventful journey home. She said she was now looking forward to a good long sleep, following which she was planning on ordering a Chinese takeaway and then sinking into a long, luxurious bubble bath. My mouth watered at the thought of beef in black bean sauce, and pancakes filled with crispy duck and spring onions...but in the next breath Scarlett was complaining about freezing her bits off in unseasonably cold Manchester, which brought a smile to my face, because I really didn't miss the unpredictable weather, and the lack of a good Chinese takeaway was a small price to pay for an idyllic life on Loulouthia. It really did feel peculiar though to think that she was there, and I was here, yet only twenty four hours previously we were sharing breakfast and hangover cures in this very spot.

Even the fact that the text came from her English mobile rather than her Greek one resulted in the formation of a huge lump in my throat, but she'd uploaded a selection of photographs on to Facebook, some taken on her last night on the island, and they were all hilarious. She'd had a cracking farewell party in Sunrise – with Alex, Sofia and Yiorgos, Lauren and Andreas, Lorry, Rhiannon, Bay Bar Spiros - who clearly bore no grudges and gave Scarlett a full on goodbye snog in front of everyone - and not forgetting Mr Toothy, Young Spiros and Old Spiros, the ladies from the bakery and a whole host of holidaymakers, bar workers and locals we'd become acquainted with.

We'd had to rein it in a bit when Bobby Brown (actually Bob the middle-aged lecturer from Leicester) had decided to attempt the splits and bust out of his cheesecloth trousers and Raquel Welch (Rachel from Dorset) had fallen from the bar top and landed on Phil Collins (who actually *looked* like Phil Collins, to give him his due). Then there had been the small incident of Scarlett whipping off her skirt in the style of Bucks Fizz when 'Making Your Mind Up' was blasted out of the speakers. It was a shame she'd forgotten that she was only wearing the teeniest of thongs underneath, thus almost giving Bobby Brown a full-on heart attack.

Once Sofia had calmed the proceedings down, for the last hour Scarlett and I had been slow dancing around the room together to an album of Whitney Houston songs, declaring our undying love for one another ('I love you my little friend!' 'No! I love you more, Jessie-Wessy!'). Sofia had been the designated driver for all and sundry and had only just ejected Scarlett in time before she threw up over our little rosemary patch at the front of the house. Apparently she'd also been sick over the side of the ferry twice yesterday but had at least survived the journey home, despite being slightly the worst for wear when Darren had collected the three of them from the airport.

Yes, she was okay...she'd survived.

I just had to survive the rest of my stay, however long, on the island without my trusty sidekick, my wing-woman, and the prospect made me nervous. Could I cope on my own? Would I be okay? I guess time would tell.

Restless and agitated, alone in the house, I decided to meander down to the bar, even though it was ages before my shift was due to start; I needed to be in company, and an hour on the beach wouldn't go amiss either. A hug from Sulky Soula, who could be surprisingly thoughtful, despite her sour puss face, brought on another bout of tears, and kind words from Apostolis had the same effect. I silently cleared a few tables to assist, topped up the small bottles of olive oil and vinegar, and then waded straight out into the sea to cool down. It was comforting to taste the salt from the water and to feel it drying onto my sun-kissed skin; to watch the shoals of tiny silver fish darting around by my legs and to listen to the holidaying Greek families chattering on incessantly and playing games either side of me, the rhythmic tapping of bat against ball steadying my mind and calming my nerves.

When I sat down at a table-for-one to eat a mixed *souvlaki* with a traditional Greek salad, I was somewhat surprised to see Nikos approaching – I hadn't expected him back until after the weekend. It was good to see him, I thought, as he walked towards me and smiled, pushing his Ray Bans back into place and, thank the Lord, he'd had a haircut, and was looking less Tom Jones and more Tom Cruise again. The manner in which he almost clicked his fingers to have Apostolis fetch him over a chair and a frappé; the way his heavy gold rings and expensive Swiss watch glinted in the sun – the man exuded confidence and wealth.

'My beautiful Jessica,' he said, lifting my hand to kiss the fingertips before I could warn him they were covered with lemon juice that I'd squeezed on to my barbequed meat. I felt myself squirming a little with the simple word 'my' – he'd said it in a very proprietorial way and I didn't want to belong to him or anyone else for that matter.

'Ah, you taste of the sea and the lemons of Loulouthia...a delicious, heady combination.' Mmmm...well, actually, with those few words and that undeniably sexy voice, I was thinking now that I wouldn't actually *mind* being his Jessica, although perhaps only for one night...

'So...I have missed you very much while I have been away...and I apologise that I was not here to say goodbye to your friend Scarlett. However, I now have a proposition for you.'

Oh god, maybe it was like that film, 'Indecent Proposal'- maybe he was going to offer Lorry a shit load of money to step back so he could do his worst with me...or maybe he was going to offer ME a ton of money to get down and dirty between the sheets with him. To be fair, the way he was gazing at me now, he would probably only have to get me lathered and bung me fifty quid, and I'd be happy to oblige.

'I know you will feel lonely and adrift without the company of Scarlett and that her departure means you are now solely responsible for the rent and other bills...but I have an apartment in Town that will be empty from September. So, I am thinking, that maybe you would like to stay there for the remainder of the season, rent free of course, rather than in your dilapidated house half way up the mountain, alone and sad. It would be better for you financially, I think, and you may use my other car, if you so wish, to travel to work...to hang on to this job that I know you love so much. What do you think, Jessica Rose Woodward from England? Would you be up for it?'

A move to Town. Away from Chaliki. It would make good financial sense, as he said, to take him up on his offer, but my heart was screaming 'NO!' Apart from Scarlett and Lauren, nobody knew of my intention to stay on Loulouthia once the season was over; this should have been the moment that I spilled the beans to Nikos, but for some inexplicable reason, I didn't want to let him in on my closely-guarded secret just yet. If I moved to his apartment, he would probably expect me to stay there indefinitely once the season ended, and then I might never be in a position to return to Chaliki. And would I feel obligated to enter into some sort of relationship with him if I moved into his place and didn't pay rent?

'It's a very generous offer, Nikos, but can I have a little think about it? I do love it here, in Chaliki, that's true, and I would be sad to move on, even if it is only a few miles down the coast. But I know I would be crazy to turn down such an opportunity...'

'Of course! You must consider my offer carefully...and I will only need your answer by the end of the month. Right now, I am overheating after a busy morning dealing with mechanical problems and I desperately need to cool down. When you have finished your lunch, we will rest for a short while on the beach and then I think I would like to take a dip in the sea with you...'

By 'taking a dip' he did, of course, mean that he would turn into Octopus Man, pouncing on me the instant we were in the water and grabbing hold with his tentacles (yes, I did say *tentacles);* his lips sucking on mine and barely giving me a second to come up for air. It wasn't an altogether unpleasant experience though - his body was solid and his washboard stomach put mine to shame; when I was squashed against his glistening wet torso and I could feel his arousal in his shorts, I couldn't deny it felt thrilling and dangerous, and my head was full to the brim of pornographic pictures of the two of us writhing around in his four-poster bed, where he would put those tentacles to good use and I would be left wilting with exhaustion, yet still begging for more.

The reality was that I still pushed him away before he thought it was a given thing that I would have sex with him that day. When he tried to slip his fingers up inside my swimming costume, I squirmed out of his reach but rewarded him with a thorough drenching with sea water and told him he needed to go home and take a cold shower. He laughed and reluctantly agreed; after he dropped me back at the house I had a cold shower of my own before drip-drying whilst snoozing on the terrace and then strolled back down to Sunrise to begin my shift – at this rate I would have legs like a racehorse.

Feeling thoroughly out of sorts, I was relieved to see Sofia and Alex had already arrived at the bar – they were familiar, they were unthreatening, they *understood* me.

'How are you today, Just Jess?' Sofia threw her arms around me and I could smell an expensive Dior perfume sprayed liberally on her wrists and other parts of her body, and I resolved to treat myself to another bottle of my favourite Coco Chanel when my financial situation was a little easier, say, in about five years' time.

'I'm okay Sofia,' I replied, as she was slowly releasing her grip of me. 'I miss Scarlett already and I still can't believe she's gone home, when we still have almost two months of the summer season remaining, but I understand her reasons for doing so. At the end of the day, she has family over in England and she misses her children, and sometimes she...she really struggled over here...'

'Scarlett Fever was loud and lazy,' Alex interrupted abruptly and I felt my hackles rise and my face flush in annoyance as I turned to glare at him. 'No, no...let me finish,' he continued, stepping back, presumably in case I was about to slap him. 'She was loud and lazy but I liked her a lot. You two are like sisters – the sensible, thoughtful one and the naughty, spontaneous one. She is good for you, I think – she gives you confidence and makes you see that you can do anything, if you just put your mind to it. And you keep her out of trouble, as best you can. I am sorry that she has left now, but I think she has done the right thing in returning to England. That doesn't mean to say that we won't all miss her infectious laughter and the joy she brought to Loulouthia.'

Okay, I suppose I would forgive him. I sighed and hopped on to the nearest stool positioned at the bar, and he came and sat next to me, side by side, as I continued.

'I know Scarlett has her faults – she would be the first to admit it – but she's been through so much in the past. Her childhood was really difficult; her mum and dad drank a lot and they fought like cat and dog. There was never enough money to pay the bills and there was always a money lender or bailiff banging at the door and threatening to take away what little they had. Scarlett and her sister, Viola, were like two little urchins until they were old enough to find part time jobs, to try to drag themselves up out of the pit of poverty they'd been born into. Dad and I always felt desperately sorry for them. Viola was out of that house as soon as she turned sixteen and she bagged herself a decent job and flat and has made something of her life. Scarlett met Darren, they married and settled down with the kids and the mortgage and the jobs. Except she couldn't quite break that cycle; ringing in to work and pretending to be sick was the norm for her mum and dad when they were in a state from the previous night's heavy drinking – when they actually had jobs to go to - so Scarlett thought that was okay. And she was terrible with money; Darren worked so hard but she was spending it faster than he earned it. But, worst of all, even though she loved the very bones of that man and would have laid down her life for him, she used to pick arguments all of the time and goad him, accusing him of all kinds, and they'd end up pushing and shoving each other and screaming blue murder every weekend.'

'Is that what ended her marriage?' Alex asked softly, placing his hand on mind as I began to tear up again.

'Yes, basically, it was. Darren tried everything to keep the peace but she constantly pressed the self-destruct button and wanted to fight with him – because it was all she'd ever known. He even dragged her along to counselling but it was useless – the bloody counsellor couldn't get a word in with Scarlett yacking on – you know what she's like! When they'd both had far too much to drink one evening, they had a massive argument; she pushed him and he shoved her back and she went flying over the coffee table, he was horrified and said enough was enough. He's such a gentle guy normally, you see; he wouldn't hurt a fly. But their relationship had become toxic because of Scarlett's insecurities, and so he packed his bags and walked out – even though he loved Scarlett, he truly did, she had pushed him as far as he could go, and he could take no more.'

'A sad story. Poor Scarlett. Poor Darren.'

'My heart ached for them both, and their children. But Darren has always provided for those kids – financially and emotionally – and he's a great father. He eventually met someone else and fell in love, but Scarlett never did. Yes, after a while she had boyfriends – usually bloody idiots who took what they could from her and left her in a mess – but she's never loved anyone the way she loved Darren; she never really got over losing him. Do you know, he actually paid for her ticket home? He'd sworn he was done handing money over to her, unless it was specifically for the kids, but she'd had him worried - gallivanting off to Greece for the summer with an almost empty bank account - so he agreed to fund her flight home.'

'A good man, I think. This is what you need also, Just Jess - a good man.'

'Mmmm. I sometimes think the last thing I need is *any* man!'

'Then maybe Lawrence of Arabia is not what you are looking for. And neither is Nikos with all of the money. If one of them does not make your heart pound and your body ache, then maybe you are wasting time with the wrong men, Just Jess. Maybe you should open your eyes and look elsewhere.'

'Maybe. Maybe Mr Right is over on Corfu, sat fiddling with his worry beads while he's waiting for me to find him - I just don't know. Perhaps it would be better if I never looked at all and I resigned myself to a life of dinners-for-one and wine-for-two. Alex, can I ask you something?'

'Sure. You can ask me anything – you know that.'

'Well, this might seem like a strange random question, but why do you call me 'Just Jess'? Why am I not named after some famous Jessica, or Jess, or even Jessie? Everyone else who comes in here gets allocated a cute celebrity nickname and I get nothing! I feel kind of deprived!'

'Ah well, listen in, because there is a very good reason. You see, Jessica, you are no imitation of some so-called celebrity. You are the 'real deal', as they say – a one-off who should not be compared with anyone else. You don't have to pretend to be someone you're not – you are unique, and you are perfect just being the beautiful, kind woman that you are. Just Jess. That is all.'

My god, it was one of the loveliest things anyone had ever said to me, and when Sofia came over and affectionately squeezed my shoulders, I was seriously moved, by just how kind and giving this amazing couple were.

Hugging them both in turn, I thanked them for always being there for me; for listening to me and looking after me and for being so much more than just my employers.

Vacating my stool, I greeted a couple of regular customers whilst giving myself a serious internal bollocking for wallowing in self-pity and not appreciating just how fortunate I was, and then I set about enjoying my evening at work, scooting around from table to table, and even getting stuck into the allocation of celebrity names for some new arrivals. Martin from Basildon became the silver fox himself, Martin Kemp, and Rolf Bilsborough from Lancashire became...well, I struggled with Rolf to be honest, as all I could think of was Rolf Harris, which was clearly highly inappropriate...until Alex came to my rescue and Rolf became Ralph...and Mr Bilsborough became Ralph Lauren, for one week, and one week only.

*

Once I'd accepted that Scarlett had really gone, and discovered that I could expect daily texts and phonecalls from her, demanding to know all the gossip from the island - meaning some days we would actually speak more than when we were living together, when often we were like ships that passed in the night because of our jobs and our men - I truly settled into my new Greek life.

After the frantic all-hands-on-deck peak season, the departure of the majority of the Greeks and Italians saw the island returning to its usual relaxed state. The British people drank more but sat back and chilled out more, and if anything went wrong, in general they would say, 'Oh well, never mind, we're on holiday.' We still worked long hours in the sweltering heat but had more free-time to visit the beach to cool down afterwards.

Nervously, I'd informed Nikos that I didn't want to move into his apartment in Town after all, however shiny and new and free of charge it might be. He was a little perturbed, as he'd probably been expecting me to snatch his hand off but, as I'd explained, my heart was in Chaliki, and that was where I intended to stay.

I think he viewed it, quite simply, as a rejection and was subsequently sulking like a spoilt brat, so I'd seen an awful lot less of him. To be quite frank, it was for the best, as when the cool evening breezes of September drifted in, the Tom Jones polo-neck top made a re-appearance and even the sight of it made me squirm and want to run for the hills. We'd kissed a fair old bit over the previous month or so and he'd also taken to sliding his hands under my clothing to explore what lay beneath (hot sweaty skin and a nasty heat rash under my boobs for most of August). When he'd gazed meaningfully into my eyes and said in a deep, raspy voice, 'Jessica, I cannot wait much longer...I am truly ravenous for your body and I am desperate to rip off your clothes and devour every inch of you,' I'd actually laughed out loud in his face, which didn't exactly make his day, but, god love him, I knew he was simmering over with frustration and it was only a matter of time before I was given an ultimatum or he transferred his affections to somebody less picky.

Lorry was much more patient. I'd tried to cool it off with him, to explain that I wanted nothing more than for us to become the best of friends but, he never gave up, and he was constantly trying to hold my hand or slide my bra straps down as he was kissing me goodnight.

The stress was killing me; even though I'd been upfront with both of them from the beginning, it felt cruel and so out of character for me, to be juggling two men who never quite knew where they stood...so I'd decided to put a stop to it all.

It had been incredibly flattering, I had to concede; all the attention and affection, and gifts of flowers (Nikos) and kebabs (Lorry, of course – who says romance is dead?). It was all new territory for me; I wasn't used to men fighting for my heart and body, complete with all of its flabby bits and wrinkles. When Simple Simon had dumped Scarlett and she had been devastated, through her fast-flowing river of tears she'd howled at me, 'It's not fair! Look at you with all the gorgeous men chasing after you! They're literally lining up, dribbling at the mouth, wanting to take you out and shower with you presents and attention, and here's me – desperate to find a decent man and all I attract is moronic dickheads!'

But I truly didn't want any of it; all I desired was to clear my head and immerse myself in the local way of life without having to worry about anyone else. I often asked myself if there *was* actually something wrong with me – rejecting the advances of two gorgeous men who most women would give their right arm to be involved with. Maybe my heart was defective and I didn't have it in me to let anyone take it from me.

But then there were times when I missed the sex and I longed to fall asleep and wake up with that special someone who would kiss me and say 'Good Morning beautiful'; who would look at me with such love and devotion in their eyes. I didn't really want to die a lonely old spinster who'd never experienced that depth of feeling that everyone else seemed to reach so easily.

I was so lucky to have been given a second chance at life and I had a wonderful future to look forward to here on Loulouthia – it would be a damn shame if I couldn't share it with that one elusive person who did indeed make my heart swell.

Chapter 19

All men issues screwed up and tossed aside, throughout the next three weeks, I literally had the time of my life.

I loved my job and my workmates, and even when my feet were hot and swollen from being on them for eight hours solid; when my eyes felt heavier than a truck-full of lead from lack of sleep, it was a pleasure to work at Sunrise and to meet and mix with the customers. At the end of a shift I would often ease my worse-for-wear sandals off my throbbing feet to paddle out into the sea - just to stand there and breathe, in the darkness, by only the light of the stars and the neon signage of the bars. Sometimes Alex or Sofia, or both, would join me, but we wouldn't say much; we would just look up into the night sky or down at the water lapping around our toes, each of us deep in thought and decompressing after the long, hot, busy day.

I'd finally confessed to Alex and Sofia that I wanted to stay on the island once the season was over and they hadn't been the least bit surprised, pulling me into a group hug, with Alex promising to show me the ropes during the Greek winter. They warned me of the rains which would come and advised me it was essential that I moved house as the one I was currently in was not fit for the cold and the damp, with no form of heating and being slightly off the beaten track; there was a recently refurbished house in their village and they were to make enquiries on my behalf.

I had serious reservations about moving out of my first real home on Loulouthia and would miss being so close to Lauren. However, I'd been surprised to hear that there was a small track, unpassable by car, only a few metres from Lauren's house, which led straight through to Alex and Sofia's village, so I wouldn't be far away at all. Apparently it had once been one continuous road that linked up the two halves of the old Chaliki village, but a small earthquake and a huge landslide had more or less divided the two many years ago.

Lauren now had the luxury of a day off each week and she drove us up and down the island in Andreas' old banger of a car and we explored places I would never have reached on my own. We also took the jeep safari with Yiorgos up into the mountains and I bought honey and nougat and an exquisite handmade white, lace tablecloth that I would probably never ever use in my whole entire life, but there you go.

We sunbathed in quiet, secluded coves that I hadn't known existed and could only be accessed by precarious paths, and we swam in waters where there was not a single other person, and the sea was calm and soothing to the mind and the soul.

She often joined me on my terrace and we would get tipsy on cheap vodka on my occasional night off and laugh about all the strange sights you are confronted with on a small Greek island, such as Mr Toothy propping his gun up against the wall outside of the shop while he popped in to buy cigarettes – as if it was the most normal thing in the world. *We* knew he was about to go off hunting up in the mountains, but I'm sure there were some tourists who thought they were about to be a victim in some bloody massacre which would be the headline on the late-night news.

She doubled over with laughter when she discovered me chasing two wily old goats around the garden after the little bastards had chewed right through my favourite pair of jeans hung on the washing line - and left holes in my two best towels.

When the weather briefly turned and there were a few unexpected showers one day in early September, we danced in the rain in our swimsuits and shorts, enjoying the blessed relief of the dampness on our skin and hair that for once wasn't sweat. Andreas' father, passing by on his incredibly noisy tractor at the time, looked at us if we were quite mad and shouted, 'You crazy English people!' while we sang and cheered as he chugged off up the hill.

And we were sometimes joined by Andreas, who would put his arm around Lauren, have a few sips of a can of lager, and then announce that he 'must go and mend the fence now.'

Occasionally, I would follow the path up to Lauren's house; it was a good, steep hike but, despite all the gyros and chips, my fitness levels had definitely improved and I wasn't panting and sweating as much as I used to do when I first arrived. They had a smallholding set-up going on, as did most of the islanders, and seemed to be surrounded by fruit trees and vegetables, chickens and goats, as well as dogs and kittens of course; so far I had resisted the temptation to take on a puppy but it was only a matter of time now I was staying – although I was told most landlords wouldn't allow pets actually inside their houses, and that just wouldn't do at all.

Now I knew that Alex and Sofia weren't far away, I would wander over to the almost hidden track and gaze over at the higgledy-piggledy rooftops I could just about make out in the distance and wonder which particular one was theirs. Once Lauren and I had put the world to rights, I usually left with an overflowing bag of eggs and figs and tomatoes and goodness knows what else, but always with a huge smile on my face.

Towards the end of September, on a fairly nondescript, quiet kind of day, I had a surprise visit from Lauren, at a time when I would have expected her to be on duty at the hotel, and I immediately wondered if something was amiss. She'd found me lady-shaving my legs out on the terrace – over the summer I'd got in the habit of doing all kinds of tasks al fresco; the

Greeks cooked outdoors, ate outdoors and washed their clothes outdoors...so I thought, what the hell, and everything from eyebrow plucking to ironing was performed at the front of my house.

'Hello you, what are you doing here on this marvellous Monday morning? Surely it's the busiest time of day for you to be making a break for freedom from behind that reception desk?'

'I've had a lot of stuff to sort out,' she told me, pulling up a plastic chair, slipping off her shoes and wiggling her painted toes in the fresh air.

'Oh well, I know how long it all takes here, with the bureaucracy and paperwork and endless visits to offices with queues a mile long and...'

'Jessica, I'm leaving.'

'Say what? Why would you leave the Diana? You have a great job and I thought you liked it there better than anywhere you've worked...'

'No, you're not listening to me. I'm leaving here, Loulouthia. This afternoon. I'm going home.'

For a second I was dumbstruck, positive I must have misheard her words or misunderstood the situation.

'But this is your home!' I eventually almost shouted, in shock. 'You can't leave! Your home is here, with Andreas, and all your animals. Your life is here, your job is here...what are you talking about?'

'I can't stay any longer Jess; if I do *I'll* be the one grabbing a gun and wiping out half of the village; honestly, I have to go.'

'But *why*? You seem so settled here with Andreas; I thought you were happy – I thought you loved him.'

Her eyes shone with tears then, as she said, 'I do love him Jess, and I always will, but I can't stay here and he won't come with me – so there's no solution, except that we go our separate ways.'

'But why would you ever want to leave this beautiful island? Who in their right mind would want to swap all of this for a dismal, dreary life back on the treadmill in rainy old England? Have you gone mad? You LOVE this place.'

'No, I don't...actually...I don't love it. *You* fell in love with this island, and that's why you're here. *I* fell in love with Andreas and that's why I'm here – there's a huge difference.' She spoke quietly, blinking away the tears, and she looked like her heart was breaking as she tried to open it up a little; I just didn't get it.

144

'Why in god's name do you want to leave though? What's changed that makes this village, this island, this *life* so unbearable now? Me and you...we've have had such a great laugh these last few weeks and you never showed any sign of being unhappy with your lot – not one. And if you still love Andreas, as you proclaim to do, then how can you just leave him behind and move on? Am I missing something here Lauren?'

'Aw Jess...I wouldn't know where to start even trying to explain - there's so much you don't know, and I've always thought that's for the best...and it's so incredibly complicated. I've given it a great deal of thought, trust me – I've thought of nothing else for so long now - and I have good reason for wanting to see the back of this place. Despite what I feel for Andreas; despite the fun that you and I have had together recently and the sisterly love; despite the wrench it will be to leave the animals behind...it's all the rest of it that I can't deal with. Not anymore.'

In disbelief that she actually seemed to mean it, I was the one who started to cry then – I couldn't believe this was happening and knew whatever had taken place, I had to do everything in my power to try and change her mind.

'Why won't you tell me what it is Lauren? I thought we were friends!'

'Of course we're friends, you dipstick! I'm sorry Jess, that I've kept you in the dark about everything, but it just hurts so much to talk about it. You're obviously going to try and talk me out of this but it isn't a snap decision – I've thought about it long and hard and I'm leaving today, and that's final. I'll miss you babe...you know I will...and I hate to leave you, especially now you've decided to stay...but this is something I really have to do.'

The tears were flooding now; I couldn't hold them back.

'But what will I do without you? First Scarlett, now you. I don't think I can survive here without you...we've become so close in such a short period of time and when I've needed you, you've always been there for me and looked after me - you're my rock...you're my...guardian angel...'

Something I said then seemed to have tripped a switch inside of Lauren; her eyes closed, she lowered her head and spoke quietly, but deliberately.

'I understand, Jess, I really do. You see, I had my own guardian angel when I first came here who was MY rock and always there for me - an English girl who'd arrived the year before me. Her name was Juliette. But I had to adapt, to learn to survive without her.'

Her voice became almost a whisper, as if saying the girl's name was too painful, and I could see she was lost in a raft of memories.

'Juliette? I've never heard you mention that name. What happened to her? Did she leave as well?'

'No, she didn't leave Jess. She died. Here on Loulouthia.'

'Oh my god, that's terrible! What happened to her?'

'She had a horrific accident...came off her scooter...on the winding road that takes you almost down to the port; you know the one – it's really steep and sometimes the sun is blinding, depending on the time of day, and renders you incapable of being able to see anything in front of you.'

'Jesus...that's awful...now I remember why I hate those bloody moped things so much. Wait a minute – is that the girl Sofia's mentioned a couple of times, the friend who had the accident?'

'Yes, she knew her. But she was more my friend than hers.'

She seemed almost angry that this poor Juliette girl should have any connection to Sofia.

'Jeez...what a terrible thing to happen. Was it a collision with somebody else or did she lose control?'

'We think she just momentarily lost concentration; her mind was on a ton of other stuff and she clipped the curb and was catapulted clean off it. Technically, she died of internal injuries received in the accident, but we all knew the truth...we all knew that *he* as good as killed her.'

He? She'd lost me now – I didn't know what the hell she was talking about. She was clearly angry and referring to a man being instrumental in Juliette's death in some way, but when I questioned if she meant another driver, or maybe someone on foot who'd misjudged their timing when crossing the road, she went puce in the face and clenched her fists angrily by her sides.

'NO! I mean HIM! Fucking Kostas...the evil bastard who made her life an absolute misery. He may as well have inflicted the injuries himself – it's what he usually did.'

Christ, who the hell was Kostas and surely she didn't mean he'd been violent towards the poor girl?

Lauren could see I was clearly baffled and it was obvious she was wrestling with whether or not to fill me in on all the gruesome details. In the end, through her tears, she chose to go there.

'He used to beat the living shit out of her and none of us ever knew. On the outside he was Mr Happy-go-lucky with a line for everything and a dazzling smile, and all the while he was making her life hell. And Juliette was the sweetest, most beautiful girl you could ever meet – so pretty and dainty and tiny...and much younger than him – she didn't stand a chance. She was so funny and kind as well, with a heart of gold; she sort of adopted me when I first arrived, even though I was the elder one, and we had such great laughs and I just couldn't have coped here without her. Do you know, she used to run errands for half the village and in particular for a little old couple who lived just up the road from her and who had no surviving family on the island – their health was failing and they struggled to get out so she made sure they always had shopping and often delivered homemade bread and cakes to them. And I used to call her Doctor Doolittle because she took it upon herself to feed half the stray dogs on the island. She was that sort of girl.'

I didn't speak, wanting her to continue; to unlock the mystery of why she could no longer bear to stay on the island; how she had been affected by the terrible demise of her friend.

'Of course he belted and punched and kicked the spirit out of her. Not at first, when they lived with his parents. He was good as gold then when they were in earshot of his mum and dad – a right little mummy's boy. He was a lazy bastard as well – always dodging and weaving so he didn't have to do any work and letting his brother pick up the slack and shouldering the responsibilities that should have been his. But on the surface he was so likeable; we had such a laugh, the six of us - always together, whether it was just kicking a ball about on the beach or taking off up the mountain with a picnic. But all that changed when he sourced them a new little house of their own – fucking miles from anywhere where no one could hear her cry and scream.'

This was horrific, and so at odds with all I'd ever known on the island. I wasn't sure I wanted her to continue but she did; it seemed once she'd lifted the lid off the story, she wanted the whole sorry mess to pour out.

'She was so bloody happy and animated when I first met her...and even after the abuse had started, she was still a bright, shining little star who managed to cheer the rest of us up if we were having a crappy day. She hid it well, you see, and the next summer it was difficult to keep up with her to the same degree, because they'd moved away from the village and HE decided they were also going to take over a bar down Skafos where he had her working like a dog, while he swanned around chatting up the girlies and lording it about like the big 'I Am'. So I didn't know what was going on – none of us did – and I just reckoned she was too tired to be bothered after work when she made excuses for us not to go out. Even though HE was full of himself and a work-dodger and a bragger, it never, ever crossed my mind what he could be capable of behind closed doors. So when she went off sick from work for a couple of days with a stomach bug, I didn't know it was because he'd punched her so hard in the gut she was coughing up blood. When she said she'd slipped off her bike and badly twisted her leg, I accepted that was why she was walking with a limp, rather than realising it was because he'd deliberately tripped her up and then stamped on her thigh. And when she told me she'd returned to the UK to see her family for a week I had no reason to disbelieve her, when the truth was that she was hospitalised on Corfu, recovering from her latest injuries. I never knew Jess, I swear, I never knew.'

The sound that escaped from Lauren's mouth then was like nothing I'd ever heard before – like the agonising howls of an animal caught in a trap – and I jumped up and wrapped my arms tightly around her as she cried continuously and repeated the words, 'I never knew...I never knew...' It was heart-wrenching to witness and a long time passed before Lauren re-surfaced and was able to conclude her story.

'He did, of course, avoid touching her face for a long time, but when she came out of hospital he was furious. A nurse there who had cared for Juliette, had seen through the story she'd fabricated to cover up why she'd really ended up in that hospital bed; her name was Ioanna – Joanna in English – and she had been abused in a previous relationship and therefore recognised all the signs. She was so kind to Juliette and when they were alone she repeatedly told her she *knew* she was a victim of domestic violence and, despite the threats Juliette may have received from Kostas, there was *always* a way out, and she promised to help her, quietly and discreetly. She ordered that Juliette memorise her mobile number, even though she was still insisting her injuries had been acquired accidentally, and Ioanna told her that when she was ready, they would formulate a plan and she would ensure she was forever free of this man. Kostas didn't know what had been discussed, but unfortunately discovered that the nurse had spent many hours at Juliette's bedside and he was scared as hell that she'd let something slip. So she took the brunt of his anger when she finally returned home.'

My hand flew to my mouth in horror; I felt sick thinking of the fear that must have been ever-present for this girl, who had done nothing wrong other than to fall in love with the very worst of mankind.

'What did he do?' I asked quietly, bracing myself for the answer.

'It's awful Jess...so awful. That piece of shit sat her down, knowing she was still in so much pain, on a chair in the middle of the kitchen, and made her play 'I spy'. 'After a few normal rounds of it, he suddenly said, 'Something beginning with F,' and when he'd tortured her by making her guess until she was all out of answers, he laughed and said 'No! 'F' for fist!' and then he punched her full-on in the face, knocking her clean off the chair and banging her head on the corner of the kitchen unit. And while she was lay there, covered in her own blood and writhing about in pain, he kept on laughing, the fucker...he just laughed.'

'Oh Lauren, I'm so sorry...I feel sick just thinking about it and I didn't even know the girl. It's hard to believe this kind of thing goes on in today's day and age. But how did you find out about it all, if he'd silenced her with fear? Did she finally open up to you one day?'

'Not really, no. You see, she was absolutely terrified of him. He'd threatened to kill her and then go after her younger sister in England. And her self-esteem was so low; he'd made her believe that she couldn't manage without him – that no one else would ever want her. So, no, she didn't voluntarily tell me anything. It was after she came out of hospital on Corfu – when she'd supposedly just returned from her holiday in England – I started to wonder if something was going on. I'd gone to the bar to catch up with her and he told me she was off sick, again...and it was just the way he said it – it made me uneasy – I knew I had to see her for myself. So I confided in Andreas and made him go to the bar a couple of nights later – when she still hadn't appeared – under strict instruction that he just act normally with Kostas, but he was to ring me immediately if Kostas left the bar at any time. And then I went up to her house.'

'And was she was there? Did you get to see her?'

'I banged and banged on the door but she didn't answer it, and of course I tried the handle but couldn't get in – the fucker had locked her in and taken away her phone. But I remembered from when they very first moved in that one of the old shutters didn't fasten properly and I managed to yank it open. I knew she was definitely in there so I yelled that if she didn't open the bloody window I was going to put a rock through it, and then there would be a whole heap of trouble, so eventually, reluctantly, she emerged out of hiding and opened the catch and I managed to climb in. Ripped my trousers to shreds as it happened, but that was the least of my worries when I saw her. Her face....'

Lauren's tears came thick and fast again then as she described what she'd found on entering the room.

'...her beautiful face...it was a swollen mess...broken nose, black eyes, cuts, bruises, scrapes – there was barely an inch of it that wasn't damaged in some way. He'd yanked a big chunk of her beautiful blonde hair out as well and her scalp had bled and was all scabbed over. I won't lie, I ran to the bathroom and I was actually sick. Everything fell into place then – her absences from the bar, her reluctance to meet me whenever I tried to get her out of the house, her withdrawal from our group of friends – and I hated myself for having been blind to what was going on; for allowing my friend to suffer at the hands of this vicious bastard for so long. I tried to hug her but she wouldn't let me – in case he smelled my perfume on her clothes and knew that I'd been there. That's how bad it was. She wouldn't tell me anything at first but eventually I persuaded her to confide in me and it all came spilling out – the physical and mental cruelty – everything.'

I couldn't speak, I was so choked – how could I say anything that would make Lauren feel any better?

'She told me about Ioanna and the phone number and I wrote it on the back of my hand. She made me promise I wouldn't say anything to Kostas or behave any differently with him, for fear he would kill her – and I actually think he would have done. The worst thing was being forced to leave her there that day; to climb back out and drive away, knowing I was leaving her with him.'

'Did you ring that Ioanna woman then?'

'It was the first thing I did, before I'd even arrived home. I cried like a baby down the line to her, but she was so calm and understanding. Not only had she been through it herself but she'd apparently secretly helped others to escape their abusers when she'd lived on the mainland so wanted to do all she could to help Juliette. She asked me a ton of questions about Kostas and his relationship with Juliette and said the more she knew, the easier it would be to put together some kind of plan, and then she assured me she would be in touch very soon to move things forward as quickly as possible – I think she was worried that if we left it much longer it would be too late for Juliette. And then I messaged Andreas, told him everything was okay, to say nothing to Kostas, but that he should return home and I would speak to him then. I didn't want him to give anything away to that bastard so I pretended everything was alright.'

'So you filled him in when he got home?'

'I did. And he just couldn't believe it – Kostas was his friend and he wouldn't have it at first that he could have done all that to Juliette. Until I showed him a picture I had taken of her smashed up face and he broke down and wept – I'd never seen him cry before and it was horrible. Then he got angry and I had to prise his car keys out of his hands and beg him not to go after Kostas. Practically every man on the Greek islands owns a gun, for when they do their Rambo hunting stuff over the winter months, and I was shit-scared either one of them would end up dead. Obviously I didn't give a toss if that was Kostas – I wanted to kill him myself – but I didn't want Andreas spending the rest of his life in a Greek prison. And I was scared for Juliette – if Kostas knew the game was up, I didn't want her to pay the price.'

'Good god, I don't know how you managed to keep it a secret though. What did you do next?'

'Ioanna and I hatched a plan. Kostas was into flash cars and had always wanted to own a Porsche, so we set about faking an online advertisement offering one for sale in pristine condition for a stupidly low price. And then Andreas basically said to him, 'Look mate, have you seen this? For sale on the mainland...and it's a bargain!' So Kostas, as anticipated, rang the number and enquired about buying this car and Theo, Ioanna's husband, told him yes, it was a very good price, but 'you must come to Athens today to collect it.' Andreas made out he was desperate to go with him to see this classic red Porsche in all its glory, and they agreed that he would be the driver and they would leave on the next ferry, just a couple of hours later.'

'Which gave Juliette the opportunity to escape?'

'Yes. Ordinarily he would never leave her long enough for her to be able to get out and raise the alarm, and he always threatened her that she would never get away in time – he would come after her and drag her back from Corfu or however far she'd managed to get, and then he would torture her and kill her. And he never ever left her long enough to get away, anyway. Obviously, he made his usual threats as he was rushing off and he locked her in – she had visible bruising again and he really didn't want anyone asking any pertinent questions if he allowed her out to work in the bar. But as soon as I knew they were safely on the ferry, I raced straight up to the house, opened the shutters again and Juliette threw her stuff to me and climbed out. She was shaking like a leaf but I assured her everything was going to be okay and bundled her in the back of my car. We left the house looking exactly as he'd left it; I wanted the piece of shit to unlock, walk in and wonder where the fuck she'd gone; how she'd managed to escape.'

'Did she even have her passport?'

'No, but we knew where it was. He'd taken it off her long ago and hidden it in one of the outbuildings, but she'd stumbled across it one day when she was searching for one of the kittens. Not wanting him to know she'd discovered its whereabouts, she'd left it where she'd found it, and in his haste to rush off and bag himself a bargain Porshe I don't suppose he'd thought to go and retrieve it – he did, after all, think Juliette was safely locked up in the house.'

'So it was all going to plan and...what next? Did you intend to leave the island that same day?'

'Yes, it was all going according to schedule and we were going to leave on the next ferry. I took Juliette straight to Ioanna's safe house and it was the first time I saw her relax. Andreas had messaged and said they were on their way to Corfu and Juliette smiled properly for the first time in forever and said to me 'It's all going to be okay, isn't it? I'm going home to my family, at last.' And she showered, and changed her clothes, and we waited. And then she realised she hadn't said goodbye to the old couple – the one she'd always taken bread and supplies to – although she'd struggled to do that more recently, after Kostas had moved her away from everyone. Anyway, she'd become really fond of them and she wanted to check they were alright before she left. She knew Kostas was on Corfu by then, making his way to his next ferry, and she asked to borrow a scooter, so she could nip up to the old lady and her husband, to take them some bits of food and hug them goodbye. The last time I saw her, as she straddled the scooter and turned around to say she would only be gone half an hour, she was so happy and relieved and relaxed; it was so wonderful to see her almost carefree after all the horrors she had endured.'

I didn't need to ask what happened next; I knew then that this brave young woman had lost her life before she could make it to safety. The freedom that had dangled like a carrot in front of her had been so cruelly snatched away; her life snuffed out as she lay in the road, her body broken and twisted; robbed of the opportunity to see her family again and to live her life without fear of this monster.

'When she didn't come back after an hour, we started to panic. I messaged Andreas just to double-check that they were definitely still en route to Athens. We were worried that Kostas had somehow got to her; that he'd had her watched – or that she'd panicked, fearing he would somehow catch up with her, and returned to their house. The ferry was due to leave at five-thirty and time was getting on. We were half way up to their house when I got the call from Andreas' aunty, who said there'd been an accident and that the passport that had been in the handbag found with the body had been Juliette's.'

'Oh Lauren I'm so, so sorry. You must have been heartbroken. And for Juliette to be so close to freedom as well. It must have been devastating.'

'I was inconsolable Jess. And I felt so *guilty*. I shouldn't have let her go off on her own like that. I should have got her out of there sooner. I should have *realised* earlier for fuck's sake just exactly what was going on. What kind of friend was I? She'd been my guardian angel...but ultimately, who'd been there to guard her?'

'It wasn't your fault Lauren; it was HIS fault, not yours. You had nothing to feel guilty about.'

'We all felt guilty though; it consumed us. Ioanna. Andreas. Sofia. And especially Alex. He couldn't bear it.'

'But it was no one's fault but that bastard's. And, I know you were probably all great friends, but why on earth would Alex, in particular, feel so bad?'

She stared at me, curiously, frowning as she leant forward and said, 'You don't know, do you? Really? I can't believe it's never slipped out when you've been cosying up to Sofia and Alex.'

'What? What are you talking about, Lauren? What never slipped out? For god's sake, tell me now!'

'Kostas...and Alex. Christ, you really don't know, do you? The thing is, even though Alex has tried his hardest to forget, he's unfortunately tied to Kostas and always will be...by name and by family. They're related, you see. They're siblings, Jess.'

'Kostas is Alex's elder brother.'

Chapter 20

Everything seemed to have altered in the last half hour; Lauren and Andreas were breaking up and she was leaving; an innocent young woman had been terrorised and lost her life; I'd discovered that the people I was closest to on the island had once all been friends with each other but now couldn't bear to even be in the same room together. Oh and Alex had an older brother that he'd never, ever mentioned - but, then again, if I'd been related to a violent, manipulative scumbag like Kostas, I'd probably have kept it quiet too.

'I'm not surprised, I suppose, that he hasn't spoken of him,' Lauren continued, 'but by choosing to do that, it means he's also never talked about Juliette, and presumably Sofia hasn't mentioned her by name either, and to be quite frank, that pisses me right off.'

'But, to be fair, *you* never mentioned her! None of you have! I've been completely clueless about all of this!'

'Oh Jess, I *wanted* to say something, to you of all people...but you were so excited and thrilled about moving here; I didn't want to put a massive downer on everything for you...and I'd promised Andreas faithfully that I would try and move on, for all of our sakes, especially after what happened in the aftermath of Juliette's death.'

She leant over the table, flicking away a leaf that had drifted down from one of the nearby trees, and took a deep, controlled breath. I couldn't hurry her, but I did wonder how it had all panned out, after this beautiful girl had departed from this earth and left a big gaping hole in all of their lives.

'I supposed I'd better finish, now I've started. To begin with, when I found out about Juliette, I was beyond hysterical and I rang Andreas, crying and screaming down the phone to him - not caring if Kostas was by his side. Andreas couldn't take it all in, not really and had struggled to understand what I'd been saying. They were just about to board the ferry to the mainland when he broke the news to Kostas that Juliette had been killed in an accident, although the details were sketchy. Apparently Kostas went as white as a sheet – presumably wondering if she'd taken her last breath as a result of any injuries he'd inflicted, and scared that he might be under arrest if the authorities caught up with him. Then Kostas answered a call from his own father, who informed him Juliette had actually died in a scooter accident, and his relief was blatantly obvious. He was even considering the possibility that they might continue their journey onwards to pick up his new car! Andreas was disgusted and gave him a real mouthful though...and then Theo, still posing as the mysterious car dealer, rang him to tell him the sale was off, and although Kostas was raging about being led on a wild goose chase, he realised he had better turn around and return home to put on a show of the grieving partner.

'The slimy prick! I hope he got what was coming to him when Andreas finally got him back on Loulouthia!'

'His father picked him up at the port and of course he instantly put on an act, playing the devastated boyfriend, collapsing in his mother's arms when he arrived home. And, as Greek families do, they came en masse to his parents' house, bearing flowers and condolences, and he fucking lapped it up.'

'What about you though? How did you cope with it all?'

'I couldn't cope, I was so angry! Ioanna was in a real state. Her husband arrived on the island on the same ferry as Andreas and Kostas – although he didn't know who they were amongst the crowd, and it was perhaps just as well – and he took Ioanna back to Corfu with him. She was in a terrible state when she left. No way was I prepared to let that arsehole get away with it though...I just had to do and say *something!* So I stormed over to his parents' house, barged in and let rip, screaming in a garbled combination of English and Greek that he was a murdering bastard; that she'd only died as a result of fleeing for her life from HIM; that I had pictures of her injuries and I would be interested to see what the coroner had to say about the other bruises, scars and welts on her body. Kostas, revealing his true colours, jumped up and went for me, but Alex waded in and ordered me to leave, which I was about to do anyway – but not before I'd shown them all the photograph of Juliette's face, when he'd beaten it to a pulp, and I yelled at them that I was going to the police.'

'Good! I hope he got put away for life!'

'It never happened, Jess. Firstly, his mum cried out and then collapsed on the floor and I thought she was a goner; she turned a horrible colour, as if all the life had drained out of her. Dickhead just stood there gaping, but Alex was by her side in seconds; she was conscious but clutching her chest. Andreas dragged me out of there and took me home; we were just heading up the little track to our house when we could hear the sirens in the distance, and I prayed it was the police as well as the ambulance. We didn't hear anything all day but Andreas stayed by my side because I was in such a terrible state and I think he also wanted to protect me, in case Kostas showed up wielding his fists or a gun.'

The whole tale was so shocking and disturbing, it was easy to imagine the scenes of confusion and terror, although so at odds with all I'd ever seen of the island and its people.

'We eventually received a message to say their mum was safely in hospital and was alive, but very poorly; Kostas stayed by her bed of course, playing the doting son. And then Alex paid us a visit, and I've never seen him so angry – berating me for the unnecessary pain I'd inflicted on his mother and father who were getting on in life and not in the best of health anyway. Then he shouted and bawled at me that it wasn't possible; that his brother, his own flesh and blood, could have beaten and abused a beautiful, innocent girl like that, without even showing any remorse. And then he sank to his knees and wept and screamed as if in acute agony, crying for Juliette, and begging her invisible presence for forgiveness – for being oblivious to what had been going on; for being so busy with his own life and his own family that he hadn't been able to stop the abuse and had been unable to save her. It was heartbreaking - Andreas and I knelt down on the floor with him and we all huddled together and wept; it was a night I'll never forget, for all the wrong reasons.'

'And then...?'

'And then...the next few days passed in a blur. They transferred Juliette's body over to Corfu, and her Death Certificate apparently stated that she had passed away due to the various internal injuries she'd received at the scene of the accident. No fucking mention of the old bruising, the cigarette burn on her leg, the fucking scars on her arms. Nothing. And her parents arrived – oh god her parents – that completely broke me. They were shattered; their lives destroyed. They had been expecting her to fly home the previous day, and now...now...they were accompanying her body back to the UK; repatriating her. It was horrific. I'll never forget their faces Jess – the despair, the incomprehension, the loss.'

'Did you tell them Lauren? Did you tell them what that bastard had done to their daughter?'

'How could I? How could I reveal everything he'd done to her, when they'd just lost Juliette in such horrific circumstances anyway? It would surely have killed them. And besides, I'd promised Lauren that I would never tell them, or anyone in her family - she didn't want anyone to know. Her dream was to return to some sort of normality and not have her life defined by the actions of one man. The funeral – I flew back for it – was just awful, but beautiful at the same time. So many pictures of her as a little girl, with curls in her hair and missing half of her baby teeth! And her sister bravely struggled through such a beautiful reading; it broke me, I won't lie.'

'Surely to god Kostas didn't attend the funeral though? If her parents weren't aware of the truth, then there would have been nothing to stop him flying over, as the grieving boyfriend.'

'He didn't even want to go! He said he was too devastated to make the lengthy journey to England and that he would grieve in his own way here on the island. Juliette's mum and dad took me aside at the wake and asked me personally why he hadn't made the trip; they didn't understand, if she lived with him, and they'd been in a serious relationship, why he was absent from her service and burial; why he didn't want to be a part of the celebration of her life alongside her family and other loved ones. To this day, I don't know how I kept the truth from them; it took everything I had not to blurt it all out, but I kept picturing Juliette's face when she pleaded with me to keep her secrets.'

'I get that. If it had happened to me, god forbid, and my dad had still been alive, I would have wanted to shield him from it. No one would want to put their parents through that kind of pain. But this worthless piece of shit should have been arrested and incarcerated for what he did! Please don't tell me he's got away scot free – that's he's living somewhere here on the island!'

'Well, you're half right – he got away scot free. When I came back from England, I'd heard he'd been out partying already and had been insinuating that Juliette had been sleeping around with a whole host of different men and he was spreading all sorts of nasty shit about her. I wanted to kill him Jess; like a woman possessed, I drove down to the bar, and in front of all of his cronies, I screamed at him over and over again that he was a liar and an abuser and that Juliette had died because of him. You should have seen his reaction; his face contorted in rage, he flew at me and grabbed me by the throat. Unfortunately for him, his dad and brother were also there, and Alex gave him a real pasting; he only stopped because his dad begged him to. They returned to the house and the next morning Kostas was gone.'

'Gone? Gone where?'

'He'd left the island for good. His parents, on the proviso that he never contact them or any of us ever again, gave him practically all of their money and he left to start a new life, somewhere near Thessaloniki on the mainland, I'm told. So he never paid any price for what he did to Juliette. Instead he was handed a big wedge of cash and the chance to start afresh.'

'But that's awful! Where's the justice in that? He could be doing it again – he could be tormenting and punching the life out of some other poor woman right now, as we speak!'

'Quite possibly, and there's nothing we can do about it. It wasn't the first time, you know. I only found out later. Apparently he had a son with an Irish girl who fled back home with her child after he'd whacked her on more than one occasion – sensible woman.'

'Christ...people like him shouldn't be allowed to have kids!'

'Oh, don't worry, he's never seen his son since the boy left the island with his mother. I don't think his ex would have allowed it anyway, but he made no attempt to maintain any contact. Andreas said Kostas' parents were devastated when the girl fled with their grandson, but he didn't give a toss.'

'Those poor people. That's terrible - what he's put them through. Oh my god! That's why Alex and Sofia's son doesn't have the same name as his grandfather, isn't it? I always thought it was strange that they'd broken with tradition and called him Yiorgos after Sofia's father, rather than Lambros, after Alex's dad – but that name was already taken!'

'That's right – Kostas' son, who had a lucky escape and hopefully lives a much happier, safer life in England, is named Lambros, after his paternal grandfather.'

Certain things were starting to make sense now – Alex's reluctance to discuss his family, although he clearly loved his parents; the unusual choice of name for his son; Lauren's distant demeanour when we first met; the tense, awkward atmosphere when Lauren was in the same room as Alex and Sofia.

'After losing Juliette, the revelations about Kostas and his sudden departure, our whole little group was blown wide apart. We hadn't been together so much in the months prior to her death but I'd always expected that we'd just resume regular contact after the craziness of the summer season and that there would be lots more memories for the six of us to make together. What was left, when our numbers were reduced by two, were four individuals consumed by guilt, who were mourning the loss of their friend - each truly believing that they could have done something to save her. Andreas went off into his own little world, surrounded by his animals and olives – he didn't always used to be so quiet, you know. Sofia was heartbroken, hid away in her house and cried for about a week solid, but then she had so much other stuff going on that her mind was often elsewhere. Alex threw himself into his work and concentrated on building up the bar business and then they opened up the restaurant – he thought he could hide his sadness behind the smile that's permanently fixed to his face, but I always knew it was there. And me – well I just tried to soldier on as best I could but I was so filled with hatred for everybody and everything - the anger was just eating me up inside.'

'I always thought you was weird around Alex...the atmosphere was always so fraught between the two of you, and you just wouldn't look each other in the eye. Do you know, I actually considered that you might have had a clandestine affair with him in the past!'

'Oh god, NO! I would never do that to Andreas. No, the problem is, when I see Alex, I see Kostas. They're so similar - they look more like twins than just brothers. And, I know it's not fair, but when I look at him, it's almost like Kostas is stood there in front of me, and I feel this fury build up inside and I want to leap on him and smash his face in – not just because of the similarity to him actually, but because I really feel like he should have *known* more than he did – he was his brother for fuck's sake! And I get that Alex had to look after his parents first and do what was best for them, particularly when his mother was so ill, but at the end of the day, he didn't prevent Kostas from leaving. He fucking should have done; he should have killed the bastard, or at the very least, dragged him off to the police station and at least we could have hoped that justice would have been served.'

'I can understand why you feel that way Lauren...but Alex *isn't* Kostas; he can't help the way he looks or being related to that arsehole. And as you say, he had his parents to consider, as well as his own wife and child, not to mention getting his head around losing Juliette as well and dealing with the shock of finding out *what* his brother was. You can't blame him for what happened, and he had to deal with it in his own way...no one was to blame other than Kostas...'

'I know Jess; it's irrational and unfair how I feel, but I can't help it. You know what makes me angrier than anything? No one even *talks* about Juliette any more. No one ever mentions her name! No one remembers the woman who did so much to help everyone else; who was such a lovely, lively member of their local community. It's all been brushed under the carpet to allow people to get on with their lives, and in the process it's like Juliette's been forgotten – like she never existed; like she was never here at all on Loulouthia.'

She was getting het up again and her eyes were blazing. Gently squeezing her hand, I gave her a moment to compose herself and then tried my best to comfort her, although no words could ever take away her pain.

'Lauren, I can't see how people *could* forget such a special person; she'll be remembered by everyone in their hearts and their minds; they just don't talk about her, probably because it brings back all the tragedy and heartbreak again - because it makes them feel sad.'

'Well, they fucking should! I used to keep dropping her name into every conversation because I couldn't bear it, but people immediately changed the subject or looked at me as if I'd just uttered some nasty swear word, so in the end even *I* stopped mentioning her out loud. But I was determined I was going to *make* them remember...so I regularly lay flowers outside of the house where they lived and also at the spot on the road where she lost her life; sometimes Ioanna travels over from Corfu and does the same. These fuckers will SEE these flowers, and they will NOT forget Juliette!'

I recalled noticing a bunch of flowers laid out at an unusual spot by the side of the road near the port. It had stuck in my mind because although there were flowers growing absolutely everywhere on this island, and pots and baskets decorating everyone's balconies and terraces and streets, these particular flowers were tied up and left on the ground, spread out like a fan. I had thought they must have been placed there deliberately – and now I knew why.

'That's so beautiful Lauren; so poignant. I'm sure Juliette would have loved that...'

'I miss her, Jess,' she sobbed, her face crumpling. 'I miss her so much. And I'm so sorry I was so inexcusably rude to you when you first arrived, but I was trying to self-preserve. I'd built so many defences and walls around me and I was determined that no one would be able to scale them. Fear prevented me from becoming friends with any other English woman – fear of somehow trying to replace Juliette...but I could never do that; she was irreplaceable. You're so lovely and feisty – you kind of remind me of how she used to be before he started to lay into her. I've loved spending time with you these last few months – you've been a real breath of fresh air, making me laugh again and reminding me that life is for living. But I can't live that life here; there's too much to remind me of the badness and pain; it's like a little worm inside of me eating away and I have to get away from this island before there's nothing left of me; before I'm rotten to the core.'

'But, Andreas...?'

'If life was fair he would be able to leave with me and we would build a new life together in England. But life's not fair. His family are here; he's an only child with a shit-load of responsibility, and his life here is on the farm, helping his parents and making sure they still have an income and their house is maintained and the animals don't starve. What would they do without him? And what would he do without Loulouthia? He's never known anything else, never wanted anything more. He will always carry the sadness about Juliette around with him but he is tethered to this island and he can't just up and leave. And I understand that, and he understands my position; we understand each other. He is devastated that I'm leaving and we've agonised over it all and he has of course begged me to stay. The only reason I've hacked it so long is because of Andreas but, although it breaks my heart to leave him behind, I can't take it any longer – I have to go.'

'But if you love him so much...'

'I do, I really do. And the thought of not seeing him every day; not living with him, not being loved by him...that's the killer. I've never known anyone like him; I was so lucky to find someone as special as him and we've had such wonderful times together, and I'll probably cry into my pillow for months when I get home, pining for him, but that's something I'll just have to deal with. And so will he.'

'But it's just so wrong! It's too awful to contemplate you two being separated when you're so obviously made for each other – like Alex and Sofia – hopelessly in love and perfectly in tune with each other...even though *I* never came here looking for love, I have to admit I'd give my right arm to have a relationship like yours, or Sofia's.'

'Sometimes, all is not as it seems, Jess. Everybody is happy on the surface, but underneath...well let's just say there is so much more going on. Let me give you a piece of advice before I leave; Lorry and Nikos – you like them both but you think you have to make a choice soon between the two of them before it's too late. In my humble opinion, you have already made your choice – the very fact that all summer long you've been unable to pick one above the other; that you haven't been drawn to one of these two men and fallen completely under their spell – well, that says it all. I know, and I think you do too, that neither of these guys is the one for you, so don't feel guilty about letting them go. You've kept them both at bay because deep down you know you've got no future with either of them. You're not in love with them and you never will be.'

Blunt, but very astute, she had voiced out loud emotions that I had concealed inside – feelings I had tried to suppress because, quite frankly, I was scared of losing these two men, not only as potential lovers, but as treasured friends; I was terrified that no one as good-looking and lovely as them would ever fancy me again, and there would never be anyone to share my bed and my life with. The future looked incredibly bleak without them in it.

'I know you're right,' I admitted, 'but I've been struggling...professing to be loving the single life while all the while I've been having these nagging little doubts and thinking that maybe I *do* want the whole relationship thing; deep down I *do* want to find the love of my life - although I've never said that to anyone before...probably because I'm only just admitting it to myself. Maybe there is something intrinsically wrong with me though - to get to this stage of my life and still be single. I was so badly hoping that Lorry or Nikos would be the one...everything would be so much simpler if I'd fallen for one of them...'

'Sometimes you have to swerve the simple things in life and open your eyes and see exactly what is around you. Okay, so Lorry and Nikos weren't 'the one', but who knows, this elusive man of your dreams could arrive on the next ferry...or maybe you've already met him and you just don't know it yet...'

'Well, I fucking hope it's not Mr Toothy or Toilet Duck!'

Toilet Duck, poor man, was the guy who emptied everyone's cess pits or sceptic tanks – mains sewerage being low on the list of essential requirements it would seem on this island – and once smelled, never forgotten. He had a nice smile but I didn't think I could cope with the stench, day in, day out.

Lauren laughed – it was good to hear, because I knew there would be many more tears to follow.

'Give over, you dipstick! I would say it's one hundred percent not one of *those* two men! But trust me, when I tell you, he is definitely out there...and when you're with him, at some point you will realise, you can't live without him and you'll just *know*.' She squeezed out a smile through her tears, and as I watched her I realised how much I was going to miss that smile, when I didn't see it every day.

Of course, I tried to change her mind – I begged her, I tried to reason with her, I used emotional blackmail, I reminded her all of the billion fabulous things about Loulouthia, but nothing would sway her.

'I know there'll come a time when I'll wake up, open the curtains and I'll see rain and the housing estate sprawling in front of me, and I'll remember what it was like to witness the sun rise over the Ionian Sea; to know that I'm missing out on wall-to-wall sunshine for over six months of the year...and I'll yearn to be back amongst the animals, up the hill, with Andreas by my side. One day I will miss the scent of the flowers and the sun beating down on my skin and the sound of the waves breaking on Ammos Beach...but right now even the noise of the cicadas is doing my head in...and I would be quite happy if I never saw another fucking lemon for the rest of my life. I think it will be a while before I have any kind of yearning to return to Loulouthia; it will be some time before all I can remember is the good rather than the bad; when it's not soured by everything that's happened.'

In the end, I had to accept that she made her choice, and we cried and hugged and promised to always keep in touch and then it was time for her to leave – because she had packing to finish and wanted to spend her last few hours alone with Andreas, before their worlds were ripped apart.

As she started to walk away, my eyes blurred with tears and my heart was somewhere down in my shoes, when she suddenly stopped and turned around. Noticing for the first time how her face looked tired and drawn, and how her once-bright and sparky eyes looked miserable and empty, for a brief moment I thought to myself that yes, she needed a break from Loulouthia; she needed to get away to mend her shattered heart – please let her return though; please don't let this break last forever.

'Jess...one more thing. I have a favour to ask you before I leave...but please don't feel obliged to say yes - I know it's a lot to expect of anyone.'

Hastily wiping tears away with the back of my hand, I smiled and nodded, knowing I would do anything she asked of me; nothing was too much trouble for this beautiful, fragile woman who had been such a good friend to me in the short time I'd really known her.

'Anything for you, you know that my lovely Lauren.'

'Could you please...if it's not too much trouble...could you occasionally take flowers to Juliette's old house, to leave them where I've always done? It's empty now - abandoned after Kostas left the island - and it's peaceful there; you won't be disturbed. I know it's silly, especially as no one's likely to see those flowers but it's massively important to me. Andreas calls it the House of Horrors, but I've always kind of sensed her presence there. If I send you directions – and Ioanna's number, in case you have any problems finding it – could you please just nip up there when you have some free time and leave her something, from me?'

Struggling to respond without breaking down, my mind blown and my heart shot to bits, I nodded again, replied that of course I would, and then blew her a kiss and waved her goodbye one final time as I watched her make her way on foot slowly back up the mountain path and out of my life.

Chapter 21

Completely and utterly crushed, I immediately took to my bed, shell-shocked and staring into space, the heavy silence only interrupted by further torrents of tears. My heart disintegrated for a second time that day when I heard the noise of tyres crunching on rubble – Andreas' car in slow motion; the sound of Lauren leaving her Greek home forever. She was on her way to the port and would soon be exchanging those emotional goodbyes with Andreas before boarding the ferry to Corfu, while he returned to his farm and his family and tried not to dwell on the hole in his heart by resuming whatever life he had lived before his heart was captured by the absolute loveliness of Lauren.

At some point I must have fallen asleep because I didn't hear his car driving by on the return journey, the passenger seat empty, Andreas making his way home without Lauren.

When a text arrived from her simply saying '*Luv u...take care my lovely Jess*', the tears came again and just wouldn't stop – I was crying, it seemed, for everything and everybody...so much sadness, so much loss.

I cried for the loss of my mum when I was just a young child; I still remembered the way she chuckled and sang to me at bedtime.

I cried for the loss of my dad, who'd been devastated when mum had passed away but who had dedicated his life to bringing me up; I hadn't become a brain surgeon or some massively successful businesswoman or in fact even followed any worthwhile career path, and I didn't have a husband and children and a fantastic house in one of the Manchester suburbs that we'd often driven out to and admired, as we'd sat munching sandwiches in the car together...but I hoped he was still proud of me.

I cried for Christian; for having lost someone who'd genuinely fallen for me in the beginning but who I ultimately hadn't been able to hold on to...and maybe during the time I'd wasted with him, I'd missed out on actually meeting Mr Right.

I cried for Scarlett and her sorry upbringing and all she'd lost when Darren had finally ended their marriage...and for my own loss, when she'd returned to England - and all the fun times we'd shared in our ramshackled house halfway up a mountain became merely fond memories to look back on and cherish.

I cried for Lorry, who I knew would be sailing away from Loulouthia in only a few weeks time, before the weather became more unpredictable and the ferries not so regular. I would miss his friendship and his touchy-feely, protective way and I was sure my life would be much quieter and duller without him.

I cried for the loss of Nikos – because I was absolutely certain I would lose his friendship once I admitted that I had no desire to be his girlfriend or even bed partner. He would cut me loose; that was a given thing. It would be his pride that would stand in the way of us remaining friends...and I'm sure my replacement would be waiting somewhere in the wings, keen to be seen on the arm of this handsome, charming man.

I cried for Alex, Sofia and Andreas...who had been left traumatised by the revelations and the death of their friend – each one of them trying to deal with it in their own way, often badly, but as best as they could. And for Alex's parents who had never recovered from the unexpected departure of their grandson, Lambros, and who had effectively lost a son when they had rid the island of the downright evil that was Kostas.

I cried for Lauren, of course, my other best friend, who was on her way back to England and who was unlikely to ever return to Loulouthia, because it was just too painful for her to live in paradise...where such horrors had taken place and everything reminded her of her guardian angel; where she was consumed by guilt and fury and memories. I hoped she found some kind of peace in England, but leaving the love of her life behind was a heavy price to pay for that peace. And I would miss her so very much and always hope that I would see her again one day.

And most of all I cried for Juliette – a vibrant young woman who had arrived here on holiday, met the man of her dreams who had turned out to be the monster of her nightmares...and who had gone from living her best life to living her absolute worst. A woman who had been treated so badly; who had been on the receiving end of so much physical and mental pain, who had seen a glimpse of freedom and a future but then had it so cruelly ripped from her grasp...and the island had been left a poorer place for her absence. So much loss.

The house had become stifling hot, so I threw open all of the shutters and windows and curled up in a chair outside on the terrace for a short time, watching the ants scurrying about on the tiles, efficiently carting off a precious crumb that I'd missed when I'd been sweeping earlier, while the breeze blew through the house and lowered the temperature indoors. The sun, coupled with the tension, resulted in the mother of all headaches though, so I closed the door again and returned to my bed; lethargic, exhausted, depressed.

'Jess! Just Jess! Where are you, my darling?'

I awoke to the sound of Alex's instantly recognisable voice on the terrace, and a glance at the time on my mobile phone told me why he was here; I was astonished to see it was already nine-thirty and my shift at Sunrise should have started two and a half hours earlier. It appeared I'd also missed several calls from someone at the bar, presumably ringing to see where I was and if there was a problem.

Yes, there was a big problem...in fact there were lots of little problems that made up a huge, complex, insurmountable one and right now I didn't particularly want to see or speak to anyone, so I ignored Alex when he persistently called out my name.

The rattle of the front door as it opened signified that I hadn't locked it earlier when I'd briefly been out on the terrace; I quickly pulled the sheet up over my body and drew my knees up to my chest as I heard Alex close the door behind him and his familiar footsteps as he searched the house for me. It didn't take him long; it was a very small house.

'Just Jess! You are there...my goodness, are you okay? We were worried about you and I am the search party, sent to see if you are sick or need help...because you did not show up for work, and that is not the Jessica we know and love.'

Yes, good old Jess...infinitely reliable and eternally single...that was definitely me.

'I'm fine, Alex,' I said, although I clearly wasn't. 'Please, go back to the bar as Sofia will be struggling on her own...and pass on my apologies that I couldn't make it in tonight...because...something unexpectedly came up.'

'Sofia is not in the bar tonight; she is...busy. Young Demitris from the bakery is keeping two eyes on it for me, in exchange for a beer, so all is well.'

'It's 'one eye' Alex, not 'two eyes', and is Demitris even old enough to be behind a bar?'

'No! Of course not, but he is a good boy; he will not rob me blind. And the policeman...he is...distracted, shall we say...with an Australian widow, who has a purse full of money and big, bouncy breasts...so he will not bother us tonight.'

Even through my sadness, Alex always managed to raise a smile, but it didn't last long as I remembered why I was feeling so blue and found myself blurting out, 'She's gone Alex. Lauren has left; she's returned to England and I just can't cope with it all – first Scarlett, then Lauren, and soon it will be Lorry, unless I give him a reason to stay...it's just all too sad for words and, I know I have friends here, but it's not the same, and Lauren's departure tonight has changed everything for me.'

Ignoring my request that he return to the bar, Alex sat gently down on the end of my bed, removed his sunglasses and sighed.

'I am sorry that Lauren has chosen to leave; I know you will miss her terribly. We all will. I saw Andreas drive past the bar earlier and he was speeding and all over the road – very out of character for him, as you know. I did wonder if there was something wrong. He will be devastated that Lauren has gone – she was his world and he will be truly lost without her...although I am surprised she stayed as long as she did.'

'I know about Juliette. She told me everything.' The words were out before I could stop them; hopefully Lauren didn't mind me raising the subject - she had been enraged that Juliette's existence seemed to have blotted out from the history of the island...so perhaps she would be glad I was actually talking about her.

I wasn't expecting what came next. Initially, there was a lightning flash of anger in Alex's eyes, but this was quickly followed by the colour draining from his face, as he squeezed his eyes shut and a low moan escaped from his throat.

'Juliette.' He said her name then, almost in a whisper and, shielding his face with his hands, he began to cry quietly into his palms; his shoulders shaking as the pain he masked seeped out and presented itself before my very eyes.

My own pain forgotten for a moment, I closed the space between us and gently removed his hands from his face, locking my eyes on to his, where I saw a glimpse of the agony he had been through and the overwhelming guilt that was festering away inside of him.

Still holding his large hands in my own relatively small ones, I whispered, 'Tell me about Juliette. I've heard a lot from Lauren today about her...but tell me what she was to you.'

Halting from time to time, to catch his breath or swallow a sob, he opened up then and described this young woman to me; a woman who was beautiful inside and out, and who'd reminded him of Kylie Minogue as she was so dainty but sparky; this woman who'd caught the eye of his confident, party-loving brother, who'd never settled down, having supposedly been abandoned by his Irish girlfriend many years earlier, when she'd apparently just disappeared off the island with his son one day, never to return.

'Keeley seemed like a nice girl...he met her on Corfu and brought her back here...but she kept herself to herself and didn't seem to want to integrate. So, we weren't particularly close to her...and we didn't see much of young Lambros really but he was a gorgeous chubby, little boy, and my parents worshipped him; their first grandson. They were devastated when all contact was lost and even now they keep his framed photograph in a drawer in their bedroom.'

He went on to paint a picture of a brother who he had hero-worshipped but who had transformed into a real ladies man, who'd spent more time trying to impress the girls than he did mucking in on his parents' smallholding or working in the bar that his father had originally opened in the 1970s; responsibilities that he should have shouldered being the elder son, but which instead fell to Alex, on top of looking after his own family and trying to earn enough to keep them all fed and clothed. Kostas seemed to get away with everything, was held accountable for nothing and was the apple of his mum's eye – but Alex understood; she'd lost two babies prior to delivering Kostas and his had been the treasured miracle birth. Alex had been the unexpected but very welcome younger brother who they adored, particularly as he was the baby of the family, but he didn't possess the same ability to be able to charm his way out of a tricky situation or dodge putting in a full day's work – not that he would ever want to. What you saw what was basically what you got with Alex – equally as handsome but kind and thoughtful, hardworking and straightforward.

'When Juliette arrived, her love of life enhanced all of *our* lives, and it was a joy to see her together with Kostas; they looked like any other couple who were in the first throes of love and we truly thought she would be the making of him. We became a tight unit – myself and Sofia, Andreas and Lauren, and Kostas and Juliette, and we had great fun together...so many memories made. When Kostas moved out of the family home and rented a house with Juliette out in the stacks – sorry, *sticks* - even though they were only probably fifteen minutes away, we didn't see so much of them. He extracted himself from our family business and rented a building in Skafos, transforming it into a sports bar and he and Juliette were there most of the time. We just figured he was trying to prove himself; to make an independent life for them both. And we were so busy in Sunrise and with the restaurant...and Lauren and Andreas were occupied of course, holding down jobs with long hours, as well as working on the land and taking care of their animals. But it was all to be expected during the crazy summer months...so we did not suspect a thing.'

He paused then, struggling to contain his emotions as he remembered the circumstances he would prefer to forget.

'Go on,' I whispered, squeezing his hands, encouraging him to let go.

'When we visited the bar and he said she was sick at home, we did not think anything of it – people become unwell, particularly when they work such long hours in the summer months without a break. When we heard...about the accident...we could not believe it! How could this have happened to Juliette? We were broken-hearted by her death...but what came next – we struggled to take it all in. Kostas seemed genuinely devastated at the time; he was my brother and I believed him – we didn't realise what a good actor he was back then – but when Lauren burst in and screamed, and shouted, and produced this awful, sickening picture of

Juliette taken on her phone, and my mother collapsed and was rushed to hospital...it broke my family apart and I think I did not treat Lauren so well...'

'It's understandable...you were in shock...'

'My mother was so sick and my father was horrified...and I could not get this image of Juliette, with her beautiful face, all smashed in, out of my mind, nor the haunted look in her eyes. Every time I closed my own eyes I saw her cuts and bruises and look of despair. Once I knew my mother was off the danger list, we went to see Kostas at the bar and it immediately became apparent that he had deceived us all; that he was indeed guilty of such heinous crimes and had been covering up his actions. He was showing off and behaving very strangely and was not a man in mourning...and then Lauren arrived. She yelled that he'd been saying terrible things about Juliette...and I knew *she* was telling the truth. Like a woman possessed, she lunged at him and he retaliated by immediately grabbing her by the throat – if I'd had any doubts before, then that one violent action told me everything I needed to know about my brother, who'd conned everyone into thinking he was a good, decent man.'

Alex went on to describe how he had caught hold of Kostas and belted the living daylights out of him; how he, with the assistance of his poor father, had dragged him home and how his parents ultimately decided that turfing him off the island with as much money as they could give him, was the best course of action to take, to keep everyone else safe and to try to hush up the scandal as much as was possible.

'I feel in my heart that it was a bad choice...that he should have been imprisoned for what he did...but I had to comply with the wishes of my parents. They were truly devastated about losing Juliette and thoroughly ashamed that their own son could have beaten and tormented her...but on this island, in this small community, to have a good name is everything. My parents could not have survived if everyone knew and blamed them; and if Kostas had stayed here then there would only be one of two outcomes – one of us would have murdered him, for sure, or, he may possibly have been arrested, charged and jailed for what he did – and that would have killed my mother. They had to do what was best for them, even though it broke their hearts...and Yiorgos, Sofia and I were all they had left, and I couldn't put them through anything more.'

How this generous, fun-loving man had managed to contain all of this anguish inside of him without the mask ever slipping, I would never know. Bridging the gap between us, I cradled him in my arms as he cried and I tried my utmost to reassure him.

'You did what you could, faced with horrendous circumstances. You were...you *are* a good son and you did your best, even though you yourself were in so much pain and your wife was absolutely distraught. You lost Juliette and you lost your brother...and you ultimately lost the friendship of Lauren and Andreas, which was tough for you all.'

'I felt so guilty, Just Jess. I couldn't look at Lauren, knowing she blamed me for not uncovering the truth before it was too late and for allowing Kostas to flee the island. And of course Andreas wanted to protect Lauren and would always be on her side, so he had to keep his distance. I can't bring Juliette back though, Jess...and I despise myself for what happened to her...'

'No! Don't you dare blame yourself! Kostas, he's just scum...nothing more. *I* hate the man and I've never even met him. You know what, I kind of want him to return to the island so *I* can make him fucking pay for what he did.'

'Don't say that Jessica! I don't want him to come back...for many reasons...not least that if you saw him – if you looked at us side by side - I fear you would hate me too. We are so alike, you see...Kostas and I...and you would despise me for it...and that I could not bear.'

My hand automatically reached up to tenderly stroke his face – the face of an honest, decent man who had been so kind to me – and I quietly said, 'I could never hate you Alex. You are YOU, not your brother, and there is such kindness in your eyes; such goodness in your soul. Right from the outset, you and Sofia have been so protective and caring towards me and I will be forever grateful and always feel such love for you both. Don't you worry - if Kostas was stood by your side right now, the difference would be blindingly obvious – because he...HE is NOTHING...and YOU...you are EVERYTHING.'

As I wiped away his tears, I hoped my words would reassure him that he could not be blamed for the actions of his brother and that they were worlds apart.

He gently kissed me on my forehead, said 'Thank you, Just Jessica – you are a very special person,' and in that moment I felt such deep affection for this strong man, who had been almost beaten down by the consequences of his brother's actions, but who had come up fighting. However, the events of that evening had truly shaken me up, and I had arrived at a decision, and I wanted Alex to be the first to know.

'I'm returning to England, Alex. With Scarlett gone and Lauren's unexpected departure...I think it's a clear sign that I should go too. Lorry will also be leaving soon, although if I just gave him the nod, I know he'd stay...but I can't; it wouldn't be fair on him. And I can kiss goodbye to Nikos when I tell him I just want to be his friend, and nothing more. So...I think the best thing I can do is to pack up and return to the half-life I had in Manchester. You've all been so good to me...but you and Sofia have each other...the other English and Irish girls are flying home from Corfu towards the end of the season...and it's not as if I'm Greek – despite

170

the connection I feel to this island and its people; that I've always felt in my heart. What's the point in being alone here, just surviving, when I can be alone back in the UK, picking up the pieces of my former life? I've just been kidding myself Alex...I don't belong here – I never have - and it will be a long, lonely winter by myself. It's been a beautiful summer; one I'll always remember...but I think it's high time I accepted that it's over.'

'No, Jess! No, no, no! You *do* belong here; you are an honorary Greek! With your dark curls and your even darker eyes, accompanied by your spectacular tan, you look like a local now! I promise you my darling, you are accepted and loved by everyone who has met you on this island and I think that here you have finally found your home. It could never have worked out with the child-like Lawrence of Arabia and definitely not the money man, Tom Jones, because you did not feel in your heart that it was right...and they did not deserve to be loved by you!'

He was suddenly quite forceful, and it was his turn to reach out to trace the outline of my face with his fingers, as he pleaded with me to remain on the island.

'Please stay, Jess, please,' he begged softly. 'There is so much more you do not know...and maybe the right man for you is already here on Loulouthia. Trust me when I say, nothing is as it seems.'

Hadn't Lauren said something similar to me earlier? What the bloody hell was going on, here on this docile, snoozy little island? How many more secrets had been squirreled away? How many more confessions were to come? Who did I really know here?

'Please don't go, Just Jess, I beg you. It would make me so sad if you were to leave, when you have only just begun to settle here, now you have finally found a place to call home. Your heart is on Loulouthia and so your life should be. Please darling. Please stay.'

Chapter 22

I stayed.

Alex was extremely persuasive, even cajoling me into returning to the bar with him to speak to Sofia, although they both insisted I remained on the other side of it as a punter, rather than a member of staff, on this exhausting evening. There was a hushed conversation between the two of them, and I guessed Alex was informing Sofia that Lauren had departed and that I knew all about Juliette.

When she joined me later for a cocktail, she simply said, 'Juliette was a lovely girl. And we are all culpable in our own way. But life goes on, for us, and we have to make the most of that life and not squander it because of one vicious, pathetic little man. I do not want to talk about him, because he is a disgusting waste of breath, and you must not dwell on the situation. So, today has been a difficult day for you and tonight you will drink and be sad...but tomorrow you will pick yourself up...unwind on the beach for a few hours...and we will party in the bar into the night, and you will laugh until your face and belly aches! Okay, Jessica?'

Okay.

Surviving without Lauren's support and friendship seemed impossible, but I did it. She texted regularly; she seemed relatively happy and certainly relieved to be back in the bosom of her family, and she had of course visited Juliette's final resting place to pay her respects, feeling a sense of peace and positivity that she just hadn't been able to capture on Loulouthia. Coping without Andreas was another matter altogether; her heart was shattered and she still loved him as much as she ever had, and wished more than anything that he could have made the move to England with her.

Andreas looked thoroughly downcast and lost without Lauren and, after Sofia expressed her concern about his gaunt, haunted appearance, Apostolis practically dragged him into the bar as he was passing, challenging him to a few games of backgammon with the oldies. Alex also regularly disappeared off up the mountain to sip tiny measures of the strongest ouzo imaginable with Andreas, to ensure he didn't disappear completely off the radar. If nothing else, tensions seemed to have eased between the two old friends and it was heart-warming to watch Alex embrace Andreas and shove a plate of complimentary *Calamari* under his nose or all but force-feed him a portion of *Beef Stifado* and home-made chips in a quiet corner of the restaurant.

It was getting to the stage where Sofia was more absent from the bar than present...but we'd also gone past the point where I felt able to ask where the bleeding hell she was disappearing to several times a week. She didn't *look* ill, so I'd come to the conclusion that she was either disguising it well or was taking off to Corfu or the mainland on a regular basis to dabble in a spot of money laundering. Maybe she had mafia connections – who knew? Despite my close bond with the couple, I felt too embarrassed to ask as so much time had elapsed and no one was volunteering any information.

Most nights it was just me and Alex running the bar; we were silly and we were naughty and we had an absolute ball; I didn't think I'd ever laughed so much in my life, which was a welcome relief after Lauren's revelations and the fast-flowing river of tears. Alex was most definitely the host with the most and people were just drawn to the bar from all around the island, and we were constantly run off our happy feet.

At the end of each shift we would retire to the beach, to share a well-earned beer, or often a large Baileys on the rocks, and we would chat late into the night about our younger years, including the antics we got up to as teenagers. On one occasion he even brought a few old photographs from his parents' home to show me, presumably so I could take the piss out of him and his longer swept back hair or his Fruit of the Loom pink t-shirt. It would appear Sofia had always been a glamourpuss though, even in her teens and twenties – I'm guessing I wouldn't have looked quite so hot in the same red boob tube and white palazzo trousers; some lucky sods are just born with those genes, I suppose. It was funny to see Andreas as a gawky teenager in jam jar glasses and also a younger Yiorgos who was a right little chubber before he hit puberty.

One particular photograph amongst the eye-opening collection hit me like a ton of bricks, completely taking my breath away. Shoved carelessly into a photo wallet, there was a crumpled, dog-eared picture which had obviously been taken in more recent years; it showed a group of happy, smiling, seemingly carefree adults – arms around each other, faces glowing, eyes shining. Alex and Sofia, Andreas and Lauren, Kostas and Juliette.

Juliette was everything Alex and Lauren had described her as and more – so very pretty and waif-like in stature; her almost white-blonde hair, which was scooped up in a messy ponytail, absolutely shone, her eyes sparkled and she was sporting a mega-watt smile, dressed in a baggy checked shirt over a tiny camisole top, denim shorts revealing toned, tanned legs. God love her, she looked like the sort of best friend everyone needed – lucky Lauren. And there, beside her was Kostas, also smiling, but even then holding on to her firmly and proprietarily – as if she was a possession; something he owned that he could treat how he saw fit.

Out of the corner of my eye I saw Alex swallow as he caught sight of the picture – he'd clearly been unaware that the photo had been tucked into the wallet or else he would probably have disposed of it...or at the very least torn Kostas right off the corner or defaced it in some other way.

As I tentatively placed my hand onto his bare arm, I felt him flinch under my touch and immediately knew what was bothering him.

'It's okay, Alex,' I whispered. 'You have a look of each other but that's where the similarity ends. Your eyes are kind, respectful and warm and your smile is genuine and lights up the room. Kostas has a smug, privileged look about him; a smile on his mouth that doesn't transmit to his eyes, which are cold and hard. You are a handsome, wonderful man whilst he is a fake, unfeeling lowlife. You could never be mistaken for him; I've seen him now and it hasn't changed my opinion of you or altered my feelings for you at all...so you have to let it go, and hope that one day he will come up against the wrong person and finally get what he deserves. In the meantime, I propose a toast to Juliette...for the incredible person that she was and for the incredible way she made everyone around her feel. Let's raise our glasses and send her all our love, wherever she is now – pain free and at peace for always.'

'Yes, let's,' Alex replied, picking up his glass and clinking it against mine. 'To Juliette...until we meet again.'

'To Juliette. And tomorrow I'm going to make a special trip up to the house where she last lived...to leave flowers on behalf of Lauren. In a way, it seems rather odd to be visiting a place of so much suffering, but Lauren specifically asked me to do it, because it's somewhere she felt closer to Juliette...and the flowers left there and at the port are important to Lauren, because she wants to ensure that Juliette will never, ever be forgotten on this island.'

'I will take you, Just Jess,' responded Alex in a gruff voice, crammed full of emotion.

'No, no. I don't want to put you to any trouble or resurrect all those painful memories for you. My only intention is to fulfil my promise to Lauren and pay my respects to this wonderful lady who I had never had the good fortune to meet.'

'No. I insist. I will drive you, but I will wait in the car. It would take you hours to get there if you travel by bus and then I think you will collapse if you have to walk up that very steep hill in the sweltering heat. So don't argue, Just Jess; it will only take us fifteen minutes by car...and I *want* to take you and need to keep *you* safe from harm.'

And so he became my driver for the day...and I was relieved in the end because where Juliette had lived was way out 'in the stacks', as Alex would say...beyond Skafos and all of the low-lying villages, and then up some ridiculously steep, barely passable track you could hardly call a road, where the goats wandered about as if they owned the place and it felt like time had stood still. I'm not even sure I would have found the house by myself, despite Lauren's comprehensive instructions.

When Alex stopped the car at the end of the track and switched off the engine, he seemed too choked to say anything but indicated instead that I should follow the somewhat overgrown pathway which forked to the left and then disappeared out of sight. Rather than allowing me to purchase flowers from a shop, Alex had insisted on picking a selection from his mother's garden, and I was touched that he had gone to the trouble, feeling sure that Juliette would appreciate the personal touch.

If I stuck to the centre of the path, it was easier under foot, where the weeds had been slightly flattened down by a previous visitor, who I could only assume had been Lauren, because I couldn't imagine that anyone else would have wanted to venture up there. The pathway led to a huge jungle of a garden, in the centre of which was a single-storey house that had clearly had no tenants since Juliette and Kostas, as it was in a sorry state and clearly uninhabitable. Through the mass of weeds and wildflowers, I could just about make out that the door was ajar and a window was broken, but it appeared the property was currently only occupied by chickens, who freely wandered in and out, clucking and crapping - probably highly delighted with their detached luxury abode.

The contents of the garden more or less obscured the detail of the house but I shivered involuntarily as my eyes darted around, taking in what I could, as I recalled some of the atrocities that Lauren had relayed to me - how much suffering and fear there had been within these walls.

I wondered where on earth Lauren had laid her flowers amongst all of these weeds but then remembered her instructions that I should look for a narrow opening round the back of the abandoned bee hives – thankfully no swarms of bees around to descend upon me – and then follow the even narrower path round to the rear of the house where I would find a tree with a swing seat, which had been Juliette's favourite place here to sit and daydream, when she was allowed out for good behaviour.

Swatting away the bugs and flying insects that were determined to zoom in and lodge themselves in my ear canal, I made my way round and gasped as I almost stumbled across the said tree and the many, many flowers that had been laid beneath it and were decomposing into the surrounding earth. Adding my own flowers to the mix, I nervously sat myself down on the rickety old swing seat and gently swayed back and forward as I tried to say a few words.

'You don't know me, Juliette, but I've heard so much about you – all good, by the way – that I *feel* I know you; you had such an impact on the life of everyone who met you. I'm assured that you were an amazing girl – one of a kind – and I'm so sorry we never met in person but maybe one day, in another life, we could be friends. In the meantime, I'm here to deliver some pretty little flowers that Alex picked for you this morning, on behalf of Lauren, who's unfortunately had to return to England. It seems a bit daft – me, sat here talking to fresh air - but I made a promise...and I promise, with all of my heart, you will never be forgotten here. Just because they don't talk about you so much, I can tell you, you're never far from their thoughts...they're just struggling to find the right words and trying to muddle on with their lives as best they can. So...anyway...Lauren, Alex, Sofia and Andreas all send their love and I'd like you to have a little of mine too.'

I hoped she could hear me, wherever she was. I hoped she knew how loved she was.

Easing myself off the seat, I brushed dust and dirt off my white shorts, and used a scrunched up tissue to wipe away the line of perspiration that had formed above my top lip.

'I'd better go now, as Alex is waiting for me, and I know it's taken a lot for him to come up here today. Goodbye, Juliette. Sleep well.'

I couldn't stay long – the place was strange and eerie and I'm sure Juliette wouldn't have wanted me to be scared shitless, hanging around, expecting someone to pounce on me at any moment. Taking one last look at the house, I decided I was glad that it was surrounded by wildflowers - Juliette had apparently loved *loulouthia* – the island and the flowers - and it was kind of a fitting tribute that the place had been taken over by them, and not forgetting Mr and Mrs Chicken and all their extended family.

Climbing back into the car, relieved to be in Alex's company again, I thanked him for bringing me and spontaneously gave him a hug – he looked in great need of one.

'You know Alex, although Lauren's intentions were good...she shouldn't have been making the pilgrimage up here all of the time. Christ, this place smacks of misery and despair. I do think there should be some permanent tribute to Juliette here on the island though...then the locals will *never* be able to forget her, and the tourists will also ask, 'Who was this Juliette?'...and we can tell them - she was a wonderful woman, who did oodles of good...but who was taken too soon. What do you think Alex? Shouldn't we have something positive to commemorate her life rather than remain forever bitter and angry, stuck in a permanent state of mourning?'

'You have become so wise, Just Jess,' Alex reached out and gently squeezed my forearm, smiling for the first time since I'd met up with him that day. 'Yes, that seems like a much more fitting tribute...we will get our heads together and have a bit of a storm-brain.'

'That's great...I'll speak to Lauren about it. And it's 'brainstorm', just so you know.'

We sat in comfortable silence for most of the way back to Chaliki, until I asked him, 'Alex, if you don't mind me asking, what was your celebrity nickname for Juliette? Or didn't she have one?'

'But of course she did! She was Juliette Lewis – after the famous actress – although Kostas did not like this – I think, because it was NOT a name that HE had given her...it was something he could not control. I ignored him and still used it anyway...and Sofia made a point of using it ALL of the time because she knew it grated on his nerves! Although after our beautiful friend died, somehow it did not seem right. We only called her Juliette then - nothing more.'

'Oh, okay. I see why. Maybe it would have felt disrespectful to use her nickname so soon after her death. But do you know what? I think we should revert to calling her Juliette Lewis now...enough time has passed. Everyone here always adores their nickname and I'm guessing it probably made her smile...and if HE hated it, then surely that's a bonus. Let's do it to piss him off, in his absence! And that lovely woman will smile down on us from heaven every time she hears us say those words.'

'Yes, of course...that's a brilliant idea! She will always and forever be Juliette Lewis and from now on we will only smile when we think of her. No more grief. No more tears. Thank you Just Jess...for helping to shift the fog and allowing me to see clearly for the first time since that darkest of days; for making me see that while we have lost Juliette, we still have our lives to live and we can incorporate our memories of her in everything we do. It is truly liberating and I feel like we should be going somewhere now to celebrate in some small way but alas, I'm afraid we must return to Chaliki to open up the bar, before all of our thirsty customers stage a riot!'

*

A few days later, I found myself sat side by side with Lorry on a sun lounger looking out to the sea, as I took a breather from the bar and grabbed the bull by the horns; forcing myself to stop being so cowardly and to have 'the talk' with him. He'd arrived a couple of hours earlier with the annoying Australian guys, and also a group of hyper young girls, all sassy and stunning and skimpily dressed. One in particular had draped herself all over Lorry, and there was no way in hell I could compete with this flame-haired, bronzed, leggy beauty – not that I had any inclination to even try – and yet, incomprehensibly, Lorry's eyes still looked at me longingly and eagerly, hoping today might just be the day I changed my mind.

It was time to be cruel to be kind; only fair to put the poor lad out of his misery, so I led him out to the beach and told him that although I'd loved hanging out with him all summer, and that I'd always treasure our friendship and the memories, it didn't feel right to take it any further, so the kisses and the handholding and all the other stuff would have to stop. He looked at me sadly and said that it was a 'real shame' – because he apparently knew in his heart and in his pants we could have been great together, and then asked if it is was because of Nikos.

'Naw,' I replied, shaking my head, which created a welcome draft underneath the curls closest to my neck. 'He's also a nice guy and, like your good self, is incredibly handsome, but he's not right for me either. And, I have to confess, from time to time I still see Tom Jones, the Welsh singer, gyrating in front of me, rather than Nikos, the Greek businessman - and that's never good.'

We both smiled and then Lorry tenderly reached out and stroked my hair for one last time as he said, 'I'm sorry it didn't work out between us, but it's been a blast, Jess. I hope you find what you're looking for here – whether that's a man or just a brand spanking new life to live. I would have stayed, you know, if you'd asked me to...but never mind. Just please take good care and always be true to yourself...because you're amazing, you are, with so many special qualities and the kindest of hearts. I'll always remember you. Be happy, Jess.'

It truly was one of the longest speeches I'd ever heard Lorry make. Lovely, sweet, funny, adorable Lorry whose smile would always light up my memories and whose friendship I would miss when he was gone.

We were just reminiscing about experiences we'd shared over the summer - such as the time Lorry had ordered egg fried rice at the new Chinese restaurant in Town, and rice had indeed been delivered to the table...but with a greasy fried egg sat proudly on top – a slightly different interpretation of the dish than we were used to back home - when the flame-haired, beautiful person popped her head out of the bar and shouted, 'Hey! Lorry! The Greek dancing's just beginning and I think I'll need to hold on to you to if I'm going to keep up with the steps in these killer heels!'

'Go on,' I smiled, as I saw him practically slavering at the mouth, eyeing up her tiny bikini-like top and miniscule orange hot pants. 'Go and do your worst...and show your new friend a good time!' I knew his single bed would be full that night, and they would probably have lots of amazing, orgasmic sex, but I honestly didn't mind.

'Thanks Jess,' he said, leaning forward to give me one last brotherly kiss on the cheek before sloping off into the bar, wiggling his bum for effect and making me laugh out loud in the process. He was a cheeky bugger, and I loved him for it, as a friend.

Nikos was next on my list. He had requested that I join him at his massive crib to share an evening meal and, reading between the lines, quite possibly a bed. Fumbling around for decent excuses, I told him I had to stand in for Sofia at the bar (not entirely untrue) so could only manage a quick catch-up, and after a few tuts and shrugs of the shoulders, he reluctantly agreed to meet me in Town for a coffee.

His mask of confidence slipped a little as I told him that I was sorry, but I could offer him no more than friendship. He swirled the dregs of his coffee round in the cup a few times, cleared his throat and finally said, 'Jessica...beautiful Jessica...if we cannot be lovers then yes, we must be friends.'

He hadn't demanded reasons why not or seemed interested in continuing the conversation further. In fact, he then proceeded to make his own excuses and left quick smart, kissing me on both cheeks whilst saying, 'Yes, we must meet up for a coffee again, one day soon.'

I smiled at him sadly as I watched him go; we would never be friends. His ego had taken a real battering and I would be lucky if I got a quick nod of the head if I passed him in the street in the future. A shame really – I liked him a lot and I would miss his charming ways and wicked sense of humour...although not his Tom Jones wardrobe and his curly grey wig. It didn't bear thinking about, what his *downstairs* body hair would look like. Eugh.

The island resorts were winding down in September, even though the season wasn't due to officially end until the last week in October, and I could almost hear the collective sigh of relief from the workers as the tourist numbers dropped dramatically and family life in and around their homes beckoned.

Lukas returned to Albania – we knocked back a few too many farewell drinks together late one night – and, as the latest in a long-line of waitresses packed her crappy job in and buggered off back to Scotland, Tassos was forced to close his restaurant doors for the season. It was a bloody good job I'd found a decent pizzeria in Town to grab my fortnightly fix of a large deep pan and small garlic baguette. I often passed Tassos on the street and was actually now able to greet him politely without wanting to wring his scrawny neck, so that was progress, but I'd think twice before dining in his restaurant next year for fear of him tampering with my grub.

A few of the other seasonal staff had already departed and it really felt that summer was finally coming to an end; everyone was exhausted and burnt out and definitely ready for some much needed peace and quiet – although I'd been warned that the freedom of the winter season was really a double-edged sword.

On the one hand there was time to travel further afield to visit the secluded bays and historic earthquake remains, and also the few remaining restaurants and bars which stayed open in the winter for the locals. Families would be reunited and able to celebrate Name Days and religious festivals and enjoy quiet nights at home in front of their log burners. The men were free to go off hunting and fishing and the women seemed genuinely pleased that they would be able to get their houses in order again – painted, fixed up and thoroughly cleaned. In many households it was like travelling back in time, when Man went off to catch something for dinner...while Woman was chained to the kitchen sink...but everyone seemed happy with their lot and feminism was almost a dirty word in these Greek island communities.

On the other hand, no work meant no or very little real income and by early spring locals were itching to return to their businesses again; to repair any damage caused by winter storms and to paint, plan and count down the days until the first bunch of tourists arrived on the island, and the whole cycle began again.

Hotel Diana was due to close during the first week of October so I made the most of the pool facilities there while I could, taking a refreshing dip at lunchtime most days. Lauren's replacement was a smiley young Greek girl whose manners and appearance were impeccable, but I missed gossiping with my fabulous friend as I perched on a stool at the bar, knocking back an ice cold bottle of beer or wolfing down a Chicken Club Sandwich as she skived off her reception duties, pretending to be on the hunt for a particular hotel guest or member of staff.

The days were still relatively hot and sunny but the nights had turned rather chilly and I was glad of the multitude of cardigans that Scarlett had left behind. We even had a day or two of rain – not so good for the tourists but most welcome by the locals and workers – and it was on a wet Wednesday in the middle of October that I caught a bus down to the port and said my goodbyes to Lorry.

He seemed to have hooked up with the flame-haired stunner over the last couple of weeks so he was leaving with a huge grin on his face. We hugged for a long time, promised we'd never forget each other and I waved him off from dry land as the ferry eased away from Loulouthia. There were no tears; I had a little lump in my throat but I was alright. I was just happy that I'd met him and, whilst I didn't think he had a long-term future with the young redhead, I hoped he would find true love back in England, or wherever he ended up. We hadn't said we would keep in touch and I didn't think I would see him again – Loulouthia had been a chapter of his life that was firmly closed now and he was moving on, whereas this island was the whole book for me, and I didn't want a sequel that took me elsewhere.

As the bars and businesses closed around us, Sunrise remained open until the very end. As Alex explained, there were still a very small number of tourists left in the resort and it was hardly fair for them to have nowhere to eat and drink - although the restaurant menu had now become limited as ingredients ran out and weren't replaced. And if we stayed open, we made a little money, which was better than none – especially when everywhere else was shut – and of course Alex and Sofia didn't have any rent to pay, as it was their property on their land, inherited from Alex's grandfather.

My birthday rolled around quietly but I shied from mentioning it to anyone; that just wasn't me. Not wanting to make a fuss or be cast in the limelight, I'd decided to treat it like any other day – let's face it, there were worse places you could be when you turned thirty-nine - except I'd promised to treat myself to a coffee and a pastry at one of the harbour-side cafes before splashing out on a new dress from a tiny little boutique I'd spotted down a narrow alleyway at the rear of the museum. I suppose I could have requested a night off from work, but it would have seemed fairly pointless as Sunrise would be the best place to hang out on my birthday and, besides, I didn't want to be completely alone all day and night.

However, after an early morning wake-up call from an out-of-tune Scarlett warbling the Happy Birthday song and demanding to know why I hadn't yet received the present she'd packaged up and sent over (my experience of the postal system thus far told me I could expect it to arrive in approximately another three to five weeks), I then received a lengthy text from Sofia, giving me a real dressing down because I'd tried to keep quiet about my big day – apparently Scarlett had messaged her earlier to spill the beans after she'd suspected I hadn't told a soul on the island, and she wasn't having that.

Refusing to let the day pass without me doing *something* of significance, Sofia insisted that I join them for lunch at their house, and although it was a change to my plans, I had to admit I was quite excited. I'd never been there before and I was looking forward to checking out their home if it was every bit as perfect and polished as Sofia was. I fired off a quick 'Love to!' response and mentally searched my wardrobe for something suitable to wear – my favourite whimsy, flimsy floral dress would be ideal for a celebration lunch with friends.

I'd just stepped out of the shower when my lovely Lauren rang to wish me Many Happy Returns; it was good to hear her voice and it didn't seem like she and Scarlett were so far away after all, and I basked in the warmth of their love and friendship. I had expected a cool reception from Lauren once I mentioned the invitation to spend lunch with Sofia and Alex but, to my surprise, she merely ordered me to have a wonderful time and said that I should allow myself to be spoiled, for once in my life.

The house was smaller than I was expecting – only one storey - but it was definitely perfectly formed and was painted in a dusky pale pink colour on the outside and decorated beautifully and tastefully inside. It was approached by a long (and winding) road, lined with other houses of all shapes and sizes and the area had the feel of a quintessential Greek village, particularly with the beautiful old church stood proud at the top of the hill, and the small, dilapidated shop set back from the road, where someone's granddad slouched outside, sipping ouzo and swinging his worry beads around, while the sheep wandered around him.

The modest-sized house was fronted by a huge balcony; a large plastic table stood at one end, surrounded by a multitude of chairs, one of which was occupied by a tiny black kitten who appeared to be in a deep sleep, but I had no doubt he or she would spring at me if I ventured too near. The table was protected by a citrus fruit patterned, wipe-clean covering and had a vase of pretty pink flowers in the centre of it. Six places had been set for lunch.

Of course! I had expected Yiorgos to be there, but not Alex's parents, which was silly of me, as it was their house after all, and the Greeks were all about family. I initially expected the atmosphere to be tense as I thought I would struggle to hide my distaste as to how they had handled the whole Juliette and Kostas situation, but the old couple were so lovely and welcoming and I thought, my god, Alex's mum was so small and fragile-looking; how painful it must have been for her, to lose two babies, for her grandson to be snatched away for his own safety, to deal with Juliette's sudden death and to lose another son in the process. Fragile, but with an inner strength it would seem.

They both spoke little English so it was a bloody good job I'd been practising my Greek, and they seemed genuinely delighted that I'd been putting in the effort and could tentatively attempt some conversation with them. I just hoped it wasn't like the time Scarlett went to the butcher's in Town and mistakenly ordered two kilos of liver instead of just enough to fry up with onion gravy for our tea. We stored some of it in our tiny freezer compartment but the remainder had been left to fester and stink in our fridge until we'd had no choice but to throw it away. It had put me off liver for life. Mind you, it didn't help that Scarlett kept referring to it as the 'placenta in the refrigerator'. Bleugh.

Thankfully no liver that day; it was a simple but tasty meal of *pastitsio,* with Greek salad and Village Sausage and 'greens', which were delicious, although I'd been shocked to find out they were basically just weeds. It was to be hoped they'd been bloody washed properly first – there were an awful lot of cats and other species wandering about on this island. Anyway, they'd all put me at ease and I really felt like a proper local now.

When Yiorgos nipped over the fields to feed the assortment of animals and Alex accompanied his father on a short stroll down the road - where I suspected his father smoked a crafty fag - Sofia disappeared inside to the bathroom and I was left alone with this dignified and gentle old lady. Smiling, hesitantly, I offered to take the dishes into the kitchen to clear up but she startled me by suddenly catching hold of my arm and saying, in a raspy voice, in broken English, 'Kostas...my son...is bad man. Juliette...good girl. Very good. Lauren...she say I forget...but I never forget. I always remember. Always.' She placed her hand on her heart and I was horrified to see tears slip from her eyes and instinctively reached out to tentatively touch her other hand.

'I know,' was all I could say. 'I know.'

As if the moment had never happened, she quickly wiped away her tears, clapped her hands together and said, 'Cake!' and then disappeared into her kitchen, leaving me wondering how she knew that *I* knew. Had Alex or Sofia mentioned something? Perhaps she'd heard on the grapevine that Lauren and I had become firm friends and had figured it out for herself. How decent of this lady to stand up and admit that Kostas was a thug, when he was her own flesh and blood. The woman had a backbone, that was for sure.

When the others returned we shared a huge, homemade chocolate cake, which had more than a hint of coffee in the sponge, and I had a feeling I would be twitching all night rather than sleeping after the heavy caffeine intake. It was delicious though – a very special kind of birthday cake - and when it was time to go, I thanked the old couple profusely and promised I would be back again to visit them soon.

Surprise number two came in the form of a small gathering that had been hastily organised for me at Sunrise later that evening. Most of the attendees were locals, already wrapped up in their multi-layers as if they were about to embark on a mission to the North Pole, but there were a handful of workers and a few end of season tourists who'd we had some fun with throughout that week. It was a bit raucous and very loud but a good time was had by all, and when I was handed a beautifully wrapped gift (paper, bows etc courtesy of Sofia, I should imagine) and opened the box to reveal a pair of exquisite gold earrings, in the shape of two tiny scrolls, as was so much of the expensive traditional jewellery sold on Loulouthia, it touched my heart and rounded the evening off perfectly. If I hadn't felt like I was accepted on the island before, then I certainly did from that moment on.

Chapter 23

There were fewer hours available for me at the bar as the season lazily drew to a close; Sunrise would re-open again at weekends throughout the autumn and winter months, but right now was being wound down so that Alex and Sofia could have a decent, well-earned break. The restaurant had already closed its doors for the last time and the hatches had been battened down to protect it against the elements.

Dwindling customer numbers and the ever-present Alex meant my services were only required for the odd hour here and there but it was perhaps as well, as things had started to get spectacularly weird.

Something had changed, massively.

I didn't know how, when or why but somehow I was swamped by all of these unexpected feelings that had suddenly risen to the surface and erupted; emotions I'd never even come close to experiencing in the past and which had completely blind-sided me. There was a fire lit inside of me and the flames were burning higher and more intensely as every day passed...and, if I'm honest, I was struggling to keep it all under control; it seemed there was no possibility of dampening it down.

On the last Thursday of the season the bar had been extremely quiet and it had just been myself, Andreas, Alex and three couples, accompanied by two holiday reps who were due to travel home the very next day. The more forward of the female reps had done her utmost to entice the quiet and thoughtful Andreas but of course his heart remained with Lauren; he was, however, happy to while away the evening listening to this girl chatter on incessantly, while her vivacious and *extremely* curvy friend, was getting very touchy-feely with Alex; her eyes undressing him wherever he was in the bar, whatever he was doing. He may as well have been strutting around his boxer shorts all night as far as she was concerned, which would have been a sight for everyone to behold.

The laughs were aplenty; everyone wanted to let their sun-bleached hair down one last time and end the season on a positive note. Andreas slipped away quietly, but the small party continued, and just as Alex was howling with laughter at Confessions of a Holiday Rep., Part 1, I wandered over to the lively group to join in with the conversation. Before I even had the chance to pull up a chair, in a split-second Alex had playfully hauled me on to his knee and to my surprise I felt a stirring within me, the likes of which I'd never known before; something had definitely been awoken down below, and if I wasn't mistaken, there was definitely something pulsating coming from Alex's trouser region.

Jesus Christ, what was wrong with me! This man was my friend – okay, he was absolutely gorgeous and his body was in terrific shape – but his wife was ALSO MY FRIEND! In the circumstances, I should have politely excused myself and clambered off, faking an urgent toilet trip or a mad desire to finish clearing up behind the bar...but the unpalatable fact was that I just didn't want to. Breathing heavily, I tried to ignore my traitorous heart beating loudly through the wall of my chest and the heat of Alex's hand penetrating through the fabric of my jeans – *penetrating!* Dear god, my head was full of filth – and I tried to concentrate on giggling and drinking along with the rest of the group, but it was tough to keep my mind on track.

And when Alex dropped me off at my house, was it my imagination or, when he leaned in to give me his usual goodnight peck on the cheek, did his lips hover there just a tad longer than usual? Was he actually contemplating kissing me on my mouth, or was that merely my overactive imagination? Or me willing him to do it because of the way I was feeling?

The next morning I told myself what an absolute gobshite I was being and attempted to put all of the horniness down to the fact that I had been pleasantly pissed and it had been a ridiculous amount of time since I'd had sexual relations with anyone; I was clearly becoming desperate. Just why had these feelings not popped up previously though, when I was under the influence of alcohol, with either Lorry or Nikos...or anyone else for that matter? Even Christian! For the first year of my relationship with my ex, when clubbing and drinking featured heavily on our agenda, I was pissed most of the time and never felt like *this*. Maybe it was because I was *too* pissed on all of those occasions in the past. Yes, that would be it.

But when Alex came to my house the next day bearing gifts in the form of two halogen heaters and a television that looked like it could have been the very FIRST television - so that I wouldn't freeze to death or be bored off my trolley, or so he said – stone cold sober, it still felt like there was something simmering between us that was about to ignite and catch fire any moment. There was no denying it, but where the hell had all of this come from?

'Just Jess, are you going to stand there all day staring at the clock on the wall, or are you going to make me a mug of strong coffee and offer me one of those chocolate biscuits that I know you have hidden in your cupboard?' He cocked his head to one side and treated me to his awesome smile before pretending to pant with thirst...and then this bloody vivid picture popped up in my head of him panting and perspiring after riding me good and hard, and it rendered me barely able to speak, let alone make a brew. Mother of god! What was happening to me?

'Speaking of standing, Just Jess...are you proposing to do just this while you are watching your new television?' New! Good joke - it was about a hundred years old, and I was only surprised it wasn't a black and white set, but I didn't like to say so for fear of sounding supremely ungrateful. 'Do you only have the plastic chairs to sit on? Well that is not good enough! You cannot relax on one of those, especially when the weather becomes cooler at night; you should be warm and comfortable in your own home during the long months to come. I have an extra settee up at my house – I will bring it here, to sort you out.'

Was it getting warm in here? Because it certainly felt like it was heating up; he really did need to choose his words more carefully.

When he was about to leave, I ensured that I dived in first, leaning in to give him a quick peck, in an attempt to avoid us straying into Inappropriate Territory. Except, when I homed in to give him the teeniest of kisses on his cheek, I found myself wondering where the hell I'd always put my hands when we'd done this previously, and thus ended up practically cupping his bum cheek, whilst his lips brushed my ear. If he noticed, he didn't say anything, only that he would be back the next day with the promised sofa, and that I should take a stroll along the beach later while the weather was still good, as there was definitely a storm brewing. Greeks – every one of them a weather forecaster. But usually pretty accurate, to be fair.

The strange moments continued. A touch here, a squeeze there, a smouldering look or an excuse to drop by. Often Sofia was present, so I did actually wonder if I was completely losing the plot and imagining it all; Alex had always been over the top in the bar with all of the customers - flirtatious, attentive and suggestive – I was, of course, reading too much into it. And he would never do anything to hurt his wife or his son, or to bring shame on his family, particularly after all they'd been through. I'd merely developed a silly, little crush on him because he'd been so thoughtful and caring towards me and we'd been working in such close proximity over the last few months and, let's face it, who wouldn't fancy him as he was *hot* and *sexy* and filled out those jeans of his a treat. No, it was pure fantasy, and it's not as if I'd ever act on any of those feelings...it was all above-board and completely harmless and would certainly never in a million years go beyond flirting.

*

Never, ever drink the vino collapso from the traditional wine factory up in the mountains because it messes with your mind and your body, let me tell you.

I'd only had three glasses – the first in the factory when Alex had taken me on a guided tour to show me where the grapes were crushed and his favourite fruity red was produced; the second on my terrace where we'd admired the incredible shades of purples and pinks that painted the sky once the sun had set...and where all flirting had remained mild and incredibly safe; but then one last (large) measure relaxing on my newly acquired sofa in the living room whilst watching Die Hard, in English with Greek subtitles, which was a rather odd experience. Of course, it necessitated me sitting beside Alex, thigh to thigh, as there was only the one, two-seater sofa and the plastic chairs were still outside on the terrace...

The flirting definitely cranked up a notch when we headed indoors; Alex casually rested his hand on my leg and once or twice I gave into temptation and dared to trail my fingers up and down his bare arm, just to gauge his reaction – he swallowed and I felt his body stiffen and his breathing become raspier and faster. Even his bloody arms were beautiful...so strong and manly but not over-muscley, and I loved the downy, dark hairs that covered them.

And then I can't say who made the first move, although I have to confess it may have been me, but the next thing I knew, Alex was kissing me passionately and urgently and I was frantically unbuttoning his shirt whilst trying to work out how in the hell I was going to relieve him of his leather belt as it looked as if it was going to be a complicated procedure.

I needn't have worried; he'd stood up and whipped it off while I shrugged my top over my head, praying I'd had the good sense to put on my best white lacy bra that morning (I had! Praise be!), and then Alex was tenderly caressing my face whilst whispering 'Jessica...extraordinary, delicious, beautiful Jessica,' and I remember thinking that he wasn't calling me 'Just Jess' for once, and how erotic it felt to hear him say my full name in that deep, dangerous voice of his.

His tongue was doing wicked things inside of my mouth – flicking, pushing, probing - a promise of what was to come when we were horizontal, and all the clothes would be shed along with our inhibitions. His fingers slid around to the nape of my neck and then were trailing through my hair, tugging on my curls, as all the while he kissed and tongued me...before he transferred those kisses to my collarbone and I involuntarily threw my head backwards – resulting in the gentle tugging becoming insistent, hard pulling, but my god, I liked it. The nibbling on my breasts that followed, I liked even more, and as he expertly unfastened my bra and it fell to the floor, I practically ripped his shirt off his shoulders to reveal the top half of his beautiful body; his chest tanned and firm with just a sprinkle of body hair.

Before I could delve into his jeans, he led me to the bedroom, lay flat on my bed and quickly dragged me down on top of him, groaning as my kisses trailed down to his navel, and he roughly pulled down my own jeans and white lacy knickers (someone was definitely smiling down on me – it was the first time in months I'd worn matching underwear).

I finished undressing him, with my eyes as well as my mouth, and as I gazed in wonder at what had previously been contained in his tight, black jockey shorts, he quickly shifted positions; sliding out from underneath me and swiftly climbing on top, pinning me down with his weight as I practically whimpered and begged him to take me.

The last thing I remember as he expertly complied, hard and fast, and I was consumed with pleasure I'd only ever thought was possible in my dreams, was hearing him growl, 'Fucking hell, Just Jessica. What have you done to me?'

Chapter 24

That bloody cockerel was in fine voice, unfortunately for me, as its sodding cock-a-doodle-doing rang through my ears and penetrated my skull at stupid o'clock the next morning. Actually it must have been later than I'd first thought as I'd already heard what I now recognised as the humming of the farming machinery in the distance, high up on Andreas' land...but still, I had nothing to get up for, so I would snuggle up for another couple of hours under the covers and make the most of my free time, now the bar was closed for a short while.

As I curled up like a lazy doormouse into the tangle of sheets, a familiar woody scent pervaded my nostrils...ah yes, I recognised that...it was aftershave...good quality aftershave, if I wasn't mistaken...it was Alex's aftershave....HOLY FUCKING SHIT!

I jumped out of the bed like I'd been stung, as pornographic memories of the previous night came rushing back to me, but a quick, panicky glance down at the bed confirmed that Alex wasn't actually in it, and in my half-awake state I ran naked, from room to room, checking to see that he wasn't hiding away in some cupboard somewhere, consumed by regret and remorse. When I realised that the house was most definitely empty, I quickly pulled on some mismatched clothes and did a swift check of the terrace and garden too - just in case - but he had definitely departed, which would explain why my key had been in the middle of the living room floor – he'd clearly locked up and then slid it back underneath (no letterbox – this was a fairly primitive Greek island and I was more likely to find my mail shoved in one of the plant pots on the terrace, when the postal service finally decided I'd waited long enough).

Oh well, at least he still thought enough of me to make sure I wasn't at risk of being murdered in my bed, even if he had done a runner at dawn. A quick check of my phone revealed I had two messages from him – the first merely saying 'I have to pick up Yiorgos. I must go to town. Insurance for the cars!xxxxxxxxx' which I thought sounded quite abrupt but I was placated somewhat by the line of kisses he'd signed off with.

The second text brought me crashing to my senses though, as I read out loud, 'Beautiful Just Jess. Wonderful night. Same time same place this evening?xxxx' and I thought, Holy Shit, what a selfish, treacherous, *stupid* bitch I was. What had I done?

Sofia had cared for me, listened to me, employed me, looked after me and welcomed me into her family, and I had slept with her husband and stabbed her in the back without even giving her a second thought. I was so ashamed! She was one of my best friends, for fuck's sake...how could I have done this to her? What had happened to Girl Code? All thoughts of loyalty and restraint had disappeared as quickly as my knickers!

My head in my hands, reeling from the shock of my own duplicity; disgusted with myself for having betrayed the loveliest of women and buggered up my cherished friendship with both her and Alex, I moaned as I recalled sex with him not once, not twice but three times during the previous night – each time more personal and passionate than the last...all amazing, fast, furious, perfect sex that had taken my breath away and made me realise why I'd held off from climbing into bed with Lorry or Nikos or any other man throughout the long, hot summer.

It had never entered my head that Alex could be anything more than a friend, as he was strictly off limits, being happily married, in a relationship with an equally gorgeous woman who was more than his match...and they seemed such a perfect couple; they fitted so well together and I had often commented on the fact I would give anything to have what they had.

Of course he was fit as fuck, and handsome and funny and kind...and if he'd been single I would have probably have attempted to mount his leg or something within the first week of meeting him – even though he was clearly out of my league and I couldn't have imagined he would have given me a second glance, what with all the scores of beautiful-bodied ladies queuing up to have a go on him.

But he *wasn't* single; he was very, very married and had seemed such a loyal, decent, trustworthy guy that I was equally as mad at him that he'd been unfaithful to Sofia. Unless this was a regular occurrence with him - maybe he was a serial philanderer who put it about it in the long, quiet winter months...perhaps he'd been shagging half of Loulouthia throughout the summer as well! I honestly didn't think so though...he worked such long hours and had never shown the slightest bit of interest in whipping his kit off for any up-for-it holidaymaker who gave him their best come-to-bed eyes. And there had been a lot of those. And when he wasn't slugging his guts out in the bar or running around after his own family, he was helping everyone else out...especially me, a quiet voice in my head said, especially me.

He'd driven me around everywhere and always made sure I arrived home safely or sent Sofia to do it in his absence; he'd initially procured my little house for me and had recently been on the lookout for somewhere else with heating and double glazed windows; he'd sorted out my Tassos issues to the best of his ability and, along with his wonderful wife, employed me in his bar and allowed me to work when I really wasn't needed sometimes, purely so I could earn some rent money; he'd listened to me and offered me advice and always been so generous with his heart and his time, often calling up to the house to bring me lunch, or to show me how to make frappés, or to fix my outside lights or oversee a water delivery when the local spring was off or being diverted to the resorts.

Far too late, I realised that he'd been there for me on many, many occasions and I'd probably spent far more time with him than was considered appropriate, him being a married man and all. But how much of it was *filoxenia* – generosity to strangers – which was such a biggy on this island? And why hadn't Sofia put her Armani-clad foot down if he'd been allocating me too much of his precious time? Perhaps because she was so similar in nature to him - so kind and giving, and she was being such a good friend and trusted me implicitly.

I shook my head, my bouncy curls in a particular state of wild disarray after my night of hot, needy sex – I just didn't know. All I did know was that somewhere, sometime during those frantic, flaming hot summer months, this friendship between Alex and I had intensified and feelings had been developed and nurtured without me even realising it – although I wasn't sure how much Alex was aware of and how I stood as far as *his* feelings were concerned.

Unfortunately, I had now completely and utterly fucked everything up, and no matter how much I loved this beautiful, enchanting, flower-filled island, I had to get away. And I had to do it fast before Sofia returned from her trip to Corfu on the late afternoon ferry.

Glancing at the clock on the kitchen wall, I knew I could probably catch the morning ferry off the island if I rang Yiannis the taxi driver straight away and he was available to come and collect me. He was, and he had a tendency to drive like Lewis Hamilton with the wind behind him, so I quickly shoved clothes and shoes and make-up and trinkets into my case and bags, sobbing as I threw in the little box containing my gold, scroll earrings. If I had any decency, I would return them. Clearly I didn't, as I couldn't bear to part with them.

There were a great many things I had to leave behind; it's amazing how much crap you acquire over five and a half months. It was to be hoped I hadn't left anything important, apart from, oh, my shattered heart that would always remain on Loulouthia.

Hearing the honk of Yiannis' horn as he screeched to a halt outside, I took one last, heart-breaking look around my compact little house, hoping that the landlord wouldn't think too badly of me for leaving it in such a mess, with food in the fridge and sand on the floor, swallowed down a huge gulp of misery, and closed and locked it behind me for the very last time. I buried the key in a massive geranium pot to the side of the terrace and Yiannis squeezed all my gear into the car boot and then chivalrously opened the door for me to hop in the front passenger side. Not wishing to offend him, I climbed in, although I had hoped to slip onto the back seat, where I could more easily duck down as we were driving through Chaliki. As the tears began to fall, I cited a family emergency as the reason for my misery and my hasty departure, and then turned to stare out of the window, as Yiannis' car whizzed through the resort and I saw the bars and restaurants and the joyful, wondrous Sunrise, disappear from view. Thankfully, there was hardly anybody about and only Tassos was on the main street, furiously banging nails into wooden shuttering that was to cover the side of the restaurant which was more likely to be beaten and blown about in any storms or heavy winds. Yiannis tooted on his horn again as he raised his hand, and Tassos looked up and mirrored his greeting, no doubt clocking me on the passenger side, trying desperately and failing miserably to sink down into the dirty footwell.

The journey to the port took no time at all and once there Yiannis emptied the boot of all my belongings, bade me a fond farewell and a safe journey in his usual cheery manner and sped off with a squeal of his wheels and a '*Yassoo!*' Choked up at the sight of the freshly cut flowers placed at the scene of Juliette's accident, presumably by the inspiring and devoted Ioanna, who I hadn't yet been able to meet – and now I probably never would – I could only nod my head in response.

My ticket to Corfu was purchased with minimum fuss now I was slightly more fluent in the Greek language, and I made it on to the ferry with only minutes to spare before it was due to depart. As the boat eased out of the harbour, I openly cried hot, salty tears as I looked back at the island that I had adored and expected to call home for the rest of my life; I would miss the people and the flowers and the lemons and the beauty of it forever. There was still so much of it that I hadn't yet been able to explore; so many views I hadn't seen, so many miles of its rugged landscape that I hadn't walked.

As many others visited the island and left again, I felt sure I would soon be forgotten – people move on and memories fade.

It was a long, miserable sail over to Corfu, on choppy waters that did nothing to settle my stomach and the waves of nausea kept on coming.

My heart was literally crushed; my future destroyed all because of one amazing night. And it really had been amazing. Not just the unprecedented, unexpected, unrivalled steamy, sweaty sex. It was also the words of endearment whispered by Alex; it was the gentle kissing and tender caressing; it was being wrapped up in the warmth and safety of his arms, my head on his chest, listening to its rise and fall, as his fingers gently stroked my forehead and his lips brushed against my hair. All my life I had been devoid of these intense feelings and emotions – all my life I had been searching for this man, but I just hadn't known it. Unconsciously, I had been falling in love with Alex, slowly but surely, over the last weeks and months and the thought of spending the rest of my life without ever seeing him again, without ever feeling his touch on my skin and listening to his heart beat in tandem with my own...it was more than I could bear.

Whilst I knew I should have been hanging it in shame, I tried to hold my head up high when I disembarked the ferry and made my way to the designated stop where the bus to the airport was due to depart from. After standing there for about half an hour, cursing bloody Greek bloody public transport, whilst loud, animated locals and weary travellers milled around in disorganised chaos, a kind elderly gentleman stopped to inform me that there had been a nasty accident on the main airport road – two coaches had collided and the whole area was blocked, with all the emergency services in attendance, and it would most likely be hours before the next bus made it through. He swiftly moved on as I burst into tears again and collapsed on to my suitcase, wondering what the hell I was going to do now.

Alone, disoriented and desperate, I just had to speak to someone; a friendly, unjudgemental voice who would sympathise with me, remain impartial, and possibly offer up some assistance in my hour of need.

Two missed calls from Alex and one from Sofia, I discovered as I pulled out my mobile from the inner side pocket of my bag. Fantastic.

Sofia knew. Of that I was certain. She never rang me for *anything,* always preferring to message, or turn up at the house instead. *Of course* she knew - Loulouthia was a small island; everyone knew everyone's business and she'd probably been up to speed before we'd even removed our underwear and commenced our night of passion.

Sobbing, as I pictured Alex in his underwear, I chose to ignore the three missed calls and the seven messages that I'd apparently received, according to the notification on my phone, and instead I scrolled down my contacts list and selected Lauren's English number; she would be the best person to speak to. In a relatively short space of time we'd got to know each other so well, and at one time, of course, she had been firm friends with Alex and Sofia...but she had successfully created distance between herself and the pair of them...and the island itself...so hopefully wouldn't be too disgusted with me - and I hadn't shagged *her* husband.

'LAUREN!' I sobbed as she thankfully answered her phone on the fourth ring. 'I've done something terrible! I've done a really, REALLY bad thing and I'm a horrible, horrible person and I'm making my way home...back to England...'

'Jess, is that you? Jesus, what's the matter? Are you okay? Are you hurt? Tell me, Jess, what on earth's happened...'

'It's Alex,' I cried. 'I had all these feelings for him and I didn't even know it...and Sofia's been so kind to me...and they're such a wonderful couple...but I couldn't help it...I'd fallen for him...and...oh Lauren...I've only gone and slept with him!'

'What? Did you say you've slept with him? Bloody hell! Jess, calm down and take a deep breath...listen to me! Where are you now?'

'I'm on Corfu...I hot-footed it from Loulouthia before Sofia came back and beat me to death with her designer handbag for being such a shitty, disgrace of a friend and I was forced to live as an outcast! But I've arrived here and there's been a sodding accident on the main road to the airport so there's no buses for hours...and I don't even have any money on me, just my credit card...and I *need* to get a plane tonight, away from here and out of Greece...but I'm stuck here at the bus stop and I'm steaming hot and haven't a clue what to do and...'

'Jess! JESSICA! Listen to me for god's sake. The first thing you need to do is calm down and then get yourself straight to the information office - you'll see the signs for it – and the staff there will tell you exactly what the situation is with the buses. When you have a better idea of what's going on, haul your arse into an air-conditioned cafe and grab yourself a bite to eat and a cold drink while you listen out for further announcements and updates. Make sure that you don't leave on an empty stomach though because the last thing you need is to be puking your guts up on that bus to the airport – trust me, I've learned from experience. And listen, as far as Alex is concerned, you have to know....'

Silence.

Followed by more silence.

'Lauren...LAUREN! Are you there? *Laauuurrren...*'

No amount of calling her name made any difference whatsoever, as the line was dead. One look at my mobile told me I was completely out of battery and in dire need of a charger...except the charger was still plugged into the socket at the side of my bed, in my lovely little house on Loulouthia.

I couldn't even cry then, I was so depleted and desolate and broken. Hoisting my heavy bag back up on to my aching shoulder, I took a deep breath, grabbed hold of the handle of my case and wearily began to tug it along behind me, as I took heavy footsteps in the direction of the information office, whilst struggling to hold the other two bags in my left hand, even though they were cutting off the circulation in my fingers. By the time I reached the office I was even hotter and sweatier and I think I nearly passed out twice as I queued, to eventually be told that they expected the debris to be cleared from the road in question within the next couple of hours, after which the bus service would resume as normal.

Resigning myself to a late night flight, but at least relieved that there was some end in sight, I staggered over to the nearest cafe, which was thankfully air-conditioned and accepted credit cards. After plucking a can of coke from the fridge and ordering a ham and cheese toasty, the old lady behind the counter took payment from my flexible friend and I installed myself at an empty table by the window, where I would be tucked away from the rest of the world.

Trying not to think about all of the delicious meals I'd devoured on Loulouthia and the lethal cocktails Alex had concocted in Sunrise as he'd jiggled about like a shaking and stirring young Tom Cruise, I thanked the tall, skinny lad who delivered my toasty before half-heartedly taking a small bite of it, as I stared blankly out of the window. I watched the tourists and travellers go back and forwards, wondering if they too had overwhelming problems; if any of them were heading home to a life of nothing, having lost everything that was precious to them.

As I knocked back the last dregs of my coke, and wondered how I was going to make use of the toilet facilities when I was loaded up with luggage, the sight of a familiar red coat in the crowds outside caught my attention through the glass. As the palpitations came thick and fast, I squinted against the sunlight to ensure my mind wasn't deceiving me.

Holy fuck! It couldn't be...it was! It was Sofia, and she was walking towards the cafe! She had clearly spotted me, sitting in the stupid bloody window seat and she was coming in, looking none too cheerful, and I had nowhere to escape to; nowhere to run and hide. If she was planning on slaughtering me for sleeping with her husband, I hoped it would be over quickly as I was pretty damn sure I'd already suffered enough.

Realising it was time that I womaned-up and accepted my punishment, I braced myself as she burst through the door and headed in my direction, as immaculate and elegant as ever, dressed in a cream silk shirt and black leather trousers under her expensive red jacket; as always a vision with her hair perfectly coiffed and coloured and her make-up expertly applied so that, naturally, she was glowing and faultless, while I looked like a stinking bag of shit, in a creased purple t-shirt that clashed with my dusty, yellow shorts. I was beyond caring what state my hair was in and whether my skin was greasy and spotty – it hardly mattered any more.

'Jessica,' she said to me in her heavily accented, sultry voice. 'We need to talk.' She seemed remarkably calm for a woman who'd just discovered her husband and friend had been getting it on behind her back.

Nodding silently, I crossed my fingers underneath the table and prayed that she wasn't party to all of the sordid details; that she'd perhaps just heard a rumour but hadn't yet had it confirmed.

As she sat down opposite me, her thick gold bracelet clanked noisily on the table-top, whilst her heels scraped the floor as she leant in.

'So, you decided to flee to England then, rather than hang around to speak to myself or Alex?'

'Yes,' I replied, meekly. It appeared I was a coward as well as a bloody slut. 'How did you know I was here, on Corfu? How on earth did you know where to look for me?'

'Lauren. She rang me a few minutes ago and said I would find you here. Luckily, I was only around the corner, as I was about to board the ferry back to the island.'

Brilliant. Thanks Lauren. Well that's you off my frigging Christmas card list.

'So...last night...while I was here on Corfu...you had sex with my husband.'

Oh. My. God. No beating around the bush then; I wondered if Lauren had also provided her with *that* information. Me and her were bloody going to be having words, I could see.

'This is true, yes? While I was here on Corfu, Alex came to your house, and he spent the night with you...and now you are feeling guilty and ashamed.'

Guilty and ashamed? That was the understatement of the year.

'Yes,' I squeaked, feeling my cheeks colour and a hot flush rise up from my chest to my neck. 'I'm so sorry, Sofia. I truly am. It was unforgiveable of me, after all you've done and the trust you put in me...to pay you back in this way makes me the lowest of the low. But I'm leaving now; I'm going away and I'll never come back and I hope in time you can forgive Alex and...'

'Do you love him, Jess?'

Wow, straight to the point then; no messing about. I toyed with denying my feelings first of all, to spare hers; by telling her that I'd just made a god-awful, stupid mistake because I was drunk, as was Alex. Maybe it would give them the chance to re-build their relationship at some point, when she could learn to trust him again. But that would have been an insult to how I felt about Alex – to imply it had only been about the sex and that there had been no feelings involved...to turn it into something seedy and meaningless.

In the end I plumped for the truth.

'Yes,' I sobbed. 'Yes, I love him...I really do. I've just been in denial, I think, trying to pretend that all these feelings were purely platonic and that he wasn't the only man I'd ever truly fallen for. I'm so sorry, I honestly am. I can't believe I let it happen, knowing he was married to you, especially when you've been such a good friend to me. The last thing I would ever want to do is hurt you, but I know that no matter how many times I apologise it will never be enough. So I'm clearing off, and I promise you'll never see me again and I won't ever try to contact you or Alex in the future...'

She held up her hand then and said quietly, 'Please stop, Jess. Wipe your eyes and take a moment. There are many things I must tell you; there is so much that you do not know.'

I had heard that said somewhere else, by someone else, and, despite all of my fear and my head telling me to run away as fast as my little legs would take me, I was intrigued to know why (a), she wasn't screaming and shouting at me like a bat-shit crazy woman and (b) what the hell else did I not know?

So I took a napkin and dabbed my eyes, blew my nose so loudly, they could probably hear it on Kefalonia, and nodded that I was ready for her to divulge her innermost secrets.

'Okay, Jessica...for you to even begin to understand, I think I must take you right back to the beginning of our story. Alex and I have known each other all of our lives; we were raised in the same village – where our home is now - and we were classmates in the same school; friends to begin with, who started to fool around a little too much once we were in high school. When we were only seventeen, inevitably we got carried away...one thing led to another and I became pregnant as a result. It was a huge shock to us both, we were barely adults ourselves and certainly didn't feel mature enough to cope with raising a child...and then there was my father, who was absolutely furious...and who threatened to kill Alex with his bare hands.'

'Oh my, I didn't realise you'd had a shotgun wedding!'

'I don't know the meaning of that phrase – but if you mean that we were forced into marriage because I was expecting a child, then yes, we had one of those. Although my father almost turned his shotgun on Alex.'

'But you loved each other, right? So it was all okay in the end?'

'No. No, I'm afraid we did not love each other – not in the way we should have done; not enough to become husband and wife and bring a child into the world. As I say, we were friends and that's how it should have remained but...well...we were both inquisitive about sex and I desperately wanted to see for myself what all of the fuss was about...so I encouraged Alex to take things further one evening, making it difficult for him to resist.'

'I can't imagine anyone ever resisting you, Sofia. But you were blessed with Yiorgos and surely you wouldn't change that?'

'Yes, of course - I would not alter that part of my life for one second, but it was very tough in the early days. As soon as I discovered I was having a baby and I broke the news to Alex, he immediately offered to stand by me, even though he was scared - but my father's threats would have made it impossible for him to walk away, so it's not as if he had any real choice. We had a wedding that was arranged very quickly, mainly by my parents, so that no one would know and it would not bring shame on my family. Except everyone did know of course and my father was very angry. It didn't stop him organising the huge celebrations though and spending a ridiculous amount of money on my wedding dress and the rings and the gifts and everything else...and not forgetting a party for almost six hundred people.'

'Bloody hell, were there even six hundred people living on the island back then?'

'Yes, but I think almost every islander received an invitation to our wedding,' she smiled, as she remembered the day that Alex became her husband – lucky old Sofia.

'Everyone said it was a magnificent occasion and it was the talk of the island for months afterwards, so that at least pleased my father. And Alex made a good husband; he worked hard and asked nothing of nobody - and he took care of me when all I could do was cry and eat cake.'

That sounded like a wonderful plan to me – I might give it a go once I arrived home.

'I was so terrified of giving birth and looking after a child of my own, but Alex was there for me every step of the way. After I had Yiorgos, I was not allowed to leave the house for thirty days – as is the custom in Greece – and I thought I would go stir crazy, but Alex was a real pillow of strength for me.'

Keep your mouth shut Jessica – not the time to point out that it was 'pillar', not 'pillow'.

'So we had our gorgeous baby boy and he brought us both so much happiness and joy, and we tried to be the best parents we could. Yiorgos could not have wished for a better daddy than Alex.'

I got that. I'd witnessed father and son working and playing together, the bond that existed between them was obvious for all to see.

'But what I don't understand – and I know it's probably the last question you want to hear from me of all people – is why you didn't love Alex, for goodness sake? I mean, let's look at the facts here. Handsome – yes. Hardworking – yes. Funny – yes. Kind – yes. He ticks all the boxes, Sofia. What's not to love? And how could he not fall in love with you...I mean, have you looked in the mirror recently and noticed how gorgeous you are...as well as being generous and thoughtful and entertaining and interesting...all the things I'm not?'

'Stop that now, Jessica! You *are* all of those things and so much more. But, let me tell you, beauty is skin deep, Jess...and I'm afraid I was not the person back then as I am now; I was far too selfish and not so kind to others. When you have children it changes you forever – if you treat someone badly then you imagine how you would feel if someone hurt your child, and it truly makes you a more compassionate and decent person. So...Alex liked me, and he cared for me and he loved me as a friend but no, he did not fall in love with me and I...I could not fall in love with him.'

'But why ever not? I just don't get it...when he's so very easy to fall in love with...'

'For you...yes. For me...I loved him as a friend and knew that he was a special man with a wonderful heart...but I could not *fall in love* with him...because...my sweet Jessica...I had lost my heart to another man.

I was already in love with someone else.'

Chapter 25

'Pardon? I'm sorry but I must be having a funny turn or something because I'm sure I just heard you say that you were in love with someone else when you married Alex?'

'Yes, you heard correctly, it is true. With an older man. His name is Theo, and I loved him before I was married and I have loved him throughout my marriage. He is the love of my life in fact, and although I have great affection for Alex, as the father of my son and as someone who has proved himself time and time again to be a worthy, wonderful man...our love is like that of brother and sister, whereas my love for Theo is that of a woman for a man; it is all-consuming, it is sexual, it is powerful and it is eternal. And he loves me also – since the moment we met when I was just sixteen years old.'

'Okay, so I know you had to marry Alex because you were expecting his baby, but why the hell didn't you leave him once the dust settled, to be with this older guy? Why have you stayed with Alex all of these years?'

'You wouldn't ask that question if you knew my father. He was an intimidating man and I was frightened of him and he continued to resent Alex for the shame he had brought on our family; he would have found a way to blame him for any separation, even if I was the one walking away from the marriage. And if I had abandoned Alex then it would have been impossible for me to stay on Loulouthia; I would have been forced to leave the island, but Yiorgos was young and needed his father and I could not have torn him from his arms. And there were even bigger problems, Jess. You see, Theo was my father's best friend and he was also a married man; we could not be together – it would have been frowned upon. He had apparently been around when I was a very young child, although I have no memories of those times, but had left Loulouthia to work in Athens; when he returned to the island when I was sixteen, he found an attractive young woman in place of that child he remembered...and from that first meeting we were immediately drawn to each other, not just by looks...there was chemistry between us and we both so desperately wanted to be together.'

'Wow. You were only a young girl then when you first fell for each other - that *would* have set the tongues wagging if you'd hooked up with him when he was married and you were only just of age! Did you give in to temptation though, or did you manage to keep your hands off each other in view of the circumstances?'

'I did not sleep with Theo or even share one stolen kiss with him before I married Alex. I wanted him so badly but any relationship would have been out of the question – a married man with a family, who was in his late thirties, and a naive, sixteen year old slip of a girl – can you imagine my parents' reaction if they had found out? No, we tried to accept that it could never be, and Theo temporarily returned to Athens for business. In the three months he was gone, Alex and I spent most of our free time together and consequently we became much closer. I was so confused, trying desperately to move on and bury my feelings for Theo...so I had sex with Alex and the rest, as you say, is history. Shortly after Theo returned, his family received the invitation to my wedding...and he tells me it was the worst night of his life - watching me spin around the dancefloor in the arms of my new husband simply tore him apart. My heart ached for him when I saw him that night, but I was too caught up in the wedding...and after Yiorgos was born, for the sake of my son I decided I must keep my distance again from Theo. But he was always there, at social occasions and whenever I visited my parents, and our feelings were stronger than ever. We tried so hard, but in the end, we could fight it no longer...and it was everything I'd imagined it to be. Blissfully wonderful.'

'Poor Alex then. I know you said that he didn't love you in *that* way but I'm sure he would have been unhappy if he'd known you were being unfaithful? If nothing else, it would have hurt his male pride!'

'Although most Greek men would have gone crazy, Alex is not that kind of person. I realise these revelations cast me in a very bad light and you will think that I have been very selfish. But before we were married, when we knew we weren't in love and admitted it to each other, I confided in him about my feelings for Theo; he wasn't surprised – he had seen the connection between us with his own eyes. And later, after Alex and I were married and realised that love was something that could not be forced, I confessed to him that, if anything, my feelings for Theo had deepened and were tearing me apart. It may sound strange to you but Alex and I were completely honest and open to each other about our feelings right from the start; we never lied – each one of us respected the other too much to talk bullshit. When I became intimate with Theo, I told Alex soon afterwards – not the finer details of course, but the basic facts so that he would never, ever hear it from anyone else first. He had the option to leave of course, always, but he didn't want to live in a different house to Yiorgos or for our son to come from a broken family...and he knew it would make life very difficult for me if it all tumbled out – my affair with Theo; my relationship with a much older, married man. I could not leave because of my father...and it's not as if Theo and I could be together at that stage anyway, as he had his own wife and two sons to consider.'

'My god, I could wallpaper every room in my house with the secrets you lot keep on Loulouthia...'

'I don't understand...you do say funny things, Just Jess.'

'So...you were sleeping with both men at that stage, Sofia?'

'My god, Jess! What do you think I am! Of course not. In the very early days, yes, I had sex with my husband, but as soon as my relationship with Theo progressed...I never slept with Alex again. In fact, we have had separate bedrooms for the last fifteen years.'

'No way! And I always thought you were the perfect couple! But surely to god Alex has had a little fun of his own during the last decade and a half? A man like him must have had girlfriends and lovers?'

To even say those words out loud made me nauseous - to think of him making love to anyone else after the night we had spent together, but I had to ask.

'Jessica, in view of the circumstances, I think all of this is something you should discuss in great detail with Alex. But, all I can say is that there was never anyone of significance for Alex; he had a short relationship with a girl from the mainland who came over to stay with family, many years ago, and he has had flings with a couple of British girls in the past, but those brief holiday romances never amounted to anything serious. Although, even though he was upfront with both girls, I did hear that one of them was devastated when her holiday ended and desperately wanted to stay here with him; she wrote to him and pestered him for months afterwards and he felt awful that she'd developed such strong, unreciprocated feelings.'

I didn't want to think about that either. Alex, with a British girl. Two, actually. And one whose heart he had unintentionally broken; a bit too close to the knuckle that.

'Don't look so worried, Jess. He was completely truthful with this girl and tried to let her down gently, but she still pinned all her hopes and dreams on him. After that upsetting experience, he said 'No more'. He didn't want to be the man who broke anyone's heart; to give someone false hope and be responsible for shattering their dreams. Since that disaster, I do not believe that there has been anyone else, which makes me sad, actually, as he deserves to be truly happy – to find someone who makes him feel so alive and fulfilled, the way Theo makes me feel. I have always wanted Alex to find love...to meet someone special who will treasure and adore him...because no one deserves that happiness more than him.'

'I hope he meets that special woman too,' I whispered. 'Someone who appreciates his humour and his zest for life and his kind heart...as well as that handsome face and spectacular body. I really hope he does...'

Sofia shook her head and tutted before closing her eyes and laughing out loud.

'Jess, you are so silly sometimes! All these years Alex has been alone and never found the right person; never fallen in love...that is, until now! YOU are the special person, my friend; YOU are the woman who makes him so deliriously happy! Are you so blind that you cannot see what you have done to him? You have stolen his heart and his soul and now you must make it your mission to keep them both safe.'

My heart was pounding, my hands were shaking and I was rendered momentarily speechless.

Not only did she not want to rip me to bits for bedding her husband, it would appear that she was practically handing Alex to me on a plate! Was it all just too good to be true? From somewhere within, I found a tiny, nervous voice.

'Me? Why would he feel that way about me? When a man like him could have anyone he chooses, I really don't think he would pick me. We had a wonderful time together last night – sorry about that, again, you know, because I hadn't heard any of this last night and I shouldn't really have jumped into bed with your husband while I actually thought he was happily married to you - anyway, as I was saying, last night was fantastic and it has been a joy getting to know him over the last few months, but I really don't think I'm special enough or beautiful enough to keep a man like Alex. Yes, I admit it - now I know it myself – I *do* love him, and I wish more than anything that the feeling was mutual...but I don't see how it can be. I can't even begin to compare with the likes of you, Sofia. What would Alex – a definite 10 on the universal scale of hotties, see in ME – when I'm probably just about scraping in at a 6 on a good day?'

'Just Jess, you are talking absolute nonsense. I have watched the two of you together over the last few months and it has been wonderful to see Alex so happy and to witness him finally falling in love. At long last I can move on – we both can – now I know that Alex will be happy and settled and taken care of by an incredibly special woman like you.'

'Moving on? You've just given me a litany of reasons as to why you can't move on!'

'Ah, well, our situation has changed somewhat. Firstly, my father is older now and had a serious health scare quite recently; he is not the man he was and I am no longer scared of him. Besides, he is calmer now and more accepting, shall we say, of non-traditional circumstances. He will be very upset that Alex and I are separating, but there is little he can do about it – and when he discovers that I am in love with Theo, and Alex is in love with you, he will know for sure that there is no going back. Also, Yiorgos is much older now, he is an adult himself...and he has wondered for a long time why his father and I do not share a bed. We have both had a long talk with him and he is happy as long as we are happy – he is a good boy – and he will also speak to his grandfather about our situation; he will listen to Yiorgos more than he has ever listened to me.'

'And your father won't mind when he finds out that his best mate has been playing hide the sausage with his precious daughter all of these years?'

'Ha, ha! Hide the sausage! I think you picked up that phrase from Scarlett, am I right? Yes, I thought so. Well, of course, my father will mind – he will hit the roofs! But Theo's own circumstances have changed now – his sons are older and he is separated from his wife – and he moved here, to Corfu, eighteen months ago, to be away from the glare of my father's eyes, and has been waiting for me to follow him, on a permanent basis, ever since. He has a beautiful villa at Kassiopi and I have been slowly moving into it, bit by bit.'

'Oh, *now* I get it! That's why you've been bloody back and forward to this island every two minutes...that's why you're here now! Oh Sofia, I thought you were dying of some nasty disease that no one dare talk about...or you had some shady mafia links and I was going to come out one morning and trip over a horse's head on my doorstep, just for having struck up a friendship with you!'

Sofia laughed her socks off then; I don't think I'd ever heard her actually snort with laughter before...but it was a good sound to hear because I think it meant she was truly happy and didn't bear any grudge against me – in fact, she seemed to be positively *pushing* me in Alex's direction.

'So what will happen to the restaurant and bar if you bugger off over here with your lover? What will become of Sofia's and Sunrise? You and Alex always made such a good team – if only in a working capacity – and I can't imagine him trying to manage everything on his own...and it just won't have the same atmosphere, without you there at the helm of the ship.'

'Oh, but I think it will, lovely Jessica. I think you and Alex will run the bar magnificently together...you have already been doing it for a good proportion of the last few months. And you are a natural when it comes to thinking of names for our customers; I saw you make that wrinkly old man's day when you called him Guy Ritchie...even though he was more Guy Fawkes, in his patched-up jacket and scruffy trousers! And you have the added bonus of the electricity that flows through the air and sizzles when the two of you are close together...it all makes for the perfect ambience. I'm only surprised that it took the two of you so long to cement your relationship...and I know the bar will be in safe hands with you both in charge.'

'But what will happen with Sofia's? How can you leave it behind when it's your baby?'

'No, Yiorgos is, and always will be, my baby. The restaurant had my name above it, but it was just a restaurant. And besides, the name is to be changed very soon, now I have signed everything over to Alex – another reason why it has been necessary for me to come to Corfu; to complete all of the paperwork.'

It was so much to take in. I could feel myself blinking furiously as I tried to get my head around the fact that Alex and Sofia had never been a 'couple' in the truest sense of the word. That all of the front they had put on when they were working in the bar and wherever else they were in company had really just been an exercise in smoke and mirrors.

'My god, all change! Has Alex thought of a new name for the restaurant then? I can't imagine it not being Sofia's! And are you just planning to be a lady of leisure over here on Corfu or have you something else lined up for your future?'

'Slow down Jess...so many questions! Firstly, you will have to speak to Alex about the choice of name for the restaurant as it is really just down to him now as he is the sole proprietor...however, I have a feeling you will be very much involved in any future decision making. Although, we have discussed a possible name that we both like very much – if you agree, then it is a done deal. And as to your second question, my wonderful Theo is a successful businessman and has made a small fortune in shipping, so it is not essential that I work...but I do want to. YOU, my darling Jessica have inspired me to resurrect my ambitions and I am therefore looking to open my own beauty salon in Corfu Town. We already have the premises and I have met a marvellous woman who is a talented stylist and make-up artist and she is going to work for me and we will employ others. Once we are up and running you must visit us Jess, and we will indulge you with a complimentary massage and pampering session!'

A bloody good pampering session wouldn't go amiss right now, what with all the stress and shocks and panic and revelations. This was all too much to take in. Yesterday I was Just Jess, single ex-pat who worked in a bar in the summer months; today I may possibly have acquired a partner, a business and a whole new life for myself. What the hell was going on?

'Are you sure this isn't some sort of wind-up, Sofia?' I asked, wondering how long it would be before my head exploded and they were scraping bits of me off the drinks fridge in the far corner.

'Are you sure that you're not just lulling me into a false sense of security and that you're not about to leap over the table to do me some serious damage? And are you absolutely positive that Alex wants ME and you haven't got me confused with some stunning, young babe with big tits and a fabulous arse? Because none of this seems real or possible somehow.'

'Wait!' Sofia held her hand up before scooping her mobile out of her stylish, ruby red handbag and scrolling down her contacts list. When the phone rang out and was answered I could faintly hear my lovely Alex's voice and then Sofia spoke to him quickly in Greek but translated for my benefit. 'Tell her how you feel, Alex,' she instructed, before handing the phone over to me. 'She needs to know.'

Feeling actually quite sick and apprehensive, my shaky hand took the mobile from her steady one, and I held it to my ear, just in time to hear Alex say, 'I love you, Just Jess. That is all.'

Chapter 26

The return ferry to Loulouthia seemed to take an interminable length of time, but thankfully, the sea was less choppy and the journey was much smoother. I hadn't even realised that I'd nodded off until I awoke to find my head on Sofia's shoulder and she said, 'Aah, sleeping beauty is awake. I think you needed to rest, my darling, after your traumatic day, but we are nearly there now; almost home – your home, not mine that is; my real home is on Corfu now.'

I sat up quickly, after I realised that I probably looked like death having cried buckets full of tears, almost succumbed to seasickness on the previous journey, feared that I was going to be bashed up by Sofia, and sweat out several litres of Greek wine and most other bodily fluids. Not to mention that I'd been awake most of the previous night, assuming various positions with Alex. I smiled, blushing berry red as I remembered the ecstasy and the orgasms and the way Alex had looked at me in wonder and confessed that he had often watched me when I was bending over in the bar and imagined me naked and in his bed.

Stroking him while watching him gasp, I had told him he would have to make do with *my* bed but offered to bend over for him so we could both fulfil our fantasies. Where had that brazen hussy come from? Dirty talk was even more foreign to me than the Greek language and yet, there I was, bold as brass, not giving a fig that all my wobbly bits were on show, making him groan with my words and actions. It just shows you what the right man can do to you...my god, I couldn't wait for Round Two. Ding ding.

As our beautiful island drew ever nearer, the whole moon lighting up the harbour and offering us a clear view of the mountains and the villages, I swiftly reached into my bag for my face powder and lipstick. If Alex really was as captivated by me as Sofia assured me he was, I didn't want him changing his mind at the last minute when I hopped off the ferry and him thinking, 'Jesus, look at the state of her...what a dog!'

After practically inhaling a packet of polo mints that had been festering under the lining of my bag for the last two months, I braced myself for seeing Alex again, and cursed the port staff who didn't seem the slightest bit interested in the fact that I was desperate to get off this boat and retrace my steps back to the promenade.

He was there.

Waiting.

Looking as fit and handsome as ever, dressed in stonewashed jeans and a flimsy open white shirt – despite the coolness of the evening and the wind which was blowing in from the sea – nervously biting his bottom lip and running his hands through his mop of dark hair. I resisted the temptation to cry out, 'Stop that! That's my job now!'

Sofia delivered me and my slightly worse-for-wear luggage to Alex's beautiful feet, before pecking him on both cheeks, winking at me, and then running to a waiting car, which I noticed was being driven by Yiorgos. Waving to both myself and Alex, he happily drove his mother away, leaving me with his dad; his delicious, sexy, Greek god of a father.

'*Yassou*, Just Jess,' he growled, kicking my bags out of the way whilst reaching for me without a moment's hesitation, and before I could even respond, I was back in his arms and my hands seemed to have a mind of their own as they caressed first his shoulders, then his back and then glided down over his shapely bum.

I buried my head in his chest. This was *my* harbour – where I feel safe and calm on gentle waters, rather than always being thrown about by a raging, tempestuous sea. This island, this community, this man - *this* was where I belonged – and if I got lucky, like the crescent of boats bobbing around behind me, I might just get tethered up as well.

'*Yassou*, Alex,' were the only words I could seem to find, as I saw the glint in his eyes and felt his heart pounding fast and loud through the almost sheer fabric of his shirt. I so badly wanted to kiss him, but thought better of it, in such a public place, when the people of the island weren't even aware of the dissolution of his relationship with Sofia, let alone his new romance with this English floozy.

Although, I'm guessing Alex thought, 'Bollocks to that', because he wasted no time before his lips sought out mine and we had the sweetest of kisses – no tongues, no probing - just his mouth covering mine and the pleasure was all in the tasting.

When we finally broke apart, barely a second passed before he cupped my chin with his hand, stared meaningfully and longingly into my eyes and said again, 'I love you, Jess.'

Without an ounce of doubt, without a second thought, I replied, 'I love you too, Alex. I think I have loved you for a very long time without even knowing it.'

It was true; love had crept up on me unexpectedly and I had fallen for the very person who I had always believed to be out of bounds. But Alex had known it, sensed it and bided his time, and here I was, drenched in those feelings and I honestly reckoned I was the luckiest woman alive.

'Alex - my lover, my friend and my soulmate - tell me you love me again, please. But this time, let me hear it in Greek.'

'Of course, my beautiful and wonderful Jessica. Anything for you.'

He took both my hands and my heart, as he said what I needed to hear.

'*S'agapo,* Just Jess.'

*

We quietly dismantled the original signage to the restaurant, Alex and Andreas having knocked up a temporary replacement – the new boarding would be ordered and erected for the beginning of the following season, in time for the influx of holidaymakers.

Sofia's uncle had also engraved a small plaque for us and we'd arranged to meet her and Theo, together with Andreas and Yiorgos on the stretch of beach fronting the restaurant, along with Ioanna and her husband, both of whom I'd only ever spoken to previously by telephone. To my surprise, the lovely Ioanna – a huge woman with a huge heart and snow white hair that had been clearly tightly curled with rollers the night before – had brought along an elderly couple who she had apparently collected on the way to our rendevouz. In fact the old couple were positively ancient, and the lady struggled to keep her footing on the sand.

I was choked to find out that these were the two oldies who Juliette had ran errands for, who had been distraught when they had discovered what had become of their English Angel.

An even bigger shock was the arrival of Alex's mother and father, in the back of Yiorgos' little runaround, both dressed like eccentric Eskimos, with Yiorgos carrying a huge, overflowing pot of flowers as they approached our little party assembled on the beach.

Alex's mother quietly said something to him and Yiorgos turned to speak to me directly, to bring me up to speed.

'My mother, she says she had to come today to pay tribute to Juliette; to make amends for being unable to help her in life and to remember her beautiful face and spirit. Also, she wanted to apologise for what her son - my uncle - became; she fears they may have spoiled him as a child and this possibly contributed to his attitude and his sense of entitlement. She is asking for forgiveness.'

Oh good grief. The ensuing silence was broken up only by Lauren's sobs - by request, she was present via Facetime, as she didn't want to miss our little gathering for the erection of the plaque or the unveiling of the new name for the restaurant. However, her cries were the undoing of Ioanna, whose howls of anguish could probably be heard from the other side of the island, as her shoulders shook and she swayed from side to side.

When the crying had died down, although Alex's mum still continued to sniff and dab at her eyes, Alex cleared his throat and paved the way for my little speech by saying in both English

209

and Greek, 'Please, we must not be sad any longer. Juliette would have wanted us to remember her smile and to celebrate today. So please, do not cry. Now, my lovely Jessica will say a few words.'

Even now, I still couldn't believe that I was His Lovely Jessica and that he in turn was all mine. Squeezing his hand to say thank you, I nervously stepped forward. Public speaking was not my forte, but in the absence of Lauren, I knew I owed it to Juliette to step up and stop being such a wuss.

'Thanks for coming everyone.' I paused to allow Alex to translate for me.

'You all knew Juliette, but I didn't – not in person anyway. I feel like I've come to know her a little through everything that Alex and Lauren and Sofia have told me about her, and it seemed like she was a hell of a person to have been around. You were all lucky enough to have called her your friend; I wish I'd had the chance for her to have become mine. For a long time now, Ioanna and Lauren have been laying flowers for Juliette, in an attempt to remind everyone on this island what a special person she was...but we think the time has come for a more permanent memorial, and what better place to have it than here, on this wall, that separates the restaurant from the golden sands. I'm told that Juliette loved to sit at her favourite table on the other side of this wall, to gaze out to sea, and also her second favourite place was down there on the beach, breathing in the sea air and watching the waves sweep in. So, whenever any of us needs to feel closer to her, we can come and stand here and look at her plaque, which reads...'

'In memory of a beautiful woman who lived, loved and laughed.
Just Juliette Lewis. 1994 – 2017.
Forever 23.'

*

There were many more tears before we retreated to the warmth of the restaurant, Chef having peeled off his camouflage gear, set down his gun and returned from the hills, to open up his kitchen to prepare a one-off, out-of-season special. Apparently he spent most of the winter either hunting with his dogs or building walls and gateposts, so we were fortunate to have him.

Eventually, the tears turned to laughter and we were able to celebrate Juliette's life as we had intended to. Andreas disappeared fairly quickly, to check on and feed his animals, and to be alone I would surmise; after hearing Lauren's voice he had retreated into his shell and was struggling to contain his emotions. I hugged him as he left, needing him to know he wasn't alone, and that sometimes time and space had a way of making everyone see clearer. There didn't seem to be any middle ground for him and Lauren and she was right, he would never leave the island; he was Greek through and through. I hoped and prayed that some day she would come to realise that she only needed Andreas – nothing more and nothing less – and that she would return to Loulouthia and be happy again.

Ioanna was next to depart, holding tightly on to her husband and thanking us for such a beautiful tribute to an astonishingly brave woman. I promised to meet her for a coffee in Town when she was next on Loulouthia and we joked that we would do everything in our power to persuade Lauren to return, using the tried and tested methods of bribery and blackmail if necessary. They almost forgot to take the old couple with them; I think the pensioners were having too much of a good time to notice that they almost missed their lift back to their village. To be fair, they had looked slightly bewildered throughout the whole proceedings, but then I think they had a combined age of about two hundred, so I wouldn't hold it against them.

Yiorgos, his grandparents, and Sofia and Theo followed. I was amazed that Alex's parents had been so accepting of the situation and hadn't been fazed when Alex had explained that Sofia was moving to Corfu with Theo, and that he and I were now an item. They had simply said that they would always love Sofia, as the daughter that they had never had, but they would love me too, and that all they wanted was for everyone to be happy. And who could ask for more than that?

Sofia's father hadn't taken it quite so well; in fact, I think his words were, 'Leave my house with this *pervert* and never come back...or I will fire bullets into you both.' I think he did actually still see himself as some sort of gangster who could control his wife and daughter, ruling by fear. Perhaps someone should point out to him that he was knocking on a bit now and the only thing his daughter and partner were frightened of was his false teeth flying across the room when he was in a rage.

I actually really liked Theo – he was smooth and he was confident and not bad for an old guy – he was knocking on a bit - at least in his sixties - but I could see what had attracted Sofia to him, and her face positively lit up every time he glanced in her direction. The bond they had between them was obvious for all to see and he plainly adored her, treating her with respect and reverence, as if she was about to be snatched from under his nose at any moment. Mind you, he had loved her for twenty years and been apart from her for most of them, and she was simply stunning, so you could hardly blame him.

Eventually, when the revving of Chef's motorbike signalled his departure, and there was just myself and Alex left inside the restaurant, I slid over and on to his knee. I thought back to how just a short time ago I had sat in that very spot in his lap and had become all hot under the collar as I'd started to suspect that my feelings for him ran much deeper than I could ever have imagined.

Fortunately, it was impossible for anyone to see us through the boarded windows, as Alex slid his hand up my leg and under my skirt, seeking out a part of me that he knew ached for him. I could feel his arousal through the denim of his jeans and my hand crept over it, as my cheeks burned, imagining him hoisting me up on to the low counter-top, pushing me back and taking me there and then, amongst the unopened packs of napkins and the condiment sets, as he called out my name and made me writhe around in ecstasy.

I was on the money – we did it on the counter-top and it was fast and furious, yet equally tender and loving. Even after he'd reached his crescendo he stayed inside me for as long as he possibly could and then proceeded to kiss almost every inch of me, whilst I gasped for breath and wondered how I could ever have settled for less than this in the past. In time, we fastened up our clothes and returned to the seating area but I couldn't keep my hands out of his shirt, raking his skin and leaving almost a grid of scratch marks across his chest, but he was moaning in pleasure and tugging at my nipples in response.

Exhausted after the events of the day, I was more than ready to head for home...but not too tired to have finished with Alex yet. I had a whole range of massage oils on the shelf in my bedroom, courtesy of Scarlett's Special Delivery that had finally arrived the previous day. She had been gobsmacked to hear that Alex and I were now a couple, but once she'd recovered from the shock she told me I was a 'Lucky dog' and that she knew just the present that would be perfect to post out to me. Blushing with embarrassment when I opened the box, I soon decided that I liked my/our gifts when I caught the naughty look in Alex's eyes and knew he had plans for me later. Yes, we would make good use of the oils, and the stockings and the other eye-popping items Scarlett had purchased without any shame. God I loved that girl and hoped she would find somebody soon who would look after her and cherish her, so I could somehow return the favour.

'Come on, Alexander the Great,' I said to him, using his new nickname that suited him down to the ground. A woman would struggle to find a greater man than Alex.

Pulling him up to his feet, I kissed him firmly on the lips once more, before we slipped our coats on, locked up and padded down the sandy steps and on to the beach. The silence was comforting, the air was cleansing and the stars in the sky seemed keen to guide us home. As I removed my socks and boots, wanting to feel the sand between my toes even if it was freezing cold and damp, now the heat of the summer months had long gone, I turned around to admire not just the magnificent man by my side, but the very special plaque on the wall that had been put there with love, before taking a last glance up at the temporary signage, complete with its new name for the business – a name that had been decided emotionally and unanimously by myself, Alex, Sofia, Andreas and Lauren.

'JUST JULIETTE'S'.

Just perfect.

Also by Antonia K. Lewis

I Called Him David

Your David, My Dave

KEEP IN TOUCH with

Antonia

Visit

www.antoniaklewis.com

for exclusive news, blog and photographs!

You can also find *Antonia* on

Facebook

and

Instagram

Or follow her Tweets

www.twitter.com/AntoniaKLewis2

Antonia K. Lewis is the author of *I Called Him David* and *Your David, My Dave.* She lives in the North West of England with her husband, children, dogs and chocolate stash.